GIVING UP

STONEVIEW STORIES BOOK THREE

LOLA KING

Copyright © 2021 by Lola King
All rights reserved. No part of this publication may be reproduced, stored or transmitted in any form or by any means, electronic, mechanical, photocopying, recording, scanning, or otherwise without written permission from the publisher. It is illegal to copy this book, post it to a website, or distribute it by any other means without permission.
This novel is entirely a work of fiction. The names, characters and incidents portrayed in it are the work of the author's imagination. Any resemblance to actual persons, living or dead, events or localities is entirely coincidental.
Designations used by companies to distinguish their products are often claimed as trademarks. All brand names and product names used in this book and on its cover are trade names, service marks, trademarks and registered trademarks of their respective owners. The publishers and the book are not associated with any product or vendor mentioned in this book. None of the companies referenced within the book have endorsed the book.
All songs, song titles an lyrics contained in this book are the property of the respective songwriters and copyright holders.
Special Cover edition
Cover art by Wild Love Designs

To all the women who read smut books in public and post it on social media.
To all the women who read them in secret.
To all the women who touch themselves to those books we love so much.
To all the women who enjoy sex unapologetically, to all the ones who are open about their kinks and the ones who keep them to themselves.
To all the women, enjoy yourselves, you deserve it. I wish you more orgasms than you can count.

And to Chad, fuck you.

Nobody is a villain in their own story. We're all the heroes of our own stories.
  George R. R. Martin

TRIGGER WARNING

This book is not recommended to readers under the age of 18. This is a dark bully romance and contains dubcon / noncon sexual scenes, bullying scenes, age difference, drug use, mention of child abuse, rough sex, and other scenes that some readers may find triggering. The characters are no heroes, and some characters in this series are unredeemable. If this is something you are not comfortable with, please do not go any further.

I'm happy to say that this book doesn't end in a cliff-hanger, however this is JAMIE's story, and some characters' stories are not concluded in this book. To me, Stoneview is a *world*, not a series, everyone will get their story in due time.

If you've followed Jamie's story until now, from the bottom of my heart, *thank you*.

Enjoy!
    Lots of love,

Lola ♡

PLAYLIST

Godless - BANKS
Numb to the Feeling - Chase Atlantic
We Did Not Make Sense - Presence
It Ain't Me - Kygo, Selena Gomez
Us - James Bay
Glad He's Gone - Tove Lo
Into It - Chase Atlantic
Youngblood - 5 Seconds of Summer
NUMB - Chri$stian Gate$
Yes girl - Bea Miller
Without Me - Halsey
Bad ones - Tate McRae
Not alone - sadeyes, Lil Xtra
DEVLISH - Chase Atlantic
Wreak Havoc - Skylar Grey
Ghost Of You - 5 Seconds of Summer

Red Roses - Call Me Karizma
I Think I'm OKAY - Machine Gun Kelly, YUNGBLUD
Traitor - Olivia Rodrigo
911 - Ellise
Gods & Monsters - Lana Del Rey
Shadow Preachers - Zella Day
If You Want Love - NF
I Found - Amber Run
Paralyzed - NF
Arcade - Duncan Laurence
Give Me A Reason - Jillian Rossi
Cruel Summer - Taylor Swift

PROLOGUE
JAMIE

Godless - Banks

How does one describe heartbreak?

An impossible task that could be a mythological punishment from Zeus in order to sentence someone to an infinity of sorrow. An eternal self-destruction.

There is the physical way my chest constricts, stops me from breathing, and barely rises before crashing on itself again. How long until I can take a breath of air without feeling like my lungs are burning with a hellish fire?

There is the way my throat is in a constant fight with itself, leaving me with a trembling voice, with an impossibility to swallow not only food but simple nothingness.

My hands are always cold. That's something I didn't know was a symptom of heartbreak. My cold hands, desperate for the touch of the man who broke me.

My stomach can barely hold air, let alone anything concrete. I've been cursed to feel cemented anxiety and grief deep inside me.

My heart is where the physical crashes with the realm of

emotions. I *felt* my heart break. I felt it tear apart, somewhere among the tissues of the muscle, something happened in some sort of scientific impossibility. At the same time, my subconscious prepared for an eternity of distress and 'what if'.

Sometimes, people are taken away from you. Life, death, the unavoidable cycle of what we're put on earth for, the safety of being unable to change fate. Sometimes, they decide to leave you. That's when the worst part starts. Intellectual obliteration of the self.

What did I do wrong?

What if I was prettier?

What if I had made more of an effort?

Is it someone else?

Why am I not enough?

Why, Jake? How could you?

You were the light of my life. You were my dawn after an eternal night in the darkness. Before you, I was crawling aimlessly through life. I was surviving trauma, I was pretending to be strong. You crashed through my perfectly concocted lie of a life and forced me into genuine happiness.

I fought it. God knows I fought against our fated, toxic love. For you, I gave in, I took a leap of faith like never before. I put my trust in you, I gave you my love, my tears, my whole. I was nothing but an extension of you, I existed through and for you.

You were nothing but my everything.

Just like discovering the acid taste of lemon for the first time, the acrid taste of a first cigarette, the sting of our first fall, I believe the first heartbreak is the one that teaches us how dangerous love can be. It creates and it destroys. And you, you used it to break me. To wreck my heart, to decimate my inner bliss.

You decided I was not worthy of your love. You decided I was not *good enough*.

If I wasn't good enough for you…

Then without you, I am nothing.

I. Am. Nothing.

I gave you everything.

And you? You gave me up.

And so, after our beautiful journey in the light of love, dusk sets down again. I close my eyes and when I open them again…you won't be there.

1

JAKE

Numb to the Feeling – Chase Atlantic

New Year's Day, morning....

"This Wolf, boys," his finger jabs the picture, "is Aaron Williams." His smile turns smug when he adds, "I heard you both fucked his little sister, Jamie."

My eyes go from Bianco to Nate in panic. I want to focus on Aaron Williams, but all I can focus on is the fact that he just said Nate had fucked Jamie.

It's like my brother can read my mind.

"Easy, Jake," he chuckles as he raises his hands in defense. "I'll have you know, Mateo, that I personally never fucked her."

I hate that I feel slightly better. But shit I do.

Now the not-so-missing brother problem.

I want to jump at Bianco's throat, but my body is too battered to move. How? How did he find him? How did he know he was still alive? How did he know to even look for him? Mainly, how can Aaron work for Volkov? That's impossible.

"Isn't the kid dead or something?" Nate tries to act casual.

"He disappeared three years ago," Bianco explains. "I'm sure you can imagine that if a bitch had both of you pussy-whipped, I had to look into it. She's a pretty little thing, isn't she?"

He looks at both of us, his eyes bouncing between my brother and myself, dying for a reaction.

"And honestly, you can tell Rose, well-tried. She did try to put me off by saying she was just some random chick you were fucking. Gotta give it to her, she sees things coming from far, doesn't she? Of course, I was naïve enough to believe your sister, as always. It might have worked if Jake had stopped dating Jamie." His eyes stay on mine and there's no smile on his face anymore. He's all serious talk now.

I look at the picture again and my heart breaks at the thought of Aaron being alive. Jamie would give her life to be able to see him again...but not like that. I already know her world will crumble when she learns that he was working for Volkov all along. There must be an explanation to this, but Bianco would never give it to me.

"So what?" Nate asks. "You want us to kill him or something? That's fine with me."

Bianco chuckles and looks back at my brother. "You were always the ruthless one, you know that, son?"

Nate shrugs but I know he's bluffing. He would never hurt Aaron, he cares too much for Jamie.

But Bianco shakes his head. "I don't need you to go puppy hunting any time soon. *However*... I've had my most trusted Stoneview people dying left, right, and center. Just at the same time as some of our ground guys have seen this little fucker hanging around Stoneview."

Nate nods in agreement and runs a finger slowly behind his ear. "Okay, he's killing your guys. We'll kill him, no need to involve his sister."

"Let me explain more clearly." He's angry now, we're not giving him the answer he wants. "How the *fuck* do you think this guy knows who to kill? Only a few of us know who is truly important in this family. You two included. You date the girl, she spies on you, and suddenly her brother knows exactly who to kill?"

He runs his hands through his hair, pulling at the roots slightly. He looks completely paranoid. "This girl is not on our side. Her family is with our rival, which makes her our rival."

"She hasn't seen him in three years, Mateo, she doesn't even know he's still alive," I snort. His speech is ridiculous, and I'm done listening to him.

"I don't give a shit when she's next going to see him and when she last saw him. I won't have two of my guys playing with her. My men are dropping like flies and I'm taking all the precautions necessary. That's how family works, Jake. I won't take that risk."

I don't miss the double meaning.

"I don't think you understand that not everyone is tied to a gang. Just because you decide to bring everyone spiraling down with you in your dodgy business, doesn't mean every family does that. It might come as a surprise, but people usually prefer their family members to *escape* any sort of illegal activity. I'll let you think about it," I conclude as I rise from my chair.

"Sit your ass back down," he scolds as he gets up too.

My brain wants me to leave but my body refuses,

knowing it couldn't take more pain. I reluctantly sit back down, I'm not exactly looking forward to another beating right now.

"Listen..." Nate starts. I know he's going to try and convince Bianco the same as I just did.

"No! You listen. Both of you. None of you are going to be fooling around with the bitch. Am I clear? Because, believe me, if you do there's going to be consequences. And I have my ways. I like punishment," he smiles, "and your girl will get plenty of it if I see any of you around her again."

He leans over the desk and his smirk turns pure evil. "I like inflicting pain, boys, and the two of you have seen nothing. If you doubt me, ask your beautiful sister how bad it gets."

I don't think, I pounce from my chair and grab his tie hanging above the desk. I pull with all my strength, my broken thumb begging me to stop.

"I'm going to kill you," I seethe. "Watch my lips, Mateo, you're going to die from my hands. I promise you."

Nate grabs me and pulls me back softly enough to not hurt me. He's not trying to get in a fight with me, just stop me from getting in trouble.

"Jake, stop," he whispers calmly to me.

How? How can he be so calm when the bastard is threatening Jamie, when he's taunting us with all the ways he must have hurt our sister. This is my own personal hell and I need to get out of here. I'm not able to stop it, but I need to at least delay it as much as possible.

I want to go back home to Jamie and keep her safe from all this.

Over my fast-beating heart, I hear my brother saying that Jamie is innocent in all of this and that the two of us were just fueling our long-time feud when we fought over her.

Mateo doesn't change his mind, though. Even when Nate says that we just had built-up anger. Even when he says that we'll stay in line from now on. No more fighting over Jamie, no more involving her in anything. He promises him to keep her away from any business-related topic, anything involving Bianco.

I'm shocked at how much my brother is fighting for this. I'm furious that he loves her so much, but I don't stop him.

"That's enough, Nate," Bianco stops him in his rant with a voice of steel. "I hear you, she's a great girl. Do you know what I do with good girls like her? Do you know how much my customers would pay for her at the club? Some tiny thing like her? So sweet, so innocent, so breakable?"

Mateo sits back down slowly, rearranges his tie, and rests an arm on the chair. "A fortune. I apologize if I didn't spell it out correctly for you." He leans towards the both of us standing, watching him, desperately needing him to tell us he'll leave her alone and perfectly knowing he won't. "I am *not* above kidnapping. I am *not* above selling. I am *not* above pimping out little sluts just to keep you two in check."

My ears are ringing so hard I might pass out. I think I'm having a panic attack. Is this what it's like? I don't remember, the last one I had was too long ago. My legs are shaking, I doubt they can hold me much longer.

"I seem to recall this is not my first warning to you, Nate," Bianco threatens.

My mouth feels like cotton, but I still manage to cut off my brother just before he replies to his boss.

"I'll break up with her."

Nate turns to me in shock, his face hardened. I think I

can feel some energy coming back to my limbs. I have to end this. I have to protect her.

I don't know why I thought this could ever work. Especially now that we signed the papers. I should have known the second Sam found us that my life would be turned upside down. Being in love is not part of who I am anymore. It can't be.

I push away any emotions from my face, I build back the walls, I cement them and bulletproof them against everything and everyone again. No more feelings, no more risking anyone's life just because I thought I could escape the past.

"She might be important to Nate but she's not all that to me. She can be replaced by another bitch tomorrow."

The smile that spreads on Bianco's lips is highly punchable but I don't move. No more emotions, no more reactions.

"Replaceable, huh?" he insists.

He probably knows I'm acting, but at least his threats got him the response intended. First, I shut down myself when he threatens my loved ones, then he can mold me back into whatever he wants. It's only the beginning of real fun.

"Yeah, replaceable," I confirm. I look around to find Bianco's assistant still sitting on the couch against the wall, right behind me. "Here, she'll do. What's your name again, sweetheart?" I smile at her and it must be freaking horrible seeing the state my body is in.

Her eyes widen and her gaze flickers to Bianco, Nate, then back to me.

"Uh..." she starts.

"*Anne*," Nate cuts off, "is four years your elder, Jake. Be good and stay in the kids' section."

"Four years?" I scoff. "That's funny, it didn't seem to bother you when you were trying to fuck my girl."

Our staring contest is cut off by Bianco. "Break up with

the bitch. It won't be too hard since you're going to California anyway."

"I'm what?" My heart stops. *Did I hear this right?*

"This is where most of my fights happen now. I don't want none of this business on this side of the country, it's too easy to link it to me. Except the Death Cage, but you're not being put in there. I love you too much for that."

"I'm not going to the West Coast. You need to re-think your plan, Mateo."

He laughs at me for a good while, so much that he hits his hand against the desk. "God, Jake...you're fucking hilarious, you know that?"

"Mateo, you can't just send me to California. I have school, I have a life here."

"And how was the good life?" he deepens the knife. "About time you come back to reality, don't you think?"

My brain is working too fast for my mouth to catch up and I end up stuttering my sentence. "I-I-Mateo..."

He chuckles mockingly at me. "I hope you'll be a little more confident than that in the ring, son. Off you go."

2

JAMIE

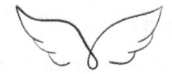

We Did Not Make Sense – Presence, Wovy

March...

"Bad girl," Jake says as he slaps my ass, making me moan harder.

He pulls at my hips, and I go on all fours for him. I feel him shift behind me and something touches my lips. I don't think, I open. He slides something in, wraps it twice around my head, and ties it behind.

It's silky, it's...his tie. The tie he wore to that luxurious restaurant he took me to for dinner.

Happy with the way he gagged me, he slips his next words in my ears. "Your mom is in the living room, make another sound and I'll choke you with this tie. Nod."

I nod.

He kneads at my ass cheeks before I feel his teeth against my right one. I do my best not to scream in the gag, but I still moan around it. Thankfully it's muffled.

He steps away and the next thing I feel are the tips of his fingers grazing my clit. It starts soft but every tap is a little harsher. In less than a minute I'm writhing, shifting my hips, and desperate for him to rub.

"Look at how desperate you are for me, baby. That's a very needy pussy you got, you know that?"

I nod again, but I don't think he cares, he's too lost in his lust. I'm lost in my own too, the pleasure is burning in my toes, traveling up my legs and my spine. It's curling in my lower belly and giving my heart palpitations.

His fingers leave my clit to spread wetness from my entrance. He rubs his knuckles against my pussy and I whimper with need.

I need him to fuck me so much right now.

But he takes his time. He slowly inserts one finger and I clench so hard around it I'm surprised he can even take it out. He slides another one in, and the third one makes me moan loudly.

The harsh slaps to my ass make me jump. "Angel," *he growls.* "Don't make me put my threats into action."

I nod.

"Be a good girl for me, baby." *He slides his fingers out.* "Show me that wet pussy."

I put my cheek to the mattress, arching my back, and spread my legs, offering myself to him. Ready for him to end me.

"Atta girl," *he groans with need.* "Do you want to be fucked, Angel?"

Not being able to answer, I grind against the air, and I arch my back more.

"Such a needy girl," *he chuckles.*

He places his hard dick at my entrance and starts pushing in slowly. Oh, it's slow. Too slow.

I whimper against the gag and try to push against him, but he grabs my hips to keep me in place. "Good girls wait for it, Angel."

He pushes a little further and I uncontrollably clench around him, making him hiss with pleasure. "Fuck, you are way too fucking tight. You'd be a saint's demise, Jamie."

Further. "But I'm far from a saint," *he chuckles to himself before entering me all the way. It's harsh enough to make me scream against the gag.*

He slides a hand under and pinches my right nipple. The pleasure overwhelming me makes my muscles spasm. He plays with my nipple without moving in me and I desperately try to get some movement in my hips.

"Jake," I mumble around the gag.

He starts his motion, not fast, but focused. He fucks me relentlessly, bringing me the kind of pleasure I didn't even know I deserved.

He fucks me with so much love and animosity, the mix of both bringing me to the edge of the cliff.

"Angel," he growls behind me. "You're never getting away from me. You're mine, you hear that?"

I moan a 'yes'.

"My personal little fuck toy."

He accelerates the pace and brings his fingers to my clit at the same time. He rubs me with a control I would never have, and I explode against him. I tighten and force his own orgasm out of him.

"Fuck," he pants as he slows down. "My angel to love forever."

Except...forever is very short in Jake's book, isn't it?

"Jamie, are you listening kiddo?"

I snap my head up from my notebook to look at Coach T. This is embarrassing. My cheeks burn as I try to push memories of Jake and me away. Next to me, Luke tries to help me catch up by tapping on his own notebook, his finger dancing along the words 'permission slips'.

"Oh, the slips," I reassure Coach with a smile. "Ciara gave me hers today." I dig it out of my backpack and hand it to him.

"I'm still missing one," he insists.

"Yes. Rose's. She..." I bite my inner cheek. "She..." Was forced by her psychopath of an older brother to sign him as her new guardian and I'm assuming the bastard isn't planning on signing the permission slip any time soon. "She needs more time. I think."

Coach T. gives me a look and I know exactly what he's thinking. We can't not have Rose in the tournament.

"Jamie." He pauses to reflect. "How do I put this..." He looks right at me with his hard eyes surrounded by waves of wrinkles. "If we want to win this tournament, I need my two best players. I've got your slip. This is my last season. I want this trophy. I won't lose it to Lady Anne again."

"I know, Coach. You won't."

"Get me Rose's slip, kiddo. I already lost one White. I want my other scorer."

"I will, Coach," I sigh.

"Dismissed," he grunts as he puts his reading glasses on and grabs a sports magazine that was lying on his desk.

Luke and I get up from our seats and leave Coach Thompson's office.

Both Jake and Rose missed the first week after the Christmas break. Rose came back.

He didn't.

He didn't pick up my calls, he didn't reply to my texts and, slowly, I stopped trying.

I tried to talk to Rose. She promised me she didn't know

where Jake was. She said it's just her and Nathan. I didn't insist. After learning everything Bianco put her through, I don't see Rose the same way. I'm not saying I see her as a victim. Simply that her list of things to worry about must be a mile long and she doesn't need me asking questions on top of it all.

It's sad to see that Chris has become this impassive brick wall and no one can get through to him. He's been robbed of both his siblings. His best friends.

And Luke...well here he is, replacing Jake as our lacrosse team captain. Trying desperately to keep things normal, to keep what is left of his group together. To pretend everything hasn't gone to complete shit. He is a pillar. Not mine, though. I don't really talk to him now that he and Emily aren't together anymore, but he tries and that is amazing of him.

"I'll talk to Rose. I'm seeing her tonight," Luke tells me. His bright baby blue eyes seem to have gone a shade paler since his best friend left all of us behind. "I don't think Nate's going to sign. She has to forge his signature."

My teeth decide to attack my inner cheek again. This just isn't a good idea. Not when I know what Nathan is capable of.

"I don't want her to get in trouble," I admit.

Luke chuckles sadly at me. "You really think Rose is scared of getting in trouble? Have you met her?"

"Yeah. I guess not." Except Luke doesn't know how bad Nathan can get. He might have heard but he hasn't witnessed it.

He didn't witness him beating Jake to a pulp. He didn't see when he grabbed his younger sister by the hair and slammed her against the coffee table. He didn't see how afraid she was when she signed. If she forges his signature and he catches her... A shiver of fear runs through my spine and I zip up my coat.

"I just don't want to put her in danger for a lacrosse tournament. I love Coach T. but it's not that big of a deal."

"Lacrosse is her full ride to Duke. It *is* a big deal."

"Duke?!" I choke. This is worse than I thought. I had no idea Rose was getting a lacrosse scholarship, and to Duke University as well.

I mean, she's a great player but she's also a freaking genius. If there is a reason a college should pay her to study there, it should be for her brain.

"Does Nathan know?"

Luke shrugs at my questions. If Nathan knows Rose could get away thanks to lacrosse, it's pretty clear why he's not signing. The last thing he would want is for her to leave Stoneview and get away from this mess. Because he's that kind of selfish.

"You got a ride?" Luke asks as we stop by his G-Wagon.

I nod and dangle the keys to my bike lock in front of him. "Always."

My phone rings in my pocket and I take it out. I glance at Luke and notice his eyes going to my screen.

"That Em?" He sounds so desperate when he says her name, my own heart breaks all over again. Oh, how I know what it's like to be dying for someone to come back to you. My face painfully turns into a sorry grimace as I shake my head.

"It's Cole."

For the strangest reasons, Cole and I got much closer in the past two months. I think Jake had truly scared him away from me before the Christmas break. I mean, he broke his nose because Cole asked me to the ball. That is toxic 101.

Since Jake is not part of our lives anymore, he can't

threaten anyone for being too close to me. Good. It's a part of him I don't miss. He was too possessive, too bad-tempered when it came to sharing. Too caveman. I don't miss that.

Lies. Lies. Lies. Jake comes as a whole. The good and the bad. And you miss all of it.

It doesn't matter. My head is not in the right place for dating, neither is my heart, and I'm thankful that Cole and I became friends. We're great friends and I love spending time with him. I tend to take a step back every time his behavior turns slightly flirtatious, but he never pushes. He respects me and my boundaries and I'm happy to finally be hanging out with someone honest and kind without any expectations on either side. He still doesn't lift a finger when it comes to being co-president of the student council, but we've come to make a joke out of his jock behavior.

I wave bye to Luke and answer my phone as I head to my bike.

"What's up, loser?" I smile into the phone.

"*Hey, Queen bee. How was the meeting with Coach?*"

"Bad news, you've been kicked off the team. I think they said it has to do with your freakishly small feet."

Cole laughs on the other end of the line. "*You really want to talk about small things? I called 'cause I was worried you'd blow away with all that wind.*"

It's my turn to laugh. What an idiot.

"*Anyway, I was wondering how you'd feel about homework together. I was planning on rewarding us with sushi.*"

"You really know how to use my weaknesses against me, huh? If you think you can trick me into doing your homework in exchange for sushi...you're absolutely right. Where should we meet?"

"*I could come to your house? Would dearest Caroline like some sushi?*"

"You can't bribe my mom with sushi. She hates it."

"*I guess I'm gonna bribe her with her favorite pastries again then.*"

"I guess," I chuckle. "Come around five. Bye, loser."

I snatch Emily's car door open and climb up with as much enthusiasm as if I was sitting down on the electric chair. I push my backpack to my feet and the deepest sigh leaves my lungs. I don't mean to be dramatic, I'm just exhausted. Exhausted and heartbroken.

"Another night crying?" my best friend asks.

"I can't help it," I reply, my voice stuck in my throat. My eyes feel puffy and my throat raw.

"Did you call him?"

I shake my head. The whole of January and beginning of February, I tried calling Jake so many times, I was scared he would file a restraining order. How is one meant to react to their first heartbreak? He promised me the world, he left me on my own.

I stopped calling on the fourteenth of February. Not because Valentine's Day reminded me I was now single, but because it was Aaron's birthday. I simply had something else to cry about and, suddenly, the school's number one fuckboy breaking up with me didn't seem so bad. The last birthday I spent with my brother, he turned eighteen, two months later he disappeared. He turned twenty-one this year.

I didn't just have to deal with being left behind, with the realization that my and Jake's relationship had shattered to pieces. I also had to deal with Camila, Beth, and the people who usually don't care about me and suddenly did because I was Jake's girlfriend. All those people, they now whispered things about me, probably started by Camila.

He didn't just break up with her, he left Stoneview, how bad can she be in bed?

You should have improved your blowing skills, Goody, want me to teach you?

How clingy are you that he had to skip town so you wouldn't follow him?

People can be mean. Breakups hurt. Aftermath hits hard.

"At least we're not taking steps back, babe. It will pass, I promise you," Emily reassures me. In all this, she's the one constant in my life that hasn't changed. My safety net, my unconditional love.

"How are you so...okay?" I don't want to drag her down with me but I'm certain Emily is in denial. "You're in love with Luke."

It's her turn to sigh. "I think I'm still too angry at him. At both of us, for letting ourselves fuck it up."

There's a long silence while we both think of our own broken hearts. Emily finally starts the car and we're on our way to school for another day without Jake.

We end up having to park in one of the furthest spots from the entrance. This is what happens when you take too long sulking, you're late.

Stupidly it makes me even angrier at Jake. Not only have I given him the power to break me, he also still puts me in trouble after he's left me behind. He doesn't even need to be in the same city as me to ruin my life.

Everyone is already inside, and we're power walking

across the parking lot when Nathan's Porsche Cayenne drives onto the lot and stops at the drop-off, not far from the entrance. My heart plunges hard enough in my stomach to make me miss a step. I haven't seen Nathan since that famous night at the Murrays. Since my birthday, two months ago.

Emily and I are close enough to the car that we can hear the shouting going on inside, not the exact words but the raised voices. They don't even have a window open. The passenger door opens, and a furious Rose comes out.

"Fuck you!" she shouts as she grabs her bag. She slams the door multiple times, re-opening it every time just to slam it harder. "Fuck you. Fuck. You. Ugh. *Fuck. You.*"

"Shit," Emily whispers, and I don't understand why until I see that Nathan has come out of the car as well. He walks around, his face as passive as usual. His self-control truly is impressive. Which is why it makes it so much worse when he hurts people; he does it purely out of pleasure.

I still feel strange when I see him, there will always be leftover memories of when he was my sweet Nathan.

Memories of lies.

Nathan grabs Rose by the back of her neck so suddenly I don't think she even had time to expect it.

"Go on, make your life harder, Ozy. Fucking do it," he growls at her. She's not scared though. She keeps fighting and tries to get out of his hold. Vainly.

I instinctively take a step forward to help, but Emily tugs me back straight away. I'm about to complain when she points at the school doors with her chin. Chris and Luke are running down the stairs.

"No need to get involved, 'Me. Not in this. Not anymore."

I could tell Emily how close Rose and I have become in the last couple of months. I could explain that Nathan kicks her out of the house every time his boss, Mateo Bianco, spends nights talking business in Nathan's mansion. I could explain that she sleeps in my bed when she would otherwise be on the streets because he won't let her go back to the Murrays. That I'm still more involved than I should be.

Except if I did that, I would also have to explain *why* Nathan kicks her out. That it's his way of protecting her. I would have to reveal that Bianco is obsessed with inflicting pain on a seventeen-year-old and that he's been doing it for years. That he truly, deep down, believes he owns Rose as if she is a personal trophy. And that is not my secret to tell.

So, I stay silent and let my best friend believe that I'm not involved with the Whites anymore.

Nathan gets away from Rose before Chris and Luke reach them. I don't think he wants a fight, he's just desperate to affirm his power. That's just what he does, isn't it?

"You care more about your car breaking than breaking *me*. You fucking asshole," she spits as Luke leads her inside. Nathan leaves in a screech of tires and Rose is still raising her middle fingers at the wind once the car has disappeared.

"Let's get to class," Emily says as she squeezes my arm.

I nod but struggle to take my gaze away from the group of three going through the doors.

While all of this is happening here, where the hell is Jake?

3

JAMIE

It ain't me – Kygo, Selena Gomez

I read Cole's text for the third time.

> Cole: How would you feel if I asked you out to the movies this Saturday?

I slide my phone across the mahogany table and let my best friend catch it. Our cafeteria is so Hogwarts, I love it. Em's eyes widen at the sight of my screen, and she looks up at me with a huge smile on her face.

"That's two days from now. 'Me, you should go!"

I shrug my shoulders and grimace. "I don't know. I mean, yeah Cole is hot-"

"Uh, yeah he is. I can't believe he's hitting on you. I thought you guys were friends," she whispers loud enough for me to hear but not the people at the table next to ours.

"It's not the first time. We've been borderline flirting since the end of January. I just...I always retreat whenever we're about to cross that line."

Chapter 3

"Damn, I didn't know Cole was hitting on you on a daily basis."

"Not on a daily basis," I laugh. "We've always talked. Student body presidents and all. We were meant to go to the Christmas ball together then..." I trail off remembering the day Cole canceled on me and Jake insisted I go with him.

I was still with Nathan back then. Still with Nathan and dying to be with Jake. How wrong was it of me to like how possessive he was? That he wouldn't let any other guy near me. So damn wrong. I'm selfish. So is Jake. We're both so selfish and wrong and perfect for each other.

"Then what?" Emily insists.

"Then Jake happened," I sigh.

"Fuck Jake. Cole is so nice! And *so* hot." She grins at me, but I shake my head again.

"I don't know...My head isn't in the right place and I..."

She senses my hesitation and pulls her chair slightly forward so she can get closer to the table. "What is it?"

"Is this really how things are meant to go?"

"Oh yes, my bad. You're used to hating each other before fucking each other." She straightens and imitates the voice of someone teaching a kid. "Well, when a guy doesn't bully you into being his girlfriend, your thing with Cole is usually how it goes. Friends then more."

I laugh at her dig because I know it's true. "I *meant*; we have a great friendship. Why ruin it with more?"

"Because the only reason you have such a great friendship is the sexual tension between you two. If you weren't attracted to each other, there would be no friendship."

"Huh..." I say as her words get me thinking.

Maybe she's right. Cole and I wouldn't be friends with each other if we didn't like each other a little too much.

"Friendships between boys and girls don't exist, 'Me. It's a myth. There's always something underneath. There's always one who wants to fuck the other. Even better when it's both."

"Rose is friends with boys."

"It doesn't count. Everybody wants to fuck Rose."

"I wasn't talking about everybody—"

"Oh come on, Jake doesn't count. Chris is her foster brother and Luke well...he already fucked her."

I laugh at the stupidity of the situation.

"This is a good thing," Em says. "A step toward moving on. It doesn't have to work, but you'll never know if you don't give it a shot. I was friends with Aaron my whole life before anything happened, and I wish it had happened earlier."

I don't think for another second. I grab my phone and send a text to Cole.

> Jamie: I'd feel really good.

His reply comes straight away.

> Cole: Would you like to come to the movies with me Saturday? ;)

> Jamie: I'd love that.

> Cole: I'm warning you, it's a date.

I smile to myself and look up just to see him across the cafeteria. He's sitting with the rest of the lacrosse team, including Luke.

> Jamie: Even better.

Chapter 3

I look up again just to see him look at his phone and up. His eyes meet mine and the smile that forms on his face is priceless. I smile back, tucking my hair behind my ears. We stare at each other for a good moment before I go back to my plate. *This feels good. It feels really good.* Or maybe the more I say it feels good, the more it will. That's the first step of moving on.

I push my front door open and come face to face with my mom putting her coat on.

"Where are you going?" I ask, surprised.

"Closing the shop," she says in a short breath. "I haven't made any food. Can you handle it?"

"Mom, you left me alone for months. I survived, didn't I?"

She pauses from zipping up her coat. "You dated a gangbanger, had someone in my house that shot a bullet in my shelves, and got your heart broken. Do you call that surviving?"

"Ouch. That was so uncalled for," I rasp.

She takes a deep breath. "Sorry. I'm sorry, sweetie. I'm...stressed."

"Anything I can help with?"

"It's your aunt. She's out of the hospital to...to pass comfortably at home."

"Do you have to go?"

"No. I can't leave you. Not again. I said my goodbyes. Look, 'Me, I have to run. Please make dinner so I have something to eat when I get back."

She leaves in a haste, and I close the door behind her. Her words were harsh but true.

When she came back on my birthday, she got everything out of me. I was in such a state, everything came pouring out. She got angry, sad, but mainly scared for me. She put me back on my feet, she took care of me like the amazing mother she is.

Now, she feels she made a mistake leaving me alone. I dated Nathan, I got attacked at the shop, Jake and Nathan had a fight in this house, Rose fired a gun. She knows it all and she's terrified to leave me on my own.

She trusted me and I broke that trust for selfish reasons. I broke her trust to have a liar in my bed and to share a relationship with Jake. One that he threw away after he got what he wanted. He walked away like it meant nothing. It probably didn't.

I'm barely done making dinner when someone knocks on the front door. Filipino pancit noodles, like my dad taught me. Except I cook mine without celery. I hate celery.

I walk around the kitchen bar and the few steps that take me to the door. Mom finally had a peephole installed after everything that happened. I recognize the face on the other side straight away and open the door wide. I gasp as soon as I see her. I hadn't noticed the black eye through the peephole.

"Shit, Rose," I gasp.

I step away from the door to let her in. She's got a sleepover bag with her, and I just know it's one of those nights.

"Don't swear," she says as she gets in. "It looks ugly on you."

I chuckle before walking to the kitchen counter. I should have never told her my dad hated cursing. I know she's following, and when I turn around, she's dropping her bag by the sofa.

"Are you hungry," I ask?

"Nah." I watch as she grabs a cigarette from her pack and goes to the kitchen door. The one that leads to the tiny backyard on the other side. It's about big enough for three people. "Back in a second," she states as she unlocks the door and goes out.

When she comes back, her voice is even raspier from the smoke, and she smells of cold cigarettes. I've put pancit on two plates despite her reluctance to eat. She locks the kitchen door and I'm right behind her when she turns around, holding both plates.

"Shoes," I growl looking at her feet.

I'm probably the least threatening person to her. Our height difference is laughable, and I have to tilt my head back to look into her eyes. I'm wearing pastel pink fluffy pajamas and she's in her usual black jeans and a gray sweater under her black leather jacket. Her go-to winter outfit outside of school.

I'm so non-threatening, yet she still hurries to take her black combat boots off. That's the thing with Rose, she doesn't do things because of threats. She'll listen if she likes you. Period.

God, my dad would have freaked out if he had seen her walk around the house with her shoes on. It's a big no-no that my mom took years to get used to. Yet now she can't stand shoes in the house either.

"You need to eat," I order as I walk to the sofa and put both our plates on the coffee table.

"I'm not hungry." She slumps on the sofa, next to me, and grabs the TV remote. "Desperate Housewives or Kim Kardashian?" she asks.

"It's called Real Housewives, not desperate housewives," I chuckle as I grab the remote from her.

"They always seem pretty desperate to me," she laughs back.

"Whatever, it's a Kardashian kind of night anyway."

She nods and takes her leather jacket off. She grabs her phone from her back pocket and puts it on the table before settling comfortably on the sofa.

If someone had told me in September that Rose White would be watching reality TV with me on my sofa, I think I would have checked them into a mental institution.

"Oh, wait," she says as I'm about to press play on my favorite VOD service. She searches for something in her bag and reappears a second later. "For you," she smiles. That gorgeous smile that looks exactly like her twin's.

My chest pinches as I grab the paper she's handing me.

"No way," I choke as I unfold it. "He signed!"

I look again at Nathan's signature on the lacrosse trip slip and back up at her. Her long legs are stretched under the coffee table and she's lazily resting her head on the back of the sofa. My eyes automatically dart to the fresh purple bruise on her face. Her ocean eyes look so dark in the dim light.

"Stop looking at me like that, Jamie. Just ask already."

"Is that why?" I point at her eye. "Because you asked him to sign?"

"No. It's because I was at the house when Bianco showed up without warning. I forged Nate's signature. The tournament is four days. As if he would let me out of his sight for that long."

I struggle to swallow and have to grab a glass of water. My throat always tightens up when she mentions Bianco. I can't imagine what it does to her. I wouldn't know, she's too strong to show that kind of weakness. That drunken moment when she spilled everything was only because she was on the verge of overdose.

"Are you okay?" I ask.

She runs a hand through her hair. She's gotten even skinnier in the past two months. Chris has been trying so hard to get her to eat but he's getting more and more frustrated each day.

"I'm fine," she lies.

"Please, eat," I insist. "Let's celebrate that freakin' lacrosse slip."

She smiles and goes into her jacket pocket. She pulls out an already rolled joint. "Did you just say celebration?"

"Promise you'll eat?"

"You know I get the munchies...bad."

I eye the joint in her hand for another second before sighing. "Fuck it, yeah okay," I tell her.

"Language," she grunts as she gets up.

When Mom walks back into the house, Rose and I are cuddling on the sofa, her flowery scent lulling me to sleep. Our plates are empty. So are the packets of chips and the microwavable pasta dish for four that we ate our way through.

"Jamie," mom scolds as she approaches the sofa. Rose and I are sluggish in our movements. The giggles and red eyes are long gone, we're just walking zombies now.

"Oh hey, Mom," I yawn.

"Gosh, 'Me, I said to make food for us, not for a whole regiment."

"Hi, Mrs. Williams," Rose says as she sits back up next to me.

"Rose," Mom coldly replies as a hello.

She's so conflicted when it comes to this White. She knows she hates Jake and Nathan. She hates them deeply within her soul for what they did to her little girl.

Rose, however, mom isn't sure how to feel about her. She knows she doesn't have the best influence on me. She knows she's up to no good most of the time, that she's rough on the outside, and has limited social skills.

Thankfully, she is also painfully aware that Rose is just a teenager who grew up abused, who's currently going through a rough phase, and is an orphan who's been ripped away from the only family who ever truly loved her.

I never went into details of what Nate has done to her in the past or anything regarding my friend. I only ever covered my side of the story, but she isn't stupid. She's a mother, after all, she feels these things deep down even when she doesn't know the details.

Mom turns the living room lights on and we both wince.

"What have you two been up to – Oh dear Lord, Rose!" Mom's eyes widen as she notices my friend's bruise. I turn to her, her eye has doubled in size on top of the ugly dark purple color.

Rose seems to remember she was hit and brings her fingers to her eye, feeling the swell. "Oh, shit," she mumbles.

"Language," Mom snaps.

I laugh as Rose loses her sass. "My bad," she says as she rolls her lips inward to stop herself from cursing again.

"I'm guessing you didn't put ice on this," mom asks as she opens our small freezer. She gets a bag of frozen green peas out and hands it to my friend.

"Thanks, Mrs. Williams."

"Rose is staying over tonight."

"Yeah, I figured that out," she deadpans.

Chapter 3

. . .

My mother is in the kitchen when I reappear. Rose is in the shower now that the swelling has gone down a little.

"Jamie," she sighs, and I already know where this is going. "You never said it was that bad."

"I know, Mom, but she doesn't need us to get involved. She just needs a place to sleep occasionally."

"That's twice this week."

"I know."

"And *where is* that twin of hers? Where is he hiding while all this is going on?"

It hurts to answer, it's humiliating but I push the words through. "I don't know."

"I thought she didn't get along with her foster family, not that they were hitting her. This is another level, Jamie."

"Mom– "

"No. There's no 'mom'. This is a dangerous situation here. What kind of adult—hell what kind of *mother* would I be if I didn't do something about it. We need to let the police know or at least social services."

"Please. It's just not how it works."

She pinches her nose with her thumb and forefinger. "Jamie..." she sighs.

"There's no need to worry, Mrs. Williams," Rose's hoarse voice cuts through our conversation.

"You showed up to my house with a black eye, Rose, I think it's time to start worrying."

"I got in some stupid fight with some girls from NSF. You should see *their* faces." She winks but mom shakes her head.

"That's a lie and you know it, young lady."

"Mom," I groan. "Please let it go."

My mother looks at us for another moment in complete

silence. I can see the battle going on in her mind. She's a good person, truly.

"Bedtime," she concludes. "Both of you."

Rose smiles her gorgeous smile and nods. "Thanks for having me again, Mrs. Williams." Her eyes are shining with respect for my mother before she heads to my room.

I hang back slightly, perfectly knowing Mom has more to say.

"Does she really hang out on the North Shore of the Falls?"

I don't know. This girl doesn't say anything to anyone. She disappears on a weekly basis, and no one knows what the hell she's up to.

"She's got friends there," I lie. It's not the best, but at least it covers for Rose's other lie. "She doesn't usually get in trouble."

Lies, lies, lies.

"Sure," she replies, not believing one bit.

I head to my room with heaviness in my heart for lying to my only parent.

I almost slip on the red carpet as we leave the theater. Cole watches me stumble and laughs. I scowl at him, but he knows I'm only joking.

"Were you always this clumsy?" he laughs.

"No! Who put this stupid carpet here?" I rearrange my bag on my shoulder.

"Do you remember in elementary school when we had this show for our parents?" he reminds me. "Everyone had to dress in navy blue. I was so happy to go and sing on stage on my own, Mrs. Larban said I had the voice of an

Chapter 3

angel. I caught my feet on the blue carpet they had put on the floor and fell in front of everyone. My mom was recording the whole thing. My parents show the video every Christmas."

I laugh as he recounts the story. "I remember." I hit his arm, taken with the giggles at the memory of young Cole falling face-first on the stage of our posh elementary school. "Aw, Cole. How's your singing now?"

"I will never sing, ever again. Fuck, no."

My laugh doubles as he recounts the last time he watched the video with his parents.

I didn't like the movie, I don't like gangster films, but I really enjoyed spending time with Cole. We didn't kiss, though I felt like he wanted to a few times. I still can't cross that line. We shared popcorn and held hands and it felt good but I'm not there yet.

He's too nice.

I try not to listen to the voice in my head, but I can't help thinking it's shouting the truth. Cole is nice. Too nice and I don't get the excitement with him that I got with Jake. My stomach doesn't twist like it did with him, my heart doesn't jump in my chest and my mouth doesn't get dry.

Cole's fingers thread through mine as we head out of the theater. He grabs my hand tightly.

"I had such a good time, Jamie. I'm sorry I couldn't pick you up and drive you here. My dad doesn't let me drive outside of school. Strict like that." He looks truly sorry, and I smile in return.

"Don't worry. I'm fine taking the bus. I had a lovely time too."

"Let me get you a taxi. Or should we both hang out at your place or something?"

"I'm spending the evening with Mom. It's the only night

she's not working this week. And you know I'm not Stoneview's royalty, I'm fine being on the bus."

"Will you send my regards to Caroline, then?" he smiles.

"Sure, I will. She loves it too much when you think of her," I giggle.

He hugs me tight, and I hug him back. I love Cole, as a friend for now. And when his lips hover over mine, my eyes are wide. That's how I notice the white Range Rover slowly driving past us. I don't look where it goes but it startles me, and I take a step back. Cole's eyebrows shoot up and he takes a step back as well.

"Shit, Jamie...I'm sorry. I shouldn't have..."

"It's me...I'm sorry," I whisper. "I don't know what's wrong with me."

"Nothing! Nothing's wrong with you. You're getting over a breakup and I'm overstepping the boundaries. I'm completely out of line. I really don't want to ruin our friendship. I don't want to push you away."

"You're not. I love what we have, Cole. I just don't want to rush things. If anything ever happens, shouldn't it be because we're both sure it's a good thing? Both sure we'll make the other happy?"

"Of course," he confirms.

"Right this minute, I'm not sure I could make you happy as anything more than friends."

He doesn't seem upset by my explanation. He seems relaxed actually.

"You're so mature, it's unsettling," he chuckles.

"I'm not. I've just been thinking about us a lot lately."

"So have I," he says in a last smile. "Get home safe."

We hug each other goodbye one last time before heading our own way.

When I turn around, my eyes automatically look for the

Chapter 3

white Range Rover. It's nowhere to be found and I might have imagined it. Or it could have been anyone's. Not every white Range Rover belongs to Sam. I make my way to the bus stop to take the rare bus back to Stoneview.

"Forty-five minutes?!" I choke as I check the bus app.

I should have gotten into a taxi with Cole. I was just feeling too awkward after our failed kiss. I need to let Mom know, she'll freak out if I'm late. She's been a lot less understanding since she came back from Tennessee. I dial her number and start talking as soon as she picks up.

"Hey Mom, my bus is going to be late, but I'm on my way." I barely have time to hear her 'okay' that the call cuts off and I bring the phone back in front of me.

Shit.

My phone died. I click on the home button a couple of times as if it's going to change anything and let out an annoyed sigh. I'm going to be in so much trouble.

"Need a ride, beautiful?"

I startle at Nathan's voice. Slowly turning around, I'm not really surprised when I see the white Range Rover. So it *was* them.

Sam isn't paying me much attention. Not like Nathan is. His ocean eyes are right on me, making me feel like he can see right through me. His dirty blond hair is in its usual bun and he's casually resting his elbow on the open window.

"No." My answer is so cold his eyebrows shoot up. I can feel my nostrils widening as I'm trying to contain myself.

"I was only trying to be helpful. You're right on the edge of NSF, young girls shouldn't hang around here on their own. I think your new boyfriend didn't get the memo," he smiles.

It's cold and calculating and I want to punch it off him so

bad it hurts. I'm not even going to tell him Cole isn't my boyfriend. Hopefully, it hurts him.

For one second, I think I'm going to ignore him. Then the anger deep inside takes over. I take a step over and place both my hands on either side of his elbow, grabbing the windowsill tightly.

"I saw what you did to Rose, you piece of shit, so don't talk to me about protecting young girls. How about you and your bestie go on your way, doing whatever little gang shit you love doing and leave me the fuck alone."

I don't think I ever swore so much in one sentence. This guy...he brings out the absolute worst in me. He's the devil incarnate and burning in hell would be a vacation for him.

There's a beat before Nathan explodes laughing and Sam turns to me, an eyebrow raised. When Nathan decides to open his door there's not much else I can do than take a step back.

He steps out and I immediately have to look up to face him. He's slightly scarier once he's standing up. I had forgotten how fit he is. He's not big but his muscles are cut and toned like a professional MMA fighter. He's a little taller than Jake, that I remembered. He towers over me as he calms down from his laughing fit and my heart beats like a rock band drum solo in my chest.

"Are you extremely stupid or extremely brave, Jamie?"

It takes me a second to swallow the dryness in my throat. His eyes are hard on me, and I'm thrown back to the first time there wasn't any love for me in his gaze. The night I thought he was going to kill his own brother.

He's actually scary.

His eyes dart to my neck and he reaches slowly. I'm too petrified to even move when he reaches out and grabs the heart pendant with a 'J' engraved in it. The one Jake gave me for Christmas, the one that has 'I love you' written on the other side. The one he wanted me to wear every day.

I can't get myself to take it off. I keep telling myself it's because it's a beautiful piece of jewelry. Truth is, I still can't process that it's truly over. I'm hanging onto the hope of him coming back to me like my last breath.

Nathan chuckles as he grips the necklace tighter and pulls on it, forcing me to come close to him. I don't want it to break. God, please don't break it.

"Nathan," I seethe through gritted teeth. "Let go."

From an outside point of view, we look like two friends, possibly a couple, close to each other. My chest is flushed against him and I'm tilting my head far back so I can look in his eyes, so he can see the fury in mine. His hand is tight on my necklace, so close to my neck I can feel the heat from his fingers despite the freezing temperatures. The humidity of our breaths in the cold air is mixing with each other. Everything about him is screaming danger, particularly the self-satisfied smile on his face.

"You're only hurting yourself by keeping this on. He's not coming back."

"You're the one who sent him away, didn't you? He wouldn't just leave. I know he wouldn't."

I know deep down that Jake truly loved me. I know what we had wasn't just another one of his fuck fests. It was raw. It was beautiful. It was pure love.

"You don't know shit about him. I told you you were making a huge mistake by choosing him, didn't I? I told you he was worse than me. You should have listened, beautiful."

I let out a sarcastic snore, enough to make Nathan raise his eyebrows in surprise.

"You know, Nathan. Jake *bullied* me. He *blackmailed* me. He pushed me past limits I wasn't even aware existed. He crossed the line so many times. Hell, he threatened me with a gun. And yet, he's not even on the same scale as you when it comes to disappointment. He–"

The growl that rumbles from his chest cuts me off and makes me shiver in fear. I've angered him and it's impossible to forget what he gets like when he's angry.

"You're being a very stupid girl, Jamie. I'd suggest you stop talking now."

"You know what? I am stupid. I was stupid giving in, I was stupid getting involved with Stoneview's number one fuckboy. And I might have been taken for a fool and, *yes*, I got my heart broken. But at least it was real. Nothing like our fake relationship. Nothing like the lie you had built for us. Such a good liar, aren't you?" I taunt.

Stop! Fucking stop!

Keeping on with this conversation is basically suicidal. But I'm angry. I've been raging inside for two months. Jake isn't here for me to take out my anger on and at this moment it doesn't matter because Nathan deserves at least half of it.

I know there is a reason Jake left and it *has* to be linked with Nathan. If he wanted to break up with me, he would have simply done so and kept on going with his life. He would have flirted with other girls in front of me without a care in the world. He wouldn't have just left.

I startle when Nathan's other hand lands on my hip in a tight grip. It's big enough to grab me easily even though there's not much feminine shape to grab on me. I'm tiny, he's big and his firm squeeze reiterates that fact well enough. He slowly hardens his grip, crushing me enough that I can't help a quiet whimper from escaping my lips.

"Stop," I breathe out.

He ignores my plea and keeps going with his trail of thoughts. "You think you're better than me? I'm a liar, am I?

Chapter 3

Who was the little slut seeing someone else behind my back? Granted you didn't know he was my brother, but you shouldn't have been seeing *anyone*." His grip tightens on the last word, and I squirm under it. "Fuck, I *loved* you, Jamie." His voice breaks slightly as he says his last words and my heart somersaults in my chest.

"It was all a lie," I whisper. I don't know if I'm saying that to make myself feel better. To take some of the guilt off my shoulders or if I truly mean it.

"Nah, beautiful. That part wasn't a lie."

He shrugs his shoulders as if it didn't mean much when it truly does. I know it because his eyes are back to the ones I used to know. They burn so brightly with love for me that there's an ache in my chest.

The flame disappears as fast as it came. "So get off your high horse. You're one of us, Jamie, you're one of the *bad* people. You hurt others, you use them, and you *love* for your own selfish reasons. You're no better than me."

His truth hits hard and I struggle to find my words. Is he right? Am I as bad as him? When I was with Nathan, I was eaten with guilt from what was happening with Jake. The thoughts that were running through my head about Jake were sinful.

That guilt disappeared when I learned of the lies and the manipulation, when I understood who Nathan really was, what he did to his siblings. But that doesn't make me a better person because I still had those thoughts, and I still entertained a possibility with Jake *before* I knew all of that. Nathan is all sorts of wrong, but I'm not far behind.

I've always known I wasn't a good person deep down. I've never been the *Goody* everyone calls me. I respect the rules, I like studying and I am a decent person because that is how my dad raised me. These things were so important to him, and I know I wanted to respect him by being the best person I could be.

But deep down I've always been jealous of people with a personality like Rose's, even if hers was forged out of abuse and roughness, she's not sorry for who she is. She doesn't give a shit, she's rude when she feels like it, does whatever she wants, and doesn't care who she hurts or how. It's tough but you know what you're getting. I wish I was like that.

Instead, I've always had this good girl façade and I'm a big disappointment when people find out that I'm just as selfish as anyone. I'm not good. I know that. This is why Nathan became more interesting to me once I knew he was the bad kind.

Mainly, this is why I was so tempted by Jake. This is why I'm attracted to him and his black soul. He's my soulmate. He's broken and wicked and it satisfies me. I could never be with someone like Cole, he's too moral. Deeply moral. Too different from me.

Nathan grasps my attention again when his hands leave my body. He takes a step back and I let out a ragged breath.

Too close.

He was too close.

His gaze is behind me, and I turn around just in time to see a scantily clad girl coming our way. I turn back to Nathan, and I know he noticed my 'o' shaped mouth about to ask him who she is when he answers my question.

"Jamie, Emma, Emma, Jamie. Emma works for me."

"Works for you," I scoff.

"It's done," Emma says, ignoring me.

"Nice bra," I mutter, looking at the piece of rag she uses as a top.

She scowls at me, and I shake my head at the situation. I

shouldn't be giving another second of attention to Nathan and whatever business he's got going on.

Emma's chest is covered with colorful tattoos, including a dagger that dips low between her breasts. The letters NSC are tattooed in black on the handle.

North Shore Crew.

Nathan is using the small crews from the poor side of Silver Falls to reinforce his nationwide gang. How ethical.

What's funny is Mom and Dad used to live on the North Shore when Aaron was a toddler. It was before Dad became Sheriff. They moved to Stoneview when Mom was pregnant with me. If Dad was just another police officer, Aaron and I would have grown up not far from where I'm currently standing. One bridge separates the North Shore from the South of Silver Falls, the richer part is where the trail to the falls is. Where there is a nice theater and the huge mall Emily and I go to so I can buy myself clothes I could never afford in Stoneview.

I can't help another shake and I become too aware I've been staring at Emma with sorry eyes.

You could have been her.

I don't know. I don't think I would have the backbone to be some badass bitch from the North Shore. I probably would have been the kind that tries to be invisible so she doesn't end up being involved with NSC or their rivals, the King family. I would also probably have been truly bullied for being the daughter of a cop.

At Stoneview Prep, the boys call girls like Emma NSP. They're North Shore Pussy to the lacrosse privileged *dudes*. No more, no less. They think they're cool when they brag about catching one of those fishes after inviting them to their mansion parties.

Stoneview boys rarely go to North Shore houses to get

their fill, they're too scared to get robbed or stabbed. Except for Jake. I know he used to go because Luke, Rose, and Chris went with him, and Chris has told me about it before; Jake trying to avoid Camila by going to a place where she'd never go. Her red soles would get too dirty.

"Hop in the car, Emma. I'll drop you." He pauses as he turns to me. "Unless I'm driving you back? That ride is still on offer, beautiful."

"I already said no." I turn to leave, and his voice almost stops me.

"I'm available anytime you need a reminder of who you truly are." I can hear the smile in his voice, but I keep going. "Just like me," he insists louder as I walk away.

Asshole.

4

JAKE

Us – James Bay

Fuck.

I know this fight is over for me before his fist even lands on my jaw. I already expect the click and the blackout. He's so fast but somehow, it's all going in slow motion in my head. I don't move on time and the pain lasts for a second before I fall unconscious on the floor.

When I come back, I'm already on the doctor's bed in the locker room. Billie is standing right beside me as I squint to adjust to the light. I can hear her foot tapping incessantly on the linoleum floor, her shoes squeaking on it as she shifts position. She's nervously playing with the chain around her neck, and I smile.

"Why are you all stressed out?" I ask in a raw voice.

"Fuck," she startles. "You fucking scared us, you asshole." She smiles at me as she squeezes my arm with a shaking hand.

"Shit, that was bad," I growl as I try to sit up. My head feels heavy, it's like it's screwed onto the shitty bed.

"Don't sit up," she orders in a strong voice. "Doc said you got a bad concussion from the fall. And a fractured rib by the way."

Oh. So that's why it hurts to talk. And to breathe. And to be alive.

"I understood it was bad when you didn't open your eyes right after passing out. You usually only go for a few seconds. You should have seen me jump in the ring. Had to knock out a bitch myself," she chuckles.

Billie is a really fucking strong girl, despite being the size of a small child. That much I've learned since I've met her. Growing up in her little gang, surrounded by tough guys on the North Shore of Silver Falls, she understood from a young age that if she wasn't strong, she was dead. Or worse.

The first day we both spent here, she was desperate to spar. I tried to go easy on her, but she was angry. Raging, actually. She needed to fight someone, and she needed someone to fight back.

I felt like shit after I gave her a black eye. She felt fine when she gave me a nosebleed. In the end, it did both of us a lot of good.

I wish I was as strong as Billie. The girl had to leave her family behind because Nate decided the North Shore Crew had to prove their loyalty to Bianco, and she never complains about it. She never even talks about them.

"Don't say *usually* like I get knocked out dead at every fight. I've won more than I lost."

"But every time you lose, it's that jaw click isn't it?" She winks at me like she knows me by heart and my heart pinches.

She really doesn't and even if she picked up on things since I've met her, I don't want her to. My habits and my

Chapter 4

behaviors are for Jamie. I only want her to know me like that.

You're such an asshole, Jake. If you miss Jamie so much, why do you fuck Billie?

Because I'm never going to be with Jamie again, and maybe if I bury myself deep enough in Billie, I won't see Jamie's face while I do so.

"You really scared me out there," she murmurs as her hand moves to my chest. "Don't do that again."

She sounds sweet right now. She isn't. She's not sweet, she's not falling for me, she's not a little breakable thing like her appearance portrays. The only thing that gives her that innocent look is her big, brown eyes. So huge, they'd fool anyone. In reality, she's so rough and so wrong for me. She's the kind of girl that could never make me happy. She's exactly what I deserve.

"Turns out it's a bit harder to fight big dudes in the ring than a small North Shore girl at training."

I thought she'd smile at my words, but she shakes her head instead.

"You're not invincible, Jake. None of us are. Please remember that."

I grab her hand tightly because, even though she shouldn't, it means a lot that she cares.

"I know. Don't worry. I'll get better, train harder. And I'll be more careful."

She sighs as she nods and for the first time since we've been here, I can sense that she's sick of it.

"We'll make it through," I insist, squeezing her hand. "At least you won all your fights. You're doing so good, Billie."

She sits on the wooden bench opposite where I'm lying and plays with her chain again.

"Can I ask you something?"

"Sure," I nod as I manage to finally sit up. I instinctively hold my side where I now know my rib is fractured and wince at the pain.

Motherfucker got me good.

"Are you related to Mateo Bianco?" She must notice my surprise because she quickly adds. "I mean, Jake *White*, Mateo *Bianco*. It's pretty self-explanatory, isn't it? Means the same but it sounds like you altered your name to distance yourself from him or something. I don't know. Maybe I'm assuming shit."

I watch as her fingers twist around the simple silver chain around her neck. There's no pendant on it, nothing. I hesitate for a minute or so. I don't actually know Billie, we just ended up in a shit situation together. I also genuinely don't think she's a bad person. She's tough, but deep down she's good and if she's asking personal questions, I'd assume it's from a good intention. So I decide to be honest.

"Kinda," I reply.

"No fucking way," she cuts me off before I can explain. "Is he your uncle or something? Shit, he's not your dad, is he?"

I shake my head no. "Chill out," I chuckle. "He was my foster dad for a few years. He bribed shit tons of people to turn my name into the Americanized version of his. He's a megalomaniac like that."

I almost say it was the case for my sister as well, but I can't get myself to talk about Ozy. My chest aches way too fucking much when I mention her name, my throat gets too tight. Billie knows her, they've met before, she's smart enough to understand she's included in everything that happened to me.

"He adopted you? That's so fucking crazy."

My jaw tightens painfully at the A. word. God it drives

Chapter 4

me insane when people don't make the difference. Bianco ain't shit to me, and I'm not fucking adopted.

"He was my legal guardian. There's a difference," I reply through gritted teeth.

"Gee, I'm sorry," she chortles. "You get a bit sensitive after being knocked out, you know that?"

I can't help the smile back. She's so annoying, in the best way.

"Anyway, I thought you must have been related somehow. That you weren't like me."

"Not like you?"

"I mean you're not some random kid who fights for him. There was the name, and now the tattoo. It was starting to add up that you knew each other."

"The tattoo?" I ask confused.

"Yeah, that tattoo you got on your back. He's got the same on his hand, doesn't he?"

I'm about to confirm when it hits me.

"Wait, when did you see Bianco?" I ask.

Billie is some girl from North Shore of Silver Falls. Bianco has never set foot there; he's not interested in what random white trash is part of his ever-growing organization. He sends Nate for that. She's never met him before. Or so I thought.

She gives me her brightest smile before answering. "He's here tonight. I met him just as you were coming into the ring. Dickie introduced me as his best fighter, can you imagine?"

Dickie is our coach, but that's not the point. My heart drops in my stomach hard enough to make me feel like I ate cement for lunch. Bianco is here on the night I got knocked out like a little bitch in the ring. Could it have been worse?

Billie doesn't notice my reaction because she keeps

going like a fangirl about to meet her favorite boy band. "And he came with that hot guy who's always with him."

"Nate is here?" I try to keep my voice as normal as possible but the more Billie talks, the more it starts to shake. I don't know if it's anger or fear. Probably a bit of both. It's a mix of fury and the memory of what used to happen when I lost a fight.

"Nah. Nate's the guy who picked me up from North Shore, isn't he? I'm talking about the other one who's always with him. The hot, *hot* one."

I roll my eyes realizing who she's talking about. What is it with girls close to me liking the asshole?

"The big one," she happily insists. "He's like his bodyguard or something. You know? Tall, dark, and handsome with all the tattoos?"

"Sam. His name is Sam, sweetheart. And he's an enforcer, not a bodyguard." Bianco's mellow voice is loud and fills up the entire room, making it feel two times smaller.

Both me and Billie turn to the entrance. Bianco is standing proud in his white suit, Sam behind him like the fucking wall he is. Big, quiet, and useless.

"Hi, Mr. Bianco. We met earlier." Billie beams as she sees him, painfully reminding me of how unaware she is of the bigger picture, or who I am.

She has no idea what Bianco really is like or the fact that Sam is a number one heartless asshole. Fuck, she probably doesn't even know Nate is my brother. She's just glad her little gang now has Bianco's protection and money. What a fucking mess.

Bianco ignores her hellos. "Do you know what an enforcer is..." He raises an eyebrow.

"Billie. My name's Billie, sir. And yeah, kinda."

Chapter 4

She blushes as Sam's gaze hovers over her whole body. He doesn't react though. Plain, old Sam. I hope Billie doesn't expect to get something out of him.

I never knew that was what Sam does for Bianco. He's not one of his 'kids' but he's always been *there*. I always assumed he was just Nate's personal bitch. His bodyguard or something. Even if my brother doesn't really need anyone to fight for him, he needs someone to watch his back. Well apparently, he doesn't need anyone to do that either.

I would be lying if I said I wasn't surprised at how important Sam actually is to Bianco's business. He's a fucking enforcer, that's why he's such a lethal bastard.

"An enforcer," Bianco starts again, "is someone who works closely with me. He does the jobs that need a bit of strength if you see what I mean. If someone keeps making me lose money for example." His gaze is on me as he finishes his explanation and my own hardens.

I get up from Doc's bed so I can have more height to myself. I'm in pain but I've been worse, and Bianco doesn't need to know that anyway.

"Billie, how about you and I get to know each other better over a glass of wine?"

"Wine?" she asks in surprise.

"She's a fucking high school junior, how about you have a drink with someone your age?" I growl.

I can see the confusion in Billie's eyes but now is not the time to explain that Bianco is much more dangerous than she thinks. She looks at me, silently wondering why I'm being so rude to him but she's smart enough to know she shouldn't be asking anything right now.

Billie is the definition of street smart, and she can smell a problem from miles away.

"Well, she can have a soda. I need an excuse to get her

out of the room so you can have a little chat with Sam. That's the fourth fight you lost, Jake. Did you know?"

I don't even respond. He knows I know.

"You get Sam to have a 'chat' with me now? You never had a problem doing it yourself before," I taunt.

"You're stronger than you used to be, and I'm only getting older," he smiles. The fucker isn't even going to deny that he used to beat the shit out of me. "Billie?" Bianco insists.

She turns to me, and I can tell she's about to say that she'll stay with me, but I cut her off. "It's fine."

She only hesitates another second before leaving with Bianco. What a smart little cookie you are, Billie.

The door closes behind them and Sam turns to me, as silent as ever.

"Try to avoid my ribs, they're already fucked," I tell him deadpan.

The last thing I expected was for him to gift me with an actual answer.

"Keep your snarky comments to yourself, mate. I'm taking you back to Stoneview," he tells me in his ugly-ass British accent.

There's a long silence as I try to process if this is a bad joke or not.

"What?"

"I'm taking you back to Stoneview," he repeats with no change in his voice whatsoever. Fuck, how can anyone be so shit at making conversation?

"Care to explain?" D- fucking -uh, Sam. I didn't ask 'what' because I didn't understand the words you said, I'm confused as fuck here.

He sighs as he walks my way and sits down on the bench Billie was on a minute ago.

Chapter 4

"How were your last four fights?" he asks.

I kind of want to punch him in the face for reminding me that I got knocked out in my last few fights. Then again... when do I not want to punch Sam in the face?

"I'm sure you know," I rumble in response. I sit back on Doc's bed as I wait for Sam to explain where he's going with all this. I thought I was meant to get my ass handed to me.

"Yeah," he confirms. "That's a lot of knockouts in a short amount of time. I hope you don't get permanent damage." He couldn't sound less honest if he tried. There's even a slight movement at the corner of his lips. Is that his smile? Is that the best he can do? If you're going to mock me, at least do it all the way.

He continues talking when he realizes I'm not going to say anything.

"I picked the lads myself—"

"You're a serious asshole, you know that?" I rage. "I was doing what I was told, wasn't I? What sort of grudge do you have against me that you feel the need to send your toughest guys on me?"

This time he chuckles, showing he knew exactly what he was doing.

"You were doing a little too well," he explains. "Bianco would have wanted to keep you here if you kept bringing him money. That's all he cares about. And *I* need you in Stoneview. Look how fast he comes now that you're putting a dent in his boxing budget."

"So you give me a good beating and then what?"

He runs a tattooed hand in his hair. It's always gelled back, the opposite to mine always in a mess. So stuck up this guy.

"We can pretend the beating happened. The important

thing is, I convinced him to bring you back. If you want to, of course."

I shake my head in disbelief. It can't be that easy.

"Alright. So where's the catch?"

"There's no catch, there are conditions."

"Sure," I snort. "Call it what you want."

"Bianco insists you can't go back to Stoneview Prep. You've got to make yourself useful so he's putting you in Silver Falls High. He wants eyes on NSC."

"Fucking great," I mutter. "Being Bianco's watchdog for the North Shore Crew. My lifelong dream."

"Better than getting knocked out, isn't it?"

"Whatever. What else?"

"The Jamie thing, that would still be the same."

"Are you fucking kidding me?!" I explode as I get up. "What's the fucking point of going back if I can't see her anyway?"

I'm close enough to him and angry enough that he senses a threat. I can see it in his eyes. He gets up slowly, asserting his height on mine. He's so much bigger as well. What a fucking scary bastard.

"I think you should take what you're given, mate. I'm not going to try to bring you back to Stoneview again. It's your one and only shot."

"Yeah? And what could *you* possibly want me in Stoneview for? You all got an agenda and I'm just here doing everyone's dirty deeds while y'all fill your pockets with blood money. Go on, Sam, what do you *need* bad enough to bring me back to Stoneview?"

There's a change in his gaze. I see it straight away. He's worried. The fucker is worried to death. Not about me, I'm sure. He runs another hand through his hair and when he talks again, his gaze is behind me, avoiding mine.

Chapter 4

"I need Rose safe." He scratches his throat and puts his hands in his pockets to act casual. He's anything but.

The loud laugh that escapes my lips is so cold, I'm pretty sure the room temperature drops a few degrees. My brain doesn't control my body anymore. Only anger does.

I push Sam so hard he staggers back and falls on the bench.

"*You* don't need her to be safe. You don't need her fucking anything," I rage. "Don't talk to me about her. I don't want her fucking name crossing your lips."

He's back up quickly but I'm quicker. The punch to his temple barely bothers him, because this time he was expecting it. He pushes me back but doesn't hit. Good, I'd probably be in big trouble if he tried to. Fuck, it felt so good to finally punch him.

"You're being a fucking idiot, you know that?" His voice barely changes. There's only a quiet strain to it that shows he's getting angrier. "I'm trying to help here."

"I don't need your fucking help. You don't get to decide who keeps her safe. *I* do!" I'm shouting so loud my voice breaks. The fury coursing through my veins has numbed all sorts of pain I was feeling.

"Don't you think maybe *she* does?"

Of course he had to point out what a possessive fucker I am when it comes to the ones I love.

"She's a fucking mess, Jake. I pick her up, drugged off her face every weekend from North Shore." He shakes his head. "You Whites and your fucking need to control everything. You want to make decisions? Fine."

He puts his hand in his back pocket and brings out his phone. He throws it to me after tapping on it a few times.

"Enjoy yourself," he says quietly.

My mouth drops open when I look down. The latest

message is a video of Rose with a few NSC guys at what I'm assuming is some party on the North Shore. She's wearing a bra only, showing her tattooed arm and the other few on her hip and ribs. One of the guys has a hand on her lower back while she's bent down snorting a line.

The camera pans, showing all the other men around. They're looking at her like some piece of meat. As soon as she straightens back up, my heart picks up in anger again. Her left eye is bruised a deep purple and I know exactly who did this to her.

"Fuck," I whisper in a broken voice.

She's so fucking skinny, she looks exactly like the last time we lived at Bianco's: bruised and with ribs popping so bad through her skin you can count them. Except this time, instead of eating nothing, her diet is cigarettes and coke. Who knows what else?

The video stops and I look down at the text. It's from some guy called '3'.

> 3: Ain't that your girl, bro? You need a tighter leash.

I feel like I've been put through a fucking washing machine. Shit, I feel so fucking sick. The mix of the punches I took, the stress, the news. It's all lethal.

"She's not your girl," I tell him through gritted teeth but it's almost a question. Who knows what happened in the last two months?

He grabs his phone back and looks at me deadpan. "She's not," he confirms. "I'm glad this is what's worrying you right now."

"Where's Nate when this happens, huh?" I rage. "Isn't he meant to be taking care of us? What a great guardian."

"Nate has no idea what she's been up to. You think any of

Chapter 4

them would still be alive if he did? Bianco is keeping him so fucking busy he barely has time to sleep."

He looks down at his phone again, tap-tap, and gives it back to me. The texts from my twin break my heart into a million pieces.

> Rose: I'm drunk af. Pick me up.
>
> Rose: Ok maybe more than drunk.
>
> Rose: I punched 3 in the face for that text. I think he hates me now.
>
> Rose: If you don't pick me up, I'll happily partake in a gangbang.
>
> Rose: 3 doesn't hate me anymore. The power of good pussy.
>
> Rose: Do you think Jake would get jealous as fuck if he knew I sleep in Jamie's bed when Nate kicks me out?
>
> Rose: I hope not.
>
> Rose: I love him.
>
> Rose: I miss him. Please tell me where he is.

My throat tightens so hard I have to scratch it. The pressure building behind my eyes is unbearable.

> Rose: I know Bianco is keeping him away.
>
> Rose: If he doesn't let him come back soon. I'm gonna kill myself earlier than planned. Tell Bianco I will do it. I promise I will.

"Earlier than planned?" I murmur, my heart breaking.

I'm brought back to reality when Sam snatches his phone back.

"That was last night by the way. Since you're so keen on making the decisions yourself, I'll give you the evening to think about it. My plane leaves at eight tomorrow morning."

He walks to the door, and I get the feeling it's because he feels the same as I do.

"Sam," I say as he's opening the door. He slightly turns to me. "That 3 guy–"

"Is dead," he cuts me off, and I can feel the fury rolling off him.

"Was it an 'accident'?" I ask, voice dripping in sarcasm.

I thought he'd at least pretend it was. At least pretend he wasn't a jealous bastard obsessed with my sister.

"No. I put a bullet between his eyes." He leaves and closes the door quietly as if not a worry in the world.

For some reason, I don't hate him as much as I used to.

5

JAMIE

Glad He's Gone – Tove Lo

I grab my red pen and look at the essay Cole just gave me.

"Ouch, Cole. There's a grammar mistake in every sentence," I murmur.

"Do you really have to use the red pen," he sighs.

It makes me giggle and I look up at him. "Focus on eating and I'll focus on your essay. Little boy gotta become big for the tournament." I eye the two plates in front of him and he laughs.

"I eat a lot, okay? I need the energy."

"My position on the field requires more energy than yours," I tease. "You don't see me eating twice my weight in fries."

Playing center is the ultimate tiring position on the field. I go from one end to another for the whole game. Cole plays defense on the men's team. I'm not saying it's lazy, but it's definitely not as hard as center.

"That's because it takes about two fries to energize that tiny body of yours."

I laugh again and our eyes lock in comfortable silence for a few seconds. It always feels so good to spend time with him.

"Whatever," I chortle. "This is due on Monday, should we work on it tonight?"

He puts his cutlery down and looks at me from across the table, that cheeky look shining in his eyes.

"Actually," he says. "My parents are finally out of town so I'm throwing a party tonight. You'll come, right?"

"Oh," is all that leaves my mouth.

"Come on, Jamie. I really want you there."

"I don't know," I sigh.

Emily chooses this moment to sit next to me, practically throwing her plate on the table. I look at the content and frown at the few salad leaves.

"Not hungry?" I ask.

"Mom's got me on a new diet. Don't wanna talk about it," she mutters.

"Another debutante ball coming up?"

"Don't want to talk about it, 'Me," she sing-songs in annoyance.

"Sorry, sorry. Cole was telling me about a party at his tonight. How does that sound?"

Cole smiles at me and nods at Emily. "Everyone's gonna be there," he confirms.

"Including Luke?" Emily queries.

Cole's mouth twists as he nods. "Probably, the whole team is gonna be there. But so are the cheerleaders so you're gonna have lots of friends there."

"Yay, the cheerleaders," she replies, her voice sarcastic enough to make both me and Cole grimace. We exchange a look and I nod at him as we read each other's minds.

"I'll go if you go," I smile at Emily.

Chapter 5

A night out would do Emily some good. She's finally past the anger phase of her breakup with Luke and is truly heartbroken. She already told me it was too hard to be around him.

I look up to where Luke is eating. His younger sister, Ella, sat with him today, leaving her cheerleader friends behind. The usual gang, Chris, Camila, Rachel, and Beth are eating with them and my stomach twists in pain. Jake is still missing and we're all assuming he's decided to leave. What if something happened to him? Like it did to Aaron. A burst of pain tears my chest apart and I have to put down my fork.

I feel sick.

That's something sweet Cole can't take away. He could never because I *need* Jake.

The cafeteria heavy wooden door opens loudly, bringing me out of my self-pity, as Scott Johnson runs in.

"Yo, guys!" he calls out to his lacrosse teammates. Some are at Luke's table. Some the table over, and Cole is with me. They all look up on cue, united and aware that Scott would only really mean them when he addresses his 'guys'.

"Rose's brother is fucking up Jas'!" he shouts.

There's a brief pause where my heart free falls in my stomach and my eyes lock with Chris' before all the lacrosse players get up in unison. Ready to get in a giant fight with whom I can only assume is Nathan.

"'Me," Emily begs as I get up. "Don't."

But I'm already gone, and I know she's after me, following the pack of angry lacrosse players. I'm quickly followed by the rest of the students, desperate for a bit of tough action at Stoneview Prep.

I manage to make my way to the parking lot at the same time as Cole. It's a sad sight to see Jason curled up on the floor, Nathan practically stomping on him.

"Touch her again and see what happens, you piece of shit." Nathan is fuming.

"Where's Rose?" I ask Cole.

"That car," he points at Sam's SUV where Rose is angrily knocking on the window. Cole is already following his teammates.

Fear courses through my body. Nathan is strong, but not strong enough to take on half a dozen lacrosse players on his own.

"Shit," I whisper, already hating myself for going headfirst toward trouble. And for who? Fucking Nathan White.

Rose is already back from the car, raging at her brother. "Tell your fucking pet to come out here! You two are fucking cowards, I swear."

Nathan gives another kick to Jason, whimpering on the floor. I can see from the corner of my eyes Scott, Luke, and Cole helping Jason back up, his big form all hunched over. It seems the other players are not as brave as one expected.

It only takes a split second for Nathan to turn to his sister, grabbing her by the lapels of her uniform jacket.

"You're a real fucking stupid girl, you know that?"

"Nathan!" I shout in shock. Rose is already shrugging off his bloodied knuckles from her jacket.

"Fuck off," she growls. "You wanna tell me that was for me as well? I feel so fucking safe, thanks!"

I grab Nathan's shoulder, pulling him away from Rose and putting myself between them. "That's enough," I order. "You're losing it completely!"

But it's not only Nathan that needs to be held back. Rose is burning with hate and before I know it, she's trying to push me out of the way to claw at her brother. I hear Chris and Luke talking to her, trying to calm her down.

"I'm gonna fucking kill you, you know that? Second time lucky, motherfucker!"

"Rose, stop," Chris begs, desperately trying to control her.

I have to put two hands on Nathan's shoulders as he makes it to go past me again. He's clearly not truly trying, or he would easily push me away.

"Why would you do this?" I ask him. My voice is drowning in despair. Jason didn't deserve his wrath. Rose deserves some freedom.

Nathan answers my question when he addresses Rose again, pushing slightly against my body.

"Do you know what Bianco would do to you if he caught you sleeping around like a fucking slut?!"

He takes a step back, dejected and I'm surprised when one of his hands lands between my shoulder blades, bringing me with him. I end up head against his chest and I hear his heart galloping wildly.

"I'm trying to keep you alive here," he barks at her and if I hadn't had my ear right against his chest and his hand tightening around my uniform jacket, I would probably not have realized how true those words were.

I hear the tremble deep in his throat and the skip of his heart. I hear that famous scratch when he tries to hold back fear. I hear the frozen vocal cords when someone tries to keep down the tears.

Nathan White is scared.

And I'm the last one who would have thought it possible.

But Rose didn't hear what I heard, and she is far past the point of reason.

"Fuck you, Nate," she rasps. "You're the worst thing that's

ever happened to us. And where's my brother, huh?! The important one! The one that fucking cares!"

It takes a few minutes for Chris and Luke to talk some sense into Rose. For the crowd to disperse. And in all that mess, I'm just here, hugging Nate as his heart rate slowly calms down.

I know it's just him and me in the lot when I hear his broken voice. "It's so fucking hard."

My own heart accelerates. "What is?" I ask, desperate for clarification.

"Staying away from you."

His nose finds the crook of my neck and he inhales deeply.

And with that, he parts from me and walks back to the SUV.

Not another word.

Not a look back.

I lay on my stomach on Emily's bed, waiting for her to show me the nth outfit of the afternoon.

"What about this one?" she asks, coming out of her walk-in closet with a giant Tommy Hilfiger sweater she wears as a dress and that makes her look like the most preppy girl in town. That means something in Stoneview.

"Sure, that fits perfectly at a Stoneview party," I giggle. I stuff another chicken nugget in my mouth and carry on with a full mouth. "It's not vewy sekshi though."

"Excuse me?" she chuckles. "Manners, young lady."

"It's not very sexy," I repeat after swallowing. "Don't you want to show Luke what he's missing?"

"Luke isn't *missing* anything. We're meant to have parted on good terms."

"Right." I roll my eyes. "Are you going to have another one?" I say pointing at the nuggets. "We got these for you. If your mom could see…"

"Yes, stop eating all of them."

"But I'm hungry," I groan, rolling onto my back.

Her face appears above me, lips pinched. "'Me, bestie to bestie, are you really going to wear that? I thought you wanted to give the whole Cole thing a chance."

"What's wrong with my outfit?" I gasp, sitting up. I look down at my body and my mouth twists, agreeing with Emily's statement.

"These," Emily says, pulling at my simple blue mom jeans then tapping my red converse. "Make you look like a child. You can't wear loose clothes, 'Me, it's just not your shape."

"A bit rude but okay-"

"And this," she pinches the white tee I've put on top of a tightly fitted turtleneck. "Jesus Christ what the fuck is this?" she laughs.

"Stop being so mean," I moan.

She helps me off the bed, grabs a nugget and we both walk to the closet.

I come out fifteen minutes later not recognizing myself in the mirror.

"Really, Em? Black vinyl pants. They're so shiny, why so shiny?"

"I like the red bra," she beams. "Put this on." She gives me a tight tank top, clearly see-through.

"Have you ever worn this? It's so tight," I pant as my head emerges from the top.

"No. My mom wishes though."

"Even *I* can't breathe in it," I sigh. "Your mom is delusional."

"Now, now, that's not news, babes. See now you can wear your ugly-ass red converse. It goes well."

"We can see my bra," I hesitate, looking at my deep red lacy bra.

"Exactly, it goes really well with the converse." She puts on a pair of thigh-high boots to go with her dress and her outfit suddenly becomes ten times sexier.

"What do we think?"

"Very nice," I nod. My phone beeps on the bed and Emily grabs it before me.

"Uh, why is Rose White asking you if you're going to Cole's?"

"Oh, I can explain."

I keep to myself Rose's well-guarded secret, but I do explain that whenever she has trouble with Nathan she comes to my house.

"I can't believe what happened at school today. Jason must be so messed up. Do you know what Beth put in the cheerleader group? She said it was karma for cheating on her for so long. The girl is such a bitch, Jason is probably out of the tournament at this point."

I roll my eyes at the drama. Beth *is* a bitch and Jason didn't deserve what happened to him. At the same time, I can't help thinking Beth didn't deserve to be cheated on.

Look who's talking.

"I know what you're thinking," Emily cuts through my thoughts. "But Beth and Jason should have never been a thing. The only reason they are 'together' is because Beth's parents have lost all their money and are desperate to marry their spoiled only child to the mayor's son. You know Beth fucks Mr. Corragan, right?"

Chapter 5

"What?!" I choke on another chicken nugget. "Our calculus teacher?"

"Yeah. She is only interested in Jason's money I can assure you. So, she really *is* a bitch to put that in the group."

"Whatever," I mumble as I reply to Rose that I am indeed going to Cole's party.

Emily escapes downstairs and comes back up with two beers.

"Already?" I ask.

"Yeah, I need a drink to forget that you used to date the Whites' older brother. What a fucking mess," she chuckles.

"Thanks for the reminder. Give me that." I grab one of the open beers from her hand and she hurries to put some music from her 'let's get hyped up' playlist.

We drink, we take a million selfies on Emily's famous round bed that always features on her Instagram, and cheer another beer to finding new boyfriends, even if none of us can get over our exes.

When my phone beeps again, Emily grabs it.

"I can't even believe you're besties with Rose White," she giggles into her beer. "How could you leave me out of this? You know I have a huge crush on her."

"Maybe she can be your rebound," I joke.

"I fucking wish. She's asking if you want—" she stops unexpectedly.

"What?"

"If you want...um...Luke to drive you."

I shake my head 'no'. "No, we're going together. Give me that, I'll tell her."

But instead of giving me my phone, Emily looks at me with a glint of cheekiness in her eyes. "Let's go with her."

"You want to get into Luke's car?" This girl is on another level of confused.

"No. Let's pick her up and go with her. Come on, I'm dying to spend time with Rose. Let's do it and hopefully, it can piss off Luke. Two birds, one stone, baby."

I'm about to say no when the tipsiness from the two beers I had kicks in. "Okay," I giggle. "Let's do it."

"Oh my God, oh my God, I'm driving to Rose White's new house," Emily squeaks in the car.

"Please stop. She's a student in our school, not one of your Instagram influencers. Left here," I indicate.

"I'm only joking. So, which one?" she asks, looking at the mansions around us.

"That one with the weeping willow," I point at the house on our right.

"This is *so* weird. Did you like...do things with Nate in there?"

"Jesus, Em, this was a horrible idea. Turn around."

"You're right it was," she replies as she parks the car in Nathan's driveway.

"Why are you not turning around then?"

"Because we're adults now." She turns the ignition off and turns to me. "We put up with our mistakes and bad ideas."

"We have literally no reason to be here, I didn't even text Rose. Please, I've put up with enough mistakes this year."

"I'm feeling adventurous." She wiggles her eyebrows at me.

"Whatever." I groan as I hit my head against her headrest.

It takes Rose a while to open the door, and when she finally does, I wince in surprise, averting my eyes.

"Uh, hi?" Rose says, only wearing a towel, water dripping out on the floor.

"Apologies for interrupting your shower, we're here to take you to Cole's," Emily explains with a huge smile on her face.

"It's 7 pm," she replies deadpan. Her eyes land on me. "Jamie, what the fuck?"

I shrug. "I don't even know."

She lets out a big sigh and steps away from the door. "You two are so fucking weird."

I bite the inside of my cheek as I walk in. Emily stops dancing on the spot and hurries after me.

The hallway is just as huge as I remember and there is loud music coming from up the double staircase at the back.

"You're lucky Nate isn't here," she says as she walks ahead of us, back up the stairs and turning left into a long hallway that I've never walked before.

Nathan's room is at the end of the opposite hall, that I know for sure. I watch Rose's long black hair dripping water as we all walk to her room. I'm not surprised she took the one as far from her brother's as possible, despite the number of free bedrooms in this house.

"Where is he?" Emily asks and I have to pinch her arm. "Ow!"

'What?' she mouths in silence. This girl has no boundaries, way too extroverted.

"Fuck if I know," Rose replies without a clue of what's going on behind her. "He left with Sam about an hour ago."

Rose's room is a suite twice the size of Emily's. No bed in sight as we walk into a living room about the extent of my house. The music is coming from where I'm assuming the bedroom is.

"This is nice," Emily grins. She slumps on one of the two

red velvet sofas and rests the heels of her boots on the oak coffee table in front of her.

Rose ignores her and turns to me. "New look?"

I shrug with a smile. "Meh."

"I like it. Make yourself at home, there are beers in the mini-fridge."

"Awesome. We will, you should finish getting ready," Emily says as she gets up and goes to the mini-fridge.

Rose shakes her head in a smile as she walks through another door.

"You sure you should be drinking another beer if you're driving?" I ask my best friend as she offers me one. I grab it because I can't drive anyway.

"Whatever, we can always grab a cab." She starts looking at the shelves in the living room.

"Defies the whole purpose of coming here to drive her," I mumble as I sit down. I look at my phone to find texts from Cole asking if I'm still coming. I'm typing up a reply as Emily's comments become background.

"So many books and so much weed, I bet she has exciting evenings in here," I hear her giggle.

I lift my head up as I hear the door to what I'm assuming is her bedroom re-open. Rose comes out in her black jeans and a tight white spaghetti-strap crop top. My mouth falls open when Rachel follows after her, her hair still wet from the shower.

"Oh, shit," Emily chortles. "We didn't think we were imposing *that* much."

I put my beer on the coffee table and put my hands in front of me as a sign of apology. "So sorry, we didn't realize you were...busy–I mean had company. I mean that *Rachel* was here."

"This is fucking great," Emily laughs.

"It's fine. I wasn't staying anyway," Rachel smiles at us. She bundles up her shoulder-length blonde hair in a loose bun and goes on her toes to drop a kiss on Rose's cheek.

I feel Emily's elbow in my ribs and I widen my eyes at her in a warning. She gets way too excited around Rose and Rachel.

"I'll see you at Cole's," Rachel says in her soft voice before heading out.

"You two are so freakin' cute," Emily gushes. "Are you back together?"

"No," Rose grumbles. She grabs a light-gray hoodie laying on the sofa closest to me and puts it on. "And I'm not going to Cole's anymore," she continues as her head pops out.

"Uh, yeah you are," Emily counters. "Don't be a mood killer. I need a party. I need to let loose. I need Luke fucking Baker to know that I'm having a real good fucking time."

So much for having parted on good terms.

"Alright, party-girl," Rose chuckles. "I never said *you* weren't gonna party. I said I'm not going to Cole's."

"I don't like where this is going," I mutter.

"I like. I like very much. Tell me more," Emily teases.

Rose grabs a cigarette and lighter on the coffee table and lights it, taking her time before replying. "I'm going to the North Shore."

There's a long silence before Emily shouts in glee. "Yes! Yes, fuck yes. We're coming."

"No," Rose and I reply in unison. "I'm not going to an NSF party," I add.

"Is it with the Kings," Emily asks, jumping on the spot.

"No, North Shore Crew," Rose corrects.

"Can you hear me or what? I'm not going to the North Shore of the Falls. Absolutely out of the question."

"Better that way," Rose confirms.

Emily is on me before I can reply. "Please, 'Me, *please* I need this." She turns to Rose. "Luke isn't going to be there, right?"

Rose shakes her head 'no' as she inhales on her cigarette.

"'Me, come *on!*" Emily grabs my upper arms and squeezes.

"Ugh, Em!" I groan, my head falling back.

"Just think! Do you want to go to a boring, uptight, preppy Stoneview party or do you want to live a little? Be adventurous? We both know if nothing's happened with Cole yet it's because you need some real bad boy in your life and you will find exactly what you're looking for on the North Shore."

My stomach twists in anticipation when she mentions bad boys. I hate the term, but I can't deny the excitement coursing through my veins at the idea of leaving preppy boys behind and going headfirst into danger.

A house party on the North Shore of the Falls. It's a terrible, terrible idea. Dangerous, stupid...

Thrilling.

"Fine," I sigh.

"Great. Now with a little more enthusiasm," Emily orders. She really is pushing it, isn't she?

"Fine!" I scream. "Let's party in fucking NSF!"

"Language." Rose's raspy voice is closer than I expected.

"You don't mind if we come with you, Rose, right? *Right?*" Emily taunts.

Rose rolls her eyes. "I swear if I have to get either of you out of a shit situation–"

"You won't have to," Emily cuts her off. "We're big girls."

Chapter 5

Rose collects some stuff around the table, mainly weed and cigarettes, some cash, and turns to us again.

"This is all great but, Emily, you sure you want to show up like this at an NSC party?"

"What?" she gasps looking down at herself.

"It's a bit...Stoneview," Rose laughs.

"Well, yeah. That's the point," Emily smiles. "'Me is looking sexy as hell, she'll fit right in. You've got..." she looks at Rose's plain outfit from top to bottom "...a black eye. You'll fit right in. And I'll be the cute, innocent Stoneview Prep girl who really doesn't like gangbangers." She gives us a pout as she blinks innocently at us. Rose and I explode laughing.

We spend another hour or so drinking some more and by the time we get out of the room, I'm a lot tipsier than when I came in.

"So what made you change your mind?" I ask Rose as we pick up our coats in the hallway. "You texted me asking if I wanted a ride to Cole's party and by the time we got to your house you were planning to go to the North Shore."

"Another argument with Nate," she replies casually. "He *confiscated* my car keys like I'm some sort of rebellious teenager who needs parenting from him. I just need to piss him off a little more. What's better than showing up at a party with his little gang?"

"Great idea," Emily reacts. "And I've got my car!"

Rose cracks a laugh as she grabs another cigarette from her pocket. "Emily, you're the cutest but your Lamborghini won't last five minutes in NSF. We're gonna get carjacked the second we cross the bridge. Or it'll be stolen by the time you come out of the party."

Emily's face drops as we both struggle to understand how we're going to make it to the North Shore of the Falls.

"Stoneview cabs don't go to the other side of the bridge," Emily explains.

"Oh I know that," Rose smiles. "But don't worry, we have one car we know *for sure* no one will touch there."

Rose goes to a side room and comes back with what I'm assuming is a set of keys in her shut fist.

When she opens the white SUV outside, my heart rate doubles. The last time I was in this car, I had just spent the night at the police station after Jake's and Nate's big fight. My body shivers at the memory.

"I don't see how this car won't get robbed in NSF. It's really nice." Emily runs a hand on the white paint.

"Yep," Rose confirms as she gets in the driver's seat. I get in the passenger seat and Emily at the back. "But they're *way* too scared of Sam to touch his car."

Rose starts the car, and I can see in the rearview mirror that Emily has lost her smile.

"Are we stealing Samuel Thomas' car? The same guy that could probably take on the three of us with one hand?"

"Don't worry about that," Rose chuckles.

We put 'Show Out' by Kid Cudi loud as we get to the other side of the Falls to get us right in the mood for the party.

Tonight is going to be great. Just for one night, fuck being Goody.

6

JAMIE

Into It – Chase Atlantic

The small living room and kitchen are packed with people of all ages. I've seen more guns and bags of drugs than people over the age of twenty-one that's for sure. But hey, tonight, I really don't care. The lights are out apart from some blue and pink neon on the walls, and the smoke of cigarettes and joints is making the room foggy enough that I can barely see people's faces. It doesn't matter, I don't have anyone to recognize anyway.

This whole house looks like I've entered another dimension. People are grinding on each other, sweaty and high. On the kitchen table, there are only crushed solo cups and what looks like an empty kegger. There's broken glass but no unlimited alcohol like there is at the parties in Stoneview. No, here everyone is holding their bottles in their hands. Most have a bottle in one hand and a joint in the other. Wearing Emily's clothes, I fit right in with the other girls barely wearing anything and confident enough to rock leather pants with a bra only. I love this place.

Rose makes her way through the crowd in her casual gray sweater and jeans. Weirdly, she still looks just as cool as the other girls wearing completely opposite outfits. It's just the vibe she sends. The kind I could never have.

"Rose!" Some girl shouts over the music. I recognize 'Lightswitch' from Chaii and I'm glad to have the same taste as the person who controls the music here. The kind no one listens to in Stoneview.

Emily and I give each other a look as the girl pushes someone out of the way to get to our friend. She goes on her toes to hug Rose and we both notice the tattoo of a dagger with NSC on the handle. It's on the side of her upper arm. She belongs to the North Shore Crew. Emily's eyes widen before she smiles at me.

"Holy shit," she mouths.

I can't help a giggle. We're in this deep. Might as well have fun now.

Both girls in front of us cross the room with us in tow. They finally stop in front of a group of two guys and a girl all leaning against the wall furthest from the door. The girl, I recognize all too well.

"Emma, look who's here," the chick holding Rose's arm squeaks. Good to know she has the same effect on North Shore girls as she has on Stoneview's.

Emma, whom Nathan introduced to me only a week ago, focuses on Emily and me. Her matte blue lips spread in a grin as the look of recognition brightens in her gray eyes.

"You brought some friends, I see," she says. I can't read how she feels about it.

"Yeah," is all that Rose replies as she lights up a cigarette. I like that she doesn't feel she has to justify herself for bringing us.

Rose introduces Emily and me to Emma, the other girl, Tamar, and the two guys, Dylan and Xi.

"Nice bra," Emma teases me, repeating exactly what I had said to her in front of Nathan.

My cheeks blush at the reminder. I become too aware that my bra is more than obvious under my white see-through tank top.

She chuckles at my reaction followed by a gorgeous smile. "I'm fucking with you. It's nice to see you again."

I smile back but can see the 'what the fuck is this about' look on Emily's face from the corner of my eye.

"I hope you guys are ready to party." Emma picks something at her feet and only now do I realize the huge bright pink platforms that give her an extra four inches. Without them, she'd probably be about my height and for some reason, it makes me like her more. She comes back up in a wave of bleached blond hair and extensions and brandishes a bottle of supermarket-branded tequila, the cap already off.

"To N.S. fucking C," she cheers before taking a few sips.

There's a round of approval from the guys and some other people around us. Emma passes the bottle to Xi.

"To Rose bringing cute friends," he says earnestly.

His deep voice vibrates low in my belly, and I instinctively bite my lower lip to stop a smile when his dark eyes land on me. He takes a few sips, and the bottle passes around.

When it comes to me, I don't hesitate and take a big swig. I'm so ready for tonight.

I don't know how long has passed when I realize our circle has gotten bigger and we've all changed places.

Emily is outside of the circle, slowly grinding on Dylan.

He's clearly loving the preppy Stoneview type, and I have to take my gaze away when I notice one of his hands has snuck under the Tommy Hilfiger 'dress'.

Rose is across from me, facing me with her back against the rest of the room. She's got one hand on Tamar's hip and another holding a bottle of whiskey.

I don't know when I ended up between Emma and Xi, leaning against the wall, but I wouldn't move for the world.

Oh, how nice it is to finally truly feel something as a guy hits on me. And I'm not saying emotionally. I'm forever broken emotionally, thanks to Jake. But my pussy is finally waking up after a long, dormant period without Jake's touch.

Xi's hand has been on my lower back for who knows how long and when he finally decides to drop it to my ass, I look up at him, eyes full of lust. His are so dark they look black, and I'd happily lick his dark skin.

"There's only a mouthful left. Do you want it?" he says, shaking the nearly empty bottle of tequila in front of me.

"Of course she wants it, don't be an asshole," Emma laughs.

She's drunk but so am I. Who thought I would have talked so much with Emma? It started with her saying that my nails were in desperate need of a manicure. I had to admit that I could never afford one. I think that's when she realized I wasn't typical Stonview. Aka I am poor. She offered to do my nails and it went from there.

She couldn't believe it when I told her that my parents used to live on the North Shore. And she and Xi laughed when I said they left because my dad became sheriff. 'You would have been eaten alive here, babe. It's a good thing you moved there,' she said. And when I told her I was being eaten alive at Stoneview Prep anyway, she got all protective, telling me she would happily come to kick some preppy ass for me.

I don't know how this happened, but I think I just became friends with a member of the North Shore Crew. Fuck yeah. Tonight, I'm a bad bitch.

"Fine," Xi fakes a sigh.

I think he's going to pass me the bottle, but he brings it to his mouth and finishes it. I open my mouth to complain when he grabs my face with both hands and smashes his lips on mine.

I gasp at the shock and quickly feel the liquid pass my lips. The alcohol burns my throat despite having had it all evening. His hands on my cheeks are hot and I almost melt under him. One hand leaves my face to land on my ass cheek and grabs me as he pulls me closer. Our tongues twist together in such hotness I feel my underwear dampen in seconds.

Hell. This guy is hot as hell.

"What the fuck?! Billie is here!" I hear Emma yell behind me.

Xi retreats so quickly I almost fall over, my body turning cold at the lack of his heat.

Shit. Is Billie his girlfriend or something?

But when I turn to the rest of the group, I understand she probably isn't. Emma, Xi, and Dylan all look so happy to see the brown hair girl coming our way that I think the excitement is just general. She's followed by two guys that I can't quite see with all the smoke.

I understand Rose knows Billie too when she turns around in a smile, but I believe hers drops at the same time as mine when the two guys following appear to be Nathan and Sam.

"Fuck," I hear her groan even over the music. Tamar

steps away from Rose in a split second and I can see my friend's eyes rolling quickly. Almost imperceptibly.

"Someone's in trouble," Emma teases. "It's past your bedtime, Rose."

Rose doesn't even turn around to look at Emma to reply. "Shut u–"

I have to squint my eyes to see why she stopped so suddenly. But when it hits, time stops for me.

It takes a long time for my heart to climb the tall ladder all the way to heaven just to take the plunge and crash down all the way down in my stomach. But when it lands, fuck do I feel it.

It's the first time in my life I hear Rose White shriek with happiness. She jumps on the spot before pushing past Nathan and landing in her twin's arms.

My whole world spins and I feel like I'm about to fall. By some miracle, I manage to stay up. Everything I've ingested tonight threatens to come back up. By some second miracle, it doesn't.

When Rose finally steps away, I get tunnel vision. There is nothing else in this room. No one else. No music, no suffocating smoke, no bright neon.

Nothing.

But.

Jake.

His deep ocean eyes lock with mine and it happens all over again. I become a prisoner to his gaze. To his overwhelming power. *To him.*

I'm his.

God, I'm *his*.

I've always been, I'll always be.

Something flashes in his eyes before they move to my

shoulder and back to me. But this time, they're hard. Only now do I realize Xi's arm is around my shoulders.

So that's why my ass didn't hit the floor. Xi was keeping me balanced the whole time.

Time? How long has it been that I've seen him? Two minutes? Two hours? I've lost all sense of time, space, and everything in between. All sense of myself.

I shake my head as I shrug off Xi's arm, but Jake is already looking away.

No, no. *Wait!*

I take a first step, ready to grab him and force him to look at me. Talk to me. To explain myself. To ask all the questions that have been on my mind in the past two months.

But there is no third miracle.

I freeze when his hand lands on Billie's chin in a gentle grip. Her big brown eyes look up at him, and in a split second my whole world crashes down.

He lowers his head, pulling her face up to him at the same time, until their lips gently touch and my heart breaks in a million pieces.

A wave of nausea comes crashing until a shape comes toward me. Nathan posts himself right in front of me. His hand comes on my shoulder, and I barely manage to look up at him. He's saying something but I can't even hear him.

"What?" My own voice resonates in my head.

I think I'm really drunk.

"I said..." his voice joins the echo of my own, dancing together in my head to some techno-electro music. Am I drugged or something? Everything is so fucking blurry.

Language! I hear my dad's voice in my head.

Language! This time it's Rose's voice.

Ugh. Fuck the Whites.

'Maybe In The Summer' by Sassy 009. I giggle at the fact that I still recognize the music despite how dizzy my whole world is right now. If I can recognize Sassy 009, I'm definitely not drugged.

"Hey, 'Me." Nathan's deep voice grounds me again and my eyes refocus on him.

"I said *what?*" I articulate very clearly. Or at least I think I do.

You go girl. Fuck Nathan.

"And I said, party over for you. I'm taking you home," he fumes.

"Fuck off." This time Rose's voice is real. "We're having fun. And you're here. You'll keep us so, *so* safe, won't you?" She laughs drunkenly and I laugh with her.

"Ozy, I'm not joking around. You're both going home. *Now.*"

"Ugh," I groan loudly. "Nathan, Nathan, *Nathan.*" I pause and enjoy how both he and Rose are waiting for what's coming next when I don't even know what it is. "Fuck you, you misogynist piece of...*crap.*"

Rose explodes laughing. Nathan's face is so shocked that I can't help giggling myself.

"Have a good night," I conclude before going my way. I see Rose going the other way and Nathan is still in the middle, clueless as to how to react.

But as soon as I'm far enough, alone in the crowd, my body starts trembling.

Shit, shit. Maybe I *am* drugged. Xi? Could he have drugged me?

Panic overtakes and tears threaten to fall. I stumble to the side as some girl dancing shoulders me. I'm about to break down completely when a delicate hand grabs mine.

"I got you, babes." Emily's voice in my ear is like one of an angel.

I let her guide me out of the crowd. We bump into someone, but I can't be bothered to look up.

"Bathroom?" Emily's voice asks and a second later the smoke is gone, the light is bright and the door shuts.

"Jesus, you're not in a good state." Wait this isn't Emily's voice. It's her hand though.

I finally look up to find Emily and Emma looking down at me. Worried eyes, twisted mouths.

"Em and Em." Is all I manage to say before exploding in a laugh again. "Get it? M&M's!" My laugh doubles. It resonates indefinitely in my head. It's like I'm lost in some never-ending cave.

"I think she'll be fine," Emma chuckles.

But that's when my laugh stops. "No. No, I won't. I really fucking won't." The haze isn't gone, and it suddenly mixes with tears.

"Fuck, Em." This time I really mean my best friend. "He's here. He's here and he saw me and…he doesn't care."

"Babe…"

"There's love. There's hate and there's ignorance. He couldn't care less. And he came with someone! He shows up after two whole months and he's suddenly with someone. How…how…"

How dare he?
Break up with me.
And move. On.

There's an awkward pause as I sniffle, and more tears make their way down. "And I've been *drugged*!"

"Whoa, what?" Emma cuts in. "Are you sure? People know that shit doesn't happen at our parties."

"I feel drugged," I admit. As I say it, I realize maybe I'm

just very drunk. I've never been that drunk.

"Sweetie, you wouldn't *feel* anything if you were drugged," she explains. "I was with you all night and I watched Xi. Even if I know he would never. We all shared the same bottle, it's mainly why we do it, so we know no one puts shit in it. It's a North Shore kind of thing. That's why he took the drink before he gave it to you. It's a trust thing when you want to fuck a girl. Needed in this town, I'd know."

Emily hesitates before she turns to me. "Do you think maybe you've drunk too much?"

As both girls start taking care of me, my panic settles down and clarity comes back. They help me out of my clothes, put me in the shower and the cold water wakes me up. When I come out, Emma is on me to redo my makeup as Emily helps me back in my clothes.

"This is crazy," I chuckle as Emma puts bright red lipstick on my lips. "I can't go back."

"Welcome to North Shore Crew parties, sweetie," Emma smiles.

"I still feel super drunk," I explain.

"I know what would wake you up." Emma takes a small packet out of her back pocket and my eyes widen in shock.

"Is that–"

"Ecstasy. Will wake you up real good."

I shake my head so fast the dizziness comes back. "I'm alright."

"Suit yourself," she shrugs. "I'll be out there if you need me."

Once we're back to being alone, Emily turns to me. "How are you feeling?"

"Like my heart broke all over again."

"Babe," she sighs. "I'm so sorry. I...What were the

chances?"

My stomach twists all over again. "I think I'm gonna be sick." My mouth can barely form the words before I'm moving toward the toilet. Nothing comes out.

"I don't know what to do," I cry again. "My life...everything..." I break down completely and Emily is on me, hugging me tightly. "Everything was him, Em. I gave him everything."

Sobs wreck my chest as my best friend strokes my hair.

I feel like everything is scrambling down. All the toughness I tried to put up in the last two months. My heart aches too much to focus on any rational thought. I don't know how long it lasts before I try to talk again.

"What am I gonna do?" I whisper.

Emily pulls away in a sudden movement and holds my shoulders at arm's length.

"Jamie. You're not some sort of weak ass bitch. You're Jamie fucking Williams. You've been through worse than a fuckboy breaking up with you and ghosting you. You got your heart broken – and it hurts a fair amount – it's time to get over the asshole."

She helps me straighten up before she keeps going.

"So here's what you're gonna do. You're gonna dry those tears." She puts her hands on my face and wipes my cheeks with her thumbs. "Wow Emma's makeup is waterproof as fuck," she comments.

She takes a step back. "Now you're gonna go back out there, ignore the fucker, and enjoy yourself."

I shake my head in disbelief as I remember the seconds before Jake showed up. "I was making out with Xi *just* before he arrived. What if he saw?"

"Good!" she exclaims. "Let him see what he fucking lost! You want to have sex with Xi? Go for it! Do things for *your-*

self, 'Me. Why are you looking at him like he's some sort of God when we both know he's some fucked up devil! You're so much better than him and you know that."

Emily's words resonate in my head as I see her open her palm in front of me.

"That guy Dylan gave me half a pill. If you want to do it, I'll make sure to look after you." She winks at me.

"You do it," I sniffle. "But if we get separated, stay close to your phone. I want to be able to reach you."

"Sure, Mom," she chuckles. She swallows the half-pill. "Let's make the most of this night."

When we come out of the bathroom, nothing has changed. I can't help looking for Jake amongst the faces, but he isn't in sight. The house is exactly the same. Turns out parties don't stop functioning because I'm crying over my ex in the bathroom.

Emily spots Dylan and she looks at me, silently asking if I'm alright.

"Go get him," I laugh. "I'm fine, seriously."

And just like that, I'm on my own. I watch as he grabs her hips and brings her to him. She looks at me over his shoulder, mouthing 'I love you.'

HVME's version of Goosebumps is playing and I bounce my head to the rhythm. I feel on a little cloud after sobering a little. I sit down on a neglected sofa that smells of beer and let my head fall backward.

What the hell am I doing?

The words of the music dance in my head as I close my eyes. I feel someone sit next to me and something hard and cold presses against my leg.

"You either drank too much or not enough." Xi's voice is

Chapter 6

like honeyed whiskey. It's incredibly smooth but it sparks fire in my belly.

I lift my head back up and look at the bottle of vodka he's put between his leg and mine.

"I've been looking for you," he says. The lust in his hooded, drunk eyes burns bright.

"Really?" I grab the bottle between us and move so that my thigh is against his.

Our eyes meet as he nods and holy Jesus it's warm in here. My breath is shallow, and I can feel his on my right cheek.

"So, which one is it?" He asks.

"Huh?" I'm so lost in the two marbles of darkness that are his eyes that I completely forgot what he asked.

"Do you want to drink some more?"

I shake my head no. "I'm done drinking."

"Great. We can move onto more interesting things then?"

I barely have time to nod before his lips find mine. Xi's been starving, that's the only explanation as to why he's completely eating me out right now. I startle when I feel his hand on the inside of my thigh. It's high. Very high but it feels so good.

People can probably see us –

Shut up. Just enjoy.

His lips are on my neck, going higher and higher until his mouth is in the shell of my ear.

"Tell me, Jamie. What kind of Stoneview girl are you?" My brows furrow. I don't get it. "The kind who's here just to piss off her parents. Or the kind who is truly a bad, *bad* girl."

My heart picks up at his last words.

Fuck.

I can feel myself getting wetter and wetter as his lips trail my jaw and back on my mouth. This time, I'm the one who kisses him. Hard and violently. I push my hips toward him, forcing his hand to slide higher until he makes the conscious decision to cup my pussy through my vinyl pants.

He pulls away from my mouth, his hand still cupping me. There's a fire in his eyes when they lock with mine and the dirty smile pulling at his lips is melting my insides. The pleasure pooling between my legs doesn't lie. I love his ways. I love his roughness.

"I think I got my answer," he smiles.

In a split second, he's up and grabbing my hand, pulling me with him. I notice Billie walking past us with wide eyes as he leads me to the hallway. My smile only doubles. Who cares what the bitch thinks? She can go fuck Jake for all I care. I'm sure they've been happy to do so until now.

'Riot' by Hollywood Undead plays and the crowd gets rowdy as the music screams 'Fuck this shit let's start a riot'. So, this is what happens past 2 am on the North Shore? Some guys start a mosh pit in the living room and Xi's hand tightens around mine as he pulls us out of the crowd.

We reach the hallway, barely any quieter, and my back slams against the bathroom door. Xi put his forearm above my head and his other hand on the door handle.

"So, are the parties here different than the ones in Stoneview?"

I shrug. "I wouldn't know. I'm not a big party girl and I only came here to fuck."

I can't believe these words actually crossed my lips. They feel so liberating. Looking at the carnal smile on Xi's lips, he's happy with my answer.

"I like the music here," I randomly say. My mind feels free, courtesy of the alcohol, and any thoughts that cross it end up on my lips.

"Yeah? I'm the one who controls the music tonight. I'm

glad you like it."

"Really?"

"Yeah, my house, my rules, my music."

His lips smash on mine again and I feel his hand twist before I stumble backward into the bathroom.

I'm in a million places at once. I feel dizzy from the alcohol, from the lust fogging my mind, but my body is buzzing, my skin on fire. I haven't felt this alive in months and God it feels so damn good.

But wait.

His house?

"Your house?" I pant.

"My house," he confirms.

"How old are you?"

"Who cares, you're eighteen, right?"

I nod as his gaze eats my whole body. Up, down, up, down it goes.

"Good, no more stupid questions then. Shut that mouth and spread those legs."

His words have a one-way effect on me. I'm soaking.

Xi grabs the back of my thighs and lifts me up on the bathroom counter. I land on make-up and toothbrushes, but I don't care. He's like a carnivore eating my lips, my tongue, licking my neck. His hands are on my knees, spreading my legs apart.

I tremble under him and my hands go to his jeans. I make quick work of his zipper and grab his hard cock through his boxers. Rock. Hard.

"Fuck," he whispers above my lips. He takes a step back to take his dark green t-shirt off and is back on me in a split second, taking my tight tank top off. His NSC dagger tattoo is on his shoulder, and right above his left pectoral, he's got the Greek letter 'Xi' Ξ tattooed.

He's hot. Really damn hot.

His eyes are glued to my bra-covered breasts for long seconds and I squeeze his dick tight to bring him back to reality. He hisses and grabs my breasts in his hands.

"You're so fucking small," he breathes in my ear. "I bet you're tight as fuck."

I squirm when he rubs me through my pants as his other hand squeezes my tit through my red-lace bra.

He unzips my pants and his hand dips in my underwear.

"Fuck, yeah," he sighs in pleasure. "Stoneview's pussy, always wet for us North Shore guys, aren't you?"

I should be outraged. Ashamed, angry, and repulsed.

But I've been enough of a hypocrite this year. I came to this party because I knew I wouldn't find my fix in Stoneview.

Xi and I have the same intentions and there's no need to pretend otherwise.

So instead of slapping him across the face for his sexist comment, for his offensive portrayal of women, I happily let him slide two fingers in as I nod to his statement.

I wince at the harsh intrusion but my body melts under his movement. I have to put both hands on the counter as his fingers move in and out of me.

"You're a real naughty girl, Jamie. I saw it as soon as you walked in."

I nod again, moaning for him.

"The kind that looks really innocent are always the dirtiest ones."

His mouth finds mine and I whimper with need.

I didn't expect what came next.

Neither of us could have.

The door slams open, making us both jump. Xi's hand is

out of my pants a second later, just in time before the hand that grabs his shoulder pulls him away.

I gasp as I see him stumble backward, my eyes wide with shock when I see Jake grabbing Xi by the throat.

"That really was the wrong choice of bitch you picked tonight, Xi," Jake growls.

"What the fuck!" Xi's voice barely squeaks out of his throat.

I should really be doing something. I'm frozen on the spot, mouth hanging, and throat closed. My brain has put an 'out of service' sign up and all I manage is to cross my arms in front of me to cover my bra.

"Next time you want to dip your dick in Stoneview pussy, make sure it's not mine." Jake turns around to push Xi out of the bathroom.

He slams the door shut and turns the lock. The sound resonates in my ears. It's the last drum before the downfall. It's the hammer of a death sentence.

When he turns to me, his eyes are two black holes swallowing everything in their way, ending all sense of time. His hands are shaking and when he takes a step toward me, I finally snap out of my surprise.

I put my hands on my zipper, ready to get dressed as quickly as possible. Jake is quicker than me though. He always was. He's on me before I can move, and he slaps my hands away from my pants, an animalistic growl crossing his lips.

His right hand clamps my jaw. His hard gaze digs into mine for long seconds.

My brain goes into overdrive. It remembers everything. How he used to hold me down to fuck me, how he controlled my body, how he would make me come harder than I could ever do to myself.

All the dirty words.

All the wicked sex.

All the wrong discipline he inflicted on me.

My pussy throbs, my nipples are painfully hard against the lace.

Jake.

Is.

Everything.

He doesn't say anything. He just drags my pants down in a violent gesture. He flips me around with both hands on my hips and I brace myself against the counter.

One hand grabs my hair, pulling until I can see him in the mirror.

I think someone is knocking on the door. Banging actually. There are words being shouted at us. I can't make out what they are. All I can do is let Jake control me. Let him own me like he's supposed to.

He doesn't touch me where I want him to. He doesn't finger me, and he doesn't pinch my nipples like I desperately need him to.

He just invades me in one hard stroke.

I gasp a whimper and he tightens his grip on my hair. His eyes are wild and angry, looking at mine all along. He pumps in and out recklessly and my legs start to shake. Everything becomes sharper, the sounds, the light in the room, the two pools of dark ocean staring at me.

His other hand lands a harsh slap on my clit and I scream.

I'm going to come.

Please not so quick. Please, please, please I don't want this to be over.

His thumps accelerate and I moan in uncontrollable pleasure.

Chapter 6

"Jake!" I gasp, my voice heightened by desire.

Another slap makes me scream again. Another. Another. *Another*, painful this time. One last one and I unfold for him. I explode exactly like he wants me to. I come so hard I squeeze his own orgasm out of him. He slams into me a couple more times before he freezes.

His hand is still tight in my hair, and I wince when he pulls me harder toward him.

"What an angel," he murmurs in my ear.

My heartbeat goes wild at the mention of the nickname only he uses for me. His tone though, his tone is the opposite of his words. He is mocking me, ridiculing me at how easy it was for him to come back and take whatever he wanted.

He lets go of me so suddenly I don't have time to realize he was the one holding me up before my legs give up. I slide to the floor, pants around my ankles and my bra all over the place. Jake has already zipped up his jeans.

He looks down at me, brows furrowed. "Stay away from me, Jamie. Me, my family or my friends. I don't want you around any of us. And for heaven's sake stop using my twin to get closer to me. It's pathetic."

His voice is ice. It's so cold it freezes my heart. My throat narrows and my eyes burn as I look up at him. I can feel the tears coming.

Don't cry in front of him.

Don't.

Don't.

I'm too lost in my own focus to realize he's leaving. I only snap out of it when I hear the door open.

What just happened? What just –

"I think she came hard enough for one night, Xi. You should give up." Jake's disdain tastes like acid in my mouth. It's bitter, rank, and it destroys everything in its wake.

I thought I was going to burst out crying. I really did. But the recognition of who Jake really is awakens a deep fury in me.

He's the devil.

He always was, I was just too in love to grasp it. I was lost too deeply in his games to realize they were just that. Games.

He bullied you, Jamie!
He humiliated you!
He threatened you!
He blackmailed you!
He used you.

And worst of all…he made you fall in love with him.
Just to leave you behind.

I get up so quickly my head spins. I manage to keep a shred of dignity by putting my clothes back on in record time and avoiding being seen naked by the people in the hall. I can see Xi's worried eyes looking over Jake's shoulder and into the bathroom. The guy had no idea what he was getting himself into.

"What the fuck, Jake," I hear Xi. "Big bro becomes the boss and you think you're untouchable or something? This ain't your house, man."

I don't let Jake reply. I don't let them get into an argument or in a fight. This is *my* fucking fight, Xi. My turn to spit venom at the fucker.

Out. Of. My. Way.

I run so fast into Jake I can hear his breath getting caught in his throat. I push him hard enough that he stumbles forward. Xi has to catch him so they don't both fall, and I use the commotion to walk out of the bathroom.

Chapter 6

Of course Billie is waiting in the hallway.

The bitch is so fit I want to punch her in the face. She's wearing a bandeau top and her shoulders and biceps are delicately defined. She's only slightly taller than me but still tiny compared to Jake. Not small like me, though. Not unshaped and petite. No, her abs are distinct, she looks toned and strong. Like she does cross-country runs or mountain climbing or some other stupid sport I don't do.

Her porcelain skin is perfect and her huge doe eyes look at me in shock. Yeah, I didn't think I had the guts to tackle Jake White either but hey, here I am.

The party is right behind me, barely separated by a door frame missing the door and the wall of loud music in the living room. Jake readjusts himself quickly, standing tall in front of me.

Oh, I'm Jake, I'm big and strong and I can scare five-foot girls easily.

Fuck you.

"That was pretty stupid for such a smart girl," he says loud and clear for Xi and Billie to hear.

Xi is on my right side, still in the doorway of the bathroom. I feel like Jake and I are facing each other like in a western. Ready to shoot. Billie is standing behind him like some pet waiting to bite.

I only notice now that Jake is fitter than he used to be. He used to be big, clearly strong. He's now more defined. His shoulders are sharper, his muscles leaner. His hair is slightly longer, messier than it used to be. His face is more serious than when he was just Stoneview Prep's playboy.

Does he really have to be so hot?

"I think we've established I wasn't smart when I started falling for your idiotic games," I reply to him. The malice in my voice is lethal.

His nostrils flare and I know I'm slowly getting him exactly where I want him. I want him fuming. Out of control. And then I want to leave him here while I happily go home. Free of anger and attachment to him.

"Go home, Jamie. This is not your world. It's mine, you're not welcome in it."

I laugh so coldly he raises his eyebrows in surprise.

"Is it?" I fake pout with the voice of a Stoneview bimbo. "Is it your world? You don't want me in it, baby? Boo fucking hoo." I mock him. I take a step toward him. "You think I'm pathetic, Jake?" This time my voice is hard. "You think I'm using your sister to get closer to you? Who the *fuck* do you think you're talking to?" I push him hard in the chest but this time he expected it and he barely moves. "*I* was there for her when you disappeared. *I* was there when she needed a place to sleep. And you, Jake, where were you when she showed up at my house with a black eye?"

His mouth falls slightly open in shock, eyes wide. His fists close tightly, and his jaw stiffens.

Oh it's low. It's very low. Rose is a sensitive topic, especially because he opened up to me about his guilt when it comes to protecting her. I'm hitting him where it hurts.

I guess he shouldn't have broken my heart. He shouldn't have taken my pride away from me. Because I feel ruthless. I feel pitiless. I want to break him apart. I want him to fall.

"You want me to tell you what pathetic is? It's disappearing without a trace and then still believing you can call this yours." I gesture at my body with a hand. "It's having to wait for another guy to get me wet before you can stick it in me."

I hear Xi chuckle mockingly and I can't help a smile. Especially when I see Billie scowl in shock. Really? What did she think we were doing in this bathroom?

Chapter 6

I know his teeth are clashing together when I see his jaw muscle pop again. This time he takes a step toward me.

"You're going to regret this so fucking bad," he says through gritted teeth.

"What did you think? That you were going to leave, and I'd wait around like a good girl? Do you even know me? I'm the worst of all, you should know that by now. The innocent look with a real bitch underneath. You thought you could go away, fuck your slut, and expect me to suck you off as a reward for coming back?"

I'm not done. I have so much more to say, so much more to bring him down from his throne but I'm cut off by Billie-with-the-big-eyes going past Jake, fists raised.

"Bitch, call me a slut once more!"

"Billie—" Jake's voice is hard.

My eyes widen as I'm pretty sure I'm gonna get punched in the face for the first time in my life when I feel a hand grab my top and pull me away. Billie's fists drop but her eyes on me are sharp.

"Alright, alright, I feel like the party spirit is dying over here." Rose's raspy voice makes me relax. The girl just saved my life, or at least my nose. I didn't even know she was behind me. I should have recognized the flowery scent mixed with whiskey.

Jake shakes his head at his twin, standing right behind me, her arm now resting on my shoulder, her hand hanging right below my tits.

"Why would you invite her here?" Jake scowls at his twin. "What the fuck is wrong with you?"

"First of all, you're the one who showed up unexpectedly," she chuckles. She's more than drunk and doesn't have much argument but at least she's got my back.

"Get the bitch out of here," Billie orders. "She's not

welcome in my house. Fuck, she's not welcome on the North Shore."

So it's Xi's *and* Billie's house. They're not related though, that's clear enough. Xi is clearly Mediterranean, Greek maybe? Billie is white trash. Plain and simple. And the bitch is *kicking me out* of the North Shore.

"Ah, my bad. You control the North Shore now, Billie?" Rose lets go of me until she's standing right next to me, towering over the bitch.

"Ozy..." Jake warns.

There's no stopping her though. Rose is too stubborn. She can't be told what to do or what to say. It automatically gets countered in her mind.

And thank God for that.

"Your boxing rep might scare the little cunts around here but don't forget who you're talking to," Rose addresses her in a lower voice.

Out of all the girls who could have had my back at this party. Rose is the best I could have asked for. She's too tall, too cool, too hot, and too much of a dude for Billie to say anything back.

Or so I thought.

"Please do remind me who I am talking to. Bianco's little princess?"

Oh boy.

I don't think I've ever seen Rose get truly angry at anyone but Nathan before. I've seen her raging against him but it's cases she knows she's not going to win and there is always reserve in it. And by that, I mean a lot of voice but not a lot of action. Understandably. I've seen her argue stupidly with her friends or with Jake. But I've never seen her *truly* angry.

I guess it was about time it happened.

Chapter 6

She glances at Jake but when her gaze is back on Billie, it's deadly.

The Whites have that thing in their eyes when they snap. It takes a lot, or it takes a specific trigger that not many people know about. Jake is the quickest to lose control. Rose is close behind. Nathan is a master at it. But when they *do* snap. It's not pretty.

It's *evil*.

Rose grabs Billie and in one long strike, she's got her pinned by the throat against the far wall.

"Fucking shit, Rose," Xi sighs. "This is way too fucking hot."

The thing with not being in Stoneview, is that this kind of behavior doesn't bother anyone here.

"Shut up, dickhead," Jake growls. "Ozy, stop."

My mouth has dropped so low I have to pick it up off the floor. Xi is right. She's manic and somehow makes it look hot.

Her voice is calm, fatal. "Billie, you can't suck important people's dick and suddenly think you're invincible. That's simply not how life works."

Jake doesn't even try to stop his twin. I don't think there would be any point right now. I see Rose's hand tightening when Billie tries to talk, and my friend shakes her head.

"Nah. Don't try to talk to me again. I *will* fuck you up if I have to. I don't because I like your sister. Simple as that. So next time you address yourself to me, remind your little brain that I'm no princess, alright? I'm a motherfucking *king*. So bow the fuck down," she finishes through gritted teeth.

She pushes Billie hard enough that she loses balance and falls to the floor.

Rose chuckles low as she looks down at her. "Yeah, just like that."

She turns around and throws a death stare at her twin. "You're an asshole, you know that?"

She doesn't wait for an answer and walks straight to me, putting an arm around my shoulder. "Let's get you home, Jamie. You're better than this."

I don't know if she means better than fighting with Billie, arguing with Jake or being at this party altogether but I let her guide me away.

We find Emily and she walks us both outside.

"You can't drive," I say as we reach Sam's car on the street.

"I know that," she chuckles. That's when I notice Chris' car coming down the street.

"Oh," I say.

"You girls get home safe. Sadly, you've been revoked your rights to come to North Shore parties again. I told you I didn't want to have to get you out of trouble." She smiles at me as she says this. "I did enjoy that you finally told Jake what he needed to hear though. I'll see you on Monday."

The look on Chris' face when I get in the car is particularly disappointed.

We drive in silence for a good five minutes before I finally talk. "Jake is back."

"I know," he sighs. "I don't know if it's a reason to let him take over your life all over again though."

"No," I admit, more determined than I've ever been. "It's really not."

And I mean it.

Jake isn't getting the good side of me anymore.

It's over.

He shouldn't have come back because he triggered something in me.

I'm taking him down.

7

JAKE

Youngblood – 5 Seconds of Summer

Those eyes.

Those two golden treasures that used to burn so bright for me.

That deep green that used to swallow me whole.

That tanned skin, so soft, so warm, so safe.

Jamie is as beautiful as ever. Tonight, she was sexy as hell in those pants, with that red bra flashing bright through her tank top. She felt so good, better than she ever did. It was torture to try and make her come before I did. It was torture not to put my lips on hers, on her body, not to reconnect like I desperately wanted to.

I could see the necklace I gave her bouncing against her neck when I was fucking her, it was the hottest thing in the universe. I can't believe she's still wearing it. Her heart is so pure.

Jamie is my queen, and she needs protecting at all costs. Even the cost of losing her respect for me. Even the cost of losing her love.

I help Billie up as Xi follows after Jamie and Ozy.

"Are you for fucking real? Is that why you kissed me earlier? To make some Stoneview bitch jealous? We're not even together, I never asked anything from you."

I know that. And I do realize how shocked she was earlier when I kissed her, but I needed something to keep Jamie away.

"Billie—"

"And I swear I only didn't knock out your sister because I know I'd get my ass kicked by Bianco if I did."

Rose is a strong girl. Years of built-up anger is what can make her win fights against North Shore girls like Billie. But I have no doubt Billie could have hurt her good if she wanted to. Billie is a fighter, a boxer who spent the last two months eating, sleeping, and breathing boxing. She didn't lose one fight. And at the moment, my twin is a miserable girl with borderline anorexia.

It takes a second for my brain to remember what triggered Ozy. When it does, my blood runs cold. When Billie mentioned him in front of her, I was ready to choke her against the wall myself.

"Yeah? And how do you know that Bianco would kick your ass, huh?"

She scoffs. "I don't owe you any explanation. Not where I get my info and not how."

I laugh at her. Surely she can't think I'm that stupid?

"Until yesterday you didn't even know what Bianco *looked like*. You spend a little time one on one with him, you suddenly know it all?"

She looks away, uncomfortable under my stare and Ozy's words come back to me. 'You can't suck important people's dick and suddenly think you're invincible.' I shake my head at the hard reminder that Billie truly is a North Shore girl.

"Did you *actually* suck Bianco's dick?" I ask in disgust.

"Girls who grew up where I grew up know how to protect themselves, Jake. It's not always about knowing how to win a fistfight."

The fucking bastard, the fucking pedophile.

"This is fucking disgusting," I reply. I'm not talking about her though, my anger is aimed directly at Bianco.

"I'm a big girl."

"You just turned *seventeen*," I insist. "So what? You suck his dick and he tells you all about my family? Is that how it works?"

"No!" she defends herself. "Look, I was angry just now. Rose was making the rules in my own house, and I wanted to shut her up."

"That doesn't answer my question. What did he say about her?"

I know she can sense how angry I am. I know she's trying to avoid an argument but it's just making it worse.

"It's not what he said about her," she finally admits. "It's what he insisted on calling me when I was doing it. I corrected him once, told him my name was Billie. I didn't again after the slap it earned me. So..." her mouth twists, her lips pinch, "Rose it was." She gulps as she finishes her sentence. "Look, I didn't want to tell you. I didn't want to upset you–"

"It doesn't matter," I cut off coldly as my teeth fight each other in a clashing war.

I leave her behind, stomping back into the living room. I'm sure Ozy is still here. She might have sent Jamie home but she's not one to leave a party before sunrise.

I find her talking to Billie's older sister, Emma. No doubt

showing her a PowerPoint of why they should sleep together again. The one and only girl who never came back for seconds after sleeping with Rose, it's driving her insane.

"How's Rach?" I ask as I settle next to my twin.

Emma laughs so hard she almost spits out her drink. "You've got a gorgeous girl waiting for you in Stoneview, why are you even talking to me?"

The look Ozy sends my way would have scared anyone else. It makes me laugh. Fuck, I missed her so much.

"Billie is really fucking mad at you," I insist.

"Ugh, Jake," she groans. "Are we gonna do this now?"

"What did you do?" Emma asks in a voice that's half a warning, half worry for her younger sister.

"Nothing you wouldn't have done yourself if she'd given you the attitude she gave me," Rose muses.

Emma shrugs. "Meh, she needs a good reality check from time to time. I'll go check on her."

Once Emma is far enough and she can't hear me, I turn to my twin with a serious look on my face. "You know you'd get in a lot more trouble if half of the population didn't want to sleep with you."

"I'm returning the compliment," she mumbles as she grabs her pack of cigarettes.

I watch her light one in her mouth. Her hands are trembling slightly, the skin under her nose is pink, irritated from all the lines she must have done tonight. But the worst is the fading bruise around her eye.

Sam made me promise if I came back, I couldn't bring it up to Nate. It's really fucking hard not to right now. I can see him at the back of the room, chilling on a sofa with Sam sitting quietly on his right side and Dylan on his left, desperately trying to make friends with my brother to feel important.

Chapter 7

Sam is busy flirting with some girl I've never seen. Well, it's more like she's flirting with him and he's nodding as she talks and runs her hands over his arms and chest. His eyes though, his black eyes are on Ozy. Always watching her.

I shake my head, my attention going back to my sister.

"How did you know?" I ask.

"What?"

I don't know why she bothers to pretend she has no idea what I'm asking about. She's probably just buying time to make up some lie she won't need but just in case.

"About Billie and...Bianco," I say, disgust very distinct in my voice. Images of Billie on her knees in front of the fucker force me to shake my head again.

"Are you on something? Why do you keep shaking your head?" she chuckles.

"Just answer the question, Ozy. Come on."

"You know Sam can't keep shit from me. Why you even ask is beyond me."

"Bianco is fucking sick. He's *sick*, Ozy. I hope you've been staying far away from him."

"Bianco has always liked young girls," she replies. Her gaze is lost somewhere to my side, smoke coming out of her mouth, twirling in the air like the thoughts in her head.

I don't know where she's gone but my stomach twists in pain. I feel sick not knowing what happened between the bastard and her. Imagination is sometimes worse than the truth. I can only hope.

"Ozy," I snap my fingers in front of her eyes to bring her back. Her gaze refocuses as she looks at me. "Tell me you've been staying far from him."

She slowly shakes her head at me. "What fucking planet have you been on? Do you think I would ever willingly chill with the guy? And don't worry, Nate makes sure of that at least."

I know she's done with this topic, so I change it for her.

"Did Sam ever spill?" I ask.

She already knows what I mean.

"Fuck no. That one I couldn't get out of him. He's been hiding you very well," she chuckles.

There's a brief pause where we look at each other. We can't be separated for too long. It doesn't matter how much we bicker, argue, or even physically fight sometimes. We're two halves of the same person and I know being without me was just as hard as it was for me to be without her.

I take her in my arms again and she lets me. For years we were the exact same height, it's only after my teenage growth spurt that I got about three inches on her. She hates it. She likes being taller than most guys. Even if in our group she's only taller than Luke.

I hold her so tight and I hear her breath leave her lungs. I'm dangerously possessive of the ones I love. That's the problem with us, Whites. It's almost unfortunate to be loved by us because we become toxically controlling, too selfish to share, overprotective.

I don't know why I'm like this, I just know that whatever happens, whoever comes into our lives, she'll always have my shoulder to rest her head on.

"I can't believe you were in L.A. all this time," she says, her voice slightly muffled by my shoulder. "You could have said something."

"I would have if I was allowed to. I was trying to figure a way out. I swear," I admit.

"And how did that go?" she snorts mockingly.

"Well, I'm back here, that's one thing." I run my hand up

and down her back as I talk, and fear grabs my gut at how prominent her bones have become.

I pull away and hold her at arm's length. "I'm back now. No more letting yourself go, Ozy. I'm serious. You need to get your shit together."

"Fucking hell," she groans. "Go back."

"I'm not getting off your back until you become a little more than a sack of bones."

"Do you and Chris take the same course to be total pains in my ass?"

"Look at yourself, Billie would have fucked you up if she really wanted to."

"I doubt that," she replies confidently.

"*Bow the fuck down,*" I imitate her raspy voice easily.

We both explode laughing.

"The nerve you have to talk like that to Bianco's fighters. You're gonna get what's coming to you, I swear." I keep on laughing and it feels so good, it's better than a good high.

"I get *way* too confident on coke. I need a break from it," she cackles. "Please protect me, I don't want Billie to kick my ass." Laughing tears break from her eyes as we keep on joking about things we know would never happen.

Ozy and I are too sheltered. Nate, Sam, they'd never let anyone from NSC touch us. It's sad, but in our own fucked up world of petty gangs and organized crime, we're the privileged ones. And, ultimately, Bianco would never let anyone lay a finger on Rose. That's what scares me the most.

Our little lighthearted moment is quickly crushed when the music stops, and Xi's voice resonates around the house.

"Everyone, everyone. Listen!" There is way too much delight in his voice.

I've been ignoring him the whole night. The moment I saw him kiss Jamie when I arrived, I should have rearranged his dentition. But Nate was right there, and Sam. Watching me, making sure I keep my end of the bargain. So I let it slide, crushing my teeth and trying to stop my hands from trembling. But when Billie told me they had snuck into the bathroom, just the two of them, I couldn't control my body. Jamie's mine. She should know, he should know. Everyone should know. I might not be able to get close to her, but if she thinks I'm gonna make her life easy, letting her sleep with random gangbangers, she's got another thing coming.

Selfishness truly runs in my blood.

My eyes are sharp on Xi as he grabs some girl's upper arm tightly, right below the tattoo she has of a huge crown, showing her off to the crowd like some product he's trying to sell.

"Look who came to us!"

The crowd laughs, the 'ooh' and the hateful words being spat at the girl make my brows furrow. Ozy and I give each other a look that asks who she is but we're both clueless. The girl looks like she wants to flee the scene. The bite in her jaw and the fear in her eyes show she is determined but that this wasn't how she expected it to go at all. She tries to shrug Xi's hold, but his grip tightens.

I feel Rose shuffling next to me and I glance to see Sam settling behind her, a hand between her shoulder blades. I always think Ozy is tall until Sam gets next to her. He's a fucking monster. I don't know, six-foot-five or something.

"Let's go," he says low enough in her ear that the rest of the crowd won't hear. They're all too focused on Xi and the girl anyway.

"What? Why? Who is she?" Rose asks him.

But Xi answers for him. "King's very own sweet, beloved daughter came to us. She *came* to *us*, guys!"

The crowd cheers as I put two and two together. The

King family, that's NSC's rival; the North Shore Kings VS the North Shore Crew, always. What is this girl doing here?

"Guys, guys, listen to this," Xi mocks. "She came to ask, in the name of her *daddy*, that we put our rivalry to sleep. In peace. I'm not even fucking with you. She asked that all of this goes down in *fucking peace*." His voice is now low and serious. "Is that what they do on the King's side? They send their women to try and sweeten us into a good deal?"

Everyone laughs at the girl. She only toughens up from it.

"Hey, Kayla," he addresses her. "Is that why you wanted to keep it between you and me? Cause you're ashamed of what they're making you do?"

"They're not *making* me do anything," she growls through gritted teeth.

I can see Billie and Emma making their way through the crowd and I know that nothing good is coming for the girl.

"Shit, Jake, do something," Ozy says as she watches them, probably thinking the same as me. It's not like she's scared to defend the girl herself, she just knows I wouldn't let her.

"Emma!" Xi exclaims in delight as both Billie and her go to the coffee table Xi is using as a stage for everyone to see. The sisters stop right in front of him and Kayla, their faces hard and angry. "Emma, remember when Kay and her girls beat Billie to a pulp? They waited for her to be on her own, they lured her away from us. And they left her for dead."

I can see the struggled gulp against Kayla's throat. She still doesn't move though.

Xi pulls Kay closer before he starts talking to the crowd again. "King's crew beat up our girls, they shot our guys. They took over our turf. And now that we can finally defend ourselves, they want to leave in peace? They want it all to die down quietly?! I say fuck *NO!*" he roars.

The guys in here are getting angry. The crowd is shouting threats at Kayla, and I notice her feet shuffling slightly away from the edge of the table. The girl is shit scared and she's still holding their gaze like a queen about to be guillotined.

"Let's go." Nate's voice behind me startles me.

I was too focused on Kayla. I look at my brother, his usual bun is disheveled, the top buttons of his shirt undone, skin slightly flushed. Guess we know what *he's* been up to while a girl is on the edge of public execution here.

"You can't leave. They're gonna kill her, Nate," I argue.

When did I start caring about other people? It's seeing Jamie, it put back that stupid empathy in me.

"Not my problem," my brother replies casually.

He's got a cigarette dangling from his lips as he rearranges his dirty blond hair, so different from mine and Rose's deep black one. Every time I look at him, I wonder which of our parents he got his looks from and which I and my twin got ours from. Which one had blond or black hair? Did they both have blue eyes?

"Not your problem?" I insist.

I notice Sam's hands are now clamped on Ozy's shoulder as if he knows she's gonna escape to go help that girl out. She's unpredictable like that, isn't she?

"Is that how you rule your new kingdom," I continue, trying to get a reaction out of him. "You invade and then let them kill each other in a civil war?"

"This ain't my kingdom, little bro. I have much bigger things to handle and worry about. *This* is North Shore. Just another insignificant wrong side of the track. We use their services, in return we give them protection and more

Chapter 7

freedom to do what they want without legal repercussions. They want to get rid of their rivals? I say good for them."

"She's one girl amongst a crowd of North Shore Crew, you can't just leave her here. It's fucking immoral!"

My brother laughs in my face. "I don't know at what point you started thinking I have morals. Do you think I made it this far with morals? Are you nine again? Why are you back to being so naïve, it pisses me off."

"She's just a girl. She's probably my age. You're such a fucking piece of shit," I spit.

I shouldn't be so angry over a girl I don't know. But I am. Because what if she's just like me and Ozy? What if she never wanted to be involved in that world? And here she is tonight, sent to sweeten the enemy. It could be my sister up there.

"Kay is a big girl, she knew the risks she took coming here tonight. When I offered the Kings a sweet deal, her dad and her laughed in my face. Bet the old man isn't laughing now."

Nate throws the bud of his cigarette to the floor and looks back up at me. "If it can make you feel better, Kay there, fucked up your girl Billie so bad she was basically dead when they found her. You know why? Over some guy Emma and Kay were fighting about at school. Billie was thirteen when it happened, Kay was seventeen. You think that was fair?"

I almost wince thinking of thirteen-year-old Billie being beaten up by a group of girls over a feud she couldn't do anything about.

Sam shifts behind Rose and talks to the three of us. "Time to leave, before they start asking us for anything."

"Such courage," I mumble as the big guy starts walking through the crowd, my sister calmly in his hold. Exactly where she loves to be. People get out of his way quicker than it takes to ask them to.

"It's not about courage, Jake. It's about not wanting petty gangbangers to involve me in their useless feuds. Now let's go. I won't tell you again," Nate says as he follows.

I shake my head in dejection and follow him. But as I get close to the door, Xi's words stop me in my tracks. I look at where he's standing again. He's now right behind Kayla, an arm across her ribs and the other hand holding her jaw so he keeps her facing the crowd.

"You know," he says in a severe voice. "If Billie wanted her revenge now, she would absolutely *destroy* you. She would fuck you up so bad, Kay." I don't miss Kayla's tremble. Her whole back is shivering. "But I think tonight we're all gonna have a go at it."

He pushes her off the table so suddenly and harshly the girl never stood a chance to stay upright. Kayla falls off, in the crowd, landing right at the feet of Billie and Emma.

"Shit, this is too good," Emma laughs. "It's just perfect."

Kayla quickly tries to get up, but Emma is already on her. The sound she makes when one of Emma's platform heels lands in her ribs stops me from leaving the house.

You were so fucking close, Jake. This is not your fight.

The other three were already through the door but I'm not surprised to see my twin stomp back inside the house.

"This is fucking bullshit," she fumes. Nate is close after her.

"Ozy!" he calls.

"No! You don't want to do something about it? That's fine, I will. Go be a big, bad guy with bigger problems."

As soon as our sister takes one step into the crowd, he's after her in a 'fucking shit' sigh.

He grabs her by the hoodie before she can completely

Chapter 7

go, pulls her back, and pushes her against me. "You two are a fucking pain in my ass, I hope you're aware."

He turns back to the crowd and the guys that notice him get out of his way straight away. He's smoking another cigarette and has his bad mood face on. People don't want to be on his shit side right now. He easily reaches Xi, pushing him to the side and talking loud enough.

"Alright, that's enough," he says calmly but firmly.

By the time he gets Kayla out of the mass of people, she's been beaten up good. The fucker isn't even helping her, he's just pushing her toward the door.

Xi follows us on the streets, Emma in his tow.

"Who the fuck do you support? NSC or those fucking traitors?" Xi calls out.

Nate snaps around so quickly Xi and Emma have to stop dead in their tracks.

"I've had about enough of you two." He throws his cigarette on the floor and goes toe to toe with Xi. Watching the fucker retreat shyly puts a huge smile on my face. "I don't support anyone. I'm not your fucking mom. *You* work for *me*. End of."

"In that case, how we handle the Kings is none of your business," Emma protests.

Nate takes a deep breath and exhales loudly to show his exasperation. "I'll handle that one myself. Fear not, your little revenge against Kay will be paid in blood. Consider it my welcome gift to the Bianco family."

Nate doesn't entertain Xi and Emma one more second. He turns around and follows us down the street, catching up with Ozy as she helps Kayla walk.

"You two are going with Sam. She's coming with me," he says as we approach both cars.

"I'm not going with any of you," Kayla hisses.

She's holding a tissue to her nose to stop the bleeding. When Rose slows down by Sam's car, Kayla keeps going.

"Kay," Nate's tone leaves no choice but for her to turn around. "I said you're coming with me. We can talk about that deal you were trying to make with Xi."

"Let's go," Rose whispers to me. "You did what you could, Jake. At least she's not in there anymore."

We hop in Sam's car and leave this mess behind. I shouldn't be worried about some random girl. I should be worried about my problems with my own girl.

I lay awake way past sunrise. I hear the birds outside around six am. It feels too weird to be in this huge mansion, in a suite twice the size of the studio I was in in L.A. I picked the room three doors down from Ozy. It's not as big as hers, but it's huge nonetheless. I didn't hear Nate come back but I know Sam slept here.

At eight am I give up and open my curtains before sitting back in my bed. I felt more at home in the Murrays' pool house than in this beautiful mansion. I'm bored to death. I'm going to see the guys today, but I doubt they're ready to hang out at eight in the morning. So I do something I haven't done in months. I go on Instagram.

I have countless DMs from people asking me where I went. Lacrosse teammates, random girls, some of the cheerleaders, and of course, Camila. I tap on her profile and silently look at everything she's been posting. For someone who always threatened me that she could do better than me, I'm surprised she hasn't found someone since I left. She always thought she could get me back from Jamie. I thought she'd finally move on after I left Stoneview.

My heart squeezes painfully like every time I think of

Chapter 7

Jamie. I can't even check her Instagram like the stalker I am because I know she has no profile. I remember her telling me she deleted everything after what happened with her dad and her brother.

Her brother who...*disappeared.*

Except not all. He works for the Wolves.

I go on Emily's profile. Her most recent picture is of her and Jamie in the clothes they were wearing yesterday. They're both kneeling on Emily's infamous round bed with the caption 'Bad bitches only'. My thumb double taps before I can do anything about it. I scroll down to the next picture with Jamie. Two weeks ago. Emily is in her cheer uniform and Jamie in her lacrosse kit. 'St Anne, you're not ready for us' the caption says. God help me the fuck out, she looks so hot in her tight skort. Her legs are tanned, like the rest of her beautiful skin, and I'm dying to grab her small thighs in my big hands. I like this picture too, way too aware of the hard-on now begging to be let out of my boxers.

The next picture with Jamie in it is from four weeks ago. It's a selfie of Emily and Jamie in their pajamas, their mouths are covered in chocolate. Emily is flipping the finger at the camera whereas Jamie is mid-laugh. 'Fuck boys. Fuck Valentine's. Galentine's all the way'.

My eyes are stuck on Jamie's smile, on the melted chocolate around her lips. What I'd give to lick that off her right now. My hand instinctively grabs my cock through my boxers as I double tap on that picture. I don't even bother looking any further, my brain is already on overdrive.

I throw my phone to my side, lowering myself a little further into bed. I lower my boxers below my balls and start stroking. My thoughts stay on Jamie, on her naked petite body. All the memories I have of our sex mix-up in my head, her small hands tied behind her back, the way she mewls when she begs, how wet she gets when I order her around. My breath quickens when I think of our first time, our angry sex. I think of the times I shut up her curiosity with my cock down her throat. My brain mixes up images and I imagine the things I've done to Billie. The things I would never put Jamie through. But in my head it doesn't count, right?

So I remember what I did to Billie and see Jamie instead. 'Hurt me. Take control,' Jamie's small voice says. So I slap, and I pull, and I make her skin red. My little angel cries in pain mixed with pleasure, she screams my name and asks for more. She–

"Shit," I hiss as I come all over my stomach. "Fuck," I pant, desperately trying to catch my breath.

My dick is satisfied but the post-orgasm high isn't there. No, instead my stomach twists back in that constant state of stress I get from being away from the girl I love. From the fact that she clearly hates me and that I will keep pushing for her to hate me.

Images of her beautiful body are replaced with the words she spat at me. The hatred, the anger, the pain in her eyes. She's not stupid, she knows I fucked Billie. And while I was fucking her, Jamie was taking care of Ozy. The size of a peanut and the braveness of a warrior, that's Jamie. I chuckle at my stupid comparison. What a poet I am.

A wave of sadness washes over, engulfing me in longing for my old life back. My three-year break living freely in Stoneview. I had so much fun in that preparatory school. I had a group of friends and a family who loved me, I had a reputation, I had lacrosse.

I never for one second missed Nate. He was dead to me, and I didn't mourn him. I had no feelings about it whatsoever. I didn't use to have feelings about much anyway. I know Ozy did. She was eaten by guilt, she missed her older brother no matter what he did to us. She hides it, but she's sentimental like that, has too much empathy for the people who spent their lives mistreating her.

I run a hand over my face. There's no point being sad about it all. We're back into it now. Nate wanted to be our legal guardian, he got it. Bianco wanted us back in his life, he got it. Now we just roll with it. We learned a long time ago that fighting back only makes it worse.

I get in the shower and put pajama bottoms on before going down. There's one thing I hate in the morning, and that's tops. I can't stand material on my back when I just woke up. I get too hot.

My stomach rumbles as I walk down the double stairs. My eyes are focused on the group chat between Chris, Luke, Rose, and me. Luke and my stupid sister had a lot of fun sending hundreds of gifs last night because their lives are boring like that. I have to look up mid-step when I hear voices downstairs. One voice in particular.

My heart takes a plunge into my stomach and my brain is automatically on high alert. Cold sweat running down my neck, down my back, hands slightly trembling. The automatic response one's body gets when they're faced with an old abuser. Reflexes never go away, survival instinct never leaves your body.

Bianco is standing in the grand foyer, hands in his charcoal suit, steel eyes, sharp gaze aimed directly at Sam. I can't hear what Sam replies to him or see his facial expression, I can only see his tensed shoulders and back, tight around his black tee.

I'm secretly hoping I can run back upstairs without any of them noticing me, but my wish is short-lived when Bianco's gaze shifts to me.

"Jake," his smooth voice is already announcing manipulation. "Enjoying your return, boy?"

"Hmph," I rumble. I turn back around to go upstairs. I don't *have* to talk to him. I don't owe him shit. Being back in his world, I constantly feel like he's my guardian again. Back to being a kid. I'm not. Nate is my guardian, and I don't have to stay around when Bianco is here.

Right now, I want to go back upstairs and tell Ozy to stay locked in her room. And so I will.

"Not so fast," Bianco cuts my plan short. I'm a hundred percent sure he's going to want to talk about me seeing Jamie last night. We were surrounded by NSC guys and girls, I know he has tons of eyes and ears there. I also know if we talk about it, he's going to want to punish me somehow and I don't exactly want to know what he's got in mind.

Next to him, Sam is standing as still as a pole. His eyes are on me. His mind is somewhere else.

"Sam and I have to go on a trip tomorrow. I want to have dinner all together tonight. As a family. Just like old times."

My heart is beating too hard in my ears for me to hear myself think.

I need an excuse.
Think. Think. Think.
Anything, Jake!

"Rose and I aren't here tonight. We have a thing with friends. It's far from here, we can't cancel."

Bianco chuckles the way only he does. That humiliating chuckle that warns you to listen.

"It wasn't a suggestion. It was a request. See you tonight. *All* of you."

And just like that, he's gone.

My body is shaking from adrenaline as Sam and I cross gazes. It's almost impossible to read the fucker's mind but right now I think I'd be pretty close if I said he was worried about tonight. Just like me. Because Sam doesn't care about hanging around Bianco. He doesn't like it – he doesn't like *anyone's* company – but it doesn't scare him. However, if his precious girl has to be around his boss, it becomes a real fucking problem for him.

"Ozy, hurry the fuck up," Nate screams toward the stairs as we both put our coats on. She comes down the stairs ever so slowly, Sam walking behind her. "Come on, we've still got to drive to D.C."

Rose's hair is tied up in a tight, high ponytail and I don't control my teeth when they start grinding. Once Sam and Nate are out of the door, I grab her arm, gently holding her back.

"You don't have to do this to your hair, Ozy. Nothing'll happen if you don't, I promise."

She looks at me with that spark of sassiness she always has in her eyes when she doesn't take what I'm saying seriously.

"Don't look so worried over a hairstyle, Jake. If it doesn't suit me *that* bad just say I'm ugly," she chuckles.

"I know you're doing it to make him happy. It's okay to be scared, but you don't have to be."

She huffs loudly, emphasizing that she's not happy with the serious conversation. "Small efforts cost nothing, Jake. Mistakes cost lives."

And then she's out the door, leaving me wondering when she became so wise.

. . .

My sister and I hand our phones to Sam, pass security, and all the usual bullshit that comes with entering Bianco's organized crime sanctuary. I have to take a deep breath before we join him in the living room. This is going to be a long evening.

By the end of dinner, I'm surprised Bianco still hasn't mentioned Jamie. He reminisced about his childhood in Sicily, talked business with Nate, mentioned a name or two to Sam. People I'm guessing are now dead men walking.

He checked with Rose if she was still doing 'good at school' and earned himself an eye-roll she couldn't control. It was too late when she realized she shouldn't have but he didn't say anything. He asked me about Billie, asked if I was ready to go to school on the North Shore of the Falls. Nothing else, no complaint, no warning. Which is why I'm on edge. And when he takes a phone call at the table, I'm more suspicious than ever.

"Nate," he says in a stern voice after hanging up. "I need you two to handle a situation for me."

"Sure," my brother replies before sipping on his glass of red wine.

"Now," Bianco orders.

"What?" It takes a lot to surprise Nate, but it's safe to say he didn't see that one coming. "Where?" he insists.

"Downtown. I've got a couple of guys telling me there's been a problem with our last delivery. Something about crates missing. Go find out."

"You don't need the both of us there," Sam says as a pure statement that would have anyone else keeping quiet.

Bianco smiles his scheming smile as he replies to his enforcer. "I need someone for brains and someone for muscle. No need to tell you who's who."

Sam's nostrils flare but he doesn't reply. He just gets up

slowly, looking Bianco dead in the eyes. "We will be *very* quick," he replies in challenge.

"I hope so," Bianco grins back calmly.

"We'll leave," I say in a hurry. "Thanks for dinner, it's best if we get back home. Who knows how long they'll really be?"

Rose doesn't say anything, ever so quiet in our ex foster parent's presence.

"No. The guys can drive you back when they come back."

"I'm sure you have a spare car we can use," I assert.

"And I'm sure you can work on your patience. Sit down."

I can't help the growl rumbling in my chest as I sit back down. Between Bianco – at the head of the table – and me, Rose is playing with peas on her plate, not even trying to participate in the conversation. She hasn't eaten any of her food. I need to get her to eat as soon as we get home. I know she won't eat here.

"Rose, *bellissima*, do me a favor, will you?" Bianco asks and the uneasiness in my stomach deepens.

He's got something planned, I know he does, I just don't understand what exactly. He was meant to have all of us here and he's slowly trying to separate us. Saying I'm on edge is an understatement. My control is freefalling down a cliff.

"What?" Ozy replies unenthusiastically.

I want to die because anyone outside of this house who would ever call her sweet names without her agreement would get a kick in the balls. The grip of fear he has on her eats me up little by little.

"Sirena prepared a delicious dessert for us. We took so long to eat though, she must have gone home by now. Will you go and get it from the kitchen for us? You know where it is."

Rose looks at him deadpan for a few seconds before replying, "Sure."

I guess she's happy to leave this tense situation for at least a few minutes.

As soon as she's out of the long dining room, through the carved wooden doors, Bianco turns to me.

"Just you and me now, I guess."

I take a long sip from my glass. Making him wait for my answer. "That's what happens when you send everyone away, yes." I boil. "So what's the plan? A good scolding? Threats? Actions? Go on, don't be shy."

"Now, now, why would I need to do any of that?" He takes a sip of wine, puts it down ever so slowly, and puts the napkin that was on his knees back on the table. "Did you do anything to warrant a scolding, Jake?"

"You're not my legal guardian anymore," I assert, ignoring his question. "You don't make decisions for me. I have no obligation to do anything you say."

He laughs out loud, cackling like a goose. "You never did anything because I was your legal guardian. You follow orders because you know the consequences if you don't. You're not just a pretty face, are you? You're very smart. You know when it's pointless to fight. You know when you've already lost."

"Why do you do this?" I seethe. "Many people would be happy to work for you. There are criminals who would die to be on your side. They would be so loyal. I'm not. I'll never be. I'll leave any chance I get. You know it."

He slowly gets up as another laugh breaks from his chest, shorter this time.

"Because I *can*, Jake. You're useful to me. You and your

siblings were easy to get. You were just unloved orphans in a shit place."

He readjusts his tie. "I have no time to look for people that might or might not be loyal. I've put a lot of work into you. I raised you, I groomed you to become a soldier for me. And you know too much now. I don't want to get rid of you just so you don't spill my little secrets. I mean, I will kill you if I *really* have to. But, believe it or not, I love you kids. I love *you*, I love Nate and..."

He titters. Not mockingly this time though. It's irrepressible, the kind that comes before an overpowering truth. "God only knows how much I love Rose."

My body jumps from my chair so suddenly, everything on the table in front of me rattles. I'm panicking, I need something, *anything*. So I grab the steak knife in front of me.

"Don't *fucking* say this. Take it back. Take it back, I'll kill you, Bianco." I take a step to round the table but there are already armed men cocking their guns at me.

Still, I grab his tie and pull until his head almost hits the table. He puts his hands so his nose doesn't break but he doesn't defend himself. Why isn't he defending himself?

"Let's not both lose our lives in one night. Put the knife down. I can't take it back, Jake. No one can control love. Not even you. You love control so much, but there's nothing you can do about love. That's why you saw Jamie yesterday, right?"

My heart is beating too fast. It's palpitating. I'm panting without having done anything. I sound like I ran a marathon.

"I..." I pant. I'm dizzy. Fuck, why do I feel so dizzy? There's a veil of fog in front of my eyes.

"Are you alright? You're looking a bit pale. Do you need anything?" His words sound honest but the smirk on his face tells me he's finally getting what he wanted. I glance next to his face and look at the glass of water I just had. The one he personally gave to me earlier.

"What did you do?" My voice sounds far. I release him and take a step back.

I look around just to realize I'm losing all sense of depth. Bianco is walking around me and I'm trying to follow but his body splits into two, then four.

"You fucking drugged me," I wheeze.

"Now, now. You must be really hungover from your party with Jamie yesterday, son."

"Fu..." My mouth feels like cotton, and I can't finish my sentence. I try again. "Fu...y..."

Fuck you, Bianco! You fucking piece of shit! My voice shouts in my head but nothing comes out. It just echoes to infinity.

I hear the door opening, I see Rose coming in but she's miles and miles away from here. There's a long stretch for her to reach me, she'll never make it.

I put a hand in front of me to hold myself on the chair. I miss and my ass hits the floor.

"Jake..." her voice is a surprise far away from me. She drops the cake she was holding to the floor.

I roll to the side until I realize I'm on my stomach, my left cheek against the warm hardwood floor. All I see are feet and the cake. There are so many though. How many?

Try. Count. Focus.

Bianco's face lowers in front of me, he looks magnified. One eye is huge, one is tiny, his mouth is the size of a horse's.

"You should use that rest to think of your mistakes, Jake. Think hard again. Our agreement. Remember that?"

I want to say something so desperately, but I feel completely paralyzed. Only my eyes are still working, wide open as I watch Bianco join Rose. I watch her take steps back in fear, putting her hands right in front of herself to keep him away.

Get up, get up, get up!

I can't.

I blink and he's got her ponytail wrapped around his fist.

Get up! Fucking get up!

I hear my sister's desperate voice so loud in my ears. 'Please, don't. Mateo, don't.'

'You rolled your eyes at me, huh? You're so desperate to be put back in your place, you little whore.' His voice is fire. It burns me. It destroys everything.

'I'm sorry. I didn't mean to. *Mi dispiace tanto*, I'm so sorry, please.' Is she crying? She sounds like she's crying. Why can't I see if she's crying?

Shit. My eyes are closed.

I blink and he's dragging her with him, her hair in a tight grip. Her groan of pain is so *fucking loud*.

I blink again, this time it takes me longer to reopen. It's taking so long.

Come on, reopen!

My eyes don't reopen at all.

But Bianco's voice in my ears is clear enough that the images in my head match a form of reality.

"*Basta*, Rose. *Stai zitto*," he growls. "I hate your little whining. God, I hate it and you know it. Now be a good girl, shut the fuck up, and take it."

And then everything is black.

Black and terrifyingly silent.

8

JAMIE

Numb – Chri$tian Gate$

"Three of them?" I ask.

"Three of them, 'Me," Emily repeats. She hands me her phone and I grab it a little too avidly.

Despite my best friend's warning, my brows still shoot up to my hairline when I see 'Liked by jkwhite and 264 others'. Jake has liked the last three pictures Emily has posted with me.

"I was going to show you on Saturday, but I was busy. And on Monday you looked too good I didn't want to ruin it for you."

I finish reapplying my red lipstick and put it back in my bag.

"Are you saying I don't look good today?"

"No," she giggles. "Girl, you look fire." Her voice becomes more serious. "I just think you're not in a position where this would take you a few steps back anymore. I'm proud of you."

I look at myself in the bathroom mirror one more time,

rearrange my long chocolate hair, and roll my lips to make sure my lipstick is applied perfectly.

"Thanks," I smile at my best friend.

On Monday, I showed up to school in a skirt a size too small, no tights, long knee-high leather boots. I was determined to have Jake biting his fingers with regret for letting me go.

He didn't show up.

I still enjoyed the other guys' attention. I enjoyed their eyes on me. I enjoyed Camila's hateful stare.

He didn't show up on Tuesday and I kept going.

It's now Friday and Emily told me he was going to North Shore High. She saw it on Billie's Instagram.

I felt stupid for a second, then I realized it didn't matter. People talk, his friends are here, and Stoneview's rumor mill is the busiest in the country. He'll have been made aware that I went from Goody-two-shoes to Devil wears Prada. Hopefully sooner rather than later. I want the fucker to know I'm moving on without him. I want him to know guys are after me.

You're a whole new level of petty, Jamie Williams.

I don't care. I have one thing in mind only: hurt Jake White. Break him like he broke me.

Emily and I walk out of the girls' bathroom, and I feel like I am in a film. In Mean Girls or something.

Everyone's eyes are on us. Emily is wearing her cheer uniform and my school skirt is just an inch away from revealing my pink lace panties. Really, I'm just like any other girl in this school who feels sexy enough to show her body or the ones who desperately want guys' attention. I'm a bit of both probably. Plus, I've got revenge on my mind. This tiny skirt empowers me.

My friend and I walk together to the sports field

changing rooms. Camila and Beth giggle between themselves by their lockers and I know they're talking about me. It's impossible to miss their venomous gazes. I found a note in my locker today.

Stay away from Jake.

I can't believe Camila is back to her stupid, childish ways when I'm not even dating Jake anymore.

Emily rolls her eyes at them.

"You bitches sound like goats when you laugh."

"Desperately trying to get Jake's attention back, Goody? He goes to North Shore High now. I think the sluts over there have a little more to show than you do."

Camila's voice is always so collected when she verbally abuses someone. It makes it harder to retort. Whereas when Beth talks, it's easy to want to just punch her in the face.

"Why are you even here? You don't do any sport," Emily ripostes.

"Supporting my friend. God knows she needs it with the shit teammates she has."

I ignore Camila and start changing into my lacrosse uniform.

Ella passes Emily and me on her way out and as soon as she's out of view, my friend turns to me, slapping my arm with big eyes.

"I forgot to tell you. *Ella* sent me a text last night. Ella Baker."

"What did she want?" I ask as I pull my skort all the way to my waist, snapping the elastic into place.

"She wants help with her audition for Ms. Barry."

"Whoa, she dances?"

Ms. Barry is where Emily takes most of her dance classes. Ballet, Contemporary, Hip-Hop, Modern Jazz. Em does it all and she's been doing it at Ms. Barry's for five years. It's not just crazy expensive though, it's practically impossible to get in.

"What did you say?" I ask eagerly.

"No, of course! I can't help her, what's Luke going to think? That I'm desperately trying to get close to him or something. No thank you."

"This isn't about you and Luke. It might be Ella's dream to dance. What if she doesn't get in?"

"Then she wasn't good enough," she replies in a stern voice. "I didn't have anyone to help me when I applied. In fact, my parents were completely against it, and I had to do it behind their backs. On my own."

"Em..."

"It's too late anyway. She's sixteen. Ms. Barry takes first-time kids at the latest fourteen. She believes if you're passionate it should happen before that age, otherwise, it's not real passion. It's just a hobby."

I look at her intensely. Emily loves dancing and she loves people who love dancing. She helped Ella get a second tryout for the cheer team, she likes the girl. I know she wants to help her for Ms. Barry.

"Stop it, 'Me," she cautions. "I know what you're thinking. I'm not helping her."

"And potentially ruining a beautiful career. She's a great cheerleader. She's got moves, she's fun and delicate. She'll basically be you next year."

She huffs. "Everyone's already talking about voting her for captain. Which makes Beth hate her, which *obviously* makes me love her."

I give her another look.

"And she's so much fun," she continues. After a brief pause of her debating to herself, she finally admits, "I can't not help her."

"Nope."

"I have to."

"Yup."

"I hate you," she concludes.

"You have no reason for that," I smile.

"Yes, I do. You push me to be a good person. You're so annoying. You can try to be bad all you want, you are good deep inside, Jamie Williams."

How I wish I was.

I'm about to leave the locker room when Rose comes in. I haven't spoken to her this week. She's been skipping a lot of classes and has only been hanging out with Chris and Luke.

She's not wearing the school uniform but she's not wearing the lacrosse kit either. She's just in a pair of large, washed-out jeans and a huge white hoodie. She's actually wearing the hood up, which looks a bit weird in the locker room, and I know something is definitely wrong when I notice the thin-wire, round, golden glasses resting on her nose. She never wears them to school.

She leans against her locker but doesn't proceed to get changed.

"Are you not getting changed?" I ask as I put my lacrosse stick against the locker next to hers. I stand in front of her, my arms crossed against my chest.

She shakes her head. "I'm not coming to practice. Just here to talk to Coach T."

"We have a tournament in a week, Rose. You can't skip practice. No one can."

"How about you get off my back about practice. Just this once," she huffs.

But I don't. I've got my captain hat on, and Rose doesn't get privileges just because we're *kind of* friends under weird circumstances. I'm saying kind of because, if you're not Luke or Chris, it's hard to tell if you're Rose's friend or not.

"Coach is with the boys, how about you tell me whatever you were going to tell him?"

"I wasn't gonna tell him anything. He's the one who wants to talk to me."

"What? About what?"

"Jamie," she huffs again. She's about to say something when Beth passes between Rose and I, bumping Rose's arm with her shoulder on purpose. She winces at the not so gentle gesture.

"Oops," Beth fakes regret. She adds a hand in front of her mouth for show.

"Fuck off, Beth," Rose growls. "I'm not in the mood to deal with bitches today."

Beth holds herself high as she tries to gain some height on Rose. Impossible may I say.

"No?" she pouts. "That's weird, usually you're always up for dealing with bitches. Boys, bitches, guys in relationships. Nothing bothers a slut like you. *Usually*. I guess today is your day off then."

People have cleared the room now. It's just the three of us. I'm pretty sure Rose is going to get mad. In my head, she's going to shove Beth, maybe even slap her.

"Yeah, this slut needs a break. So run along," Rose sighs as she goes back into her initial position, against her locker.

"How's Jason?" Beth insists. "Did your druggie of a

brother beat up any other of your boy toys? I bet there's a long list to go through."

"Is this why you're such a bad cheerleader, Beth?" I interject. "Because you spend every practice bullying people in the locker room?"

Beth flips around, sharp eyes on me. "Nobody talked to you, broke girl."

My mouth falls slack at her stupid insult. The door to the locker room opens slowly as Coach Thompson makes his way in, his limp slowing him down.

"Miss Lam, cheer practice has started. Out," he mumbles.

Beth doesn't wait a second longer and hurries out of the room.

Coach sits down on one of the benches, huffing, and puffing as he tries to find a comfortable position.

"Alright, White" he starts in a stern voice. "It has come to my attention that you may or may not have forged your parents' signature on the tournament slip."

"I don't have parents, coach, I thought you knew that much," she chuckles.

But I know that kind of chuckle by now. It's the one she uses when she can't be bothered to face reality and serious conversations. The one that's a little too high for her voice, a little too fake to the ears who know her. Her chuckle is the equivalent of me biting my inner cheek. A stress reliever.

"Let's not play around with words, kiddo. If something happens to you at the tournament and your *guardian* wants to sue us because he wasn't aware that you were at a tournament in the first place, the school could be in big trouble. Now if you ask me, I only care about kicking St Anne's ass. But if you ask Mr. Parker, he has a different opinion."

Rose runs a hand below her hood and huffs loudly for

the third time tonight. She pushes her glasses up her nose with the knuckle of her forefinger.

"Principal Parker literally cannot stand me, Coach. He'll do anything to ruin my life. He's got a vendetta against me and my brother."

"Oh my, I wonder where this could have come from. You two are such exemplary students."

I have to pinch my lips to suppress a smile.

"I'll get it signed, Coach. Real one," she assures. "Can I ask who told you about this slip?"

"No. Now get to practice. Why haven't you changed yet?"

"About that." Her voice is slightly quieter now, which makes it raspier. "I can't play today."

Coach laughs and both Rose and I grimace. I know she's serious when she says that. Everyone has respect for Coach Thompson, Rose included. Every player on his team hates to disappoint him.

His laughter slowly dies down. "I'm sorry, for a second I thought you said you weren't going to train with the rest of your team *one* week away from the most important tournament of my career."

"I'm so sorry, Coach." The desperation in Rose's voice pinches my heart. She loves lacrosse and it's the only thing at this school she never misses.

"Anything to do with that?" he says pointing at her now fading black eye.

She pinches her lips but doesn't say anything.

"Coach, she really isn't feeling well today. She spoke to me about it, she wasn't in class during the day," I say, desperately trying to get her out of trouble. I owe her one for stopping Billie from destroying my face a week ago.

"Rose," Coach T. gets up from his seat and limps to our

side. He stands in front of her, raising his head slightly because she easily towers over him.

His hands are locked behind his back like anytime he's about to tell us something motivating. Rose is avoiding his gaze. I think she would play if she could. I just don't see what's wrong with her.

"Duke's scouts will be at the tournament," he finally says.

"What?" she chokes.

"I've told them so much about you and this is how you thank me? By skipping practice? You're good, Rose, you're my best player, but you're not *the* best player. They've seen countless girls like you this year, dying to get into their dream university and play their dream sport. You know how rarely Duke gives full rides. I don't need to remind you."

Rose walks in a small circle, her hands going under her hood again. She's so stressed, I can feel it in my own stomach.

"Coach, thank you, thank you so much. I won't disappoint, I promise. Just give me today, I can't. I really can't right now. I'm in too much pain. Next week, I'll train every day. I promise, every day I'll be on that field–"

"I'll help," I chime in. "I'll train with her. And Luke, Coach. I know he'll want to help. We can have Cole as well to do some drills."

If Rose loses a chance to go to college and finally have a normal life because of whatever she's got going on right now – which I'm sure has to do with Nate – I won't forgive myself for not helping. I need to help and make sure all the chances are on her side.

Coach growls some sort of 'humph' and looks at both of us, his eyes following a game of tennis between us until he settles on Rose. "I'm counting on you, White. I've got a good reputation with those guys, I only bring them people who do not disappoint. So don't."

"I won't, Coach."

He nods and heads for the door but pauses after opening it. "Oh, and White?"

"Yes, Coach?"

"Scouts do drug tests on kids they're interested in. They do it multiple times during the tournament. You didn't hear this from me."

She nods at him, not admitting or denying anything.

"Williams, get to practice."

"Yes, Coach," I shout as he leaves.

Once the door is closed, I turn to my friend. She slumps on the bench, her head in her hands, her elbows on her knees.

"Are you okay?" I ask.

I can't see her face, just the back of her hood. I hear her mumbling a 'thank you' but she doesn't come back up.

"Rose..." I try again.

She mumbles something else. I can't make out what she's saying so I put a hand on the back of her head and pull down her hood to hear her better.

"Jesus Christ," I cringe when I see the back of her neck.

I have to take a step back from her to calm my heart that just went galloping into the wild.

The purple finger marks tattooing the back of her neck dip down under her hoodie. I don't want to imagine what's under.

Tears prickle at the corner of my eyes, my throat tight enough to choke me. I force the tears back and swallow the giant ball in my throat.

You need to put up a strong face, Jamie.

"Rose, talk to me."

She lifts up her head. It's blank. No tears, nothing. I'm starting to believe she really never cries.

"I'm never gonna get out of here, am I? Not alive."

"Rose..." I crouch down in front of her. "We need to get you help. Please, we need to tell the police–"

"No cops, Jamie. When will you understand that Bianco controls all of them?"

If only dad was here. He would do something.

She stands up and I follow, but I can't keep up with her pacing so I'm the one who sits down.

"It's always so hot in here," she growls as she continues pacing. Her hair is a mess, and her face is flushed from the heat.

It's hard to see Rose like this. She has a vibe, this girl. Something invincible about her.

It is always crazy hot in the locker rooms. We always complain about it during summer. Never during winter. It's because the boiler room is only a thin wooden door away.

"Do you want to go on a walk?" I ask.

"No, you need to go lead your practice and I need to get home."

"Why didn't you come to my house if Bianco was at yours? You usually leave."

"I don't leave, Nate kicks me out. And we all went to Bianco's house. Whatever, it's a long story." She's talking fast and panicking. The bottom base of her neck is shining with a veil of sweat.

"Rose, calm down. We'll sort this out. Maybe you should see the school therapist, you need to talk to someone about this."

"Ugh," she groans but her voice is a lot deeper than usual. It's not hoarse anymore, it's completely broken. "I don't need to see a therapist, Jamie. What I *need* is to get far away from this godforsaken town!" Her voice dies down before she can talk again. "Why is it always so fucking hot in here?!" She grabs at her hoodie and rips it away from herself, passing it over in a struggle of grunts and cries.

"Jesus, Rose..." I whimper, barely holding the tears at bay.

Under the hoodie, she's in a white tank top. Her torso and arms are covered in deep purple bruises. If I thought last time was bad, I was completely mistaken. She's got pink welts on her shoulders as well.

"I need to get far away from here. And my only chance is this full ride to Duke. If I don't impress during this tournament, I'm just as good as dead."

My voice is shaking when I reply. "You will. You will. We have no choice, we'll make sure you will."

"I *have* to get a signed offer, Jamie," she insists. "If not...if not..."

I get up and grab her hoodie from the floor. "You will," I repeat, more determined than ever. "But the first step is for you to get some rest. You need to recover and be ready to practice every day next week." I give her the hoodie back and help her put it back on. "You need to go home. I'll walk you out."

She nods at me, wipes her nose with the back of her hand, and gives me a small smile.

"Jake was right. You truly are an angel."

Her words make me chuckle and we both head out together.

Outside, we wait on the steps together. Rose smokes a cigarette, her hood up and her eyes fixed on the horizon. I sit next to her, my hands desperately trying to keep my lacrosse skort from rising to my hips. These things are not meant for squatting, they're meant for running.

"What would you do if you had a million dollars," Rose asks me.

"I don't know," I shrug. "Probably spoil my mom. Buy her a house, pay her debts. Something like that."

She nods, turns her head away from me, and blows away some smoke.

"And you?"

She turns back to me and shrugs.

"I don't know. I ask myself all the time and I can't find the answer."

"Do you *have* a million dollars?" I double-check. With this girl, you never know.

"Nah. But Nate does. He's got multiple millions I bet. Freshly laundered as well. If he dies, I should inherit it."

We both laugh and it feels good to hear that sound from her.

"What are you going to study at Duke?"

"Law." She inhales on her cigarette, and I get mesmerized by her lips around it. They're so red. Just like Jake's. She exhales away from me again. "But I'm not going to Duke for now, so let's not fantasize."

She looks at the parking lot and her brows furrow.

"I'm sorry, Jamie. Chris was meant to pick me up. I don't know what happened."

I finally pull my gaze away from her lips just to find Jake's car stopping in front of the stairs. He changed his car after going to North Shore High. He's got a black SUV now. My heart picks up, like it always does whenever something related to him happens around me.

He stays in the car, and she takes another puff.

"Are you not going?" I ask.

"He can wait for me to finish my cigarette." She takes her time to exhale. "He knows."

"Knows what?"

"What happens with Bianco. He found out. It's painful to talk to him. He's becoming overprotective and I kinda hate him a little."

"Jake? Overprotective?" I reply, my voice vibrating to the sound of sarcasm.

She chuckles. "You know. More than usual." A beat passes between us before she speaks again. "I don't think I can reassure him another time that Bianco didn't rape me. Like...what does he want me to say? Not yet?"

"Please don't say this," I whisper in pain.

"What? The truth? If you think it's hard to hear, trust me it's harder to apprehend it. Knowing it's coming and there's nothing you can do about it."

Jake comes out of the car, and it takes Rose out of her own thoughts.

"What are you doing?" he questions as he walks the stairs up to us.

Is he talking to me?

No. He's not even saying hi to me.

"Finishing my cigarette. Where's Chris?"

"He's picking up some food in Silver Falls. We're meant to meet him at his. Come on."

Rose gets up and I follow. It's the strangest thing. It's like I'm a ghost, his gaze isn't even going my way. Not even a glance. He's looking right at his twin, and I feel like when you're a kid and everyone pretends you're invisible as a bad joke.

"Are you not even gonna say hi to her?" Rose tells him.

"Ozy," he huffs, running a hand through his messy hair. He finally turns to me. "Hi."

I flip my hair behind my shoulder and look at him, deep in his ocean eyes.

And I don't say anything.

"Bye, Rose," I tell her before turning around and going up the steps.

"Thanks for that, Ozy," I hear him growl at his sister.

I see Luke coming into the parking lot, his sports bag hanging over his shoulder, lacrosse helmet in hand. He's coming from the side of the building. The same way I'm heading back to go onto the field. That means the guys are finished. That means I'm half an hour late for my own practice.

Luke halts, clearly waiting for someone and my heart somersaults with joy when I see Cole. I discreetly look back to see Rose and Jake waiting for their best friend.

Cole calls my name and a smile tugs at my lips. This is basically revenge served on a silver platter.

Jake doesn't like Cole. Because Jake is a possessive man. He couldn't stand his interest in me when we were together, even if it was just friendship.

I love Rose and I'll do anything for her to get the happy ending she deserves after what she's been put through. But I owe nothing to her twin.

Nothing.

So as Cole waves at me, coming my way with Luke at his side, I hurry to him and jump in his arms. He drops his helmet to catch me, and it makes me giggle.

"Such enthusiasm, Queen Bee," he laughs. "I hope it's an apology for ditching my party last Friday."

"Sorry, I don't go to lame parties."

My remark makes him laugh and I'm glad he didn't take

it the wrong way. We still have our private joke of calling each other the opposite of what we are. We still have our friendship despite letting him down last week.

When I was with Xi, I realized Cole could never make me feel all the wrong sexual ways Xi made me feel at that party.

But Jake doesn't need to know that.

Cole puts me down.

"Can I make it up?" I ask. "Are your parents back in town?"

"Yeah, it's too late. Sorry, you're gonna have to find something else," he smiles.

"Ugh, fine," I fake irritation. "What are you doing tonight? Sushi date?"

"Nah, you're coming to Luke's party tonight."

I turn to Luke, slightly surprised. His smile is bright, welcoming. Is he happy to set me and Cole up? Despite what happened with Jake? Jake is his best friend. If Luke is happy for Cole and me to be a thing, it means Jake is truly over me. He's not faking it.

Some secret part of me hoped that with everything going on, he was trying to protect me from it all. He was keeping me away from the fiasco that is his life around Bianco. If that was the case, Luke wouldn't be happy. He'd be sad for his friend. My heart recoils as I look at Luke. He's fine with it. He thinks Jake won't care.

Maybe he truly doesn't care. Maybe he truly just left me behind and is now playing his games with Billie. I'm the new Camila, she's the new Jamie. It's hard to swallow.

"Come tonight!" Luke insists. "I didn't ask because, you know, Em and all that, but it'll be fun to see you there. It's some sort of pre-tournament party. Both teams and the cheerleaders are coming. The rule is you have to dress in

Stoneview's team color. Not a word to Coach, though." He winks at me, and his traits tighten in cheekiness.

"So?" Cole's hands on my shoulders snap me out of my dejection. "Come on, you're captain, you should be there. And you owe me."

"Yeah," I smile as I let out a forced chuckle. "Course I'll come."

"Sick, see you tonight." Luke waves us goodbye as he joins his friends still waiting by their car.

Jake gives him some sort of dude shoulder hug with a tap on the back. Luke is talking to the twins, but Jake's killer gaze is on me. Well, me and Cole. I can't read him. I don't understand him. I want to know what I'm up against. I want him to hurt. Hurt so bad.

I put my hand in Cole's and watch Jake's gaze glance down.

"Don't you have practice?" Cole asks.

"Crap! Pick me up, okay?" I say as I run back toward the field.

Coach is going to have my head.

9

JAMIE

Yes Girl – Bea Miller

"Mom," I call as I walk out of my room. "Cole is here!"

I walk into the living room, focused on my miniature handbag to make sure I haven't forgotten anything.

"What in the name of…Jamie," she scolds me.

"What?" I ask as I look up.

"What are you wearing? That is so inappropriate!"

I look down and back at her. "It's a skirt, mom, not a stripper's outfit."

To be fair, it's a very short burgundy skater skirt. I didn't think she would mind though.

"Really? Do you think I was born yesterday, young lady?"

She comes closer and opens the burgundy letterman jacket Cole had lent me, opening it to the simple dark blue bralette I'm wearing underneath.

"I'm talking about this."

It's not like we can see my nipples or anything, it's a long bralette and it stops an inch above my belly button. I feel sexy in it, and I'm not planning on taking off the letterman jacket. It's a sexy peak, nothing more, nothing less.

"I'm not going to take the jacket off," I justify myself.

"'Me," she sighs. "Why are you changing yourself? You're perfect the way you are. I know breakups are hard, but it wasn't you, it was him."

"What the fuck, Mom," I rage. "Why would you even bring this up? Maybe this is me being a little more myself, maybe I'm sick of the goody-two-shoes persona."

"Oh, okay. So you swear now? You do know I can still forbid you from going to this party, right?"

That calms me down straight away. My mother is a lovely woman, but she never lets anyone walk all over her.

When she sees I have nothing to reply, she insists, "You know your dad hated swearing."

Guilt gnaws at my insides. I wonder what my dad would have thought of all this. I had never dated, never attracted the interest of boys before. Would he have been the kind to be over-protective? To scare boys away with his sheriff badge? Or would he have had a conversation about contraception with me? What about Aaron?

My throat constricts and my mom must notice I'm upset. "Go have fun. Just...be careful. Promise?"

"I promise," I smile.

Cole comes to get me at the front door. He's a gentleman like that. He promises my mom he won't drink and will bring me back home, and we both leave in an Uber. He lied to her about the drinking, but I know he'll bring me back home. Cole's parents don't let him borrow their car and he hasn't got his own. It's not that they can't afford one, but they're strict like that. He has to bargain every party, every date, everything outside of homework and lacrosse.

. . .

Chapter 9

We walk into Luke's mansion and bump straight into Ella, his younger sister. She's put her beautiful bright blond hair into a tight ponytail and is wearing a tight, leather, burgundy dress.

"Cole!" she exclaims.

I can see she's already way past drunk. She jumps into his arms, and he hugs her only briefly, probably feeling awkward in front of me. I feel slightly guilty. Am I just using him to make Jake jealous?

We walk further into the house. Both the women's and men's teams are dressed in burgundy and dark blue only. The cheerleaders have taken over the open bar and the DJ booth, making TikTok videos and adding to their Instagram stories.

"What do you want to drink?" Cole asks as he wraps an arm around my shoulders.

"I'll stick to soda for now." After the drunken horror of last Friday, I would rather keep a clear mind tonight.

"Soda it is." He turns to go to the bar, but I grab his hand.

"Wait," I say in a panic. "Don't leave me alone."

Being surrounded by all those popular kids, seeing Camila dressed sexy in Stoneview's team colors even though she doesn't play nor cheers, makes me feel uncomfortable. Without Emily's popularity backing me up, without alcohol bringing out my confidence, I'm still just Goody. The girl who doesn't belong here.

He laughs and brings me closer to him. "Let's get our drinks together."

We hover around the bar for as long as Cole's teammates come and chat with us. Every now and then, one of them gets surprised that I'm the captain of the women's team. 'But we never saw you at pre-season parties...'

"Why have I never been invited to pre-season parties before?" I ask Cole once his friend has left us.

He chuckles and puts both the palm of his hands on my cheeks. "Do you want the truth, or should I give you a nice little lie?"

I fake pout, but I ask for the truth anyway. "You can't lie to me. Come on, I won't get upset."

"You were a little too stuck up for pre-season parties. You probably would have shut it down, screamed at your girls that they shouldn't be drinking so close to the tournament, and made their life hell at the next practice."

He lets go of my face and I can't help a laugh. "You're so mean," I exclaim as I slap his chest. "That's so not true."

"Really? Because I see you cringe every time you see Ciara take a shot over there." He points at Ciara in the corner of the room.

He's so right. Ciara's my wing. She's the link between me, center, and Rose, attack. Rose isn't here tonight, thankfully. After the week she had, and the state she's in, I would put her in bed myself if I saw her here.

"So I'm not stuck up anymore?"

He laughs. "No, you changed. In a good way."

I finish my soda, tipping the can back, my gaze looking up. When I look back at Cole, there's something different in his eyes.

"What?" I ask in a smile.

He puts a strand of my hair behind my ear and a cheeky smile brightens his face.

"What are you wearing under my jacket, Queen Bee?"

The lust in his voice makes my cheeks flush. I don't know this side of Cole. I only know the gentle and light-hearted side. He grabs both lapels of his jacket and brings me closer to him in a harsh movement. My breath instantly leaves my lungs, my eyes focusing on his as my mouth falls slightly open.

"Are you only wearing a bra?"

I nod but still manage to whisper. "It's a bralette." Because that's exactly what matters right now.

He bends down enough to whisper in my ear, "I thought you looked hot in my clothes, but I think you would look a lot hotter without them on."

He pulls away from my ear, his lips hovering over mine, close enough that I can smell the beer he was drinking, it's mixing with the smell of his cologne. He finally lets go of the jacket I'm wearing and takes a step back.

"Should we find Luke?"

I try to swallow the ball of desire that got stuck in my throat and nod.

He takes my hand and drags me with him. Maybe I'm going to need a drink after all.

Jake

Luke readjusts the triangle of cups he's just put on the garden table, and I light up the joint in my mouth.

"Kaylee, why are you not wearing the team colors?" my friend asks as he pours some beer in the cups. He sounds annoyed, but I know he's only doing this to work her up.

"Oh...I...my cheer uniform is in the wash and...I don't know, I thought red would do?"

"That's not very supportive of our team," he scolds her.

I chuckle at her blushing face. He's just desperately trying to get Chris to defend her. All he wants is Chris to fuck a girl tonight. We haven't heard one bit of information about our friend's sex life since the beginning of the year. For me, since we fucked with Jamie at his birthday party in September.

I know my foster brother; he can't last that long without having sex. He never mentions his secret girlfriend, we're so sure she doesn't exist. So what has he been up to?

The thing with Chris is he has a superhero complex. He wants to defend every creature that can't defend itself. And more often than not, he also fucks them into feeling reassured. They love a big guy with a good heart. So Luke has been rude to every girl around us, wanting Chris to step in. But he's in his own world right now, looking at the backyard every now and then, frowning, rubbing his neck. Something is stressing him out.

Luke is also not the most threatening guy around. He's our little ray of sunshine, he's not a mean guy.

"Jake isn't wearing the team colors," Kaylee retorts.

She's on the other side of the long table, teaming with Chris for beer pong while I'm teaming with Luke.

"I ain't part of your team," I reply disinterested.

If Luke wants her helpless, I can surely help. I just didn't really want to till now.

"Surely you shouldn't be at this party then?" she tells me, giving me a playful smirk. But you don't want to play with me, babe. I promise you.

"Are you talking back to me?" I tell her in a dark voice. I pass the joint to Luke and put both hands on the table, palms flat on the mosaic decorating it. "Do you have any idea what I do to bad girls, Kaylee?"

Her eyes widen and she takes a slight step back, clearly shocked. I don't even know why I said this to her.

Actually, I do know. I miss a good girl that blushes at my crudeness. I miss Jamie.

Chapter 9

Luke chuckles next to me and, fucking finally, Chris steps in.

"Jake," he growls at me. "Can you behave yourself for two seconds?"

I smile at him and then back at Kaylee. "My bad, babe. You start." I throw her the ping-pong ball and she catches it. She gives me a shy smile, her sassiness all gone.

I think that would have given me a boner a few months ago. A girl, shying away from my roughness. I don't think I could care less right now. Jamie is the only girl I want to punish with my own brand of violence. Except I don't follow my heart anymore, I follow Bianco's orders.

The image of Bianco dragging my twin away while I was passing out on his floor is engraved in my mind forever. It's been added to my bank of traumatizing moments he has tattooed on my brain.

It should be weird that I'm at a party when less than a week ago, I was in a taxi with Rose, being sent back after being drugged while she was being abused. It should be surreal, out of this world, unbelievable. Not for us. Bianco has abused us through all our young years. Get traumatized and go back out there like nothing happened. From eight to fourteen years old. It's ingrained in us, inked in our souls, tattooed on us. Literally, tattooed on us.

I know how *I* was abused. And I know my sister was beaten up. I never understood how far it went. She said he never sexually assaulted her, but that he was in love with her. *Obsessed*. That's the word she always uses when she talks about Bianco. But she never said he spends hours beating her, bruising her. I know now. She told me everything when we got home. I insisted, I was still dizzy from the drugs, I could barely stand up, but I forced it out of her because I saw how he dragged her out of the room.

She showed me her arms and her neck. Not the rest, but I could easily imagine. I didn't need to see it. I didn't say anything in front of her, I nodded, I thanked her for opening up to me. I waited for her to go to bed to throw up. Once I got over the momentary loss of control. I texted Nate, I told him what his *boss* did. What our ex foster parent put our sister through. And I concluded my text with something I had always thought but never truly believed I'd put into action until then.

We need to kill him.

He took hours to reply, and only gave me two words.

I know.

But we never see Nate anymore. He's so busy, never sleeps at home, always 'working'. Sam keeps us company at the mansion every now and then. Well, he sleeps there and keeps quiet like he always does.

The ball lands in the cup in front of me and Kaylee's laugh takes me out of my thoughts completely.

I grab the cup in front of me, down it, and grab the joint back from my friends. My whole life is out of fucking control anyway, what's a little more? Losing myself in drugs and alcohol tonight can only bring me some peace.

"Kaylee's right," Chris smiles at me. "You're not part of Stoneview's team anymore. Luke, you let the enemy on our grounds."

I laugh. Chris doesn't even play lacrosse. I throw the ball back and it lands in the cup in front of Chris. He downs it and wipes his mouth with his forearm. I think my best friend wants to let loose tonight too.

"Jakey was our captain, I can't not invite him to our pre-season party just because he now plays for N.S. High," Luke exclaims.

Chapter 9

Right on cue, my phone rings, and I take it out of my back pocket as Chris throws the ball back.

"Shit," I mumble, looking at the message I just received. I lick my lips at the treat Billie sent me and show my screen to Luke as I down another cup in front of me.

"Oh, shit," my friend agrees.

My new favorite North Shore girl sent me a picture of her in the black and white N.S. High lacrosse kit. Except she seems to have dropped the shirt. And the bra too. Looks like their pre-season party is a lot more fun than ours.

> Billie: You should be partying with your own team

I bite my lower lip and put my phone back in my pocket. She sounds pretty convincing when she says this accompanied by her boobs on display.

"Dude," Luke says. "I really don't think you should be here."

We both laugh and Chris' harsh gaze fall on us, but I can't focus on it because, behind him, Cole fucking Cooper is making his way to us.

I guess that would be fine if he wasn't holding my girlfriend's hand so tightly while he walks.

Not your girlfriend.

That's something I just can't seem to imprint on my brain. Jamie's mine. There's just nothing that can change that. Seeing her with someone else, I just want to fuck her into understanding that. But I can't.

I can't, I can't, I can't. It's just so hard to comprehend it.

"We'll take the winners," Cole announces as they both settle next to the table, halfway between my side and Chris'.

Jamie is the closest to me and I don't miss what she's wearing; that fucking jacket with *Cooper* written on the back and the number seven on it. Cole's number. It's ten times too big for her and I grit my teeth thinking she never wore mine. She never did, she hates that shit.

She enjoys being owned behind closed doors, she likes the protection and the possession. But in public? Nah, she's her own person. She would scold me for *holding* her too possessively. Can't imagine what she would have thought if I had put my last name and lacrosse number on her back.

My brain suddenly plays one on me, because while I thought she hated it, she's still doing it for Cole. He's not even her fucking boyfriend. Or is he?

Fuck, maybe I don't know her? Maybe I don't know her at all.

My palms feel sweaty when I throw the next ball and I miss. Kaylee throws back and it lands perfectly. I do need a drink. I down my third or fourth drink of the game and grab the first girl who walks past us. Jessika.

"My beautiful Jess." I give her a charming smile as I hold her waist. "Will you be a doll and get us all some shots? I think it's time to get this party started, don't you?"

She smiles and nods, giving me a pat on the chest before she disappears inside.

Yeah, shots. That's what I need.

We keep playing, and Jamie starts supporting Chris' team. I can see from the corner of my eyes Cole's hand going up and down her back. Sometimes grazing way too fucking close to her ass. I'm practically dying for him to touch it, just so I can smash his fucking face on the table. Tattoo that pretty mosaic on his forehead.

I smile to myself as I throw the ball back again. That's when Jessika comes back with a platter full of shots. Unfortunately, Camila, Beth, and a lot of the cheerleaders came back with her.

Chapter 9

"Let's get this party started," Jessika screams, accompanied by a few of the girls wooing.

I notice Jamie going on her toes to talk into Cole's ear. She's asking him to leave, I know she is because she fucking hates Beth and doesn't feel comfortable around these girls. Her skirt hikes up – giving me a great view of the midnight blue, lace shorties she's wearing under it – and Cole grabs her ass, helping her higher while he goes slightly lower to hear her talk into his ear.

Well.

Time to fuck him up.

I'm taking a step toward them when a body slams against mine and I feel a drink spilling on my white t-shirt.

"The fuck?" I growl.

"Oh my god, Jake, I'm so sorry!" Camila's fake apologetic voice is already giving me a headache. "Here, let me help." She gives a few slaps on my abs, pretending to 'dry' the shirt, and grabs two shot glasses. "Whatever, let's drink," she smiles.

I take a shot because I really fucking need it. But when I look back to where Cole and Jamie were a second ago, they're gone.

Shit.

"Another round!" someone shouts. And I go with it.

What else can I do? I'm not fucking *allowed* to date Jamie. All I can do is observe her from afar. All I can do is threaten guys like Cole to not touch her because she should be all mine. All I can do... is watch helplessly as she moves on from me.

So I go along with the party. I take one shot after the other. I snort a line or two that Camila offers. I don't know how long has passed but I don't see Jamie and Cole again.

Camila comes back to me, a drunken smile plastered on

her lips. I'm now sitting with Chris and Ella on the sofa, debating who's got more chance of winning the tournament.

"Jake," Camila drawls as she sits on my lap. I want to roll my eyes, but I'm a bit too drunk at this point. A bit too high. So that too, I go with it. I grab her waist, bringing her closer, taking in her expensive perfume, the kind that attacks your sinuses and numbs your brain. I bury my face in her neck to find more of that familiar scent I used to lose myself in.

"What's up," I say as I pull away from her neck. I push all of her hair to the other side, before playing imaginary notes on her shoulder with my fingertips.

"I'm sorry about your t-shirt," she whines. She's not. She just wants something to talk to me about, because we have nothing in common.

"Mm," I drop a kiss on her naked shoulder. "Always sorry for something, aren't you?"

My eyelids are heavier than earlier, but my brain is still excited from the coke I snorted an hour ago. I see from the corner of my eye, Chris looking at my hand that starts squeezing Camila's thigh. He gives me an annoyed look and I relax back into the sofa. I lean toward my friend while Camila makes herself comfortable on my lap and starts talking to Ella.

"I haven't heard from that girlfriend in a while," I whisper to my friend. "Does that mean you're open to sexcapades again?"

"With Camila?" he chuckles. "Don't you think if I wanted to be involved in your toxic fuckery I would have done so before?"

I laugh because he couldn't be more right. "It's not like you haven't been in toxic fuckeries before."

"It's a shit idea, Jake. Not just for me. You're going to regret it."

I don't know if Camila can't hear us or if she decides being talked about this way is worth it if she can get me in bed afterward.

I don't really care. When she leans back into me, her back against my chest, and brings one of her soft hands behind to bring my face closer to her, I let her. I indulge in it like it was the first time. I pretend I'm one of those lucky guys Camila Diaz has chosen to give attention to. So many fuckers crave that attention.

"Let me help you clean that shirt, Jake," she whispers in a sultry voice.

I wrap both my arms around her waist and hold her tight to me. "You want to clean my shirt? You think that makes it up for staining it?"

"I can make it up to you after cleaning it. I'll be such a good girl, you'll see."

The familiarity of her words stirs something in me. Pure lust. It's not something I want right now, not with her, not like that. But there's a higher force in me that takes over when it hears the possibility of complete control.

She gets up, grabs my hand, and I let her drag me to the double staircase.

"There's a bathroom downstairs," I say as we pass the door to the closest one.

"There are better ones upstairs," she replies cheekily as she walks up, my stupid self in her tow.

I can already imagine Luke and Chris' disappointing talk tomorrow morning. 'Her again?!' 'Do you know how many chicks could replace her?'

But none of them could satisfy the sick need I have to possess someone. At least with Camila, I know I'll get my fix. It will be a disappointing one, but it's still a fix. Like putting gaffer tape on a wall crack.

Camila pushes a door open, and I falter slightly. "That's a bedroom, Cam. Come on you're not even trying to pretend you want something else than a quick fuck."

"Who said quick?" she giggles.

This is one of Luke's many guest bedrooms. It has an ensuite bathroom that is shared with another bedroom.

I walk straight to the bathroom and take my shirt off. "Come clean it," I shout her way.

She pads into the bathroom, huffing loudly, sending some strands of new bangs flying up.

"I like your bangs," I state drunkenly. "Looks cute on you."

Her eyes widen, not used to compliments from me. "For real?" she double-checks.

"Yeah, for real. Now clean my shirt, little pet."

She offers me her sluttiest look, accompanied by a small smile that is nothing but pure anticipation, and grabs my shirt. She settles in front of the double sinks and opens one before rubbing soap on my shirt. I sit on the edge of the bath and watch her intently. She can see me in the mirror, but my eyes are focused on her ass.

"Take your panties off."

She stills, I watch a wide smile spread on her lips, and finally, she executes.

I get up, push her tight skirt above her hips and sit back down.

"Cam, that's a nice view, you know? Your thick butt waiting to be spanked while you wash my clothes. I could get used to it."

Her eyes are back up in a split second, something different in her gaze. She's sad. I raise an eyebrow as she stops the water flow and puts the soap back next to the sink.

"Jake," she sighs. "Don't make promises you can't keep.

Please." Her last word is a plea, but I find it hard to give a fuck.

Camila and I were never good together, but I was never the monster of her story. I wasn't good to her, but she was horrible to me too. We brought the worst out of each other, we were the epitome of toxicity.

"You don't love me, Cam. Stop acting like it," I scold her.

She violently throws my shirt on the floor and turns around fuming. "You don't fucking know that! You broke my heart, do you give a shit at all? Huh?"

In return for her vulnerable honesty and anger, I give her a predatory smile. She fucked up. She should know not to drop her defenses around me.

I walk to her slowly, giving her time to regret her words, and stop only an inch away from her.

"Get on your knees."

"Jake," she sighs desperately. "I–"

"*You* are going to get on your fucking knees, choke on my cock and think about the way you address yourself to me. Who fucked our relationship, Cam?"

She doesn't reply, looking away, avoiding my gaze. I grab her exposed pussy roughly, making her gasp. She's wet for me. Nothing unusual here.

"Who?" I insist. "Who cheated on who first, come on, admit it."

"Me!"

"That's right. So don't talk to me about breaking hearts. *You* wanted some other guy's dick in your cunt. So why are you pissing me off now, huh? Get on your fucking knees, Cam. You know there's only one thing you're good for now. So, execute."

I let go of her pussy and let her sink to her knees, her skirt still above her hips, her underwear on the floor next to us. She's unbuckling my belt when the door to the adjacent room opens.

"I'll meet you downstairs–" The voice I recognize too well stops suddenly.

Camila shrieks as she stumbles back on her feet and pulls her skirt down.

"Leave, you fucking perv!" she screams at Jamie, whose narrowed eyes hold nothing but fury.

She's not even disappointed, nor surprised. Because she doesn't expect anything better from me. I thought she had left the house, I didn't think she was here let alone in a bedroom. My heart drops in my stomach so hard I feel like I've swallowed poison. She was in a bedroom. With Cole.

"Leave," I repeat, barely any emotion in my voice.

Jamie crosses her arm over her chest, planting her feet to the ground.

"You heard him, Goody. Get your ugly ass out of here," Camila spits her venom at my ex.

My *ex*. No that doesn't sound right. It really doesn't.

"I was talking to you, Camila," I specify.

A smirk spreads on Jamie's lips as the real ex gasps in shock. "Are you for fucking real right now?"

"I don't know, do you want to test and see?" I turn to her, holding her gaze in my threatening one.

She shrieks, literally *shrieks,* curses at both of us, and storms out, slamming doors in her way.

"You didn't have to ask her to leave," Jamie assures calmly as she approaches the sink. "I'm just washing my hands."

She slowly opens the tap water, washes her hands with the soap Camila left on the side, and completely ignores me.

I watch her tanned shoulders move to the rhythm of her

scrubbing and that's when it hits me. The jacket she was wearing is gone, only leaving her with a fucking bra on.

"Are you fucking kidding me?" I growl as I approach her from the back. She watches me in the mirror as she turns off the tap and grabs a towel without moving from her position. "You wear bras to parties now?"

I put both my hands on either side of her, holding the sink. She struggles to turn around, stuck against me, but when she manages her gorgeous boobs push just against my stomach.

So fucking tiny, this girl.

"It's a bralette," she whispers. Her eyes are hooded, her gaze dragging along my neck before going back to my eyes.

She wants me. After what I've put her through, after breaking her heart, fucking, and leaving her at a party last week, she still *wants* me. Her body can't control that attraction we have to each other.

And I want her. What's wrong with a bit of meaningless sex with your ex? I'm used to that.

"And who did you wear that bralette for, Angel? For Cole?" I pretend to pout knowing perfectly what her answer is going to be.

She might have been in a room with Cole, but she wore that for me. I know she did.

My whole body shakes at the thought of what they could have been doing in that bedroom. How can she still think I'd let her do those kinds of things?

"You," she vows in a trembling voice like admitting her deepest secret.

"Me?" I ask for confirmation as a malicious smile spreads on my lips. "Prove it."

She only nods. She doesn't say anything as she drops to her knees, exactly in the same position Camila was a few minutes ago. Except when it's Jamie, it drives me absolutely insane with lust. My cock is already hard, so fucking ready to have her take me in.

I feel dizzier from her closeness than from any drugs or alcohol I ingested tonight. Jamie is my fucking drug, she's my demise, my doom. Everything about her is exactly what I want and exactly what I can't have.

Jamie is my unattainable utopia.

She undoes my pants, pulls them down, and rubs me through my boxers.

"Close your eyes," she murmurs in the voice of a mermaid, enchanting me into following her directions.

I close my eyes and entangle my fingers through her thick hair as she makes me step out of both my pants and boxers. I feel her breath on my hard dick, I feel her lips rubbing up and down, getting me ready.

I hear her throw my stuff away from us and buck my hips forward. Suddenly, her tongue is on me, making me gasp in pleasure. My lips fall open as she rubs her tongue up and down my shaft.

"Angel," I moan as I tighten my grip on her hair. "Take me in."

She keeps going up and down with her tongue, teasing me with wetness before licking the tip like an ice-cream.

"Jamie," I growl, my voice growing darker from impatience. She's teasing the fuck out of me and she's about to regret it real bad.

"Beg for me, Jake."

The sultriness in her voice makes my cock vibrate.

"Just for me," she repeats. "Show me how much you want it. Show me I mean more than she does."

She means so much more than Camila. It's not even comparable.

Chapter 9

She puts her lips around my tip but doesn't go any further. I'm dying from the teasing, so I give her what she wants. "Please, Angel. Let me in."

I feel her lips spreading into a smile and she moves me slightly deeper, finally past her lips until I feel her tongue lap at me again.

"More," I order. She pulls slightly back, and I get what she wants straight away. "More, Angel, *please*. Please just let me fuck your throat. I need this. I need you, don't you get that?"

She takes me all the way in in such a sudden movement, I moan loudly when my dick hits the back of her throat. She pulls away just as quickly.

"I want to touch myself while I suck you off," she says.

I let go of her hair and let her pull away while I assume she readjusts herself, putting her hand under her skirt and into her sexy panties.

Except...except it's taking a bit too long.

Something's wrong.

My eyes snap open just in time to watch her through the mirror. She's put my clothes in the bath and is opening the shower jet on them.

"Jamie!" I shout as I jump around and on her, but it's too late. The jet is already soaking all my clothes. I'm stark naked and watching my boxers, pants, and shirt drowning in the bath.

I grab her arm tightly and pull her to me, my hard cock pushing against her. If I thought controlling her was a turn-on, her fighting back is the fucking cherry on top.

"Let me go," she seethes.

"You think I'm going to let you go after what you just pulled?"

I drag her until I can push her against the wall, facing the tiles while I pull her wrists behind her back.

"Is that my style, Angel? Do I ever let you do any rebelling without punishing the fuck out of you in return?"

She pulls at her wrists with a strength I didn't know she had. "Let me go, Jake. You really thought I was going to go on my knees for you after what you did to me? After finding you here with Camila? How desperate do you think I am?!"

She fights me frantically. It's in vain but boy is she fighting. The beast in me is screaming with pleasure at the fact that she can't escape no matter how hard she tries.

"I'm going to hurt you now, Angel. Because that's what happens when you think you can fuck me over."

I slide a knee between her legs, forcing them apart.

"I'll scream, Jake!" she rages, squirming around.

"Stop it, you're making me even harder. And yourself wetter."

She stops for a split second, caught in the act. Of course this whole thing makes her wet.

I reach out under her skater skirt with my other hand, and I only need to feel her underwear to know I'm dead right.

"Oh, Angel. What a dirty girl you are."

She lets out a short moan when I slap her covered pussy with a flat hand.

"Stop," she growls. "I'm serious."

"Relay the message to your pussy then," I mock her.

She pushes at me again and I crush back against the wall. "No more squirming now. Or it'll hurt."

I pull her panties to her knees and place my hard dick at her entrance. I delight in her sigh of pleasure.

"No," she squeals.

"Painful it is, then," I instruct low in her ear.

Chapter 9

I plunge into her so hard, her head hits the tiles in a painful groan.

"Fuck," she whimpers.

She gets wetter, she moans, and she squirms for a few seconds but then her behavior changes.

She pushes back again, and her voice is pure rage when she talks again. "Let me *fucking* go, Jake. This is not our thing anymore, don't you get that? Things have changed. Despite what you think, I'm not. Yours. Anymore."

Her words are worse than a punch to the stomach. I let her go quicker than if her skin was burning mine and take a few steps back.

She just stabbed my heart badly enough for me to have to fight with my own breathing. How can she throw such truths at me? Like it doesn't mean shit that we're not together anymore. Like...like she's truly over us.

Like I should be.

She doesn't give me respite though; she keeps stabbing at me with no mercy.

"I'm not yours to play with anymore. I'm not yours to order around." She pulls her panties back up as she keeps talking. "You know, it's hard to admit that I loved the way you were with me. How you controlled my body into submitting. It was ecstatic, Jake. But you don't have that right anymore. If I want to fuck other guys, I will. I *dream* of Xi's dick in my mouth. You ruined it once, but you won't twice. And if I want to fuck Cole, believe me, I will too. And you don't get a say about it."

The beast in me is roaring so loud I want to put her to the floor and choke her down. But the pain she's causing is worse. It overtakes it all.

"Is that what you are now, Jamie? Some girl who gets revenge by tricking me out of my clothes and fucking other guys? That's just not who you are." The disappointment in my voice is loud enough to floor her but she doesn't let it faze her.

Instead, she laughs back at me. "I couldn't care less if you think that's not who I am. It isn't. But as long as you suffer, I don't care if I lose myself in the process."

She turns around and leaves the bathroom with a halo of calmness around her. Like she knows I'm the one left hurting after those words.

And I am.

It hurts really fucking bad.

But if Jamie Williams thinks she can get away from me *and* have the last word, she really forgot who I was. She forgot how this whole thing started. I forced her into submission once, I can do it as many times as I fucking wish.

I might not be able to date her, but if she wants to play games. Oh, baby, we will. Nothing stops me from keeping her around on the leash I've always had around her neck.

10

JAMIE

Without Me - Halsey

I only start breathing again when I walk into the backyard. Standing up to Jake is one of the hardest things I've ever done in my life. Last week, I had alcohol-induced bravery. I was fuming at what he had just done. I always tried to defend myself and always ended up giving in. I never put up a real fight.

And now I did.

So why do I not feel any better?

My heart is beating so hard in my chest I feel like I'm on drugs. My extremities feel numb, my stomach is twisted. And my pussy is wet. Always when he starts playing with me. It's a mix of adrenaline and despair. How can I say no to Jake when I'm dying to say yes? But my pride is at an all-time high, I feel powerful. Is that how he feels all the time?

Probably not, he's so used to it. Jake doesn't understand emotions the same way we mere mortals do. It's hard to know when he's genuine and when he copies human emotions to plaster them on his god-like face.

I find Cole by the pool outside, holding his jacket, ready to give it back to me. I put it back on straight away. Mid-March, the weather is still cold, especially at nighttime. Everyone barely feels it in their drunken state, and I must admit in my high adrenaline one, I don't feel very cold either.

Cole and me. I bet Jake is dying to know what we were up to in that room. I hope he thinks we were having sex. Or at least making out. I hope it burns him, eats him from the inside like it did me when I saw him kiss Billie in front of me. That's Jake, isn't it? He fucks girls right, left, and center while he expects me to wait like a good pet.

I don't understand his sick possessive behavior when he's the one who broke up with me. It only reinforces my feeling that he's doing it to protect me from Bianco. But how could I know? Jake never lets anyone in, never explains himself. He makes decisions and expects everyone to bend to them. Whoever doesn't, risks his wrath. I'm not scared of his wrath, I'm scared of losing him forever. Because after the games, the anger, and the revenge...what will there be left of us?

I wasn't having sex with Cole. I was giving him a 'tour of rich mansions'. We were just having a ton of fun walking through Luke's gigantic house and mocking the number of useless rooms or the kind of things rich people collect. I mean, Cole is rich, but he's the kind to not think too hard about it so he can take a joke.

Cole had left an open chocolate bar in his jacket and when I put my hand in the pocket it got covered in day-old melted chocolate. I gave him the jacket and went to wash my hands. It was pure luck to enter that bathroom from the bedroom. It definitely wasn't luck stumbling upon Camila about to suck off Jake. It made me sick to my stomach. I

Chapter 10

think I'm starting to understand how she feels about me. I hate her, I hate her for going back to him. I hate Jake for playing with all of us. It doesn't even cross his mind that he breaks hearts in the process.

"So, Goody, are you bringing the ladies to the top of the Mid-Atlantic league this year?" Ewan McKee asks as I settle next to Cole.

"Yo, McKee, she's got a name you know?" Cole chastises him.

But I don't let Ewan talk again. "I did last year, didn't I? Top ten," I reply, pride in my voice.

The way I lead my girls to victory is something I will always be proud of. At school, in the halls of Stoneview Prep, I'm the shy, studious girl. On the field, I'm ruthless. And they know I am, or girls who don't like me wouldn't have elected me captain for the second year in a row.

"You might have been Mid-A top ten, but you were crushed like a cockroach when you got to the nationals." Beth's nasal voice grits my ears as she and Camila come to stand next to Ewan.

They couldn't just let us have a simple conversation about a topic I enjoy. They had to come and ruin it.

"It's a different level," I admit. "I wasn't ready for it last year, but I am now."

She scoffs. "I see you train every week, Goody, you're not that good."

My nostrils flare up as I try to keep in the anger. She's just trying to work me up, I have to keep calm.

"I do my best," I smile at her. "Coach is happy."

"Jamie's an amazing player. You're gonna crush St Anne this year!" Cole defends me. I can't help but grin at him. I think he really likes me.

My happiness is short-lived when I see Jake bursting out

of the house, changed into clean, dry clothes and with a killing look on his face.

I'm practically sure everyone can hear me gulp, but I try to keep a straight face as he strides toward our group.

Shit.

He looks furious, the kind of furious that he's never shown at school, in front of his friends. He stops only a step away from me, and I think everyone can feel his anger because Cole puts a hand on my shoulder, bringing me back toward him slightly. Jake faces me, while Cole stands behind me.

"You went to one North Shore party and you think you're some bad bitch now or something?" His mouth spits poison like fireworks.

Something stirs in me, satisfaction. Jake White lost control. Jake White is showing *emotions*. And that's because of me. Poor, small Jamie Williams who could never defend herself made him beg, pushed him to his limits, and left him standing. He might be feeling rage, but he's feeling something and that's a win for me.

"You're nothing, Jamie. You're just a little girl trying to play in the big boys' league."

"Two minutes ago, you were begging this little girl," I sneer.

Jake is about to reply, but Camila cuts into our conversation, reminding me that she, Beth, and Ewan are still watching us on my right.

"Oh my God, Goody, you went to a North Shore party? Is that why you dress like a hoe now? What were you doing there, scouting your next trailer?" She and Beth cackle loud enough to push a sadistic smile on Jake's face.

"She wasn't scouting anything. She was stalking me. Somebody can't get over our break-up."

I scoff, is he for real? Trying to turn this situation around. Acting like a big, bad, bully in front of Camila and his boys.

"Aren't you the one who can't stop talking about me to your sister?" I bite back.

Two can play his game, I'm not going to fold in front of Jake anymore. He's going to have to try harder if he wants to break me.

"If you're over us, why are you finding any excuse to talk to me," I insist. "Let me enjoy my night, go enjoy yours."

I can see people starting to gather around us, they're loving the drama. Stoneview Prep feeds on gossip, on other's fallout and demise. It makes them feel important in their world of drugs and champagne parties.

The muscles popping at the jointures of his jaw bring me wicked pleasure. Bow down, Jake. You lost this one.

He steps dangerously close, and I feel Cole closer at my back.

"If you're over us, why are you still wearing this?" He grabs the necklace he gave me, and my throat tightens.

No, not this.

Suddenly, everything around us darkens. Heaviness drops in my stomach, my legs feel shaky. The adrenaline is not bringing me strength anymore, it's being replaced by fear. It's not about him or me breaking the other. This is real, this is the last remnant of our love. The truth I was desperately holding on to.

"Don't," I whisper as if there were only the two of us here, rather than a whole party watching us.

The balance tips when Jake understands he's got me. The evil in him takes over, the sociopathic creature that doesn't understand the line, the limits, the stop sign that warns him he could destroy someone with his words and actions.

"What's wrong, Angel? Desperate to hold on? You need a good reminder that you're nothing to me anymore."

He pulls at the necklace harshly. I whimper in pain as it breaks around my neck. It's more mental than physical but damn it hurts. He throws the necklace in the yard. "There, that should help."

Tears build behind my eyelids, a noose closes up around my throat.

No, no, come on, don't cry. Don't give him that.

"Jake. What the fuck, man," Cole steps in, putting both hands on my shoulders. He rubs at them in a reassuring gesture, but it makes it worse. I blink once, thanking God for still having dry cheeks.

Jake smiles at Cole before bringing his dark blue gaze back to me. The color of night, that's what they are. Nightmare-filled nights. Dark, but still blue enough to give you hope of a better day coming.

"I don't get it, Angel. Is that your new boyfriend or are you just trying to make me jealous? I see what you're doing, Jamie. That revenge, the way you're changing yourself to get back at me...it's giving me importance. It's all still with me on your mind. You're not doing it for yourself, you're doing it for me."

The truth in his words hits me, but it probably hits Cole harder.

"Alright, fuck off now. This is none of your business."

Cole pulls me back as he says that, stepping before me and putting himself between Jake and me. I let him, I'm not strong enough to fight by myself right now. When am I really? Last time, Rose intervened. This time it's Cole.

I'm so disappointed with myself.

Chapter 10

Jake's vicious smirk is now directed straight at Cole. He doesn't realize the kind of danger Jake can be.

"I could fuck you up so bad, Cooper. You know that, right? I wouldn't even have to try that hard."

Cole stands his ground despite Jake's threats. "What, like your brother did to Jas'? Real brave, bro. To your teammate as well."

"You're not my teammate, *bro*. And now that I've left, watch me kick your ass with N.S. High colors."

Cole's answer is cut off by Camila's confident voice. "Don't fight over something so insignificant, guys. If someone isn't worth it, it's her."

"I'm not fighting *over* her. I'm just trying to get her to leave," Jake jeers.

"You've been downgraded back to a nobody, Goody," Camila continues, digging the knife a little deeper.

"This party ain't for you. Go home," Jake orders triumphantly.

"You heard him. Bye-bye, tramp." I don't react fast enough when I feel Camila's hands on my side. She pushes hard enough for me to stumble to the side and fall into the pool.

I shriek when the freezing water engulfs me. Everything happens too quickly for me to grasp it. Two hands grab me to help me back out, laughs and giggles bring heat of shame to my cheeks and ears while my body trembles from the cold.

Cole's jacket is taken from me, and two warm arms wrap around my body, picking me up and letting me wrap my legs around a strong waist.

When I fully come back to my senses, Cole is putting me in a taxi. He joins me, and I don't really know how long it takes but, next thing I know, he's walking me to my house, inside and to my bedroom. He helps me out of my wet clothes and gives me privacy to get changed into my pajamas. He stays silent though.

He gets me into bed, and I sit against the wall I use as a headboard as he pulls the covers over me. I bring my knees to my chest under the covers. We stay in silence for another minute and the slight tension between us is what finally brings me over the edge.

I go to speak but he does too just at the same time, so I keep quiet.

"Jamie..." he sighs. "I...I can't do this. I can't be this guy in-between you and Jake. I think I like you too much to watch you choose him over me."

He goes silent again as he thinks of what he's going to say next, and my sudden sob breaks it all.

"I'm sorry," I cry. "I'm sorry, Cole. I..." My next words are only whispers in the dark of the night. Secrets I can't admit to myself. "I'm in love with him."

Against everything I expected, Cole sits down on my bed and squeezes my small hand in his big one. His voice is empathetically soft, "I know, Queen Bee. I know."

I completely break down into loud sobs as I let myself fall back into the darkness I was in only a couple of months ago when Jake left. My whole world crumbles around me again, my heart breaks open, bleeds out, and still beats to emptiness. It goes to a slow rhythm of nonexistence on repeat as Cole lays down beside me and takes me in his arms.

"He doesn't deserve you, Jamie. You're too good for him."

"I know," I choke between two sobs.

The spasms in my chest don't let me align more words than that. My breath clogs my lungs as Cole rubs a warm hand on my back, telling me sweet things. Telling me he'll always be my friend and be there for me.

When I wake up, Cole is gone. My eyes are swollen from crying, my cheeks sticky, and my face too warm. I look around my room and that sickening feeling in my stomach comes back tenfold. The one that warns me that I'll never get over Jake. That no matter how hard I try, my whole being just goes back to loving him with all I have.

And him? He'll stay away emotionally. I watched as he shut down his feelings, I watched as he turned back into the bully I met in September. Yeah, he'll keep his distance emotionally alright, but the beast who loves playing is back. The thrill in his eyes when he humiliated me in front of everyone was clear as day.

Jake has broken my heart, and he's still not done playing with me.

11

JAMIE

Bad Ones – Tate McRae

Church on Sunday is a good way to try and focus on something other than myself. Seeing happy people slightly takes me out of my self-pity. Mom and Pastor Gilligan talk about getting lunch together at our favorite diner after he's gone around and spoken to everyone. He always says hi to every single person who comes, takes a few minutes to speak with them and see what is going on in their lives. It's easy in a small-town church.

"Mom, I'm not hungry," I complain as we head out. "Can we even afford it?"

She shrugs. "I got it covered."

I know what that means. It means she stole from the Bakers' register.

"Mom," I scold her in a whisper. "I told you we couldn't do that anymore. We'll get caught, they're onto something."

"I know what I'm doing, 'Me," she tells me in her strong voice. The one that tells me not to talk back.

I huff a wordless complaint. I really don't want to go to

Silver's. I'm trying really hard to get over myself. Still trying to get an asshole out of my thoughts.

"Why don't you go on your own with Pastor Gilligan? It can be a date or something."

"Jamie," she blushes.

Happiness bubbles in my belly thinking of my mother going on a date. Finally. Finally something else but complete destruction.

I'm jumping on the spot when I talk again. "Go on a date with him! Go, go! Mom, it'll be so much fun."

"Fine," she laughs. "I'll drop you home and–"

"I'll take myself home. Just enjoy yourself," I squeal as Pastor Gilligan walks out of the church.

We talk for a few minutes before they both get into mom's car. This is great, I want her happy.

I also slightly want her off my back. She's been so reluctant to let me do things on my own since she's been back. She only let me go to the party on Friday, and wasn't aware of the one before that. I don't even want to know what she would do if she knew I went to the North Shore of the Falls.

I check my phone to see if Emily wants to hang out and she sends me back a picture of her trying on dresses at His&Hers, one of the most expensive dress shops in Stoneview. I forgot she's got a Debutante ball when we come back from the tournament. Her grimace on the picture makes me chuckle. She hates those things so much.

My heart skips a beat when I look up and cross those dangerous eyes I know too much. How are Nathan's so much softer than Jake's? They shouldn't be. Nathan is a literal monster. He hurts people for fun. He inflicts pain for the thrill of it.

But when he looks at me, it's like he could watch the

whole world crash and burn as long as I am by his side while he does so.

He watches me from afar, leaning against his car, a hand in his suit pocket. Always in a suit, like his job as a gangster is a fine, white collar business that requires the finest clothes. His dirty blond bun is sleek and tight behind his head. He's smoking a cigarette and observing me with focused eyes behind his black rim glasses.

Should I talk to him? Should I walk over?

I want to but he doesn't look like he's waiting for me. He's just there...watching me.

Ugh, fuck it. I'm sick of the Whites playing with my head.

I take decisive steps toward him and watch as his artistically tattooed fingers flick the bud of the cigarette, and he steps on it.

"Hi," he smiles once I stop in front of him.

"What do you want?" I question harshly. I can't show weakness in front of him. Not when I'm already so vulnerable.

"I don't want anything," he muses as he stands straight again, gaining height on me.

"Then what are you doing here?" I take a step back to keep some safe distance between us.

"Keeping an eye on you because Jake can't keep his dick in his pants."

His words push my brows together, poking at my good old curiosity.

"What do you mean by that?"

"Do you need me to draw you the meaning of not keeping one's dick in his pants?"

I roll my eyes but my body surprises itself when a short laugh crosses my lips, tainting the air with the truth of how relaxed I suddenly feel.

"I *meant*—"

"I know what you meant. If I wanted to explain to you why I'm here, I would have."

That's reminder enough for me. "Yeah, you'd have no problem lying about it either."

"Jamie," he sing-songs. "I don't want to get into another conversation about which one of us really is the bad guy in our relationship."

"*Was* the bad guy in our relationship, we're not a thing anymore."

He chuckles. "I'm dying to fix that once and for all."

"Keep dying," I scoff.

"You're hurting my feelings, 'Me."

"You're hurting your own feelings when you hang onto us."

He takes a step forward, standing close in a warning. His voice matches his stance. "Why are you trying to fight me? I was just checking on you."

"I don't need to be checked on."

He nods slowly, going back to his initial position. "It was nice to see you, 'Me."

His behavior is killing my need for knowledge. Why does he need to check on me? And why is he just dropping it?

He goes to open his car when something strikes me. I woke up this morning to a text from Rose saying Nathan had categorically refused to sign the slip for the tournament. This is my chance to help.

"You know who you should check on?" I call out as he opens his door. He looks up, raising an eyebrow. "Your sister. The way you supposedly *protect* her from Bianco is not sustainable. It's cruel and it's selfish. You're acting like you're worried for her but you're the one who brought her and Jake back into your dangerous world. You have no reason to act the way you do, except that you're a sadistic fuck. You want to do a good deed? Don't check on me, just let Rose go to the tournament."

I'm not entirely sure Nathan knows exactly what Bianco has been doing to Rose, but I can only assume he does since he's the one who kicks her out when his boss comes to his house.

He huffs, pulling his sleeves up, that thing he does when he's getting worked up. "Not this fucking lacrosse slip again."

"If you didn't want to deal with teenage stuff, you should have left the parenting to the Murrays," I grumble. "I guess you were just that desperate to become a dad."

"Well, you never wanted to call me Daddy, I had to find another way."

I pinch my lips hard.

Don't laugh, not now.

I will never get how Nathan can go from lighthearted and funny to ruthless and violent. Jake has a constant, he's cruel, he's sociopathic. I had that feeling about him before I even started talking to him, the cover he puts on only fools superficial, uninterested Stoneview Prep's kids. It's like he used to have feelings, but they've been crushed by trauma.

Nathan has feelings. He just chooses when he wants to be sweet. He knows when he does something wrong, and he enjoys it so much.

"Just sign it, Nathan."

He takes a deep breath and huffs again, showing me he really isn't in the mood for kids' stuff. But it's not kids' stuff, it's Rose's future. He looks around, his eyes scanning for some sort of imaginary danger. Well, I guess it isn't that imaginary to him. His life is probably full of looking-over-his-shoulder moments.

"Get in the car. We can discuss it some other place. I'm sure you can find ways of convincing me to sign." His voice is calm and collected as usual. He gets in the car himself, not waiting for me.

But does he not realize the kind of effect his words have on me? Or does he know exactly what he's doing?

I can hate Nathan all I want, I can be fully aware of the kind of things he does. There will always be a place in my heart for him. That spot that was reserved for my first boyfriend, my first love, my first sexual experience. The first person who made me feel safe after one of Volkov's men shot me.

My body is a mix of repulsion and titillating. My legs rub together under my Sunday dress. It's the same one I was wearing when we met, and my heart skips a beat. This is strange, there is no other way to describe it.

"Where are we going?" I ask as he drives us around the beautiful Stoneview streets.

I focus on the perfect lawns and huge iron gates that give the rich and famous privacy.

I wonder if Volkov has a house in Stoneview. He must, it's his territory. Or *was* his territory. Nathan took over now.

"My house."

"What?" I choke. "I can't go to your house."

"Why? The twins aren't there." He pauses and his eyes flicker to me before going back to the road. His right hand lands on my thigh softly. "Jake isn't there."

It takes me a few seconds to swallow the ball of anxiety and anticipation that has formed in my mouth. But I don't push Nathan's hand away. Why should I? Why should I accommodate Jake after everything he's done to me? Nothing in our relationship was ever normal.

We started with bullying and blackmail, we kept going with stupid games. Even the love we shared, I can't be sure anymore that it wasn't all fake on his side. He explained it himself, he *said* he loved me. And as much as I felt loved, did he? Did he love me?

That stubbornness he had of never sharing his secrets, never opening up about his childhood when I shared everything that happened with my dad and my brother. That way of covering every question, every shady thing with a 'I'll feed you my cock if you ask too much'. It's impossible to know if Jake loved me, no matter how much I want it to be true. And what happened at the party on Friday only confirms that.

The ride feels so much like how Nathan and I used to be. His hand on my thigh, 'Red Right Hand' from Iggy Pop quietly playing in the background. He always has the passenger window slightly open and the wind in my hair helps me cool my head off.

I hesitate again when he unlocks his front door. I shift on my feet when he walks inside his house and holds the door open for me.

"I'm not forcing you to be here, 'Me. You wanted to discuss something. Let's."

His words sound manipulative, but the comforting smile on his face and the glint in his eyes are reassuring. They're so like him. I mean, they're so like *him*. The Nathan I know.

He steps into the grand foyer and takes the first door to the left. I follow him into what looks like his office. A lot of paperwork on a contemporary desk with a structure made of steel and chrome finish. There's a closed laptop and a few packs of empty cigarettes. Empty takeaway containers, beer bottles, and used glasses. It's messy, unstructured, anything but Nathan.

"Is this where you work?" I ask.

He closes the door and turns to me. "Sometimes. But I've been in and out lately. Haven't been able to stay in Stoneview longer than a day at a time."

"I noticed," I admit.

When Nathan is in Stoneview, I know. I know because Rose ends up at my house often, or she disappears with Sam. I also see him on the main street or recognize his car driving around, dropping Rose at school. It's been sporadic since my birthday and rare since Jake has been back.

"What do you even do for Mateo Bianco?"

"Don't ask questions you don't want answers to."

I settle against the desk, crossing my arms. "I just..." Do I really want to say this? "I just want to be convinced that you're not that bad. That somehow I got it all wrong."

He walks to me, settling himself only an inch away. He bends down, putting his hands on either side of me.

"I can clarify what you got right and what you got wrong if you wish." His breath is on my cheek, adding to the warmth of my body's desire. "I lied to you and I'm a bad man who does bad things. That you got right."

My gulp rings out loudly in the room. I shift on my feet, trying to find some sort of escape after being reminded that he isn't even slightly ashamed of what he does.

"But choosing Jake over me because you thought he was better, nicer or less ruthless." His pause is accompanied by a low chuckle, mocking my mistakes. His mouth is on the soft skin just below my ear, making me shiver. "That you got all wrong, beautiful."

"Nathan..." I murmur. A mix of desire and shame overtakes me, forcing my thighs to rub together and squirm under him.

"I'm exhausted, 'Me. And, today, I don't have the strength to pretend I don't want to rip your clothes off and fuck you on this very desk."

He gathers my hair in one hand and moves it to the other side, clearing my shoulder of it. He drops a soft kiss on the bit of skin where my shoulder meets my neck and hovers there for a few seconds.

"Wh-why are you exhausted?" I ask to get us talking again. My brain needs to find a way to fight the sexual tension.

His head drops completely on my shoulder, burying himself against my neck, inhaling me. He puts his hands on my waist and lifts me up until I'm sitting on the desk. He talks against my skin, like he's enchanted by my scent.

"I've just been busy. Bianco is on my back constantly and —" he stops himself short, pulls away, and his brows furrow as if just realizing he said too much.

"Are you okay?" I check. He seems anything but okay. A little too tired, a little too tense.

"Better than okay, I'm with my favorite girl on my day off. What more could I want?"

"I should have known gangsters always rest on God's day."

He laughs heartily. Something that sounds like pure crystal. "I don't usually take Sundays off."

"Why today then?"

"It's my—"

"Birthday," I cut him off in a whisper as it suddenly comes back to me. March 21st.

"Yeah," he smiles.

"I'm so sorry, I completely forgot."

Chapter 11

He shrugs. "It's not that big of a deal. I haven't celebrated it in years. Since I was declared dead for a full minute and twenty-five seconds actually."

Aka since Rose shot him.

Still with me between both of his arms, he looks for something on his desk, his hand taping behind me, moving papers around while his face stays close to mine. Finally, he picks up a piece of paper.

"So, that slip," he mumbles. It's like a cold shower for me. "Ozy has been pissing me off so much with it I seriously thought of leaving the country."

Guilt gnaws at me as I remember what I'm here for in the first place. I'm a hypocrite, because I know I didn't get into his car for Rose. And I didn't step into his house for Rose. I did it for one simple, senseless reason: I missed our good times together.

"Why don't you want to sign, Nathan? It's just a tournament. A four-day tournament. No one's running away."

"Really? Do you know Rose? She loves when people look for her."

"Have you signed Jake's?"

A smirk appears on his lips, he knows I got him there. He's being controlling over his sister while he lets his brother do whatever the hell he wants.

"North Shore High couldn't care less if anyone signs any slip. And I don't care what Jake gets up to. I have to keep an eye on Rose."

"No, you don't," I start getting defensive. "Everything was fine before you showed up here."

He chuckles. "Really? Rose is an anorexic druggie and Jake a toxic control freak. How was the bullying before I came, 'Me? You all hate me so much, but Jake would have never been a hero to you if I hadn't turned out to be such a villain. And now that he's not the savior of your story anymore, look where you are. Right back into my arms."

It's hard to hear the truth, isn't it?

"Oh, Jamie. Jake is *fucked up*, don't you get that? He's my brother, I know him by heart. You think it's just a breakup. It's not. He won't date you, that's for sure. And he won't love you. But he *will* keep toying with you. That's what he does. And you're just such a willing toy. Why do you make this so easy on him?"

While I open and close my mouth to find something to retort, he wraps his hands around each of my thighs, slowly going up until they get caught in my dress. He doesn't stop, pulling the hem of my dress up at the same time. I can't look at him, so I look at his hands. Up and up...and up...

When he reaches the apex of my thighs, they automatically tense, trying to shut. He keeps my legs firmly spread and squeezes hard. The gesture alone makes me gasp.

"Nathan..."

"Ssh." He kisses my cheek, my jaw, my throat.

One of his hands moves to my pussy, his thumb rubs my clit through my panties. I gasp but his mouth is on mine at the same time, his lips crashing on mine, his tongue ravaging mine. I kiss him back, harshly, desperately.

I kiss him...like I missed him.

He keeps rubbing me while his other hand goes to my hair, gripping it and pulling at my head until I lean back and then until my back hits the desk.

I look up just to see as he drops to his knees in front of me, taking my panties with him. They're off the next second, just before he places my feet on the edge of the desk. Without warning, his hot mouth meets my burning core. The clash of the two makes me moan in pleasure.

His tongue is fire on my skin, ravaging everything in its

wake. My clit throbs every time he abandons it for my entrance and my pussy clenches emptiness every time he passionately tortures my clit.

I'm gasping for air, tentatively grasping at paperwork as my head hits the hard desk. Stars dance in front of my eyes from sheer pleasure. The appetite this man has for me is unmeasurable.

Two fingers dip in my pussy, rubbing against my walls and making me cry in pleasure before he gets up and sticks them in my mouth. He doesn't say anything, but I suck on them instinctively, relishing in his warmth and my arousal.

"If you would let me in, 'Me," he pulls his fingers out of my mouth and inserts them in my pussy again, his other hand coming to play with the hardened tips of my breasts through my dress, "if you were mine, I'd treat you like the queen you are. I would never hurt you like he did." His fingers curl in me and I cry out so hard my voice breaks out. "I love hurting people. But not you, never you."

He pulls his fingers out and I feel him shift. I glance at him only to realize he's putting a condom on. This is happening, it's really happening.

He presses his thumb against my clit in the perfect amount of pressure. It's heavy, but not too harsh and I start rubbing myself against him, brazenly looking for release.

I feel my orgasm building up, little needles prickling all over my body, butterflies reaching out for freedom. The tension coursing through my veins is begging to snap.

"I'm going to make you come so hard, beautiful. Make sure you scream the right name when I do."

As my orgasm unleashes in me, Nathan enters me in one violent stroke. I explode as his cock fills me, as I rub my clit against his thumb.

My broken voice reaches out of me in a high, uncontrollable moan, "Nathan!" I try to breathe, panting as he pushes into me mercilessly.

I stop rubbing against his finger and so he starts moving his thumb slowly, in complete opposite of his hip movements. I try to form words on my lips, but the only thing that comes out is a breathless, whispered, "Nathan...Na..." Thrust. Gasp. "Na..." Thrust. Moan. Deep breath. It's like my orgasm is endless.

He slows down, taking his thumb off and putting his hands on either side of my face. He pulls me up swiftly, his slow thrusts still driving me insane. His forehead against mine, I can still see the muscles in his neck straining as he controls his body into a slow pace. His shirt is undone, his tattooed, slim body working away at me. His abs tense under the physicality of our lust.

"Na–than. Try again," he smiles, his hot breath on my lips.

My hands reach out to his hair. I undo his bun, run my hand through it, delight in the long strands entwining with my fingers.

He thrusts harder, like a warning that he just told me to repeat his name. In this almost sitting position, every movement he makes hits against the magic spot that drives me insane. He repeats, hard, violent but slow between his strokes. My second orgasm comes out so suddenly, his name crosses my lips in a shriek. "Nathan!!"

He accelerates ferociously. As he comes, he grunts, "Fuck, 'Me...I love you."

He stops abruptly and kisses me so hard I fall back on the desk. He pulls out and follows, resting on me as we kiss slowly, lovingly, like none of this is wrong. Like he didn't just admit he still loves me. Like I haven't fucked up real bad.

I stay lying down on the desk, his head on my chest

while I caress his hair. His hands on my hips, his breath against my skin. I don't know how long we stay this way. His heartbeat against mine, the orgasm comedown, it all lulls me into a state of complete relaxation.

Until one of our phones starts ringing, startling us. He pulls away from me, grabbing a box of tissues and giving it to me before zipping up his pants. To my enjoyment, he doesn't button up his shirt.

I clean myself as much as possible and grab my panties from the floor, all in complete silence before he picks up his phone.

"Boss," he says in the most neutral voice I've ever heard from him.

My brain starts going into overwork. He's talking to Mateo Bianco. Regret tastes bitter on my tongue. The choking feeling of having made a huge mistake is hard to swallow.

After dating Nathan for two months, breaking up for his lies and manipulation, dating his brother, getting my heart broken, we finally had sex for the first time.

What is wrong with me?

I remember the guilt he used to feel around me, how I always associated it with our age difference. It wasn't, it was his lies. The constant buildup of them.

I go to my purse to occupy my hands, find something to do, pretend like I'm not eavesdropping on his conversation with the man who destroyed Jake's life and ultimately mine.

"Last time I saw him he was overseeing bets at the Death Cage." He pauses while he listens to the other end of the line and glances at me. He runs a hand through his hair, messed by yours truly. "I'm at home."

A finger scratching behind his ear, and I know he's thinking seriously about his next words. "So...another one gone." Another pause, there's a slight frown on his face. I'm not exactly sure what or who they're talking about, but I can see on Nathan's face that he's lying to Bianco. "Yeah, I'll let you know when I leave for D.C."

He hangs up and turns to me, but I look back into my purse. Pretending to look for something so our gazes don't cross.

"'Me...'" But I'm not listening. Because, to my surprise, I actually found something in my bag.

"The bitch," I whisper to myself.

Camila managed to put another one of her stupid notes in my stuff. This is the same bag I had at Luke's party on Friday, she must have slipped it in there then.

"What's wrong?" Nathan asks.

I keep my eyes on the note.

I said to stay away from Jake. Stupid girl.

The note is ripped away from me, and I look up at Nathan, holding it and reading it.

"Who's that from?" He asks in a serious voice.

"Jake's ex. Camila," I sigh.

"But it's not signed," he insists, concerned.

I take the note back from him and ball it in my fist before throwing it in the bin. "Yeah, well only one person is so possessive of him that she keeps bullying me even when we're broken up."

"Do you want me to talk to her? She won't bother you for long after that."

"No," I chuckle. "I can handle Camila Diaz, don't worry."

Chapter 11

He walks to me as I finish talking and slips both his hands in my hair again. He pushes the tips of his fingers at the base of my neck, forcing me to look up at him.

"What I said is true, 'Me. I still love you. I can't take back what I've done, and I'm not about to step away from the life I live. But it doesn't change the fact that you're the most precious thing that's ever come into my life."

He lowers his head, his lips hovering over mine. But when he makes that final movement to kiss me, I turn my head to the side.

His sigh of desperation hits me right in the heart. This was a mistake. I'm weak, vulnerable because I'm broken-hearted. But I can't ignore who Nathan is, what he's done.

Whenever I look at him for too long, images of what he did the night of my birthday flash to my mind. Jake's beaten-up body on the floor, the slow rise and fall of his chest, and how I prayed that it wouldn't stop. The way Nathan brutalized Rose into the change of guardianship.

Nathan might be good to me, but he is not a good person. No matter if Jake breaks my heart or not.

His lips touch my cheek as he talks. "I understand," he simply says.

I put my bag around my shoulder as he walks me to the door of his office.

"I just–" I'm cut by the sound of the front door opening right behind the office door, and the voices coming in. Jake's laugh resonates in the grand foyer, followed by Luke finishing his joke and Rose's raspy voice telling him that he's dumb.

My eyes widen as they meet Nathan's. "No," I whisper as I see the wicked smile that spreads on his lips.

He can't simply wait until they head to their rooms, he can't keep this between us. His hatred for his brother is too much, their game of attack and revenge runs too deep between them.

He opens the office door and walks out in front of me.

Jake's surprised voice is still ignorant when he talks to Nathan. "I thought you were away in—" It dies when he sees me. Still in the office, desperately trying to hide behind Nathan.

I step forward, the need to leave too strong to stay through the tension. I notice Rose, Luke, and Chris still by the door while Jake has stepped closer to us.

Rose is wearing a sweater and lacrosse skort, holding her stick with one hand. The guys are all wearing basketball shorts and Jake is topless, his jersey tucked in the waistband of his shorts and hanging off the side. God, I forgot how fit this man is. All tanned skin and ripped abs. Sweat is coating his clear skin, free of tattoos except for the one and only I know he has on his back. The opposite of Nathan who is covered in them. What mess did I manage to put myself in again?

Jake's eyes go from Nathan's unbuttoned shirt to me. I know what I must look like, I've got that just fucked look on me right now. I wince when I see his jaw click. When the muscles pop like he's desperate to scream something at us, to shout his rage and jealousy. But he doesn't scream.

Instead, his evil smile spreads on his lips, covering what I'm sure is pain deep inside of him.

"So?" he addresses Nathan. "How was she?"

"Jake—" I attempt, taking another step toward him.

"After all this time. You had to wait patiently for me to throw her away to finally stick it in her, didn't you?"

Tears prickle at my eyes, shame engulfing me. Anger follows. Why am I letting him slut-shame me? I know he's been sleeping with Billie, I found Camila on her knees for him, and I'm still letting him make me feel like shit for sleeping with whomever I want.

"Bro, let's move," Luke says, putting a hand on his shoulder. "We can go to mine."

"I don't need to go anywhere, I'm fine." Jake shrugs Luke's hand off. "Hey, Nate, did she do that thing where she begs and cries for you to let her come? Or are you just too average?"

"Fuck you," I spit at him. "Go be jealous somewhere else."

"It's my house, you go be a slut somewhere else," he growls back.

"It's *my* house," Nathan corrects him calmly. "And I don't want any of your little friends here."

"Nate, you're being a dick," Rose intervenes. "Let us have friends over. It's the least you can do."

"Did I ask for your opinion?" Nathan looks at Jake before he talks to Rose again. "You and your three musketeers can go hang somewhere else. If you stay here, no guests." As he says that, he takes a step forward and closes the office door behind us so no one can see what's in there.

Gangs to run, secrets to hide. That's Nathan White for you.

Rose is staring daggers at Nate, ignoring me completely. My stomach twists in guilt. I didn't even get him to sign the lacrosse slip. No, all I did in there was get fucked on the desk without thinking of how I could help my friend.

The tension is too much, Chris' gaze looks at every single one of us, as if weighing danger and what is worth fighting for.

"We'll leave," he finally says. "Jamie, I can give you a ride if you want."

I swallow the anxiety stone that had stuck in my throat and nod at him.

"Yeah, sure. Thanks."

Nathan slides a hand between my shoulder blades and leans toward me, dropping a kiss on the top of my head, but my eyes stay on Jake and his on mine.

"Unblock my number," Nathan quietly orders in my ear, his low voice and hot breath ringing the aftermath of orgasms between my legs.

I nod and step away from him.

I'm about to cross the door when Jake's voice calls me out again. "Why are you leaving, Jamie? Rose is right here, you can finish your family tour tonight if you want!"

I don't turn around, I just lift my hand up and give him the middle finger as I keep on walking.

How long are we going to keep hurting each other? When does the cruelty stop? How do you put back together the unfixable?

I guess some things stay broken forever.

12

JAKE

not alone – sad eyes

Glossy eyes, flushed cheeks, messy hair, and her body in utter relaxation. I would recognize Jamie post-orgasm even with my eyes closed, I would just have to listen to her calm breaths, in contrast to her usual rapid ones because she's an overthinker.

Rose shoves me in the shoulder the second the words pass my lips. "What the fuck is wrong with you?" she seethes as the front door closes.

"What?" I ask, pretending I don't get I was being a dick. "The girl likes to be fucked by Whites, I'm just saying."

"Stop being an asshole for a minute. Think you can try?" she throws back.

"Whatever," I mumble as I head for the kitchen.

The guys and I were training all afternoon to get Ozy ready for the tournament, even if we're not sure she'll be able to go. Nate won't pay for us to go to college, he doesn't give a shit about those sorts of things. Duke's lacrosse scholarship is the only way my sister will be able to get far away from Bianco, and we're not about to let her miss that chance.

I walk to the other side of the foyer and push the door to the kitchen. Ozy is right behind me.

"Jake, you can't be mad at her. You've been going back to your good old ways since you've been back. Fucking around like you belong to nobody. She's allowed to do the same."

Her words are a matter of fact as she grabs herself a glass and then the juice from the fridge. Almost like she knows I can't fight her on this and so she's not putting too much effort into the conversation.

And I know she's right, but I can't believe Jamie did this to me. I just never thought she'd have it in her to betray me like that. No matter how many times I betrayed her myself.

"Men," Rose huffs as if reading my thoughts. "You just hate tasting your own medicine, don't you?"

"Pass me the peanut butter," I grumble as I sit down at the kitchen island.

"Please, Rose, my favorite sister in the entire world," she smiles as she passes it to me with a spoon.

I'm about to reply that she's far from my favorite when she pisses me off even more than I already am, but the kitchen door opens and Nate walks in. His shirt is finally buttoned up and his hands are in the pocket of his slacks. He's redone his ugly-ass bun that makes him look like he's posing for the cover of GQ.

"Ozy," he says as he settles at the kitchen island too.

She's making herself a sandwich on the counter behind me, and Nate is now sitting right opposite me.

"What do you want," I hear her grumble behind me.

"Why do you bother training when you know I won't let you go to that tournament?"

Chapter 12

I hear cutlery clashing against her plate before her voice rises again. "Fuck you," she hisses.

We can still see the bruises Bianco left on her neck from the previous weekend and the fucker dares to tell her he won't let her go.

"Your life must be so simple, Nate," I drawl. "Living in Bianco's luxury in exchange for your soul. Abusing your siblings knowing he'll always have your back. Fucking heartbroken girls."

"There's no need to be so bitter, Jake," he smiles. "Remember I used to make her come before she even knew you existed."

Motherfucker.

I get up from my seat so suddenly my spoon ends up on the floor.

"Nate," Rose sighs.

I don't even listen to anything else she has to say, I cut her off instead.

"You know what's funny, Nate?" I seethe. "She couldn't get herself to let you fuck her when you guys were together, she had to wait to be entirely broken and for me to reject her to finally think of you as an option. I broke her heart last night, I ended her. It's the only reason she was with you today."

He doesn't say anything, he just calmly takes his phone out and starts tapping on it.

"Oh, look," he smirks. "She unblocked me. Just like I told her. She follows orders so well, doesn't she?"

"You can't do this," I growl. "You can't force me to stay away from her just so you can steal her for yourself."

"Whoa, whoa, slow down. What? Why are you forcing him to stay away from her?" Ozy asks, now settling beside me to catch up with what we keep hidden from her.

Nate's eyes flick to her before going back to me, his jaw clenches and the slightest movement of his head confirms what I already thought. She can't know shit.

"Nothin'," I mumble.

"Are you two seriously hiding shit from me?" She lets out a loud sarcastic bark. "I feel like I'm in a bad telenovela or something. Two brothers going for the same girl." Her voice goes low, mimicking our darker ones. "You stay away from her, no you stay away from her. We have to protect her." She pauses and rolls her eyes. "Jamie deserves so much better than either of you."

Nathan ignores her, we both do, there's no space for her sarcastic words in our hatred for each other.

"I didn't force you to do anything," my brother replies. "Bianco did. And I'm not stealing her, she came willingly, trust me. But don't worry, when she comes back for more, I'll make sure to do it behind Bianco's back."

This is complete bullshit. The rage boiling inside me is gut-wrenching. I feel like I'm losing sensations in all my extremities, my head is spinning.

I grab the first thing that comes to me and throw it at him with enough violence that he grunts in pain when the glass jar of peanut butter hits him in the face before crashing into multiple broken pieces on the floor. He stumbles out of his stool and I'm on the other side of the island before he can come back to reality.

"Oh here we go," Ozy quips. "I feel another smart decision coming from both of you."

Nate is hunched over, keeping his right hand just below his eye where the jar hit, and I don't let him straighten back up. I punch the side of his face so hard he stumbles back again. I push my shoulder against his stomach, pick him up, and slam him to the floor. This all happened too fast for

Chapter 12

him, and for once, for one *fucking* time in my life I got the upper hand on him.

"You think it's so fucking funny to fuck the girl I love?!" My rage explodes on him and I let truths slip past my lips, spit accompanying my broken words. "This whole fucked up situation is because of your pathetic existence!" I shout loud enough that we barely hear skin hitting skin when I land another punch to his face.

His groans are better than molly. It sends my body into a frenzy, a need to hurt him more. To finally give him what he deserves. I kick him in the ribs, and he has to go into a fetal position to avoid permanent damage.

"Jake, stop." My sister's voice is so bored one could wonder if she really wants me to stop.

I kick Nate harder, reminding myself of how it felt to have him and Carlo Diaz beat the shit out of me on Jamie's birthday. We were meant to celebrate together, we were meant to love each other, we were meant to be happy.

"How does it feel to be the one suffering for once you fucking bastard!" My voice breaks and tears spring in my eyes as I go down and hit his exposed ribs with my fists.

Nate's grunts are turning into desperate whimpers, and I revel in the pain he must be feeling. God, this feels so good.

"Guess you shouldn't have sent me away for more boxing if you didn't want to get your ass kicked."

"Okay, enough. Enough, Jake."

Rose is too skinny, too weak to truly stop me from killing Nate – and I really do want to kill him right now – but she doesn't hesitate to grab my waist to pull me away from our brother. She puts all her strength in it, and I leave him alone. Because the last thing I would want is to hurt her by accident. Unlike him, I care about her wellbeing.

When Ozy lets me go, I finally take a good look at him.

There is blood all over the kitchen tiles, Nate spits some more and rolls onto his back. His lips are busted, his left cheek already swelling. He struggles to sit up against the wall, holding his side while his head keeps lolling back and forth.

I turn to Ozy and her worried eyes are settled on him. "Nate, are you okay?" she asks in a quiet voice.

"Don't..." I throw my hands in the air, frustration keeping a tight hold on me. "Don't fucking ask him if he's okay, why do you care?!"

I'm aware I'm shouting at her while she hasn't done anything wrong, but I can't control it.

"Don't take his fucking side, Ozy!"

"I'm not taking sides." Her voice breaks as she defends herself with that sentence she always throws our way. She should, she should be taking *my* side. She runs a hand through her hair in worry and I tremble in fury.

How? I just can't understand how she can always forgive him, how she always goes back to protecting him when he should be paying for his sins.

"You want to take care of him? Go on, be his nurse then! Where were you when I was being transported to Silver Falls ER because the bastard tried to end me?!"

"Jake, you're not being fair–"

"I don't *fucking care*! Life isn't fair, Ozy!!"

What is happening to me? I push her out of the way, feeling my whole body tremble. My vision narrows, blurred by tears stuck in my eyes. I stumble in the foyer and drag myself up the stairs. My chest is constricted, and I struggle to take a breath. My back hurts as I open my door and fall onto my bedroom floor.

I shake, I whimper in pain. My breaths are shallow and I

have to crawl toward my bed. My legs feel dead, my thoughts cramping my mind.

I was dying to leave L.A. and come back here. But Stoneview has been suffocating. Everywhere I turn, one of Bianco's minions is on me. Despite Nate being away most of the time, I feel his presence weighing on me. Every day someone new asks me who is this brother we never talked about or why I don't go to Stoneview Prep anymore.

Making myself a place among N.S. High's petty gangs have been a lot of bruises and bloodied knuckles. My friends miss me, I miss them, my sister isn't safe, Bianco is on our backs constantly.

And among all that? Jamie. The forbidden fruit I had to push away. And for what? Just so Nate can welcome her back into his arms? None of this is fair, and it's driving me fucking insane. How cruel to have given us three years of freedom before putting us back in this prison of a life.

Bianco doesn't *need* us, he just loves asserting the power he has over us. He just loves keeping Rose close. A lethal shiver runs through me at being reminded of why he keeps her close.

This is too much, it's *all too much.*

My body feels too small for my soul.

I'm dying. I'm fucking dying, and no one is here to help me.

"Ozy," I choke, trying to scream her name but just like in a nightmare my voice dies in my throat.

Where is she? And where is Jamie when I need her the most? She let me go. She didn't fight for us.

Maybe it's my fault. For months I thought she was the one teaching me to embrace my emotions and let them flourish rather than feel anger and hatred all the time. What if it was the opposite? What if I'm the one who brought her down, turned her into a heartless bastard like me?

It's a contagious disease to lose your empathy. Bianco did it to me, now I've done it to Jamie. It's easier than one thinks, it's about being told repeatedly that your feelings don't matter, that the only thing that will help you survive is selfishness.

It's about understanding that no matter what you feel, shit will happen either way. No matter how much Jamie loves me, no matter how much she wants to save me, if I keep showing her she will get nothing from me in return, she'll learn that it doesn't matter what she feels. Might as well not feel anything at all. I didn't want Bianco to kill those kids, but no matter how much I cried and begged him not to, he did it, right in front of my eyes. Every time.

Flashes blind me, bangs in my ears force me to cover them.

"Stop!" I scream at Bianco.

Wait, Bianco isn't here.

Then why are the ghosts of all the kids that were competing against me laughing and pointing fingers at me?

Look, Jake. Look at them, you won, you beat all of them.

Blood. So. Much. Blood. It's everywhere, it's on my skin, in my hair. It smells like copper, it thickens the air with death.

It's the last one. Finish him.

Bianco's voice is right in my ear, and I flip around but suddenly he's on the other side of me again. *Finish him, Jake! Show me you deserve to live. Then you can go back to your siblings.*

BANG!

I scream when two hands grab me under my armpits

and turn me around. I struggle but a voice brings me back slowly. It's not Bianco, it's so much softer, so familiar.

"...down," I hear a whisper.

I try to crawl across the floor but I'm on my back now and I can't turn back around. It's impossible, my body is too heavy.

"...attack," the soft voice repeats.

I cry out when my eyes try to open and tears are flooding everywhere, drowning me in fear.

"...just...nic...okay." That voice, it's so safe.

A warm hand lands on my cheek and I turn to it as it goes to my hair and starts stroking me.

"I don't want to kill him," I sob.

I feel something on my side, it's long and soft. I turn to it and let my head rest on it.

My breathing starts to even out as I hug the long pillow next to my shaking body. Sobs still rack through my bones, but I can finally take a gulp of much-needed air.

"It's okay," the voice is clearer now. "It's just a panic attack."

Ozy.

A panic attack.

"But..."

"Ssh," she tells me as her hand goes through my hair again. I open my eyes again, now realizing I'm hugging her leg next to me. She's sitting down on the floor, right by me, and I'm lying down with the whole upper part of my body on both her legs.

"That's not how they usually feel," I rasp.

"Usually?" she chuckles softly. "You haven't had one in three years. You couldn't understand them when it was happening to you twice a week, I wouldn't expect you to remember what they feel like after so long."

Her voice is more hoarse than usual, I think I just scared her a lot, but she doesn't show it.

My heart is still hammering in my chest and my hands feel cold but I'm starting to see clearer.

"So I'm not dying," I double-check, looking up at her.

She smiles down at me and shakes her head. "No. You ain't leaving me behind like that, trust me."

I chuckle and stay tucked against her legs as I go back to looking at the rest of the room.

"How did you know?" I ask her. She was downstairs with Nate, so far from me, then suddenly she was in my room with me.

"Your hand was freezing," she replies casually as if that is an explanation in itself.

"What?"

"When I gave you the peanut butter, you were shaking a little and your hand was so cold. It might have been a while, but I don't forget how your panic attacks start, Jakey."

"Your brain..." I think about it for a few seconds, and she waits patiently. "...is weird as fuck, Ozy."

She explodes laughing and I automatically join her, the stress of the past ten minutes alone in my room finally lifting.

"I know."

13

JAMIE

Devilish – Chase Atlantic

We're all standing in the school parking lot, saying goodbye to our parents – or not for the ones whose parents don't bother about their kids' life. Mom and Emily's dad, Carl, are chatting away while my best friend and I catch up on last weekend.

"'Me...I still can't believe it."

"You think you can't believe it? I feel like crap, Em," I rasp.

"Nathan White. You slept with Nathan White. You slept with Jake's brother."

"I slept with my ex-boyfriend," I correct as if one cancels the other.

"Yup, that would be the twins' older brother."

I run a hand over my face. "Em, please stop."

"You slept with Lucifer, 'Me! I can't stop!"

My eyes widen and I look behind me to check that none of our parents heard. They're still talking, completely ignoring us.

"Shush yourself," I snap. "This isn't funny!"

She nods silently, pinching her lips to avoid smiling. She stays silent but her eyes bore into me, and I know she's waiting for something.

"Just ask already," I sigh.

"How was it?" she almost squeals.

"It was really damn good and a huge mistake. There are reasons I'm not with Nathan anymore. A few of them would include he's a liar—"

"A drug lord," she adds.

"A manipulator."

"Probably a murderer," she says looking up in the air as if she is thinking really hard about all the things Nathan could have done.

"He's older," I keep going, almost as if to myself.

"Oh, and he's Jake's brother," she nods harshly.

"And a bully," I conclude in a sigh.

"Well...that never bothered you before. That is actually probably why you slept with him. 'Me, you're a naughty girl who likes very bad boys. And that's fine, but you need to be careful. Jake broke your heart, Nathan will do the same."

I let out a huff, my heart pinches every single time she pronounces *Jake*.

"Nathan can't break my heart," I admit. Her brows rise in question, and I quickly add. "He doesn't hold it in the palm of his hands like Jake does. I never truly gave it to him."

Which is a shame, because Jake took pleasure in breaking my heart.

The sounds of the three buses' motors starting up make us both snap our heads toward where they're parked. Coach Thompson and Coach Swift make their way toward the middle of all of us and parents and students settle around them.

Chapter 13

"Alright everyone," Coach Swift calls out. "Cheer team is coming with me and Mr. Ashton in bus one, Women's team is going with Coach Thompson in bus two, and Men's team is going with Mr. Corragan and Ms. Randall in bus three."

A lot of complaints rise, as it did last year when we were all separated for the buses.

"It's so stupid," Emily mumbles to me. "It's not like we're going to do any practicing on the buses, I don't need to be with all those bitches."

She loves some of the cheerleaders, but she really does hate the others. One in particular. And just as my best friend and I think about her, she stands out of the crowd and towards the first bus.

"Come on girls," Beth's nasal voice exclaims. "LET'S GO STONEVIEW EAGLES!"

Some of the guys roar out a war scream. Most of the cheerleaders woo and shake their pompoms and Em and I look at each other.

"I'll see you in three hours," I sigh.

"Love you," she replies as she heads out with the rest of the cheer team.

I quickly hug goodbye to my mom and head for my own bus.

As I walk inside the bus, I notice Ciara sitting on her own. I can't believe Rose didn't make it to the tournament. Coach T. is so devastated about it, but not nearly as much as I am. Guilt is wrecking me.

I wanted to convince Nathan to sign the slip, instead I let him seduce me, again. I let myself fall for him and let him fuck me without even a thought toward Rose. And now she won't be able to prove herself to Duke's scouts.

I walk to Ciara and wave at her for her to take an earbud out. "Mind if I sit here?" I ask.

She shrugs, "It's not like Rose is occupying it."

My mouth twists and I put my bag on the rack above our heads. My phone beeps in my pocket and I fish it out.

> Nathan: You can thank me when you come back.

I frown at his cryptic text. I don't even know why I unblocked him. I don't wonder about the illogical things I do anymore, my pussy takes over my brain too easily.

"Oh shit! Coach wait!" Ciara exclaims.

I look up from my phone to see her facing the window. My eyes follow and my mouth falls slack as I see Rose running toward our bus, her backpack hitting against her back, her lacrosse stick in one hand and a paper I recognize too well in the other. The slip!

Behind her, Nathan's Porsche Cayenne is driving out of the parking lot.

Rose pants as she hops on our yellow bus and settles herself next to the driver, holding her ribs with the hand holding the paper.

"I got it, Coach," she pants. "It's signed. For real this time."

Ciara and I look at each other, wide smiles forming on our lips. I can't believe it. Coach walks to Rose and grabs the paper. "Do I want to double-check if this is a real signature, White?"

She shakes her head smiling. "You can if you want to, it's real."

He eyes her suspiciously for another few seconds before putting the slip in his pocket. "Take a seat, but I hope you're going to be a little fitter on the field. What a joke seeing you in this state after a short jog."

Rose chuckles and walks toward us, I step away from the

seat I was about to take, knowing she probably will want to sit next to her good friend. I take a few steps back so she can settle herself but instead of sitting she keeps going, grabs me, and hugs me tight. She straightens so high my feet lift off the floor.

"Rose," I giggle. "What are you doing?"

Her raspy voice is in my ear the next second. "I don't condone you sleeping with my brother to obtain things, and I hate you a little for breaking Jake's heart...but thank you."

I hear her thank you, but my heart stopped when she said I broke Jake's one. She puts me back down and my breathing quickens.

"I..." I start but the words don't quite come out. I don't know what to say to that. Jake has no heart. That's what I want to say, really. But she knows him better than I do, and if she says that, he must have had quite a reaction to finding me with Nate.

It's pure jealousy. He's a possessive guy, but he doesn't love you. He used to do the same to Camila, get in fights out of jealousy.

Yes, that's it.

"Let's get to our seats, Goody," she smiles down at me.

I don't really think about Ciara and how she's going to end up alone anyway. I'm just glad Rose doesn't totally hate me for what happened last weekend. I texted her countless times during the week, asking for forgiveness, saying I shouldn't have slept with Nathan. She didn't reply. Only now do I realize it's not because she was mad at me, I think she simply doesn't want to be put in the middle of our love triangle.

"You're not mad at me?" I look for reassurance once we're settled in our seats.

She lifts her head from her phone and smiles at me. "I

don't really care who you sleep with, Jamie." She chuckles to herself as she thinks over her next words. "And I'm the last one who would shame you for sleeping around. Jake broke up with you, you should be free to do whatever you want."

I sigh in relief, but she puts a hand up. "Nate is a shit guy, I don't think you should get involved with him anymore, but I also don't think that's why you feel bad. I think you feel bad because you love Jake, and you didn't want to hurt him. You did though."

I nod at her, it's true. My heart pinches because I love him so much. And if it hurts him to see me with someone else, why doesn't he do something about it?

"Anyway, I know you saved the best White for last. Let me know when you're ready to experience real pleasure." She winks at me and goes back to her phone, not even waiting to see if her words had an effect on me or not. She knows they did. Purely in a seek-for-thrill sort of way.

I wonder what it's like to sleep with Rose White. I overheard Lila from our team talk with another girl the other day. *Sleeping with Rose is like heroin, it only takes one time to get you addicted for life.* Maybe she was talking to Ciara actually?

I chuckle to myself, why am I even thinking of that? The Rose White effect.

"Have you slept with Ciara before?" I blurt out. My own eyes widen at my question. It just came out.

She laughs as she looks up again. "Jamie," she chortles.

Her arm extends to the seat in front of her and I shake my head in panic when I see her tapping on Ciara's arm. She takes her headphones out and turns around.

"What?" she huffs. I think she's a bit annoyed that Rose sat next to me.

"Goody wants to know if we slept together."

Ciara's brows shoot up and she looks at me. "Why? Are you interested in a threesome?" she mocks me.

My heart gallops in my chest as the ruby of embarrassment colors my cheeks and heats up my chest. "N-no. I-Sorry it was so rude of me to ask."

"It's fine, Goody," Rose laughs. "Ciara loved it."

"Fuck off," Ciara mumbles in return. "Biggest mistake of my life."

"Because she's in love with me now." Rose's evil smirk is so resemblant to Jake's, it frightens me for a second. They both take pleasure in watching their victims squirm.

"You're evil, Rose. I feel sorry for Rachel," Ciara rages as she turns back to face forward. The pain and anger in her voice only confirmed that she probably truly is in love with Rose.

"Your answer is yes," she tells me, undisturbed by the fact that Ciara is hurt by her words.

She calmly goes back to her phone and I have to shake my head to go back to reality. Rose can be so cruel to the people that don't matter to her. The Whites are all the same in that sense. They don't care about anyone or their feelings unless you make it to their list. Then they become controlling, addicted, possessive…and they never let you go.

Once settled in our room, I'm finally back with Emily.

"I promise you, 'Me, she just talks about him non-stop, like, it's so obvious they sleep together." She opens a can of coke zero and sits on her bed.

"Mr. Corragan isn't even that young," I say as I grab my toiletry bag from my small suitcase. "How can Beth sleep with him so often?"

"They're like, in a proper relationship. I swear if they get caught it's gonna be so bad. And Mayor Simmons will cancel her engagement to her son and her family is going to be in so much shit." Her eyes sparkle as she says that. She really hates the girl.

"Try not to sound too excited," I laugh as I walk into the bathroom.

I let out a sigh when the hot spray hits my skin. As I shower, I look down at my legs. Nathan has left love bites on my inner thigh and my insides clench with need. I don't want Nathan, but Emily is right, there's just something in the darkness that attracts me. Like I'm meant to be there, relish in it.

I like being possessed by dark men. I like submitting to them, I like when Jake holds my throat when he fucks me, I like when Nathan orders me to scream his name when he makes me come.

Emily and I go down for dinner in the hotel's restaurant. This huge hotel holds the tournament this year. All the teams that qualified are hosted and catered for. For Prep schools like Stoneview and St Anne, it's low budget. For High Schools like North Shore High, it's luxury. Oh, how the world works.

I settle with my friend at a table with Rose, Luke, Cole, Jason, and some other cheerleaders. The tables are long and spread in rows of multiple tables. Twenty teams in total, ten for women's lacrosse, ten for men's, and each school comes with a cheer team. The top three teams will go to Nationals.

I've spent nights and days planning team plays, movements on the field, starting line-up, how often we'll switch our players. Coach and I made a list of all the teams we will win easily, and all the ones we need to be careful of. We changed our starting line-up for each team we're playing. In

Chapter 13

conclusion, there are two teams we're worried about. North Shore High, we beat them last year, but they've got a new center that runs like a rocket. And St Anne, our forever nemesis. We lose to them, every single year.

Last year, we almost didn't qualify because of them, and as soon as we reached Nationals, they destroyed us. Christine is their captain, their center, an absolute bitch. I look for her in the crowd of teams eating their dinner, but instead of finding her, I find Jake.

My heart skips a beat, accelerates and I feel it in my tight throat. My insides twist as I see he's eating next to Billie. God, I hate her. She thinks she's so strong and indestructible. She thinks no one can touch her because she's part of a gang and because Jake fucks her.

That's what it does to you, being in the king's arms, letting him worship your body. You think you're above everyone else. A queen among peasants. Jake makes you feel special, invincible.

Seeing Jake sitting with the North Shore High team and wearing their colors probably doesn't only feel strange to me. He was Stoneview Prep's beloved captain, the king of our school, the God among us mere mortals.

He's talking to a teammate I've never seen before, but when he suddenly looks away from him and his eyes land on me, my heart kicks up. I'm breathless.

He is so gorgeous, it's ridiculous.

His gaze stays on me as he bends down to whisper something in Billie's ear. Her eyes flick to me and she laughs as Jake pulls away from her.

Bitch.

I refocus on my table just to find Luke and Emily talking to each other. They're exchanging about how they're going to celebrate once both teams go back to Stoneview, qualified for nationals. I can't talk about this until I know for sure we are qualified. We're good, but anything can happen.

Emily laughs at one of Luke's jokes and Cole kicks my leg under the table. His eyes widen as we both think the same thing: are these two patching things up? If not, at least they're going back to being friends.

Luke and Emily had one of those healthy breakups. Their relationship might have been a lot of trying to make the other jealous, but once they had broken up, they gave each other time to heal. The complete opposite of Jake and I trying to completely destroy the other.

After dinner, our teams head to a meeting with Coach Thompson in one of the hotel's meeting rooms. It only takes half an hour, but I'm exhausted by the time we get out. I need energy for tomorrow. Emily catches me as I head out of the room.

"So..." she hesitates. "I'm going to go for a walk with Luke. Just in the area, we just want to talk."

I laugh as she finishes her sentence. "Just a walk?"

She giggles in return. "I'll try to be good, I swear."

"Have fun," I yawn as I head toward the elevator.

I slide the card and open the door to my room. I turn around to close it and stretch myself in another yawn, still facing the door. I start biting my cheek thinking of the upcoming days.

Tomorrow morning we're watching the men's team at 9 am, our pre-game warm-up is at 10:30 am and our first game at 11 am. Our second game at 4 pm is against Edmont High. We'll beat them easily. The day after tomorrow we have an easy game in the morning, and St Anne in the afternoon. North Shore High is on our third day, in the afternoon, and on the fourth–

My thoughts are cut short when a hand slams on my

mouth from behind, giving me a near heart attack and startling me hard enough for all my muscles to tense. I scream so loud my lungs beg to explode but the whole sound is muffled by the strong hand.

My fight or flight response kicks in straight away and I wiggle, kick one leg behind, trying to get my assailant in the legs. Adrenaline is running high, and my hands feel clammy as I try to pry off the unforgiving fingers digging into my cheeks.

He doesn't make a noise, or maybe I can't hear him over my screaming attempts. His height behind me feels like I'm about to get crushed under a giant. My heart is beating hard in my ears, they're ringing, the skin on my back is already drowning in cold sweat.

I'm too focused on trying to breathe, on his hand on my mouth that I don't realize until it's too late that something slipped above my head. I only understand when my eyes are suddenly covered with something. It feels like a sleeping eye mask or something. My hands shoot up to take it off straight away, but they're grabbed before I can reach it. Someone is holding them in front of me.

Wait.

Someone. Is holding them. In front of me.

And someone. Is. Behind me.

I think deep, deep down, my subconscious was hoping that it was Jake. The hand on my mouth felt like the first time he did this to me. I thought I caught a waft of his wooden and spicy scent, the frame behind my body felt like him.

But it's not. Because there are two people manhandling me right now.

My screams double, still muffled by the hand. My knees buckle in fear but an arm wraps around my waist while the person in front of me still holds my wrists together in one mighty grip.

Tears spring to my eyes when I hear a belt unbuckling. I shake my head, the word 'no' not making it past my lips. I kick a leg in front of me, catching the person in front of me somehow.

A dark chuckle sends a shiver down my spine, but I don't stop fighting, I kick again, miss. Again, and it lands against him.

"Feisty for such a tiny little thing," the dark voice snickers again. I don't recognize it.

My God, I don't recognize it.

Tears start flowing down, not even making it past the blindfold on my eyes. This is not a sick joke from Jake, this isn't a prank, this is real.

I feel something thick around my wrists, probably that belt I heard, and I twist my body strongly. I'm starting to suffocate.

There's nothing to do. I'm stuck. I'm stuck. I can't move.

The whimper that breaks from my chest can't come out of my mouth and sounds higher in my nose.

The belt tightens around my wrist and the hand that was holding me from the front lets them go. Every attempt to break free from the binds is pointless, it doesn't move in the slightest.

"Little lamb is ready for slaughter." That dark voice again, it's mocking me. It's ready to have a good time.

I scream again when I'm suddenly dragged across the room from behind. No amount of kicking and wriggling helps. My fight is slowly dying but when I feel the hand on my mouth slightly pulling away, I'm ready to scream all over again. It's suddenly gone, and I open my mouth, dragging a deep breath to scream help from the top of my lungs.

Too slow.

I'm still taking that deep breath when the man from behind pushes some material in my mouth and gags me with it. It feels like some sort of scarf or something, digging so far in my mouth it makes me gag when he tightens it behind my head, pulling hair with it.

I go to bring my tied hands to my face, but my movement stops short.

"Tsk, tsk," the dark voice tells me.

I can hear the smile on his lips. I don't get it, he's not holding my wrist, they're only tied with the belt, why are movements restricted? Why can't I bring my hands to my face?

"Little bitches get leashes," he continues. Suddenly I'm tugged forward by the belt. That's when I understand he's holding one end of the belt, stopping me from going anywhere, from any movement. My sight is gone, my mouth is gagged, my hands are tied.

My body freezes entirely. I'm completely at their mercy. My insides tighten and the self-loathing starts. Because that's exactly the kind of situation that creates pleasure between my legs. My clit tingles while my brain shouts at me that I'm just a little whore who is going to die tonight. I will, I will die. They're going to have their fun with me and then they're going to kill me.

And yet, the anticipation in me screams at me that I should have gone and seen a therapist about getting excited by this. Too late, now I'm on the verge of dying.

I don't know where the other man has gone. The dark voice talks to me as he tugs on the belt again. "Come on, on the bed little lamb."

Another whimper slightly makes it past the gag in my

mouth. My brain releases another shot of fear in me, and it makes me shake.

This is real, Jamie, this is not some kinky game with Jake.

"Pweas..." I gargle at the back of my mouth. "...on't"

Another tug and I fall face-first on the bed, I'm on my stomach, my arms are pulled up, and the next thing I know I feel both men standing behind me, my arms taut up above my head. They must have tied the belt to the bed frame.

Knuckles run up and down my spine. I feel it through my thin t-shirt.

Reality dawns on me and the tears start again. "Please... please," I beg between sobs racking my chest.

"Mm, she's so good at begging."

Another chuckle but it's not the dark voice. No, this one I recognize.

"She is, and she loves it."

Jake.

Fucking. Jake. White.

Two hands grab my hips and pull me back, making the pull on my shoulders painful, the other slides a pillow under me. The hands on my hips are now on my jeans, pulling them down with my panties.

"*Jake!!*" I try to scream but it comes out as a barely audible sound.

Panties and jeans around my ankle, I squirm in bed as the cold air of the room meets my wet pussy.

I have no fear of dying anymore.

Now, I'm angry, *fuming* that he thinks he can do this to me. The possessive asshole who never let anyone near me now thinks we can have some kinky threesome when we're not even together anymore? No, he's just doing this to humiliate me.

Chapter 13

And I am. I'm unbelievably embarrassed that it makes me wet.

A hand rubs my naked butt cheeks and I know it's Jake's when his voice reaches my ears again.

"Angel," he croons.

I hate him. I hate him so much right now it's a storm destroying everything inside me. Everything but that deep love I have for him.

I screech behind the gag and wiggle out of his touch. The only thing it gets me is a harsh spank.

I'm going to kill you. That's what I want to scream. Impossible, of course.

I'm back to the beginning of our story. Being at Jake's mercy and getting wet from it.

"I think she wants to tell us something," the other guy laughs.

Jake chuckles darkly in response. "But I don't care what she wants to say."

He gets rid of my jeans completely and spreads my legs a little more, exposing my pussy completely. I tug at my binds, wriggle some more but it doesn't change anything. Not a damn thing.

Jake ignores my movements, he keeps talking. "Toys only exist to please their owner. Don't they, Angel?" He grazes his knuckles against my pussy, and I whimper in pleasure. "And look how much you love pleasing me."

His hand leaves me, and the dark voice talks again. "She's dripping," he whispers.

"Always for me," Jake confirms, pleasure sticking to his tongue.

The humiliation twists my insides and more pleasure pools between my legs. Another slap lands painfully on my cheek, making me scream behind the gag. I don't even know if it's Jake or the other man.

"You betrayed me, Angel." Jake's voice is now cold. He's not mocking me anymore, he's angry.

I want to shout that he's the one who betrayed me, that we're not together, that he's a piece of shit who used me and threw me away and now can't get over the fact that I'm not his anymore. But there's a reason that gag is there. He doesn't want to hear these truths.

"But that's okay, you can make it up to me tonight. And guess what? I got a text from Luke saying Emily's gone back to his room. So we have *all* night, baby."

I grunt against the gag hoping he'll take it as an insult. But he doesn't care. Jake doesn't care if I think he's a heartless bastard, he's shown me his true colors months ago and I still fell for him. I still let him steal my heart, my soul...my dignity.

"Stop trying to talk, you're gagged for a reason," he orders.

I'm assuming it's his hand that wraps around my thigh tightly, the touch feels familiar. He squeezes hard enough to make me squeal.

"The only time this thing will come off is when you'll suck my cock, little lamb."

That's not Jake. That's the dark voice. I expect Jake to say something to him, to get territorial like he usually does. He only laughs.

I hear both of them moving behind me, their hands are off me now. I try to concentrate on what I hear, what they're doing. I hear the zipper from a bag being opened. They shift around in silence, a small laugh slipping past their lips every now and then.

I feel a presence closer before they even touch me. I

understand one of them is undoing the belt from the bed frame. He pulls until I'm sitting up and keeps pulling so I'm falling on my back, my head now at the other end of the bed, my legs by the bed frame. While the first person ties the belt around something else, I feel a hand grabbing my right ankle. I jump in fear, fight back but there's no point.

When they're done with me, both my ankles are tied to opposite sides of the bed, spreading my legs wide. My head is hanging off the bed and my arms pulled taut above my head, the end of the belt is tied somewhere I don't know. All I know is I can't. Fucking. Move.

In a sudden hand movement, the blindfold comes off, the brightness in the room blinding me. It takes me a few seconds to be able to open my eyes fully.

Both men are standing by my head as I watch them upside down. Jake has his arms crossed at his chest, looking down at me with an evil smirk on his lips.

I flip my eyes to the guy with the dark voice. From down here, he's very tall. I know he's at least as tall as Jake because their shoulders are around the same height. He's got a light brown skin tone, darker than Jake, about as dark as me. The smile that spreads across his lips when he looks at me is carnal. It clashes with his deep brown eyes and long lashes. His skin looks so smooth, so perfect. His lips are on the darker side, plumped, and a shiver runs down my spine when his tongue darts across his bottom one before he bites it with pearl white teeth.

He is gorgeous. He looks Arab but I wouldn't be able to place a country. His shoulders are not square but clearly strong, just like his arms.

"This is my new friend, Lik. But people switch it around sometimes, they call him Kill," Jake's voice brings me back to him. His face lowers to mine. "You don't want to bring Kill out, trust me."

The gag is soaked with my saliva from trying to talk, but I keep going anyway.

"...uck...you..." I choke.

I turn my head to the side to realize the end of the belt is tied to the bed leg. I pull at it even when I know it's pointless.

"I think she's saying fuck you," Lik mocks.

"Tsk, tsk. Such a dirty mouth." Jake straightens up and slaps the side of my face.

It's light, almost affectionate but I know he means it in a condescending way.

"We're going to make you feel so good, Angel, by the time we take that gag off you'll be begging us to fuck you."

He bends down and grabs something, waving it at me. "Look at what I bought for you. Remember I said I'd get you one? You kept telling me that's what you put in the search bar when you watch porn."

My brows furrow. He's right, I know what this is. I've seen it in porn before, the kind I watch secretly where girls are tied up to beds. Oh, the irony.

It's a magic wand sort of vibrator, the kind with a bulbous head and that has to be plugged into the wall. I shiver in anticipation. This is not good, not good at all. Then why does my pussy clench with need?

I watch him walk to the other side of the bed until I can't see him anymore while Lik still looks down at me.

I don't know him, I don't know who he is. What is going through Jake's mind thinking this is something I would be okay with?

He doesn't care if this is okay with you, that's what you love about him.

Chapter 13

I startle when I feel Jake stretch my pussy lips and put something between them. It's the vibrator. The head is big enough to keep my lips spread and settle against my clit, covering it all. I try to close my legs, impossible.

"Lik, come check how wet the little slut is."

His words hurt. I know Jake is capable of being sweet to me, he just decided I wasn't worth being sweet to.

Lik, or Kill, or whatever his name is, smiles at me one last time before disappearing out of view.

"Fuck," I hear him hiss. "She's loving this."

Even if the gag was off, I couldn't scream that I don't love it. Because my body clearly does.

Why does it feel so good to be played with by Jake?

I feel more movement and the sudden vibration against my clit makes me squeal in the gag. The pleasure that overwhelms me wracks my body with a spasm I can't control.

"Yeah, I think she loves it," Jake confirms in a chuckle.

The vibration is almost not enough, it's on a low setting that has me moving against the vibrator in search of more pleasure.

They both reappear in my line of vision and Jake wraps a hand around my throat. The intensity of the vibrator accelerates, and I moan into the gag.

"We're taking bets, Angel. I say five orgasms before you start crying and begging to be released. Kill says four. What do you say?"

The intensity goes up again and again, and I whimper. This is too much, too sudden, I'm going to come, I can't control it.

Please don't come. Please, please. Don't show them how much you love it.

My orgasm crashes to me so suddenly I scream my release.

"We should put some music on," Kill suggests.

Jake nods and pulls away from me. As the vibrator goes back to the lowest setting, my clit tingles with need again. A long moan breaks past my throat and my eyes roll to the back of my head.

"...Jake," I groan in pleasure.

"You enjoy yourself, Angel. We'll be right here."

Lik puts some music on, not too loud as to bother the neighboring rooms but enough to cover any of my moans that might get past the door.

Then, they both settle on two chairs around the small round table opposite the bed. They watch me a little longer before turning to each other. Lik pulls his phone out and Jake takes out some weed and papers.

I watch them, my head upside down as the vibrator goes up in intensity again but neither of them pays me any more attention. My second orgasm comes crashing so hard my legs beg to shut around the torturous object between them. But I still ride it, grinding against the head, my body getting every ounce of pleasure out of it.

It stays on the highest setting past my orgasm and the pleasure overwhelms me, my clit too sensitive to take anymore.

"Jake!" I scream in the gag. My moans turn into whimpers until the lowest setting takes over.

This is pure torture. The two of them are chatting away, rolling a joint and watching some lacrosse drill on their phone while I'm tied to the bed, a panting, whimpering mess.

When the vibrator starts accelerating again, my clit screams for a break, even for at least a few seconds. But it doesn't come. The vibrations intensify but I can't come, not again. It's too much for me to take pleasure out of it a third time.

"Jake, please," I whimper, drool starting to make it past the scarf in my mouth.

It's been around my tongue for so long I've got lint scratching down my throat, suffocating me. My scream burns my lungs as the third orgasm hits me. My skin is on fire, my pussy clenching and drenching the sheets below me, I can feel my cum sliding down between my butt cheeks. I can see Jake re-adjusting his pants, but he still doesn't turn to me.

I can only catch my breath when it's back on the lowest setting, but still, the pleasure has turned into pain and my clit is too raw to take anymore. Yet, it doesn't stop.

I don't know how long it takes for me to reach my fourth orgasm, I've lost count of the number of times it went back to the highest setting, and I've lost track of time completely. All I can see is that Jake and Kill are almost finished with their joint and are now watching stupid videos.

I scream so loud when the fourth orgasm hits me, pleasure still racking through my whole body despite my clit feeling raw.

They both turn to me when I stop screaming and as the lowest setting comes back.

"I think that was four, wasn't it?" Lik asks.

I don't really know who he's talking to, but I nod my head repeatedly, hoping the fact that he would win their stupid bet means they'll turn off this fucking thing.

"And clearly she can take more," Jake replies like he's bored that I'm not begging him anymore.

But I'm exhausted, my body is weak, I don't have the strength to take any more pleasure.

The vibrations accelerate and I whimper against the gag.

My mouth has never felt so dry. My neck is in horrible pain from being pulled at the edge of the bed, my eyes feel heavy from exhaustion. And yet, my pussy is clenching, begging for another kind of release. One only Jake can bring me.

"I'm sure you can take another one. For me, Angel," Jake smiles wickedly at me.

He gets up, and the scent of his cologne brings more pleasure to my already wrecked body. The feeling of his ocean eyes on me makes my insides tighten and the next thing I know, I'm grinding against the vibrator again, trying to find a release that seems impossible.

The pain and pleasure are so strong when I come for the fifth time, my whole body trembles, spasms making me shake against the bed. The intensity doesn't go down and tears build up in my eyes, then fall against my temples.

"...please...jake!!" I scream against the gag when I understand Lik has locked the device on high intensity. "...aaaaah." Another orgasm is forced out of me and my tears double.

"There they are," Jake groans in pleasure as his thumb wipes some of my tears. How can I desperately need someone so cruel? "Gorgeous," he says as he spreads my tears against my cheek. My pussy clenches at his voice.

The vibrations suddenly stop, but my body doesn't relax. It still spasms against the bed and the need for Jake to make it all better is still here. My clit is raw, I've had too many orgasms, but I'm not satisfied. I need him. I need him inside me.

Jake's hand goes behind my head and the gag falls off. I take a deep breath as he talks.

"Tell me what you need, Angel."

"You," I whimper. "I need you, please." My mouth feels

Chapter 13

like cotton, my voice is raw, but my body is completely aware of what it needs.

Lik lets out a genuine laugh as Jake tears through my t-shirt, ripping it off me.

"Fucking hell, Jake. You've turned this girl into a complete submissive."

"I know," Jake growls with pleasure as he settles by my head again. "*My* complete submissive." My hips buck against nothing as he talks.

"Jake, please..."

He chuckles, mocking the need he put in me himself. He undoes the bind around my ankles and settles between my legs. I have to pull my head up to watch him as he gets rid of his t-shirt and jeans. He runs his knuckles on my inner thigh and I shiver with need until I realize what he's tracing. Hickeys Nathan left there.

"You betrayed me..." he growls. "Hey, Lik, what do *you* do when someone betrays you?"

"I personally put them six feet under, but I think you've found a great alternative," he replies, stroking my hair.

"I think I have."

"I..." I panic. "I can't take both of you, Jake."

I didn't expect him to burst out laughing. "Oh, don't worry. Lik isn't interested in fucking you. He's not into pussy."

"I'm definitely interested in getting my dick sucked though," Lik adds.

I feel Jake's arm on either side of me before his face appears above mine.

"Would you be interested in that, Angel? Sucking Lik while I make you come on my cock?"

As desperate as I am to feel Jake inside me, I don't know Lik and I don't want him. That much I know.

I shake my head as I talk to Jake again, "I only want you."

He smiles at me like it's exactly what he wanted to hear. "You heard her. Get the fuck out of here," Jake grunts, his voice so full of lust I'm sure he's about two seconds away from snapping out of control.

I hear the bedroom door open and closing and Jake talks again. "It's only you and me now, Angel."

He enters me in such a violent stroke I cry out, desperately trying to bring my arms on his shoulders to slow him down. But my pussy adapts so quickly to him my cries turn into endless moans.

He puts a hand over my mouth and fucks me relentlessly. He's so angry every one of his strokes has the sole purpose of showing me how dangerous we are for each other.

My brain tries to scream at me that my life is all over the place. That I can't have sex with Nathan *and* Jake. But while Nathan was a mistake, a momentary slip, Jake is meant to be. Each thrust is a reminder of how much I belong to him.

He bites my neck, inking regret into my skin. He fucked Billie and I fucked Nathan, but this right here is everything. This is love, lust, passion, *poison*.

I come so hard my legs shake uncontrollably, wrapping around his hips and forcing him to stay in me past his own release. After long minutes of silence, he finally slips words in my ear.

"How does it feel, Angel? To be worshipped by the devil?"

The shiver that runs through my spine forces my teeth to clatter for a split second.

"You're not the devil, Jake," I whisper. "You're just someone who's been broken, but I know there's a scared kid in you who has been robbed of his childhood."

I dig my gaze in his. Confusion shows in his beautiful ocean eyes, and he blinks a couple of times. His long, black lashes emphasize his lost innocence.

"Your demons could be mine if you'd let me," I add in a barely audible murmur.

His jaw tenses, cracks, and relaxes, but he doesn't reply. He gets off me, releases my wrists, and helps me sit up.

Jake joins me in the bathroom while I clean his cum off my legs. He enters the small hotel shower and grabs the jet from me. I open my mouth to ask what he's doing but he puts his thumb on my lips. He stands behind me and traces my jaw, my neck, and then my collarbone. He caresses my breasts gently like he's suddenly scared of breaking me after what Lik and he did to me.

He flicks one nipple after the other and after half a minute of him doing so, I start squirming on the spot. He presses his strong body against mine and his hard dick makes me shiver.

His hand slides down but he avoids my pussy. His fingers trace the hickeys Nathan left on me again and I almost hear his teeth grinding as his body tenses. He brings the jet down and puts the pressurized water against my clit. I jump at the shock of pleasure. It only takes a few seconds before I moan greedily.

But it's never just pleasure with Jake, is it?

He suddenly pinches exactly where Nathan had left the biggest mark. It's harsh and violent on what is already a bruise. I shriek at the pain, but he keeps the jet against my clit, moving ever so slightly, making sure the pressure is perfect.

It doesn't take me long to come undone in his arms, my

knees buckle, and he releases my bruised thigh to catch me at the waist. He puts the jet in its hold and pushes between my shoulder blades as he releases my waist, so I have to put my arms on the tiles in front of me.

He doesn't ask me anything, he doesn't check how I'm feeling. He just grabs my hips and enters me roughly. I scream in painful pleasure. He growls something I don't understand and two seconds later his grip on my hips is lethal as he lifts me slightly. My toes barely touch the floor anymore as he slams into me from behind. He's got complete control over the movements and all I can do is push against the wall so I don't hit it.

He takes his time to push into me, I feel his knees against the back of my thighs. The wet slapping is not from the shower, I know it's from me. The animalistic way in which he's taking me makes me whimper, tears of pleasure building in my eyes at the roughness.

The tension in me needs to be snapped by Jake's possessiveness. I need to give him the control so he can force me to break apart against his body.

And he does. He forces another orgasm out of me. He pushes my body to take the excruciating pleasure only he can give me. He withdraws and comes all over my ass.

I'm panting hard when he lets my feet touch the floor again. He pinches my ass cheeks and smears his seed all over them before he talks in my ear from behind.

"Why do you let me do these things to you, Angel?"

My heart skips a beat. This is a question I was dreading. It's a question I hate asking myself and avoid all the time. But I have answered it to myself before. Maybe not directly, but deep down I know.

I know from the men I'm attracted to, dark and morally wrong.

I know from the porn I watch, full of dubious scenes that always make me come in less than a minute.

I know from the things I imagine, the wicked situations I wish Jake would do and that probably never even crossed his mind.

"You think I let you do this because you force me," I whisper. "You think it's because it's you and I'm in love and stupid. You think I will regret it. But it's not you, Jake. It's me. I enjoy it, it makes me wet, it makes me come. I'm depraved and you feed my depravity."

There's a short silence while he thinks of my words.

"Yeah, well apparently so does Nate," he rasps before leaving the shower.

When I come back to the room, he's standing by the bed in his boxers.

I let myself enjoy his ripped abs and V that dip into his underwear. He slowly walks to me, still silent, puts both his palms on my cheeks, and kisses me in the least expected way possible.

He ravages my mouth with love, he plays with my tongue in ways that call for unconditional adoration. My heart picks up so fast I feel it in my ears. My extremities tingle, there are butterflies on LSD in my stomach and I go on my toes to deepen our act of passion.

He pulls his mouth away but doesn't let go of me.

"Do you think maybe...maybe we're too broken for each other?" His voice is hoarse from pain and my heart breaks for him. Because he genuinely thinks he doesn't deserve what we could have. "People like us should fall in love with people who can be lights in their darkness. Who can fix them and ease them into an ordinary life. *Normal* people."

And by normal people, he means ones who don't carry an infinite luggage of trauma with them.

It's the first time since he's been back that I find the real Jake beneath all the anger. So I hold onto him as much as I can. I show him the girl he broke, the girl that's been waiting for him to come back and tell her he loves her.

"No," I reply as a tear passes my eyelids. I have a reflex of shaking my head at the same time, but his palms gently force me to face him. "No, Jake. I don't want normal people, I want *you*. You and all the broken pieces you come with. I'll take all the darkness. I'll take all the obsession and possession. I'll give you all the control you need. I don't *care* for other people. We need each other, our broken pieces fit, they *fit*, Jake, I promise you."

He smiles but it's a defeated one. "In an ideal world, we'd escape this town and settle somewhere together. You'd go to your ideal college and become one of the best surgeons in the country. I'd watch you grow, and we'd heal each other. You'd slowly chase away the demons and I'd slowly let go of that anger that drives me. We'd be in love…unconditionally."

This sounds so good it makes my heart swell with hope, even if I know we're far from our ideal world.

"We could," I lie as the tears start flowing freely.

"No."

Ah. Welcome back, Jake the sociopath. All sort of warmth has gone from his body and the coldness of that simple word seeps through my bones.

"Don't give up on us, Jake," I beg him in one last attempt.

"We both gave up on each other. I did when I didn't fight for you, and you did when you slept with Nate. You need to stick in that smart brain of yours that any sex between us doesn't mean shit to me. Our relationship…it's beyond repair. I'll never forgive you. And when you find out…" He stops himself short.

"Find out what?" I press.

"You'll never forgive me either," he simply replies.

He doesn't talk again until he's fully clothed. "Go to bed, Jamie."

How does he expect me to go to bed after what happened? After what he just dropped on me? How am I expected to focus on lacrosse when I know Jake is hiding something from me? Something I wouldn't forgive him for.

14

JAMIE

Wreak Havoc – Skylar Grey

"White!" Coach T. shouts at Rose. "I thought I just told everyone to be quiet."

Rose gives him a charming smile and steps away from Ciara.

"As I was saying, now is not the time to rest on your laurels. I get that you girls are ecstatic about the results against St Anne, but it was a tie. You didn't win, you simply did better than last year. And guess what? North Shore High beat them by five points."

My heart drops in my stomach. We missed the St Anne versus N.S. High game because we were playing our own game at that time.

"How?" I choke. We're better than them.

"I'm glad someone is listening." He turns to the whiteboard behind him. We went over our plays yesterday, so instead of his usual drawings, there are two positions, two numbers, and two last names.

DEFENSE 13 SCOTT

Chapter 14

CENTER 20 EVANS

"Are we seriously worried about Billie Scott?" Rose chortles. "She's about half my height."

"She could be on Ashley," I mumble as I focus on both names and numbers. Fucking Billie, it wasn't enough for her to steal Jake. She also had to ruin my tournament.

We knew N.S. High's new center was going to be a challenge. I watched her play her first game and she is a fast one. But I would have never expected Billie to be a problem. She's a tiny girl, like me, she's a year younger, and it's her first time playing the tournament. I guess she might not scare Rose, but our other straight attack, Ashley Stuart, is not as fearless as my friend.

"She's strong, she's fast, and she's good at fouling without being noticed."

"Typical North Shore," Ciara huffs.

"I don't care about the little teenage feud going on between Stoneview and North Shore High, but I will be damned if you girls make me lose my last tournament because you think you're better than them. You will only beat them if you focus, if you remember our plays, and if you play hard and smart. Stuart, you're not on the starting lineup for this one. You will be useless against their new defense. Clayton, you take over."

I turn to Melissa Clayton and look her up and down. She's smiling proudly and giving a nasty look to Ashley.

"Hey," I snap. "Focus. Your aim is not to score, it's to drive their defense out so Rose can score. Don't turn this into the Melissa Clayton show because you get to start the game."

It's important to remind Stoneview girls that not everything is about them, they love the attention too much. At least Melissa is brave enough to take on multiple defense players at once if Rose goes for the goal.

A shiver of stress and excitement runs through me. I wipe my clammy hands against my kit and grab my stick. The adrenaline running through my veins at the idea of playing hard against N.S. High is making me giddy.

"White," Coach calls Rose. "Duke's scouts watched the game against St Anne. They asked about you and they're coming to see this game. They're coming to watch *you*. No fuck ups."

Rose nods repeatedly. "No fuck ups, Coach."

A bell rings in the locker room, indicating we have to make our way to the field.

"Showtime!" Coach T. shouts as he claps his hands a couple of times.

I watch my girls grab their sticks and turn to me. Lacrosse games are the only moments Stoneview students see me as more than Goody, and I am ready to destroy N.S. High with them. It's not just about winning the tournament, being the third day, it's now the weekend and families have driven down to watch the last two days. This is our penultimate game and the bleachers outside are packed with other teams, families, coaches, scouts, and locals.

"Time to show them who's boss, ladies," I smile as some girls start shouting encouragement to each other.

I hold the door open for them and they all go out, each one hitting my stick in the process as a replacement for a high five.

The rain hitting against my cheeks as we huddle up on the sideline feels like needles. I know the ten minutes we have for halftime are going to fly by and I calm everyone down as Coach enters our circle.

"Clayton, are you okay?" he checks as she sits down on

Chapter 14

the wet grass to check her knees. Billie tackled her hard enough to make her slip knees first on the floor.

"Fine," she mumbles but everyone's eyes grow wide as we watch her bloody knees.

"Not fine. Stuart, you're on. Bailey," he shouts at Ciara. "Are you fucking drunk or something? You let their center go past you six fucking times! White, that's not how you're going to impress Duke. Get your shit together." He turns to me. "Pass the ball, Williams. If I see you try to sprint past their defense one more time you're out. It's impossible, so pass. The. Fucking. Ball."

My mouth falls slack. Okay, maybe I have been raging against Billie for the first half of the game, but she's a damn monster. She fouls, she mocks, and she's really good, which makes the whole thing worse.

Every time I win the draw and try to make a run from center to goal, she's on me like glue. But what is really making me lose my mind is when we're face to face, and she's close enough to throw Jake's name at me.

He was in my room last night.

Don't you just love sucking his dick?

He's so big it was practically impossible to take him in the ass.

Of course I'm going to be destabilized, and she knows it.

Jake and I haven't spoken in three days, since he and his friend came to my room. Has he really been with Billie since then?

The whistle calls the one minute until the end of halftime and Coach finishes his talk with the girls who are now coming on the field.

I settle on my spot in the center of the field and press my stick against my opponent, the ball the only thing separating them. Evans, number 20, the feared center. She was on the sideline the first half of the game and I'm worried her presence on the field will be my demise. They're currently winning by four points. It's far from impossible to catch up, but North Shore girls are really damn tough.

We watch the ref put the whistle in her mouth, ready for the awaited sound.

"I eat Stoneview girls for breakfast, bitch. You don't stand a fucking chance."

The whistle blows and I lose my first draw of the game.

"Fuck," I curse as I go after her. I'm really not used to losing draws and she's too fast for me. No one on my team has time to get in front of her and she scores before I reach her. The walk back to center for the second draw is embarrassing. Especially because everyone at the tournament is watching this like it's the game of the century.

I lose three draws before I finally manage to win the ball and boy does it feel good to finally catch up. Rose scores the next seven goals like it's the easiest thing in the world for her. Coach is right, I should pass the ball.

The problem with finally being tied to N.S. High is that their defense starts getting nastier.

Billie and her teammate double team me and my ass ends up on the muddy ground. I lose the ball, but Rose is right behind and scoops it up in her stick. The following second, she scores from so far everyone on the bleachers gets up as they scream in shock and encouragement. She helps me up from the ground and turns to Billie.

"Crazy thing you might want to know, Billie," Rose tells her with her smug winner smile. "Being a good player works even better than foul play."

"Fucking bitch," Billie spits as she comes dangerously close to Rose. She takes a threatening stance before talking again. "You think I care about kicking your ass in front of a

Chapter 14

crowd? You won't be much of a problem for me without your brothers around."

"Please, try," Rose snorts.

"Girls, back to starting position," I jump in.

It's not that I'm not dying to see Rose kick Billie's ass, but she's being watched by Duke's scouts as we speak, and they will cross her name in bright red pen if they think she would be a problem player. Rose knows exactly where I'm getting at and takes a calming breath before turning her back to Billie to walk back to the restraining line, where she starts every draw. I walk next to her.

"Go on, princess," Billie quips. "You be a good girl like Bianco taught you."

Rose stops so suddenly she almost slips in the mud. Her back goes rigid and her jaw locks.

"Don't," I beg her in a whisper. "She's only trying to rile you up. This game can decide your future, don't fall for it."

Rose gives me the slightest nod and I know it takes all her strength to take another step. Billie knows it too, and she must know Rose is being watched by the scouts because she insists again, desperate to get something out of her.

"Hey, Rose."

The tone of Billie's voice doesn't announce anything good. She drawls like she already knows her next word will provoke Rose beyond control. And we all know how it goes down when a White loses control.

"How does it feel to know your parents didn't want you?"

My mouth falls at the nerve Billie has. She hit straight home. Rose drops her stick and is on her in a split second, looking down on her from all her height. She's raging and I run to her, taking hold of her upper arm. I can see Coach Thompson walking along the sideline, coming closer to us. He can't cross if the whistle isn't blown, he risks a free shot.

"Rose, Coach is coming. Just drop it."

But she's not listening to me, she's fuming, and her eyes are narrowed on Billie. Her words are as sharp as swords. "How does it feel to know that even without parents I managed to avoid being white trash like you?"

"At least I won't be Bianco's little bitch for the rest of my life," Billie sneers.

I don't control my fist.

My knuckles hit Billie's face so hard I'm pretty sure I broke a finger but watching her go down and hit the ground takes over the sharp pain shooting from my hand.

The gasps rising around me makes me realize how close everyone was watching our interaction.

The only problem is Billie doesn't stay on the floor. She gets up quickly and despite the redness starting to show on her left cheek, she's ready to hit back.

I'm not.

Jake

It hasn't been easy to avoid Jamie in the past three days, every team is constantly crowded with the other schools, and it seems my eyes constantly find her. Trying to stay away from her is about as easy as stopping two magnets from connecting.

After what Lik and I did to her, she hasn't tried to address one word to me and it's better this way, because when she tries to find the nice guy in me, when she begs for us to get back together...I get too close to giving in.

And I can't. I can't do that. But that's okay, because all the work Jamie has done on me, all the hours spent trying to get me to open up, trying to make me a better person, to find the empathy in me...they're quickly regressing by the minute.

I don't see Bianco as often as we did as kids, but his hold on us is just as strong. I feel exactly like I did when we lived with him. The panic attack I got after finding Nate and Jamie at my house taught me another hard lesson about letting my feelings drive me...I really fucking shouldn't.

If I let myself care too much, I get panic attacks and that teaches me I shouldn't care because it will only get worse. Every panic attack, every suffocating moment is an occasion for the demons to take over and give my mind a break.

When I don't care, when I'm my sociopathic self that only enjoys watching people suffer, my emotions can rest in some sort of subconscious space where no one will bother me.

If I don't have any feelings for Jamie, she can't hurt me. And if I don't care about her, Nate and Bianco can't use her against me.

Granted that's all easier said than done, because when I see her playing on that field in her tight skort sticking to her from all the rain, her serious face on, with only the win on her mind, I'm easily reminded of why I am desperately in love with that girl.

The girls from Stoneview have finally caught up with N.S. High and I can't help but feel happy. Not only because of Jamie but because Ozy really fucking deserves it. She's a beast on the field and every time she scores, Luke and I scream from our seats, getting up and bumping chests.

It's not just us, though. Many Stoneview students have driven down for the weekend just to watch their team play and I wouldn't be surprised if most of them have come for my sister. I can even see Nate on a higher stand, sitting with Sam and watching Rose like they fucking care.

I can't help but keep an eye on Duke's scouts. They're watching her closely, scribbling and debating every single move she makes. I watch with a smile as Jamie wins another draw, Billie and her teammate corner her, and she falls to the ground, but Rose is right behind her. She tries to score from close to the restraining line. Stupid move, it's too far she'll never make—

"Fuck yes!!" Luke and I scream as we jump from our seats. I can't fucking believe she scored, she's the best. That Duke scholarship is hers, it has to be.

The rest happens too fast for me to understand, all I know is by the time Luke and I calm down from our euphoria, Rose is on Billie and the next second Jamie's fist crashes against her face.

"What the fuck," Luke gasps as the two refs and Coach Thompson hurry toward them.

But that's not the real problem. The problem is Billie getting up and the rest of her team joining her as Jamie takes a step back in fear.

Fuck.

My sister doesn't hesitate to put herself in front of her friend and none of this is going to end up well. Especially when other girls that were standing on the bleachers – and that I know are part of the North Shore Crew – start making their way to the field.

"We need to move," I tell Luke as I start making my way down the bleachers and toward the field.

Why the fuck would Jamie do that? She just signed her death warrant. Billie is never going to let that go.

We make our way past the refs and coaches desperately

Chapter 14

trying to calm down everyone and the first thing I do is send Luke to my twin.

"Don't let Ozy get in trouble, this is too fucking important."

He's on her in a split second, grabbing her arm and pulling her from the small crowd. I hear her complain, but she'll thank us later.

I'm too late to stop Billie from hitting back. She must have punched Jamie in the stomach or something, because two of Billie's girls are already holding her arms and she's hunched over, whimpering and desperately trying to take a breath.

To say it affects me would be the understatement of the century. How am I meant to not give a shit about her if she puts herself in situations like this?

"You made yourself the wrong enemy," Billie growls. "It's always been a dream of mine to fuck up a Stoneview bitch." She draws her fist back, ready to hit her again, and I grab her wrist so hard she jumps in fear.

"Someone needs to make wiser choices," I snicker at her.

"Yes, your fucking bitch does," she hisses back.

"I thought *you* were my bitch," I pout in mockery. "Nice new blush." I poke the fresh bruise Jamie just left on her cheek and she turns her head the other way.

"Let me fucking go, Jake. If I don't beat the shit out of her now, I promise you it'll be later."

"Tell your wannabe gangsters to let her go. I'll only ask nicely once."

The two girls don't wait for Billie to tell them, they let go of Jamie as soon as I finish my sentence.

Security finally makes its way through the crowd, and everyone disperses. I let go of Billie so she can go her own way.

"Great," she says bitterly. "Now guess which kids are going to end up in trouble. Spoiler alert, it won't be the rich ones."

She leaves before security can get to her and retreats toward the locker rooms. Jamie is still here, holding her side where I can imagine Billie hit and desperately trying to fight the tears.

I'm sure she can see the rage in my eyes when I face her because hers widen in surprise.

"What the actual fuck, Jamie?" I growl. How could she put herself in danger like this, how could she make me fear for her safety when I'm desperately trying to let her go.

"She...she started it," she whimpers before taking a long-awaited breath.

"I don't fucking care who started it. Billie is a semi-professional boxer, she could have knocked you out in the blink of an eye!"

"You think I don't know that?! She was begging for a fight," she cries out. "How do you expect me to stay calm when she mentions Bianco to Rose!"

My mouth opens but nothing comes out. Wait, what?

She got herself in trouble for Ozy? She put herself at risk so Rose wouldn't have to fight Billie herself, so she wouldn't risk her scholarship.

"You..." I finally manage. "That...that was reckless and stupid, and you could have gotten seriously hurt." I try to make the words sound harsh, I try to give her a lesson, but they all come out mumbled and it shows that I don't mean any of them.

Why? Why is she so perfect? So selfless. Us Whites have brought her nothing but trouble. Nate lied to her, used her to spy on us. I fucked her over, bullied her, loved her, and let

Chapter 14

her down like she meant nothing to me. And at what point has she become such good friends with Ozy?

"WILLIAMS!" Coach Thompson's voice trembles with fury.

"You got yourself in shit loads of trouble, Angel," I smile at her.

"What are you gonna do about it?" she whispers. "Tie me up to the bed and punish me? Lik isn't welcome this time."

My eyebrows shoot up, but I can't reply. Coach is already shouting at her and telling her she has to leave the field.

When did Jamie Williams become such a bad bitch? I fucking love it.

15

JAMIE

Ghost of You – 5 Seconds of Summer

I'm walking across the lobby of the hotel when a hand grabs me. I'm pulled into a room so quickly I drop my small suitcase.

"Why do you have your suitcase?" Jake whispers.

"I've been kicked out of the tournament," I growl as I look around myself. "Really, Jake? A supply closet?"

He takes the ice pack the nurse gave me and weighs it in his hand. He shakes his head and chuckles.

"Remember that time I pulled you inside the janitor's closet at school?" he says, still looking at the ice pack.

I nod, knowing exactly what he means. That day he saw Aaron's picture in my locker.

"Yeah, after that I stopped looking for my brother. You opened my eyes."

He looks up and there's something in his eyes I can't describe. Almost like guilt, but Jake doesn't feel guilty.

"Or did you stop when Nate burnt your notepad?"

"Yeah, I guess," I agree. "A bit of both."

Chapter 15

We're both whispering like we're about to do something wrong.

We're about to do something wrong, aren't we?

"That day, I was dying to kiss you," Jake admits. "But when I saw that look in your eyes, the longing for your lost brother. Shit, it broke my heart for you."

"Why are you saying this now?" I ask, confused.

"Did you really stop looking for him?"

I nod once. Almost ashamed.

He nods back, slowly, turning my words over in his mind.

"You opened up to me so much when we were together, didn't you? About your brother, your dad, all the trauma you endured."

It sounds so weird coming from his mouth. Especially with all the arguing we've done lately, I almost can't believe we're having a practically normal conversation about our relationship in a supply closet.

I go with it anyway. "Yeah, I did. I trusted you, I trusted you wanted to help me heal."

His lips pinches and he looks away for a second, still playing with the ice pack, kneading it like a stress ball.

"No one can see us in here. No one can hear us talk," he says, his voice low.

I nod, confused. Then slowly, clumsily, I understand. He doesn't want anyone to know he's talking to me.

He's scared.

"You're protecting me from Bianco, aren't you? He threatened me, didn't he?"

He doesn't reply. I went too far in my thinking, it sounds too real to him. I take it down a notch. "You're right, no one can hear us in here. No one knows where to find us. It's just you and me and I won't repeat anything."

"Why did you want to know so much about me? Why did you always ask questions?"

He sounds childish, like he doesn't get that when you're in love with someone you want to help them become the best version of themselves. All those emotions, he doesn't really understand them.

"I wanted to get to know you, to help you grow, to work on the things that have broken you."

"There are too many," he admits quietly, his eyes so focused on the ice pack he's about to burn a hole in it. He hasn't lifted his gaze for the whole conversation.

"We could start with something small," I reassure him. "You're safe here, with me. No one will know."

He nods slowly but it takes him a long minute before he talks again. "You kept asking about my tattoo."

"Yeah, I did. Would you like to share what it means with me? It would mean a lot to me." I keep my voice calm, I don't rush him. This is the first time since I've met him that he's willing to open up to me. I'm not about to ruin it with the excitement that we're getting somewhere, that maybe, somehow, it'll all get better.

"Do you know what 1933 is?" he asks.

I think about it for a second. "End of the prohibition?" I try.

"You're so smart," he chuckles. "During the prohibition, the mafia families became prominent alcohol distributors. They made millions out of that. But the Bianco family always wanted something else. They stayed out of it, sure that it would end, and they would be ready when it did. They built their empire on weapons and women instead. When the prohibition ended, a lot of mafia families died down. They were small back then, the Cosa Nostra wasn't as big as it is now. That's when the Bianco's rose up. That's the

Chapter 15

start of their empire, 1933. When they became the kings of New York."

I nod at the fascinating history lesson, despite the sad story behind it.

"And the W?"

"The Americanized version of Bianco...White. They wanted something that represented them, but not something that would directly spell their name out. There you have it, your explanation."

I wait until he gets to the true hard part about this. Because we both know there is more to this explanation. He huffs after a few seconds.

"Only the most trusted get this tattoo." His face twists with the pain from the memories. "Unfortunately, my siblings and I inherited it. It came with Bianco's obsession with us. A tattoo each so he could mark us as his forever. Truly, forever."

I put a hand on his cheek and he finally looks up, his broken gaze fixed on mine.

"You're more than a bit of ink on your back," I tell him.

"Yeah, I'm also a fucked up kid who is stuck in his past."

I shake my head. "No. You're a beautiful man who is trying to heal from trauma. You're someone I trust with my life, who I know will do the right thing when it comes down to it. I know you, Jake. You might think you're horribly broken into pieces of hate, but I think you're a beautiful mosaic made of courage."

The light that flickers in his eyes is the most beautiful thing I have ever seen. He licks his lips and drops the ice pack.

"I want to kiss you." His whisper is barely audible.

I suck in a breath.

"I'm going to kiss you, Jamie. We're not gonna get back

together, and I'm not going to love you again. But I *am* going to kiss you and fuck you against those shelves."

"Wai—"

My single word is cut short by his lips crashing against mine. He doesn't even wait for my mouth to accept his tongue. He doesn't wait for my go-ahead. He grabs my waist and lifts me up as he pulls down his lacrosse shorts. We're both sweaty from our games, my muscles ache from running around the field. But I still wrap my legs around his hips. I still intertwine my tongue with his in a consuming kiss.

My need for him wets my underwear and I moan when he rubs his hard dick against the shorts of my skort. He pushes the shorts and my underwear to the side and slides two fingers in my swollen pussy.

I gasp a whimper and he slams a hand against my mouth at the same time as my back crashes against the wall.

"Ssh," he chuckles. "The lock is on the outside, anyone could come in."

The fear adds to my neediness. So what if someone comes in? Let them see how much I love being owned by Jake. Let them see how wet I get when he curls his fingers inside me. Let them hear me scream his name in devotion.

When Jake fucks me, he becomes the king of my pleasure.

And I'm his loyal subject begging for his grace.

He struggles to slide his dick against the tight skort and curses under his breath. I giggle against his hand, and he freezes.

"Don't," he snaps. "Don't...don't giggle. Don't show me how fucking happy we could be."

He's fuming. I try to push his hand off, but he pushes back harder. My head hits the wall behind me and I wince.

Chapter 15

"We wouldn't be happy, Jamie. We would be miserable." He enters me slowly, making me moan against his hand. "I'd hurt you, I'd take everything from you."

Once he's slowly settled inside me and I feel my pussy tightening around him, he gives me harsh, strong thrusts.

"I'd take all the control," he growls against my ear as he thrusts again.

"I'd take your freedom." Thrust.

"I'd keep you to myself." Thrust. "I'd be the selfish bastard you hate so much."

Every thrust makes me hit against the wall. It makes the shelves rattle, it makes some cleaning products fall to the floor. But the loudest thing is how hard I'm moaning. How desperate I am to scream for him, to tell him that I'm dying to be his.

"You'd hate it, you'd be nothing and I'd be your everything."

He accelerates, making all my muscles tighten and sending heat from my toes to my heart. Said heart drops in my stomach and I come from his words and harsh movements.

I want to scream for him, but he doesn't let me. My breathing is so ragged, my nostrils flared from trying to bring air to my lungs. I'm a sweaty mess, tight around him. My orgasm wrecks everything in me, and he still doesn't stop.

"I would kill anyone who looks at you, Jamie. I would *hurt* you for what you did with Nate. I'd hurt you, so." Thrust. "Fucking."

I whimper loudly at the pain that comes from the next thrusts. He's reckless with my body, punishing it for all the things he wishes we had, and we'll never have.

"Bad." He groans as he freezes against me. He picks up slowly again, but I can already feel his seed escaping me.

He comes out of me and holds me tight while I unwrap my stiff legs from around him. He waits until my feet are securely touching the floor and makes sure I'm balanced before letting me go.

He looks down at me, putting strands of hair behind my ears when he talks again. "You'd hate it...right?"

I nod.

Only because I know I have to. Only because I'm meant to hate him after everything he's done.

But no. I would not hate it.

"Good," he concludes.

He leaves me without a look back. All this effort to open up to me...and nothing.

"Disqualified?" Mom chokes as I open our truck passenger door.

Disqualified and banned from the team for three weeks. That's my punishment for standing up for my teammate. I don't even get to stay until the end of the tournament and mom had to drive all the way from Stoneview on a workday to pick me up. I had no other way to get back home.

"I'm sorry, Mom," I reply in the smallest voice possible, holding the ice pack against my knuckles.

"I am...so disappointed in you, 'Me." It hurts, because I know she means it.

I go to the back of the truck, and I'm putting my bags and stick in the back when a hand touches my shoulder.

"'Me, are you okay?"

I snap around to face Nathan.

Chapter 15

"What are you doing here?" I whisper. If my mom sees him...

"I came to watch your game against N.S. High." He pauses and a full smile lights up his face. "I didn't realize you were going to make it so entertaining."

I chortle despite the ridiculousness of the situation. "I'm stronger than I look, aren't I?"

He shakes his head, a chuckle escaping his lips. "Mm," he pretends to think, "no, I believe you just caught her by surprise."

We both laugh, only stopped by Jake's cold voice. "The cutest fucking couple in the tri-state area."

He approaches us until he's standing right next to Nathan. He's not the same man that fucked me in the closet. I can already see it.

"So eager to cockblock," Nate growls.

The Whites always get my complete attention. That's how I didn't realize Mom had gotten out of the driver's seat and came around to the back.

"What the hell," she scolds.

I jump in surprise and turn to her, my voice stuck in my throat from the fear of her confronting the two men I know she loathes.

"You..." she seethes at both Jake and Nathan.

"Ms. Williams," Nathan smiles.

"Don't *Ms. Williams* me. You two have caused enough trouble as it is. I don't want to see you around my daughter. Not now, not ever again."

"Mom," I panic in a mix of embarrassment and deep anxiety about her getting involved with the Whites. "Let's go."

She takes a deep breath, a step back, and nods at me to go. We've barely taken another step that she stops and huffs.

"No. You know what? No."

"What?" I ask, confused.

She turns around and walks back to the boys. She points an accusing finger, altering between both of them. "Let this be the first and last warning. If I see you around my daughter again, I'll have you both put in jail."

"Jail," Nathan snickers. "Now that's a bit extreme."

"You think that's funny? Because as far as I'm concerned, you're an adult and she's a child. That's statutory rape in my books."

"Mom!" I scream in shock. "Stop it, please."

"She's eighteen," Nathan retorts.

"Not when you met her, you piece of shit."

Oh my God. She never curses. It's so rare that I shrink at her words.

"I've done nothing illegal," Nathan insists.

"Ha, now that's a good fucking joke," Jake jumps in.

Mom ignores him. She's settled on Nathan...for now.

"Don't talk to me about the law. I know Judge Joly personally, and if I want to cause trouble for you, believe me, I will."

Seeing the tiny thing that is my mom stand up to the White brothers is something I never thought I'd see. She has to look up at both of them to threaten them and it would be ridiculous if her words weren't so sincere. She addresses both when she talks again.

"You think I don't see you two thugs grooming my daughter, pulling her to you, changing her, showing her a life of crime. I won't stand for it. My husband was Stoneview's sheriff, do you understand? I won't disrespect his memory like that."

"Ms. Williams, with all due respect," Jake intervenes.

"Don't. Don't talk to me. I feel sorry for the Murrays,

Chapter 15

they had hope for you. I always knew it was pointless. It's sad, but kids like you don't change."

I'm speechless. I knew my mom was a strong woman, but seeing her like this, talking about crime, and mentioning my dad. I feel like I've completely let her down.

"Jamie. Car. Now," she concludes without giving them another minute of her attention.

I hurry after her, doing my best to ignore the two pairs of eyes drilling holes in my back.

The drive back is completely silent and we're in the living room before she talks to me again.

"How could you do this to me, Jamie?" Her voice is so broken my own stays stuck in my throat.

"Mom," I let out in a raspy whisper.

"I can't believe it. You were meant to be the good kid, I trusted you when I left for Tennessee. Do you really think I needed that kind of stress added to our lives? You skip school, your grades have crashed, you date gangsters, and now you punch lacrosse girls! What's next? Am I going to find your body on the North Shore? Do you have any idea what your dad and I had to go through to make sure you could grow up here and not there?"

"I'm sorry—"

"Sorry won't cut it, Jamie! You're putting your scholarship in peril. This is the only thing you should be thinking of, not parties and boys! Gosh, Aaron was a handful, and he was rebellious, but this...If Dad could see you right now..." she shakes her head, lost for words.

I don't think she understands the impact her words have on me. I felt repentant until now, but her mention of Aaron tips me over the edge and into fury.

"You don't mention his name for three years and when you do it, it's only to say he wasn't a good kid? What the actual *fuck*. I guess you're such a saint, you know, stealing from your work and teaching your daughter how to do the same. Boohoo, I'm sorry, me and your dead son are such disappointments!"

"He's not *dead*," she shrieks like she lost all sanity.

I think we both have.

"He is, Mom! He's dead and buried somewhere amongst all Volkov's victims because Dad couldn't pick between this hell of a town and his own family! We're never going to find his body, so either grieve or forget about him but stop holding on for fuck's sake! Do you have any idea what it does to me?"

"Don't tell me how I should deal with my child's disappearance."

"Your *child* is my brother! And this whole situation you're so desperate to get me out of started because I was looking for him! God, how could I have been so stupid? You were so adamant in telling everyone he couldn't be dead that I believed it. This is all *your* fault."

There's a stretched, unbearable silence where we both catch our breaths.

"Go to your room, you're grounded. No phone, no parties, no Emily, no hobbies. Nothing. I want you at school, at home, and at the café. You're grounded until graduation. Until I move you to UPenn. After that, you can do whatever you want."

The coldness and apathy in her words break my heart completely. She's given up on me. Completely. The tears that shine in her eyes don't even match the ones flooding my cheeks.

My throat is constricted but I manage to make it to my

room and slam my door before a deadly sob wracks my whole body.

At this moment, losing Jake or Nathan pales compared to losing my mom's love.

"To our badass captain for finally teaching North Shore bitches we aren't fucking scared of their asses!!!"

The crowd of Stoneview lacrosse players goes wild at Ciara's words and everyone downs their drinks for the tenth cheer of the night. I down my solo cup full of whatever cocktail Em made me. It's sweet enough that I don't really taste the alcohol and I've had way too many of these.

I couldn't believe it on Monday morning when Emily jumped me by our lockers to scream that we had won the tournament. The game against N.S. High was pushed to the afternoon and my team won. Without me, but they won.

I couldn't have known before because I've officially been phoneless for a week. Not just that, but Mom waits for me at the door when I come back from school. She drives me to and from the café for work and I've had no contact with anyone apart from school for a whole week.

So, on this Friday night, I decided to sneak out of the house for the first time in my life. I can't even imagine Mom's fury if she finds out, but I needed to celebrate our win with everyone. Who would have thought punching Billie Scott in the face would have made everyone in Stoneview Prep love me so much? But that's not why I'm so happy.

No, the reason I'm over the moon is standing right in front of me, getting her picture taken with her signed offer of a lacrosse scholarship to Duke. It's pretty much a miracle after everything that went down last Saturday, but I'm so happy for Rose. I don't think Nathan knows, otherwise, she probably wouldn't be here right now.

Two arms wrap around my waist and lift me up. I recognize Cole's drunken voice and I shriek like the typical drunk girl I am right now.

"You're so fucking perfect, 'Me," he mumbles in my ear and somehow I know he's just being a great friend and not hitting on me.

After the pre-tournament party and the state he saw me in, I think we both unofficially agreed our relationship would never go further than friendship.

I stumble when he puts me down. I really drank too much, and so has Em. I don't know how we're going to get home...but who cares right now?

"I need the restroom," Em shouts in my ear. "Come!"

I follow her to the bathroom on the second floor of the Bakers' house. The last time I was using one of Luke's guest bathrooms, it was to get my revenge on Jake. Tonight, I don't want to hear from or see him. It's enough that my mom lost it last time she confronted the Whites, but it's also a night where I want to enjoy myself free of drama. Jake is never free of drama.

"The room is spinning," Em giggles, sitting on the toilet seat, her lace panties around her ankles.

I laugh back at her and nod my head in agreement. Talking is so hard right now. Only the bass from the music downstairs makes it up to this room and it makes it all feel surreal.

"Should we do more shots?" Em suggests as she washes her hands.

"That sounds...like a really good idea," I reply before jumping on the spot.

"'Me..." she starts seriously.

"What?" I gulp. This sounds like drama, I don't want drama.

"I can't believe you punched someone in the face."

She explodes laughing and I'm close behind. Who would have thought?

Our walk down the hallway to try and reach the stairs is not exactly the easiest. Every few steps we can't help but laugh at the most ridiculous things. We have to hold onto the walls and I'm pretty sure we both end up rolling on the floor at some point. It doesn't stop us from hearing a familiar voice behind one of the doors, and more specifically the moans.

"Holy shit, it's Camila," Em whispers.

My heart drops in my stomach instantly. Is she with-

"She's not with Jake," Em insists. "I saw him in the backyard through the bathroom window."

"Oh..." I don't want to go back to feeling so happy because I now know it's not him, but I guess I still can't help it. "How do you even know what Camila sounds like when she's having sex?"

"I just know," Em nods like an old wise man with a hundred years of knowledge.

"Did she just say spit in my mouth?!" I choke.

"Yeah," Em shrugs. "What? Luke spits in my mouth all the time."

"Oh so you admit you're back with him?"

"Nuh-huh, we're not."

I roll my eyes at her words. Just fucking, I guess.

"You're gonna tell me big bad Jake White never spat in your mouth?" Em asks in shock.

"No!"

"And the devil incarnate Nathan White never spat in your mouth either..."

"Stop!" I chortle.

"Wow, I'm disappointed. And surprised."

We both explode in giggles again.

"Are you sure you want this?" A male's voice rises.

"Yes!"

"You remember your safeword, right?"

"Yes!" We hear Camila's voice through the door. *"Fucking hurt me!"*

"Oh shit," I whisper.

"I really want to know who it is!"

"Fuck!" She screams. *"Fuck I'm gonna come! I fucking love you when you do that. Shit! AH! I'm coming!"*

Both our eyes widen as we put our hands on our mouths so she doesn't hear us laughing.

"I'm traumatized," I squeak with teary eyes. "Please, let's go back downstairs."

She nods as she still chokes on her laughing fit. I hadn't even realized we were still on the floor.

We both get up, but after a step, we fall face to face with Jake, Luke, Chris, and Rose at the top of the stairs. The laughing stops straight away. Mine at least, they're all cackling from what they've just heard behind that door too.

It's always so weird to see all of them together. I almost forget they're the kings of our school. That it doesn't matter if Emily sleeps with Luke and I'm Jake's ex. It doesn't matter that I got close to Rose and that Chris used to be my friend. At the end of the day, seeing them together in all their beauty and God-like selves, they seem so unattainable. They look like you need a private member club card to talk to them.

Rose's beautiful smug smile spreads on her lips when

Chapter 15

she sees my friend and me, and I know she notices how Em looks at her. She knows she could have her in her bed without even trying.

Luke's eyes are completely on Em but I can see he's desperately trying to look unaffected. As if he didn't care about her. Chris is looking at both of us with his usual impassiveness. He's so calm for someone whom I saw take multiple shots tonight.

And Jake.

Jake's jet-black hair is tousled as usual. His biceps are stretching his white t-shirt and he crosses his arms when his gaze settles on me. His ocean blue eyes rack over my body but he doesn't show anything. I hate when he's like that.

When he's got his mask on, at least he looks happy. But when he's empty like that, I feel emptier.

The door behind Em and I open, and Camila comes out completely disheveled and clearly just fucked. But, oh, the shock when the person coming after her is none other than Landon.

Landon.

School yearbook Landon.

The kind of guy Camila would never be seen with. Every time he comes too close to her, or someone mentions him to her she finds a way to humiliate him.

It wouldn't be the first time I think Landon has the potential to be a handsome man. His piercing green eyes are mesmerizing. But just like a lot of teenagers, he doesn't really groom himself and has an uneven amount of hair that doesn't cover the whole of his cheeks yet. He looks skinny, hasn't fully hit puberty, and he looks like he rarely washes his hair. He could also use new glasses even though they're a designer brand. He hasn't been near me since Jake had threatened him before we even started dating, but the fear on his face when he sees Jake shows he hasn't forgotten about it.

"You have got to be fucking kidding me," Jake snaps.

The shock and embarrassment on Camila's face are heightened by her now scarlet cheeks. She panics and babbles a few words looking between Landon and Jake before finally saying, "Jake don't be mad."

What? Why would he be mad?

"I don't give a shit who you fuck, Cam. But you're not bringing your fucking garbage to our parties."

Jake pushes past me and Emily and grabs Landon by the neck of his shirt. "Why the fuck would you show your ugly-ass face here? Did you not take my threat seriously last time you touched Jamie?"

"Jake," I intervene. I put a hand on his shoulder, but he shrugs me away. "Why are you getting so mad?"

Maybe there is a slight pang of jealousy in me right now. Why does he care so much who Camila sleeps with?

"I'm sorry, man. I'll leave," Landon panics.

"*I'm sorry, man,*" Jake mocks him. "Fuck you're such a pathetic little shit."

The shock that travels through my body when Jake rears his arm and punches Landon in the face is freezing. He falls to the floor without a chance of defending himself.

Luke is on Landon the next second. He grabs him from the floor and pushes him up against the wall.

"I don't even remember inviting you here. Who the fuck would invite the school perv?"

"Luke!" Emile shouts.

"She did!" Landon whimpers looking at Camila. "We've been seeing each other on and off for weeks!"

"No, we haven't!" Camila whines. "He's lying!"

Chapter 15

"Chris, do something," I yell at him. This reaction is terrifyingly disproportionate.

"Don't worry about it," he mumbles back, watching as Luke and Jake beat Landon to the ground again.

He's meant to be the reasonable one. Instead, he's leaning against the banister, hands in his pockets. My eyes go to Rose, standing next to him but she avoids my gaze as if she knows she can't control *all three* of her boys. One she might be able to, but if they all make a decision, there's not much she can do about it.

"There we are!" Jake grunts as he kicks him in the ribs. "That beating was a long time coming, wasn't it? Did you enjoy making her your little sub-slut *again*?"

I don't know if it's because I'm drunk or because I've had very mixed feelings about Jake lately, but the rage that boils inside me right this second is all directed at him. Is he really mad because of what we heard? Because Landon enjoys dominating his girls? I stride to him as he takes a step back from Landon, satisfied with the bloody face he left him, and I grab him by the upper arm.

"You need to stop, you hypocrite."

He smiles down at me in all his smugness. "Something you want to mention maybe?"

I can feel my cheeks warming to a deep blush. He knows exactly what I mean but I'm not about to spell it out. Our night with Lik was closer to my limits than we'd ever been. Or maybe it was past my limits, but I keep adapting them to Jake.

I watch Luke and Chris surround Landon as he struggles down the stairs, I'm guessing leaving the house.

Camila looks at Em, Jake, and me before hurrying away but when she walks past Rose, the other White twin catches her by the elbow.

"If you bring that piece of shit to one of our parties again, it's going to be your beautiful face on the other end of my fists. You got that?" Rose threatens in her low voice. She lets her go and Camila leaves without a word.

"Drop it, Jamie," Rose tells me like she's reading my mind.

She heads down the stairs and my gaze lands on Jake again, I hadn't realized I'm still gripping his strong arm. He eyes my hand and looks back up at me, a winning look in his eyes. It's sparkling within the marine blue.

"You should check Luke isn't finishing Landon outside, Em," he says.

"If you think I'm going to leave my best friend with her sociopathic ex, you got me all wrong," she replies.

I chortle loudly as I watch Jake's face turn serious. He's annoyed because yet another person knows he's a number one psycho.

"I'm fine, Em," I smile at her. And I truly am.

I'm not scared of Jake.

16

JAMIE

Red Roses – Call Me Karizma

I made a mistake since Jake and I broke up.

I made a big mistake.

I stopped fearing him.

I understand that as soon as Emily leaves and I'm dragged into the closest room.

"What the hell are you doing?" I rage.

"Don't ever try to get in my way like that ever again," he seethes as he pushes me to the middle of the room, letting go of me and barring me from accessing the now locked door.

"Jake, are you seriously playing the bad boy card on me again? Don't you realize this is getting old? You get me alone, you scare me, it turns me on, we have sex and don't talk until our next altercation."

His gorgeous smile slowly spreads on his lips. "Who said I was going to have sex with you?"

"My bad, you often isolate me for a little gossip over tea."

His laugh is so genuine, goosebumps raise on my skin.

No, no, I can handle bad Jake.

I can't handle nice, genuine Jake. Not until I'm fully healed from our breakup. Which will probably be never.

"If you insist, I'll fuck you. But only after you learn your lesson," he grins.

"You don't teach me lessons. Not anymore."

"I did less than a week ago." His voice is back to the dark man he can be and my pussy throbs at the mention of last week.

Damn weak, desperate pussy. She wants sex, nothing else.

And looking at the only two men I ever slept with, she clearly doesn't care who gives it to her.

"Thanks for reminding me of exactly why you're a hypocrite. Beating up Landon when all he did was play rough with Camila *consensually*. Remind me the last time you asked my opinion about the way you play with me?"

His smile drops so quickly I shiver.

"Don't fucking compare me to that freak. I know how you like it, Jamie, you just hate that I know your body better than you do."

"Landon is not a freak. He clearly likes sex the same way you do. The only difference is that people find you hot and you are popular while you all treat Landon like he's trash. Why? Because he's not as attractive as you and your friends? How stupid we all are to have put all of you on a pedestal, you're all so fucked in the head. And you? You're the same kind of *freak* he is."

"I'm not like him, so shut your fucking mouth. If you ask me to stop, I stop. Except you never do."

He looks like he's seconds away from unleashing his wrath on me. Why does he get so angry when it's about Landon?

"God why are you so worked up about the guy! That big, bad bully act is getting so old, Jake!"

He takes a deep breath and his eyes soften slightly.

" I *hate* the guy because..." he scratches his throat. "Camila cheated on me with Landon. Multiple times over the two years we were together. And then when I moved on and had my eyes on you, he made a move on you too. So no, I'm not a *big, bad bully*, Jamie. If he thinks he can show up to my parties and fuck my ex in the guest bedroom, he's got another thing coming, trust me."

I gulp a little too loudly. I didn't know that. That...that must have hurt quite a lot. I can hardly believe beautiful Jake White, king of our school, feels threatened by bottom of the school Landon.

"I thought you didn't even know he existed before that day at the cafeteria," I say softly. He's just made himself so vulnerable by admitting what happened.

"Oh, I knew, believe me." His voice turns dark again. "So instead of always thinking you *know* everything because you believe you're Nancy Drew, try to stay in your lane. You thought you were such a brave girl tonight, didn't you? Next time you try to put yourself between me and some asshole I'm beating up, I will correct your fucking behavior in front of everyone. That clear?"

Of course he has to go back to being an asshole, that talk was a bit too genuine for him. Just one too many feelings.

I let out a loud laugh, cackling like a goose to show I'm mocking him.

"Correct my behavior? You really think I'm ever going to let you touch me again?"

"I don't know," he shrugs. "But you know what's great about us? I never ask your opinion about what I do to you. I wanted you scared and you started fearing me."

He takes a step closer, and I take one back.

"I wanted to fuck you and you let me."

Another step for him, another for me. The anticipation growing in my lower belly is everything I hate about myself.

"I wanted you to fall for me and you fell like a toddler trying to learn how to walk. But you know what the best part of all that is, my little Angel?"

He takes another step but when I try to take one back, I can feel a bed behind my knees. So I freeze and look up at him, jutting my chin, holding my head high as I look at him.

"The best part is you love it enough to always come back for more. Like a little masochist desperate for me to hurt her over...and over...and over again." He pushes me hard and I fall on the bed.

"That's not true," I breathe out as my back bounces on the mattress. His strong form is on top of me before I can move back up.

Did I even try to move back up?

He puts both hands on the mattress, on either side of my face, and looks down at me, his mouth way too close to mine.

"Tell me, Angel, if you're not always desperate for more pain. Why didn't you scream for help when Lik and I broke into your hotel bedroom? Why did you let Emily leave you alone with me tonight? Why aren't you pushing me away right now?"

"I–"

Because no matter what you do to me, I want you back.

Because I still think I can change you.

Because I can't move on.

Because I still love you.

"Why, Jamie?"

His voice is so harsh right now, it's not smug anymore. I

can't even look him in the eyes. I know he knows why. It's embarrassing, but it's the truth.

"Why don't you push me away?" he repeats.

I look up at him, his eyes are so hard on me he could break me with a look. He *is* breaking me. He always does that.

"Push me away, Jamie." This time, it's an order.

I can't, Jake.

I have to look away again.

I'm weak. I'm broken. I'm a puppet who will forever let this guy do whatever the hell he wants to me as long as it means he's thinking of me. As long as his attention is on me.

"Push me away, I said. Push me away!"

His hands are suddenly on my shoulders, shaking me while I do nothing, while I just lay there, limp.

"Do it for fuck's sake," he shouts at me. "I'm horrible to you! I broke you, push me away!"

But I don't do anything, because if his hands are on me, I can live with whatever he does.

I'm a lost cause.

I like bad people doing bad things to me.

I like it even better when it's Jake.

"FUCKING DO IT!" His voice breaks as he screams his last words.

His whole weight falls on mine and we lay like that for a few minutes, his arms wrapped so tightly around me I can barely breathe.

Then he whispers in my ear, "If you don't think you should stay away, then I haven't broken you hard enough."

I don't have time to ask what he means. His hand is in my hair fast as he gets off me and drags me off the bed. I fall on the floor in a scream and he's on me the next second, grabbing my hips and flipping me around. I go to push up, but I don't know why.

Or maybe I do. Maybe I just want to make sure he wants this so bad he'll impose it on me. That's the only way to know he wants it as much as I do.

"Spread your legs like the good little slut you are," he growls.

I spread my legs as he hikes my skirt up and around my hips. He doesn't push my panties down, he rips them and disappears long enough for me to turn around wondering where he went.

He reappears from the bathroom door with lube in his hand and settles behind me again. He puts the lube on the floor and takes his belt off.

I chuckle. "You don't need lube, I thought you knew these sorts of things make me wet."

He grabs my wrists, tying them behind my back with his belt.

"You're gonna need lube for the hole I'm planning to use."

I freeze on the spot.

"Wait," I panic, pulling at my wrists.

"Looks like someone is finally taking this seriously."

"Jake, we can't do this. Not here, not now. This isn't funny."

"Oh Angel, your fun ends where mine begins."

"At least let's go on the bed," I beg.

"Bitches belong on the floor."

He pulls my hips until my cheek rests properly on the carpet and ass exposed to him.

He pinches my ass cheeks painfully and I let out a cry.

"Stop it," he growls. "You know I love it when it hurts you."

Chapter 16

"You're scaring me," I insist.

But when his fingers spread my lips and he slides two fingers in my pussy, my complaints die out, turning into moans instead.

"I often wonder why being forced turns you on," he admits. "Trauma really destroys even the most beautiful souls."

He dips his fingers in and out of me, making me writhe with pleasure. The only moment he takes them out, his tongue replaces them. From behind, spreading my ass cheeks, he reaches my clit with his god-like kisses. He flicks my clit with his tongue, he makes out with my pussy, working me up, making me grind on his face when he slows down.

He renders me a slave to the pleasure he can give me, and I let go without even a hint of regret. His tongue leaves my pussy for a second, leaving me panting and desperate for an orgasm. When he touches me again, he's spreading my wetness from my pussy all the way to my tight hole with his tongue. I jerk at the unexpected pleasure and his chuckle between my ass cheeks makes me shiver.

With my cheek against the carpet, I can feel how the bass from downstairs makes the floor tremble.

His thumb replaces his tongue against the rim of my asshole, and I feel him circling around it, my wetness making it all slick.

"God, you're making me so hard, Angel. That really is a power of yours."

I hadn't even realized he took off his pants, so the surprise is intense when he enters my pussy in one hard thrust. I scream in pain and pleasure.

"I trained your little pussy to adapt to me. I can do the same with that tight ass of yours."

It's hard to take a new breath when he starts moving slowly enough to make me squirm in all directions.

"Fuck me," I groan into the carpet.

"The only thing I'll be fucking tonight is your ass."

"Don't," I mewl. "I'm not ready."

"Tell me to stop then. Tell me I crossed the fucking line and I need to get off you. Do something about it, Jamie." He thrusts hard. "Talk to me," he orders before going slowly again. I can feel his hips rolling behind me.

"Make me come, please." I pull at my binds, desperate to touch myself.

He laughs. "What the fuck do you think this is? I don't give a shit if you come, I just want to hear you scream."

He fucks me harder but not faster, his strokes go deeper, pushing me, making it hard to stay in the position he put me in. I feel his thumb circling the rim of the tight hole again and I groan loudly when he starts pushing in. It doesn't hurt, it adds to the filthiness of our sex and it's uncomfortable. But I like uncomfortable.

His thumb goes in and out, circling and stretching, and I moan at the strange sensation. His dick never stops pumping in and out of my pussy, making me beg for release.

"When I'm done fucking your ass, Angel, make sure to remember how bad it hurt. Make sure to remember I didn't stop when you begged me to, and I enjoyed your pain. That's who I am, do you understand? I enjoy people's pain above everything else. Especially yours."

Fear grips me when I feel him spread lube over my back hole. I feel two of his fingers prepping me for stretching.

"It's not too late to tap out...push me away, Jamie. Before I go too far."

But his voice is not as convincing as when he ordered it earlier. No, now it's strained with pleasure. The words meant

Chapter 16

as a chance to stop it all sound like a plea to let him keep going.

And he feels so good inside me...

When I feel his dick leaving my pussy and lining up with my ass, I freeze.

"Wait—"

"Time's up."

He pushes in slowly, agonizingly slow. I feel the muscle spread, inch by inch as he inserts himself. It's more than uncomfortable this time, it burns, it's painful, it's unbearable.

"You're hurting me," I cry out. "I can't..." I attempt to crawl away, trying to move my body forward despite my arms being tied behind my back. His hands land harshly on my hips, holding me tightly, bruising my skin.

"Don't fucking move," his voice comes out between gritted teeth.

Holding me in place, he pushes further, mercilessly.

"Jake," I yelp. "Please..." I can't breathe.

One hand stays on my hip and the other one comes around.

My whole world turns upside down when he rubs my clit with his expert thumb.

"Shit," I moan. He's kept me on the edge for so long, this feels like a gift sent from heaven.

He circles my clit a few times as he keeps pushing from behind and the pain turns into unbelievable pleasure.

"Oh my god," I rasp as I feel myself tighten around him. "I'm gonna come..."

But his thumb leaves my clit, and he enters my pussy with his fingers as he starts thrusting slowly with his dick.

The whole thing is so overwhelming my head starts to spin.

"Please let me come," I moan. "Please..."

I'm panting hard when he starts thrusting faster with both his fingers and his dick.

"Fuck, Jamie..." he groans in pleasure, and it makes me moan harder.

His thumb finds my clit again, only the pad of his fingers teasing the entrance of my pussy and he starts thrusting harder and harder.

"Jake..." I breathe out. "Jake..."

My breathing shortens, accelerates. My skin prickles, the tension reaches its limit, my eyes roll to the back of my head, and I scream in pleasure as I come around him, squeezing him so tight I feel him accelerate and groan his release.

Everything suddenly stops but I can't seem to come back down from my high. He plays with my clit a little longer and I shudder from the aftermath of my orgasm. I have never hit such highs in my life and reality feels completely distorted.

He slowly pulls out of me, reminding me of the pain I had so quickly forgotten. I hiss as he eases himself out and I feel his cum leaking out straight away.

He unties my wrists and I hear him sliding his belt back on.

I can't move. I am too spent, in too much pain, still trembling from the unthinkable pleasure. All I do is lose the position I was in and lay flat on my front, still on the floor.

His feet appear in my vision, and I look up at him as he squats in front of me. He caresses my cheek as he talks.

"Now I'm going to leave you like this, Angel. Thoroughly used and helpless. I'm not going to help you clean up or recover, I'm not going to be sweet and it's going to break your heart all over again. That's your lesson tonight: don't let me come close to you, it only brings you pain."

17

JAKE

I Think I'm OKAY - Machine Gun Kelly, YUNGBLUD & Travis Barker

I push my front door closed with my foot, not bothering to turn around. I should have. The click of the gun behind my head makes me freeze in fear.

"Get on your knees, boy." Bianco's voice is far from the usual fake kindness he puts on.

No, it's cold enough to send my heart and my brain into panic.

I'm glad I've gone cold again. It allows me to not show anything when he pushes the gun into my head.

I fucked up. Somehow, at some point, he found out I talked to Jamie. I haven't been careful. The parties, the tournament, I've been talking to her in front of people I know I can't trust. In front of kids from the North Shore Crew.

Fuck. Bianco waited at my house to surprise me from behind. How typical of him.

Or maybe...maybe he knows I've been looking into Aaron Williams. Since he told us that he saw him in Stoneview, I've been asking around. I asked people from NSC, I asked people who fight at the Death Cage, I asked guys from N.S. High. Shit, I even asked people from the Kings' Crew. The guy is like a ghost.

If someone told Bianco I was looking for the man he thinks is killing his most trusted soldiers...

Shit.

I slowly fall to my knees in my own foyer and wince as they hit the black and white polished tiles.

"A little birdie told me you weren't taking my threats seriously. Tell me they're wrong."

"They're wrong," I say through gritted teeth.

Control yourself. It's the only thing you still have control over.

"Lie down on your front."

"Mateo," I argue. "Let's talk."

The only response I get is his gun shoving my shoulder. So I execute. The tiles are cold against my cheek, and I'm instantly thrown back to the times he would crush my head against the marble floor of his villa. I squeeze my eyes shut and open them again.

It's okay. It's going to be okay.

He's not going to kill me. Of course he's not, but the pain I know he's capable of inflicting can feel worse than death.

"Hands behind your head."

I follow his order quickly. As long as he's busy with me, he's not going to ask if Ozy is home. He won't go find her in her room where she is waiting for me with Chris.

I'm starting to understand why Nate keeps boys away from her or why he beat up Jason. If Mateo finds her with one of them, he'll hurt her. He'll hurt her badly and I can't begin to imagine that.

I feel him step beside me and he's suddenly kicking my legs apart. My breathing accelerates and it takes everything

Chapter 17

to bring it back down. Panic isn't the solution, shutting down emotions is.

He puts his expensive, leather Oxford shoes between my shoulder blades and I can't help the groan that escapes my lips when he squats, putting most of his weight on the leg that is on my back.

It's getting real fucking hard to breathe, so I stay silent. There is no reasoning with him until he decides he's done.

"Not taking my threats seriously. That's stupid," he chuckles sarcastically.

He throws some pictures on the floor, in front of my face. Me and Jamie on the lacrosse field after she punched Billie. Her arriving at this house with Nate. Her and her mom talking to Nate and me after the tournament. And the latest one, her leaving Luke's house last Friday. It was a week ago, and I still haven't heard anything from her. She's probably staying away for good now.

Shit.

"Not taking my threats seriously and then lying about it. That's damn suicidal. Did you really think I wasn't going to have her followed?" He presses harder on my upper back, making me hiss. "See that position you're in, Jake? That's how I'm going to have your girl when all my guys take their turn on her."

Images of Jamie in this same position make me feel sick to my stomach.

"I'll stay away from her. I promise," I wince.

"Do you understand the kind of danger you're putting my organization in if you let this girl close to you?"

No. I really fucking don't.

Bianco is the most paranoid motherfucker to live on this planet. He thinks everything and anything is a danger to his *organization*, and we all must pay the price of his sick paranoia.

"*Mateo!*" My sister's voice brings both of us back to reality and my heart goes back to trying to escape my ribcage.

It was almost a shriek and I already know she's going to speak to him in Italian by the way she pronounced his name.

"*Lascialo andare, per favore.*" 'Let him go, please.' Her Italian is so perfect. Mine isn't because he only ever cared about teaching her.

His foot leaves my back and I get back up, dizzy from the fear and spending time on the cold floor.

"Rose," he smiles. His voice is back to a sickly-sweet drawl but I'm sweating in fear when I see her at the bottom of the stairs with Chris.

"What are you doing here?" she asks in her high voice. The one she saves for him, the innocent one that he loves so much.

"I was just visiting. Jake and I needed to have a chat, and I missed you, my beautiful flower." His words are daggers as he finishes his sentence, "I see you were too busy to miss me."

Chris' brows furrow in confusion. He knows who Bianco is, he knows how much we loathe him, but I know Ozy never talked to him about what he used to do to her, what he started doing again. I don't even know if he's ever seen the letters he branded on the back of her neck. If he has, he never mentioned it to me.

"I hate your hair like that," Mateo insists, spitting venom at her.

Her hair is always down when she's not around him and

he can't stand not seeing the brand he left on her, whereas she can't stand showing it.

"I know," she replies in a trembling voice. Her hands automatically go to her wrists, looking for a hairband that isn't there. "I've got a hairband in my room. I'll be back."

"Don't bother." The disappointment in his voice could break a weaker soul.

"Nate isn't here," I jump in. "We talked. You can leave."

My eyes can't stop going to Chris. His seem to have lost their usual honey color and turned a few shades darker. They've never looked so brown.

Mateo doesn't reply to me. He tucks his gun back in the holster he's wearing under his suit jacket and takes his time to walk to Rose. I start walking too but her hard eyes stop me in my tracks. Why does she do this? Why does she let him get close? She knows what follows.

He's barely reached her that his palm slaps her hard enough to resonate in the immense foyer. She tries to stay straight but her hand shoots to her now bright red cheek.

"You look disgusting," he seethes. "I–" He doesn't get to finish his sentence because Chris is on him, grabbing him by the neck and pushing him until Bianco's back hits the wall.

"Chris!" My twin shouts.

"Fucking touch her again. Go on, fucking try!" My friend's voice is hoarse with anger. I've never seen him like that.

We always joke about who would finally make calm Christopher Murray flip. We just never realized it would be that bad when he did. He's much taller and bigger than Mateo, and when he grabs him by the collar of his crisp white shirt, lifts him, and slams him into the wall, Bianco hits the back of his head.

Rose runs to them, grabbing Chris' shoulder in an attempt to pull him away but I grab her.

"Let him," I growl.

"That's not gonna help us, Jake," she seethes at me, but I don't let her go.

I need this, and if I'm too weak and Chris has to take over then I don't care. As long as Bianco suffers.

"He's got a fucking gun!" she screams at me.

Looking at the position he's in right now, with Chris practically choking him into unconsciousness, I don't think he's got the strength to reach for his gun.

The front door opens to Nate and Sam, and everything happens too quickly to do anything. Nate pulls out his gun faster than I can understand, pointing it at our friend.

"Don't!" I shout at him, fear gripping me.

Sam is on Chris anyway. He pulls him away and punches him in the jaw, making him stumble back. I let go of Rose to jump on Sam. I manage to hit him in the ribs, making him retreat slightly but the whole thing is a fucking mess.

Until Mateo pulls out his gun. Everything freezes when he aims it at my best friend, my brother.

Chris steps away from Sam, raising his hands in front of him in surrender.

"Do you know what people who rise against me have to say about it?" Bianco says in a voice colder than arctic.

Chris' gulp is loud in my ears. He shakes his head in negation.

"I don't know, they don't get to live to tell the tale," Mateo concludes.

"Mateo, please," Ozy begs in a shaking voice. "Let's talk. He didn't know...he didn't know who you were."

"Is that your boyfriend?" Bianco asks her in all seriousness. That fucking pedophile.

"No!" she almost shouts in panic. "We...that..."

I shake my head with her as she speaks. "He's our previous foster brother. Mateo, lower your gun."

He wouldn't kill him, right? He can't do that. He's already ruined our lives, already tore us away from the only family that ever loved us.

"Please, just let him go home," Rose pleads.

She says another string of words in Italian. I don't catch much, she's too fast and says too much. I know she's just as scared as I am right now. If anything happens to Chris...

I swallow the rock that has formed in my throat. I can't even imagine.

"Come here, Rose," Bianco orders.

She walks to him in the least threatening way possible, slowly, almost on her toes.

"I'll let him go. But you know this is going to cost you, right?"

"I know," she whispers.

His free hand slides underneath her thick black hair and wraps around the back of her neck. "Whose initials are those?"

"Yours," she replies instantly.

"That's right."

I have to look away. I feel too sick, my throat is too tight. His other hand is still pointing a gun at my best friend, and I have to watch silently as my twin trembles from fear and disgust. My heart accelerates, the room spins, and it takes all my strength to stay upright. To not run to him and bash his head against the wall, to not put any of their lives at more risk.

"Nate. Your office. Now," Bianco concludes as he lowers his gun.

He lets go of Rose and she stands still until Nate, Sam,

and Bianco have disappeared into Nate's office. As soon as the door closes, she practically teleports next to Chris, bumping into his chest as he takes her in his arms.

"You need to leave," she speaks, her words muffled in the curve of his neck. But the way his arms tighten against her, I don't think he'll leave without her. The way his eyes won't leave mine, he won't leave without me either.

"You should go, Chris." I know he can hear the pain in my voice.

"You already know my answer."

"We can't come with you," I insist. I'm so cold, so shut off from any emotions. He should take the hint and just leave.

He smiles at me, takes a couple of steps back, and sits down on the first step of the staircase.

"I guess we can all wait until they come out of that office. Fingers crossed I won't take a bullet to the head tonight."

"Don't do this." Ozy follows him and she settles between his legs, putting her hands on his shoulders as he looks up at her. "This is nothing," she reassures him. "He doesn't scare me. He only does if I know he can get to you. You don't want to be involved in any of this, Chris."

My friend shakes his head. "I can't. I can't leave you guys with him."

My twin and I exchange a look and silently agree. We can't have Chris here. It's too dangerous. We'll put our lives at risk if it means he'll leave.

"Fine, we'll come home with you," I huff.

"We'll have to come back here tonight though," Ozy concludes.

Chris nods and we all leave.

. . .

Chapter 17

"Are you okay?" Chris asks Rose as we all settle in the den in his basement.

She nods and chuckles. "Come on. I thought you knew I'm stronger than that."

He shakes his head in return. "Guys, you can't go back," he insists.

"There's nothing in that house we can't handle," I lie.

Rose and I share a look and she nods. "What happened today..." I can see in her eyes the exact moment her heart breaks for offering a white lie to our best friend. "It never happened before."

"Don't fucking lie to me," Chris barks at the same time as his hand slams on the marble coffee table. "Do you think I never saw the initials he branded on you? You think I didn't see the bruises you desperately try to hide from everyone?"

"Your hero complex is getting real old," she growls back. She really hates being caught lying.

"You don't mind my 'hero complex'," he makes sure to air-quote the insult she always throws at him, "when you sleep in my room three times a week because you need to isolate yourself from the world. Because it gets too much. Because you feel unsafe out there. Anyone else Rose, lie to anyone else, but you know your bullshit doesn't get past me."

"It's not bullshit, he never slapped me. So I repeat: what happened today had never happened." Her voice is barely a whisper as she adds, "He never went for my face before."

"I don't *care* what he goes for. You're not going back, neither of you."

She ignores him and turns to me. "What was he doing at the house? What did you do?"

"I'm sorry," I wince, going through Bianco's warning in my head all over again. "I...fucked up."

"Does this have anything to do with Jamie?" she asks.

What *doesn't* have to do with Jamie? My whole life is about her. She's all I think about, all I dream about and every time I let my thoughts wander, they go to her...and to why I can't have her.

I need to tell Ozy about Aaron. I need to tell her the things Bianco threatened to do. I need to tell her the conversation I had with him and Nate the morning I was released from the hospital.

"Jamie needs to be kept away from all this," I simply say. "At all costs."

"Fucking around with her is not really gonna help," Chris replies.

"I know," I snap back. "It's hard, okay? I'm trying to stay away from her. But every time I let my guard down, she's there. She wants us to be together. She wants to understand things I can't explain, to know about the past."

I take a deep breath, trying to gain back control over my wild heart.

"She wants to heal me. And you know what the worst thing is? I want to let her. And I can't. So no matter what, I have to push her away."

"You're being too hard on her," Chris adds. "You're being selfish and you need to let go for good, Jake. Not just pretend to let go and then keep her around for personal pleasure."

"You know what pisses me off," I rage as I stand up. "You never approved of our relationship."

"No, never," he admits in a calm voice.

As soon as my blood starts boiling, his levels off like he's some sort of meditating monk that can't get angry.

Chapter 17

"Get over your jealousy, Chris! She was into you and you rejected her."

I start pacing the room like a crazy man and he shakes his head at me.

"I should have never let you kiss her. I should have never involved you. You kept pretending you weren't interested but you jumped on the occasion to fuck with her. So what is it now? You want me to let her go so you can jump in? Don't you have your amazing secret girl to deal with? Is her pussy not enough for you anymore?"

Ozy shakes her head at me before throwing it back in frustration. Yeah, maybe I'm losing my fucking mind.

"Don't include my girlfriend in this," he warns me in a lower voice. "I'm not jealous. I told you *and Jamie*, countless times, that I'm not interested in her. I've never been. She's a dear friend and you went in there like a wrecking ball."

He frowns darkly at me before throwing more truths my way.

"She's way too good for you and she's been through too much. I shared with you what happened to her dad and brother so you'd understand she doesn't need any more trouble in her life, and instead of doing that, you went and ruined her further. And now, even when you know she's in danger, you can't get your dick to stay down? Come on, man, if you really loved her, you would have cut all ties by now."

Ouch.

That really fucking hurts.

Probably because it's true.

I love Jamie. I am so in love with her the world stops spinning when she's not around me. Yet I can't get myself to let her go when I know I'm putting her life at risk?

I can't let Jamie love me anymore. I can't let her come back to me and give her hope by sleeping with her or even talking to her. And I know there's only one way to get her to stay away and that is if she truly hates me. I love her, and so I have to let her go.

"Let's get some food," Ozy's raspy voice cuts through my thoughts, and Chris and I exchange a look.

I nod, silently telling him he was right. He knows he's not going to get an apology from me. We need to put our heated discussion aside and jump on the fact that my sister wants to eat. Our life-long battle to get her to feed herself is more important than our argument.

"Lila's?" Chris asks Rose, perfectly knowing she won't say no to her favorite Vietnamese restaurant.

"Now we're talking," she smiles.

When the front door rings, I grab my wallet and head for the door. But it's not the food. That's okay, it's better than the food.

"Bro, that's a great surprise," I smile as I hug Luke hello.

I mess Ella's hair next to him and she sticks out her tongue at me.

"You're a child," I chuckle.

"I am when you treat me like one."

"Why are you here? Don't you have a playdate at the sandbox?"

Luke laughs as they both walk in. "Dad came for the weekend. Just him, God knows why. I've had enough patronizing and being put down for the evening."

I grimace at the light tone he uses for such a serious topic. Luke is being Luke, trying to pretend it's all fine when his dad has probably spent the entire afternoon and evening denigrating him.

"We ordered from Lila's," I tell them as we walk back to the kitchen. "Enough for an army so hopefully Ella's bottomless stomach can be satisfied."

Chapter 17

She playfully punches me in the arm in response. "But did you order enough summer rolls?"

"You're going to fight with Chris for those."

When we're all set in the dining room with our food, Chris leaves and comes back with two bottles of Jack Daniels.

"This is a bad idea," Ella mutters.

"For you maybe," he smiles back.

"This is a great idea," I beam.

"No," she insists. "You guys get unbearable when you're in these states. You all clearly had a shit day and you're going to get annoyingly crazy drunk."

"Uncontrollable drunk," I confirm.

"Start a riot drunk," Luke adds.

"And you'll be here to take care of us," Ozy chips in. "You're the sweetest."

Chris ignores our conversation as he opens the first bottle and fills up four tumblers.

He passes them around in silence and then looks at all of us. "No matter what happens, we'll always have our friendship. We'll always have each other's backs. Right?"

We all nod, bright smiles on our faces, as Ella shakes her head.

"Thanks, El's for looking after us tonight." He winks at her and downs his drink.

We all follow, downing and hitting the tumblers on the table. We down another one and start eating.

Ella shrieks as I extend my arms, lifting her up. "Don't drop me!"

I'm lying down on the faux-fur rug in the den, bench

pressing her. I can't even remember how this bet started. Sometime after we finished the first bottle of whiskey.

Ella is an amazing cheerleader, and she can easily keep her toned body in a perfect plank as I bring her up and down for the second time. She's keeping her arms straight by her side and her legs crossed over at her ankles. With a hand behind her neck and one tightly wrapped high around her upper thigh, I lift her up and down a second time.

"Fucking hell, El's. You're so much heavier than you look," I say through gritted teeth as I repeat the movement a couple more times.

I'm hot from the effort and alcohol. The tipsiness forces a smile on my face, and I laugh with her when I suddenly drop her, and she crashes on my chest.

"Jake!" she shouts, playfully slapping my chest.

"You moved!" I cackle back.

"That was seven," Luke says as he pours everyone another glass.

Everyone except Ella of course. She hasn't touched a drop of alcohol tonight, with her brother's watchful eyes on her.

"Two more than you," I smile at him.

We all down our glasses and turn to Chris who's taking his t-shirt off. My best friend really is a big guy. It's more than his six-foot-four figure. He trains two hours every morning at Stoneview Prep's gym. He's not part of the lacrosse team but he always exercises on his own. He's a runner and an amazing weightlifter, a rare combination, but that means he's zero fat and pure muscles.

"Alright, who wants to see the master at work," he jokes arrogantly.

I like drunk Chris. I like when he lets his asshole side

out, rather than the calm, boring guy who doesn't get involved in the craziness.

He downs another glass, lays down on the floor, and waves at Ella to come close. I don't miss her and my sister ogling Chris' hard-earned muscles.

"You should not be allowed to take your top off," Ozy lets out on a breath.

We all laugh at her, and she looks up in surprise.

"Did I say that out loud?" she giggles.

She fucking *giggles*. She is so drunk.

It feels amazing to be ourselves for one evening. This is better than any party, any drug-induced state. This, right here, just the four of us and Ella, is pure happiness.

Chris starts lifting Ella up and down, his hand can practically wrap all around her thigh. She is so focused on staying tense that she doesn't realize the number of times she goes up and down.

He puts her down gently as Luke and Rose jump up and down on a corner sofa.

"That's twelve! The sweet boy kicked our asses, Jakey!" Luke shouts.

I sip on another glass of amber liquid, watching as Chris stands up and pounds his chest with his right fist.

"You guys don't even compete in my category. What do I win? Do I win the girl?"

He bends over for a split second, barely enough to push his shoulder against Ella's hip, and picks her up caveman style.

"Chris!" she shrieks as her body tips upside down. She thumps her fists against his back as he goes up the stairs with her.

"Luke, thanks, bro. I'll bring her back soon," Chris says as he leaves.

Ozy is rolling on the floor laughing when Luke kicks into a sprint after them.

"Murray, I'll bury you alive." But the humor in his voice makes us all laugh.

Another bottle later, we're all by the pool. I'm so drunk, I slur enough words that it's hard to understand me. None of us is very clear to be completely honest. Only Ella is sober. She is now wearing one of Chris' t-shirts, and pants from Ozy, her hair still wet from when Chris threw her in the pool.

Chris and Ella have started a competition of who has the best hidden talent. Ella showed us some of her insane cheerleading skills and tumbled up and down the backyard. I walked the whole length of the backyard on a handstand. Ella turns to Ozy as I jump back on my feet.

"Rose, do that thing where you tell us all the ingredients in something!"

Lying face down on one of the loungers, Ozy lifts her head and looks Ella dead in the eyes before answering a plain and simple, "No."

We all explode laughing except Ella.

"Come on! The guys have the muscles, show them you got the brain."

"I don't need to show them, they know I'm smarter than the three of them combined *and* I can take them all down if I want to."

"That sounds slightly impossible," Ella retorts. "I'm pretty sure you'd fly away if Chris blows on you."

Rose raises two fingers and lifts her thumb, imitating the universal sign for a gun. She pretends to shoot at Chris. "Big target, he'd be down in no time."

"You can shoot guns?"

"Perfect aim," my sister confirms in her calm raspy voice.

I know she's gone past-caring drunk or she would have never mentioned shooting guns.

"No fucking way," Ella explodes. "That is *so* cool, Rose. I want to see!"

On any normal night, Chris would have shut the idea down. He wouldn't want Ozy to jump back into our past. Who knows what sort of PTSD she suffers from having shot her own brother? Who knows what will be brought back from her shooting sessions with Bianco?

But we're drunk, we're happy, and we're not conscious of potential danger right now.

"We could use my parents'," Chris suggests in a casual drunken voice as if this is the best idea ever. "They've got some sort of handgun in a safe in the subterranean garage. I think it's a Smith something."

His words are blurred by the alcohol in his blood system, his eyes heavily hooded by the shots of endorphins we're all getting tonight by being together.

"They've got a 9mm Smith & Wesson M&P Shield Plus. It's a handy little thing," my sister replies.

"I'm sorry *what*?" Ella says with a huge smile on her face.

"I don't want to know how you know that," Chris adds.

"Your dad showed it to me in case I ever needed to defend you two babies against anything."

Chris and I explode laughing until we realize she's dead serious.

"That reaction was priceless," Luke chuckles.

"Okay are we going to shoot shit or what?" Ella insists.

"You're the reason kids keep dying in our country, El's," her brother tells her.

"Rose said she was good at it. I just wanted to see if it was true," she pouts in return.

"Let's do this," I say as I get up from the stoned ground by the pool. "Show Ella your hidden talent, Ozy."

I don't even know how we got into the garage the Murrays have under their house. The lights were too bright and the walls too white, so we turned on the red lights and are now all silently staring at Chris as he types the code to his parents' safe.

He takes out the black handgun that is slightly smaller than mine and turns to Ozy. She grabs it, steps in front of him, and grabs the pack of bullets inside.

"I'm pouring more drinks," Luke says behind me.

A few seconds later we're all cheering together before Chris opens a hidden door to another room. We all walk in and my eyes widen at the small shooting range Thomas and Hannah Murray have hidden under their house.

"How have I never seen this in my life?" I ask my best friend.

"Meh, it's just a silly hobby of theirs. I discovered it by accident."

"So...Stoneview," Ella says as she runs a hand on the cemented walls.

There is already the black silhouette of a man on white paper on the other side of the long room. A target I know my twin is going to destroy meticulously.

"This is so cool," Ella giggles as she gets giddy on the spot.

She's standing too close to Ozy and I'm about to grab her arm to pull her back when Chris steps in, wraps two arms around her waist, picking her up and bringing her against the wall to join Luke and me.

"So what sort of cool tricks can you do?" Ella asks. "Can

you draw a heart or something?"

We all laugh as Rose loads the gun, a smirk tracing the outline of her lips.

"Whatever you want, sweet Ella," Rose replies calmly.

"Just impress me."

"Ozy, you're drunk. Be careful," I warn in a flash of consciousness. It's gone as fast as it came.

She smiles at me, turns around, and aims the gun at the target.

Bang. Bang. Bang. Bang. Bang.

She pauses to find her initial position again and lifts her aim slightly.

One. Two. Three. Four. Five.

She releases the magazine and puts it on the counter in front of her, then the gun away from it.

She presses a button, and it brings the target all the way to us. She takes it down, kisses it, leaving a mark of the red lipstick she was wearing today on the paper, and walks to Ella.

"There. Just for you."

We all look at the target, our jaws hanging low. She shot in the heart five times in the exact same spot, and in the middle of the head five times in the exact same spot. Not one bullet had a different trajectory from the other.

"That is insane. Rose wins the hidden talent competition," Ella shouts.

Up one floor, we settle in the basement den again. We dance to all the music Ella puts on, pose for group pictures, and build human pyramids to impress her with our horrific cheerleading level. We spend the rest of the night drinking way too much. I don't know what time it is when I feel the room spinning from laughing and the alcohol. What was I even worried about today? I have my friends, and I love them so much. No matter what, we'll always protect each other.

My eyes lock with my sister's. God, I love her so much. I can't let anything happen to her. She's been through so much, we both have. That worriless smile she's had on her face all night long. The giggles full of naïve happiness. This is what we deserve.

"Hug time," Luke announces.

"Let's put Ella in the middle," I add.

"No!" she complains.

We don't leave her a choice. It's just too much fun to annoy her. Chris is on her in the next second, grabbing her by the hips and dragging her to Luke and me. We all settle around her as we start huddling in a big hug until she's completely squished between us.

"You guys are so fucking drunk," she whines.

That we are.

"But you love us so much though," Chris replies just before Ella loses her footing and slips and falls to the floor, taking us all down with her.

"Shit, guys," Luke says as he looks over at the coffee table. "We drank four bottles of whiskey."

"You damn idiots," Ella mumbles. "That's one each."

There's a long comfortable silence as we all slightly drift to sleep.

I'm staring at the blank ceiling when Chris' drunken voice rises again.

"Jakey, when we wake up tomorrow..."

"I know."

"You have to let her go, man."

"I know," I whisper this time, my heart squeezing and begging me not to forget about how much it loves Jamie. "It's just hard."

Chapter 17

"We'll be here for you," Luke adds. "Always, bro."

I only nod at his words, my throat tightening, my body knowing that I will have to cut her out of my life. Completely this time. If I don't, I won't be able to resist.

"There'll be others," Ella says. "She's amazing, but you will get to meet so many other amazing girls in your future."

None like her though.

Ozy doesn't add anything, and I know it's because she doesn't agree with them. She knows Jamie enough to get what I'm feeling and how special what we had was to me.

There's only one Jamie Williams. Only one Jamie who has so many qualities and flaws that balance each other perfectly for me. Only one girl who is broken enough that she accepted me for everything I was. Who forgave me for what I did to her, who loved me despite the secret past I kept from her, despite how it has shaped me with darkness, coldness, and hardness.

No one will ever love me like Jamie did.

No one will ever love her like I do.

But on Monday, I will break her heart. I know exactly how, and she will hate me forever for it.

"Who wants tattoos?" Rose suddenly drops.

"Fuck. Jake, wake up." Ozy's voice is way too loud for my pounding head.

I grumble a complaint, grabbing a pillow to hug it tight. Why does my right arm hurt? Did I burn myself yesterday?

"I have five miscalls from Nate," my sister insists in a groggy voice. I don't think she's been awake for much longer than I have.

"Can't we just tell him to fuck off? If we hide here

forever, they might leave us alone."

"Get up," she orders. "Where's Chris?"

"Rosalind WHITE!!" Chris' furious voice rises from his bathroom.

"That'll be you," I chuckle. I can't remember the last time anyone called my sister by her full name.

She jumps out of Chris' bed and almost trips over my limp body lying on the floor. I can't move, everything hurts. Especially my arm. Probably a mix of all the alcohol we drank and sleeping on the floor next to Chris' bed. As if he doesn't have enough spare rooms in this house.

"Oh no," she whispers in panic. "I fucked up. Shit. Jake."

I sit up to find her pointing at something on her forearm.

"I can't see shit, Ozy," I mumble. "I took my contacts out, what is it?"

She takes a step toward me, and I can't help a gasp as I explode laughing. "What the fuck is this!"

Next to some of her other tattoos, she's got a new tattoo of a miniature bottle of Jack Daniel's.

Wait.

I get up quickly enough to make the room spin.

"Rose," I growl as I look exactly where my arm has been stinging.

Unsurprisingly, I've got the exact same tattoo as her on my shoulder. "What the fuck is wrong with you?!" I shout.

Sam is the one that had gifted her a tattoo gun and ink for our birthday. He used to teach her when we lived at Bianco's, and she decided to use us as her canvas yesterday.

We both turn to Chris as he walks out of the bathroom. He extends his arm in front of Rose, showing us the inside of his forearm. The same tattoo is inked onto his skin forever.

"Oh shit," Ozy can't help a laugh and she puts a hand in

front of her mouth to try to calm herself down. She's desperately trying to hide her smile.

"Rose, I'm going to end you."

"You took advantage of us," I add purely to get her into more trouble.

"Shut up," she laughs. "I offered tattoos, you all jumped on the occasion. People pay good money for tattoos like that."

"For what? Tattoos with wonky lines? This is so shit!"

"I *was* very drunk," she admits. "But I didn't force anyone."

"I need some food," I complain.

We walk down to the kitchen, dragging our bodies like zombies through an apocalypse.

Luke is already in there with Ella. He's nursing a cup of coffee at the kitchen island and Ella is making breakfast.

"You fucked up big time." Chris insists. "You know I want to be a lawyer. These things are forever. Do you really see me defending someone in court with this stupid tattoo on my arm? It's a bottle of Jack Daniel's for god's sake."

"Are you really going to go to court with your forearms showing? What kind of harlot does that!"

"I'm not joking," he chastises her. "What kind of unprofessionalism is that!"

"Would a bottle of Macallan have been more professional?"

I can barely hold my chuckle at her stupid joke. For a split second, Chris forgets how to act human as he growls at Ozy.

He pounces at her and wraps his arm around her throat from behind, pulling until her back is flushed against his chest.

"The valiant never taste of death but once," he jokes,

quoting his favorite play.

Ozy's eyes light up with more mischief, ready to act out more of Julius Cesar but Ella cuts them off.

"Chris, sunny side up?"

He lets go of Ozy to move over to Ella. "Please, Sweets," he replies.

There's a silent pause as we all turn to him.

"Did you just call her Sweets?" I say as I pour milk over my cereal.

He shrugs. "Of course I did. She's the only one that's sweet to me. Luke, why are you not complaining about your tattoo? Don't tell me you've been spared."

"I like my tattoo," he smiles.

"I don't remember doing it on you." Ozy runs her fingers through the bird's nest that has currently replaced her hair and sits down opposite Luke.

"I think I was the last one. I don't remember really well."

"Show us," I say with a mouth full of cereal.

Ella puts three eggs on a plate, her back to us. Luke gets up, turns his back to us, and lowers the gym shorts he's wearing until his right ass cheek is showing. The Jack Daniel's bottle is even wonkier than Chris'. The laughs he gets from all of us is short-lived when Ella turns around and scolds him.

"Will you please put your ass away?!"

She gives Chris his plate and goes back to the stove.

"Interesting spot for your first tattoo," I chuckle.

"Why were you butt naked in front of me?" Rose laughs.

"So you could tattoo me?"

"You had sex," Chris deadpans.

Both Luke and Ozy choke on their coffee and cereal respectively.

"I'm sorry, what?" Luke chuckles but I can see neither of

Chapter 17

them is sure of themselves.

"I mean, I wasn't there but according to the banging on the wall I share with the bedroom you slept in and according to the state Rose was in when she walked back into my room, I'd say you did. Oh, and probably the fact that she casually mumbled 'just slept with Luke he was better than last time' when she fell asleep next to me. I'm pretty sure I know what I'm saying. You shouldn't have tattooed him on his butt, look where it led."

The silence that has fallen upon us is tense.

"What the fuck?!" Ozy shouts. "Luke, why?!"

"I didn't do anything! You probably jumped me!"

"Why is your dick so small I can't even feel it today," she argues back.

"My dick isn't small, maybe you slept around too much. You can't feel anything down there anymore."

"I'll punch you," she growls.

Still, neither of them moves from their seats, too hungover to have an actual argument.

"I can't believe you guys had sex," I laugh.

"This *isn't* funny," Ozy rages. "I'm with Rach. I don't cheat on Rach."

"What can I say, they always come back." Luke winks at my sister.

"You were hands down the worst sex of my entire life."

"I'm guessing you're talking about our first time since you can't remember yesterday."

"Can you?" she fumes.

"Nope."

"What is Emily going to say?" I ask.

"Emily and I aren't together. I've got a lot less to lose than our serial cheater over there."

"I'm not..." she pauses while her brain desperately tries

to remember what happened last night. Clearly, she doesn't remember shit. "Fuck!"

My gaze lands on Ella to see her reaction. I don't miss the failed suppressed smile she exchanges with Chris. I peer at him just to see his index finger skimming his lips in a shush sign and the wink he gives her. But Ella breaks the silence anyway.

"You guys didn't sleep together," she admits. "Chris is just messing with you. I was with Luke all night." She grimaces before adding, "Even during the butt tattoo."

Rose slowly turns to Chris, her lips pressed tight. "We're even."

Chris gives her his most sarcastic bark. "You tattooed a wonky bottle of Jack Daniel's on my forearm. We are so far from even I can't even see it on the horizon."

"I was three seconds away from having an aneurysm, you made me believe I cheated on Rach."

"And who knows what I'll do next." He wiggles his eyebrows in mockery.

"If I find my car burnt down, it'll be too far, Christopher," she fake-chastises him.

"Thanks, I'll remember the hard limit."

We only get to enjoy a lighthearted, hungover breakfast for another half hour. Ella is taking a picture of the four of us lined up, showing our fresh tattoos when she grimaces.

"*Nate* is calling you," she says as she reads the name on the screen.

"Fuck," Ozy whispers.

"Just hang up," I say.

"Are you sure?" Ella insists. She hangs up anyway. "Okay, pose again guys...wait...he texted. He says to call back. Urgent. Oh, he's calling again."

"Jake, just take it already," my sister huffs.

Chapter 17

Why does reality always have to catch up?

"What should I do?" Ella questions.

"Pick up or I will. You're putting Ella in an awkward situation because you want to escape consequences," Ozy repeats.

"Fine," I snap. I take the phone from Ella. "I'm putting Ella in an awkward situation. Says the girl who tattooed Luke's butt in front of her." I slide my thumb on the screen. "What do you want?"

"I'm driving to your friend's house as we speak. If you and your idiot of a sister are not outside by the time I get there, I'm coming in to fuck everyone up."

He hangs up.

Could Nate take on me, Luke, *and* Chris? I doubt so.

Do I want to take the risk? Not even a little bit. If he's with Sam, it'll be a whole fucking mess I just don't have the mental strength for right now.

"Let's go, Ozy," I say.

"What did he say?" Chris asks, his brows furrowing into seriousness and concern.

"Nothing, he's just pissed we didn't come home last night."

We've been waiting on the streets for ten minutes when Nate stops his Porsche Cayenne in front of us. I was just going to get in, but he opens his door and gets out.

I notice the bruises on his face straight away. The badly busted lip, the stitched eyebrow, the swollen nose. He got beaten up bad and he's fuming. Scratch that. He's enraged, infuriated...*murderous*.

So when he stops an inch away from Rose, I grab her by her jacket, pulling her away from him slightly, putting a safe distance between them. Nate is a master at controlling his anger, but when it's out, he's unstoppable.

The difference between my brother and me is that I've had to bury my emotions to survive. To hide behind a cold apathy to protect myself. But Nate, he's always completely aware of his emotions. He feels everything, he knows good from bad, and he rules it all.

He weighs his decisions with a precision he's obsessed with, a control that is inimitable. Something I've always envied him for. There is a jealousy that burns in me for a sort of control I know exists, but I will never have. Had he been a good person, he would have saved the world. But he was born evil, and he has chosen to use his gift only for selfish decisions.

"What happened to you?" Rose asks.

He ignores her question. "How many times did I say, *no guests.*"

"Really? That's what matters to you right now," I mock him. "You're practically disfigured and you're telling us about house rules?"

"You're right," he chuckles. That dark one he keeps for special occasions. "Why should we care about what I say? Especially when it was only to keep Bianco from completely losing his shit and do something unimportant like hit Ozy in the face or, I don't know," he shrugs, "demand she moves back to D.C."

"What?!" My twin and I gasp. Mine is an angry, shocked gasp. Hers is a small, anxious one, her throat tightening on the word.

"Get in the car. We'll discuss it at home."

"I...is..." She's completely lost her composure, a trembling hand now resting on the car as if to keep her up.

"Is he still at home?" I ask the question I know she wants to.

"No." Is the only answer we get before he gets back in

the car.

We follow, both sitting in the back.

"Where's Sam?" Ozy asks after a few minutes of silence.

"Sam's not going to save you, Ozy," Nate answers through gritted teeth. "He's got places to be, people to kill."

"Did Bianco do this to you?" she questions quickly.

She's panic-talking, trying to get the gist of a situation we won't fully understand.

I slide my hand to the middle seat and grab hers. I'm angry, but I'm not worried because there is absolutely no way she is moving to D.C. Bianco has power over us, he's always ruled us with fear and blackmail, but he can't make her move to D.C. That's simply impossible.

"If only you had been so desperate for answers yesterday, maybe you would have stayed at home instead of running away and leaving me to handle him."

"You were always so desperate to stay with him," I snarl. "You don't need us to hold your hand, do you?"

Fuck him, even if he's right. Rose and I knew we should have been home yesterday. We were meant to have dinner with Chris and come back, make sure to be there before Bianco left. We fucked up.

"What does he mean moving to D.C.?" Ozy ignores my remark and keeps vomiting questions, desperate to understand.

"It means your old room is being cleaned and dusted as we speak."

"But...you're our legal guardian. Y-you won't allow him, right? You can't change my school and my...my," her voice wavers, and I tighten my grip around her hand.

"I'm your legal guardian so Bianco can keep an eye on both of you. Had you not pissed him off, he wouldn't want to keep a clos*er* eye."

"Who did this to you?" I insist. Nate could kill Bianco with his bare hands if he wanted. If *only* he wanted to.

"The kind gentlemen Bianco invited over to our house yesterday."

"Why?"

"Because his people *keep fucking dying*," he hisses. "And he doesn't fucking know who is killing them. He's in a never-ending punishing mood."

Is Bianco doubting Aaron Williams is the one killing his men?

"Do you?"

He doesn't respond, so I insist. "Nate, do you know who's killing Bianco's men?"

"Stop asking questions, Jake," he avoids answering again.

"Who were they?"

"A bunch of fucking strong guys, stop asking questions!" He hits the steering wheel hard enough to honk.

"I don't want to go to D.C.," Ozy says in a quieter voice.

"I fucking know that," Nate fumes. "It's not like I haven't been trying to delay it for months."

He runs a hand through his dirty blond hair. They're undone, a mess from the night he must have spent awake. Our eyes cross in the rearview mirror and I can see the desperation in them, they reflect my own. I think...I think he was genuinely trying to avoid the worst for us.

"He can't make me go," Ozy says again. "I won't go. He's delusional! He'll have to *kidnap* me if he wants me to go there."

My gaze crosses with Nate's again when my sister mentions kidnapping. The fear in them is freezing, the silence is deafening.

18

JAMIE

Traitor – Olivia Rodrigo

The laugh that explodes from my lungs makes me spit the coke I was drinking.

"You have *got* to be kidding me," I howl, my eyes not being able to leave the awful tattoo inked into Chris' forearm. "What sort of weekend did you have?" It's already Friday, but I haven't seen Chris all week, clearly he had a crazy two days last weekend.

Not the same as me, that's for sure. Last Friday had marked a whole week of Jake and I not talking after our night at Luke's – after we had anal for the first time and he left me alone on the floor. Thoroughly fucked, high on orgasms, and disorientated.

He did it on purpose, he wanted to make me feel used and discarded and he hit exactly where it hurts. He made me swear off parties for the rest of my life. At least the ones he attends. I'm not just healing a broken heart, I'm also healing a broken ego. Even today, two weeks later.

The message was loud and clear, 'stay away from me'.

He's keeping me at arm's length, he wants me away from him and he's trying to hurt me to achieve it. He's protecting me, it's never felt more like it. Except I can't keep coming back. No matter how much I love him, I can't keep getting hurt.

I've been living the last few weeks thinking I was doing a great job at staying away. Except I realized it's not me staying away, it's him. The only moments nothing happens are because he's managing to resist our fatal attraction. Every time something does happen is because he's snapped and failed himself. I'm not strong, all I do is desperately wait for him to not be able to resist me.

How pathetic.

I spent last weekend with Mom. It's not like I can do much else anyway. I still have no phone, I'm still grounded. It seems like it'll be that way forever. We're slowly talking to each other again and spending quality time together. As long as I don't bring up the harsh punishment she's brought upon me, we can get along. It's not ideal, but at least there's no risk of bumping into Jake.

You'll get over him. Let time do its thing.

I feel like I've been repeating this for four months. When will it work? The squeeze at my heart every time someone mentions his name is unbearable. How do I fall out of love?

Even now, listening to Chris recounting his last weekend with the twins and Ella brings pangs of jealousy I wasn't aware I could feel. Why doesn't Jake want me to be part of his life?

Chris is the kindest soul I've ever met. He saw Emily wasn't here today and said he would spend every single free period with me today. I can't blame my best friend for not coming, I would have if I thought it would help. Today marks the third year of Aaron's disappearance. Today marks

Chapter 18

three years of my dad's death. Today marks three years of being kidnapped and shot.

I squeeze my eyes shut and open them again. I can't get the vision out of my head. The smell, the sound.

At least it's Friday, just one day and I can shut off from the world for two whole days.

"You haven't touched your food." Chris' low voice brings me out of the nightmare. I don't even know when he stopped talking about his weekend.

"I'm not hungry," I rasp.

I tried to live today as any other day. I tried to laugh and pretend it's all fine, but the knots in my stomach, the pinch on my heart, the heaviness in my chest...it's all too much. And my scar, God it burns so much.

"You should have stayed at home today, Jamie. Emily will be excused for it. You would have too."

"I don't want to be alone," I admit in a tight voice. "She offered to stay with me today, but I don't think I want it to be just the two of us sulking."

"I get that," he smiles. "Are you working tonight?" At my head shake, he continues, "That's good, do you want to do something? We could go to the movies or have dinner in Silver Falls if you want?"

"Cole is taking me and my mom for dinner tonight."

Cole, the guy who could have stopped talking to me after I rejected him countless times and instead cherishes our friendship and acts like the brother I've been missing.

Chris nods, completely understanding as usual. "Where are you guys going?"

"I'm not sure. He's sorting it out. Blue World? Ocean World? Big Blue...something?"

He chuckles. "Bluest Ocean. It's an amazing place, you'll love it. You're not allergic to shellfish, are you?"

"I'm not," I smile. "But I'm not a big fan either, my mom loves it. I kind of guessed it wasn't a steak place anyway. Bummer."

"I'll take you for steak whenever you want. To the best place there is."

"What with your convict tattoo? I don't think so."

We both laugh, but it's short-lived as our Vice Principal, Ms. Rodgers stops by our table, her most serious face on.

"Miss Williams," she starts with a graveness that sends a chill down my spine. An awful presentiment grows in my stomach. "Principal Parker needs to see you in his office right away. It's urgent."

I stand up straight as a rod, not waiting for any more explanation.

"Take your stuff with you," her eyes dart to Chris, "and you can come with a friend if you wish."

That freezes my blood completely. Something happened. On this cursed day, I know something horrible has happened.

"Do you want me to come? Should I get Cole?" Chris' quick words send even more panic through my body. He got it too, that feeling of doom.

"I-I don't know."

"I'll come. We'll call him if needed."

He grabs my backpack before I can even think of bending down to do so. His hand is in mine the next second, gripping me tightly enough to know he's there for me, that he won't let me go through this on my own. Whatever *this* is.

Chris dragged me through the halls, the difference between his height and mine making it look like a dad in a rush to get somewhere important with his kid dragging behind. But now that we're in front of the Principal's office, he's released me so I can walk in before him.

Chapter 18

Principal Parker is sitting behind his mahogany desk, his brows kissing each other from the worry on his face. He's on the phone and scribbling on a paper in front of him. Beside him, Mr. Ashton is waiting, an arm across his chest, an elbow resting on the palm of his hand so he can hold his chin in his other hand. The emotions on his face don't announce anything good either.

"Take a seat," Ms. Rodgers whispers as she joins Mr. Ashton.

They mumble secrets to each other as we wait for the phone call to end. Secrets about me and the news that is going to break me in less than a minute.

Chris and I both sit on the dark wooden chairs, cushioned with soft, velvet, purple paddings. I rest an elbow on the armrest so I can rub my temples without using too much of the little strength I have.

Principal Parker hangs up the phone and looks at me.

"Miss Williams, thank you for coming so quickly." He looks at Chris and nods. "Mr. Murray." Back at me he adds, "I'm going to be talking to you about a very personal matter, are you comfortable with the people present in this room?"

No.

I'm not comfortable with any of this, but my head is already spinning, and I need to know. "Y-yes."

"Miss Williams, the school just got a call from the Silver Falls police station. You are the only next of kin for your mother, is that right?"

Yes, I'm all she has. She's *all. I. Have.*

Please be okay. Mom, please be okay.

I nod.

"I'm afraid your mother has been arrested on theft charges. They haven't told us anything else. She is being held in jail until further notice."

My whole world collapses.

The room tilts, my vision narrows as black spots invade the corner of my eyes.

"We can call you a cab to the station, but you won't be able to see her until her interrogation is over. What you can do is call the station and ask to speak to her. They might let you."

His voice disappears across the surface as I sink underwater. All I can hear are faint sounds as my ears ring louder and louder. My stomach tightens under the pressure, threatening to empty itself. Bile burns its way through my throat, and I desperately try to swallow it back down.

That makes no sense.

I don't get it. Can't handle it.

All sorts of scenarios run through my head as I imagine her being fired from the Bakers café, never being able to get another job. The crippling debts, never being able to pay back, my mom in prison.

I attempt to take a deep breath, trying to settle down the ringing. Impossible.

"Miss Williams?" Looking up, my gaze falls on Principal Parker again. "Would you like to call your mother?"

"I..." The whirl of doom and anxious thoughts going around in my body stops me from thinking straight. "I don't have a phone with me."

"Well, you can use the schools of course. Or if you would like to go to the station, Coach Thompson has offered to accompany you."

Looking to the side, I notice Coach T. standing next to Mr. Ashton. When did he come in?

I shake my head 'no'. "Can I...can I call, please?"

"Ms. Rodgers will let you use the one behind her desk. You'll have more privacy."

Chapter 18

I feel like the walk to her desk takes hours, like the tone of the phone is deafening. When my mom's voice finally comes on, I'm a lost child. My one and only compass in life has broken and everything has fallen apart.

"Mom?" I sob. It comes out all at once, the tears flow, the fear drowns me, the tightness in my throat mutes me.

"'Me, sweetie, it's okay. Everything's going to be okay."

But it's not. It's not and her tone says it all.

"I had a chance to speak with Mr. Baker earlier, before... before they arrested me."

She scratches her throat and I scratch mine, mirroring my one and only example in life.

"He showed me the proof. He has a document that counted all the missing money. All the money *I* took. Yes?"

It clicks straight away. All the money *she* took. She's taking the fall for both of us. I'm eighteen now, I could get in serious trouble, and she doesn't want that for me.

"Mom..."

"I have to go, 'Me. I'll call you, okay? Please, arrange to sleep at the Joly's tonight."

"I will, Mom, and I'll talk to Hope!"

"I have to go, sweetie," Mom concludes quickly before hanging up.

It's not until I've been excused for the day, escorted out of the school, and sitting with Chris in his car for about ten minutes that I say another word.

"Take me to North Shore High."

"What?" he asks, completely confused. His voice is slightly raspy from not having spoken that whole time.

"Take. Me. To. N. S. High," I repeat, pausing after every word.

"I don't get it," he insists.

But I do. I really do get it. Jake wanted to push me away, he wanted me to hate him and so he did the unforgivable. Is that what he was hiding from me? What he was saying I would never forgive?

The first time he mentioned that document to me, I discovered a new sort of fear. The kind I can't control. The kind I can't *fix*. And I'm a fixer. Not being able to do anything about what he held over me was torture.

But he made the torture so sweet, playing with my body, my mind, my feelings. Making me fall in love with him despite Nathan. Nathan might have turned out to be a manipulative monster, but that didn't make Jake less of one. That's what my mistake was all along; thinking Jake would change for me. That he would become less of a psychopath, that he would develop strong enough feelings, that he would care about me.

He doesn't. He doesn't care about anyone but himself. He doesn't care about hurting me, about my mom, about ruining my life. He cares that I'm finally not in his way anymore.

He said he had deleted it, that nightmare of a file with everything my mom and I stole from the Bakers. With our last name written in red. Our own personal scarlet letters.

And he *said* he had deleted it. It was a fresh start for us that night, finally being able to be on an equal foot. Finally falling in love with each other out of honesty. But did he? Did he ever fall in love with me? Or was he just completely set on destroying me?

I fix, he destroys.

This is so obvious to me now. We were never meant to work. Opposites can only attract when they walk the fine line of love and hate. Jake crossed that line so many times, went so far across that we'll never come back from it.

"Jamie, talk to me," Chris brings me back to the present.

My throat doesn't even feel tight anymore. I have no tears to shed, I am pure fury. Rage and hatred are seeping through my veins like poison, ready to kill.

"Start driving. I'll explain on the way."

Until today, I would never have told Chris what Jake did. The blackmailing, the threats, the bullying. But during our thirty-minute drive to the North Shore of the Falls, while Chris speeds on the highway, I let it all out. Everything Jake did to me, everything I let him do. I try to work it out out loud, over and over again: how I could have fallen in love with him in the midst of the terror he had instilled in me.

But the worst thing is, Chris doesn't even look surprised. He drives in silence, his fingers holding the steering wheel tighter and tighter, his knuckles getting white, his neck tensing to the point that I can see the tendons straining.

When he parks in front of the rundown building my stomach twists. The difference between Stoneview Prep and North Shore High is guilt-wrenching. The privilege I grew up in almost makes me feel sick. It reminds me that, had Mom and Dad not worked their asses off, had Dad not been promoted, this is where I would have gone to school. Funny how they wanted Aaron and me to grow up in an area where we wouldn't be surrounded by crime. They wanted to keep us safe. Oh, the irony.

"Stay in the car," I say as I grab the door handle. "You don't want to leave a nice SUV unattended here."

"I don't care about my car, you're not walking in there on your own. N.S. High is no fun, Jamie. People in there don't react well to strangers walking in unwelcomed. Especially when they recently had a fight with a girl from the North Shore Crew. Besides, I'd like to talk to Jake too."

"Chris." My voice is brittle when I continue, "I need to do this. Just me. Without anyone's help. Without anyone defending poor Jamie Williams. You, Em, *Rose*," I still get surprised knowing this girl likes me enough to defend me all the time, "you guys are always there, always saving me. Jake gave a document to the Bakers that is going to put my mom in jail."

It takes superhuman strength to not let the tears fall. "In *jail*," I repeat in a whisper. "I was in love with him, and that's what I got in return. I need my closure, and I need to do it alone."

He nods at me and, to my surprise, takes me tightly in his arms. "I'll be here, waiting for you. I got you."

I don't know where to find Jake, but I already know who to talk to as I walk toward the stairs that lead to the entrance of North Shore High. I don't go to the door, but instead, make my way to the group of men that look just slightly too old to be here. I head toward the one I recognize; he sees me before I'm close enough to talk to him and gets up from the steps he was sitting on.

"Jamie Williams," he smirks. "I love the uniform."

I thought my drunk brain had exaggerated Xi's hotness when I met him at that party. It hadn't. His dark hair and bushy eyebrows contrast with his long lashes which put a sort of cuteness on his rogue face. His dark skin contrasts with the other white guys around him, making him stand out as the hot one, his hard muscles showing he's the strong one in their group.

"Aren't you too old for high school?" I ask as I stop in

front of him. I don't even know his age, I just know he's older.

"I'm actually at work right now. Do you like my office?" *Work.* Selling drugs to teenagers? Waiting to beat up their rival gang?

"Jake. Where can I find him?"

"Are you guys still trying to make this work? You gotta let it go, baby."

"Where?" I insist.

"I don't keep track of him."

I roll my eyes. Great, thanks for the help.

"But I do keep track of Billie, and they're usually pretty close to the other."

I don't even have to pretend this doesn't hurt me. Jake has gone too far and him dating or fucking Billie is the last thing I'm worried about. It's the last thing that hurts me.

"Okay, well where can I find the lovely Billie?" I spread the bitchiest smile on my face.

"Probably enjoying some lunchtime fuck at the back of the building. Room 159 is her place."

He stops me when I turn around to leave. "I wouldn't go through this building in a Stoneview Prep uniform. Unless you want to come back the other side dead. Or worse. I can accompany you. It would be my pleasure, especially if you and Billie are planning on having another catfight."

"I'm fine, thanks," I mumble.

It's not hard to get inside N.S. High. They have a security guard watching a video on his phone by the entrance. I pass their metal detector, clearly from another school, without him even batting an eyelash. There's a sign indicating where the rooms are. 100-130 to the left, 131-160 straight ahead, at the end of the hallway that leads toward the back of the building.

Lunchtime. Crowds of students are by their rundown lockers. Groups of people are spread out, going about their activities. One guy suddenly pushes another against a graffitied wall, whispering threats low in his ear. No one is surprised, no one tries to stop them.

It's overcrowded in here. Too many students, not enough space. There's a tension weighing in the air between some groups, and I'm instantly taken back to Emily telling me about the tensions between the North Shore Kings and the North Shore Crew. Now that N.S.C. has Bianco's protection, threats to the Kings are at an all-time high. But that's not why I'm here. I don't care about this world. I care about mine, where my mom is in jail.

"Move out of the way, bitch," someone says behind me.

I turn to face two girls and notice their tattoos straight away. The identical ones they sport; a crown on both their shoulders. Why are they even talking to me?

"I'd like to take a piss if you don't mind."

I jump out of the way when I realize I'm standing in front of the bathroom door, blocking the entrance. I collect myself and re-focus. Time to get to the point.

I stride toward the end of the hallway and hell if I feel all those eyes on me. That uniform is some sort of target on my back. I have to push my way through thicker bits of the crowd, tighter spots where some people are reluctant to let me through without bothering me. I still make it to the other side with only dark looks and one guy shouting that he wanted to check if Stoneview bitches wore underwear under that slutty uniform.

The crowd thins out as I get toward the end of the hallway, and in front of room 159...nothing. Not one soul. It's like

Chapter 18

a different world. The loud voices from behind me become background noise. I don't know what I imagined. Someone guarding the door? People talking drugs and arms deals?

I imagine opening the door to Jake and Billie undressing each other, laughing about what he did. A new world where it's not money that makes you important and yet still a world where Jake White is the king. Where somehow, he managed to make it to the top of the food chain.

All these thoughts add to my hatred. My fire is fueled by everything Jake and I could have become had he decided to accept me into his life. Had he wanted to save me the way I wanted to save him. Had he loved me. Instead, he decided to destroy us. To destroy me. And I'm ready to end it all.

But when I push the door open, ready to confront him, it's anything but what I expected. I find myself entering the back of room 159 and recognize N.S. High's lacrosse center. Evans. That fucking rocket of a girl who told me she ate Stoneview bitches for breakfast then managed to make me lose draws after draws.

The two girls she's laughing with are the girls that were holding me still when Billie struck back after I punched her. There are two guys standing before the teacher's desk. My heart takes a plunge when my eyes meet Lik's.

I remember all too well when he and Jake came into my hotel room. When they tied me up and forced orgasms after orgasms out of me while they were just chilling. I remember the hardness in his pants despite Jake saying he wasn't interested in girls. Thinking about it, I don't think said hardness was for me. I barely have time to feel the first wave of embarrassment because Lik moves to the side with a cocky smile on his face.

Right behind him, Jake is sitting at the desk, like a king reigning on his court. There's weed on the table, a grinder, and some papers ready to roll a joint but his hands are behind his head, fingers interlocking.

His lips are slightly parted, his eyes hooded, and that breathing...I would recognize that among everything in the world. Pleasure. Utter bliss. A smug smile spreads on his lips before his head falls backward in a murmured 'fuck'. But it comes back up straight away, deep blue eyes interlocking with mine as his face hardens and his hand goes under the desk.

His arm tenses and he frowns at me. "Hold up, Billie. Can't keep my dick hard suddenly."

What?

I can feel my nostrils flare as my breathing becomes ragged with anger. Billie suddenly appears from under the desk and I must say this is not exactly what I expected, but I'm not surprised either.

"What the *fuck* are you doing here?" she spits at me.

She's on my side of the desk the next second. She laughs as she brings the sleeves of her sweater up.

"The bitch really does have a death wish," she says to her three girlfriends behind me.

"I didn't come for you," I growl back.

"You didn't come for me? Funny because I'm definitely coming for you."

"I don't *care* about you, Billie," I try to explain as calmly as possible.

A chair scrapes against the floor and my gaze goes back to Jake as he gets up, zips up his jeans, and slowly walks around the desk before leaning against it.

"I won't defend you again, Jamie. We've had countless conversations about our breakup, and I'm tired of repeating that you should accept it. Camila took it easy compared to you and if letting Billie and her girls beat the shit out of you is the only way for you to stay in your place, I'm not about to get in the way of that."

"You're a real fucking asshole, you know that?" I tremble with anger as I feel my fists tighten and my nails dig into my palms.

"I have nothing to say to you," he concludes. Or at least, he thinks it concludes our conversation.

"Nothing to say to me? Oh, Jake," I laugh dryly. "I'm not here to listen to you. I'm here to tell you that you went too far. And if you think you're going to get away with what you did, you're about to wake the fuck up. Believe me."

It's his turn to laugh and I hear the others chuckle as well. Especially Billie.

"Jamie. Let. Go." He runs a hand through his hair and shakes his head. "You can get other dicks; you've proven it countless times before."

"For the love of God, will you shut up about you and your dick?! Do you think this is funny?!" I shout as I get closer to him. "Your God complex is acting up again. You are *nothing*, do you understand? You are lower than hell. You are the biggest regret of my life! *You* broke up and *you* couldn't stay away."

He pushes away from the desk and stands tall above me.

"Jake, man, you never said your ex was a psycho. Watch out." I don't even know who said that, some guy.

"Watch out?" he chuckles. "Have you seen her? What is she gonna do, she's the size of a doll. A doll I'm done playing with."

"I'm going to out everything you did. I'm going to go to the police, I'll tell them about the blackmail, about what you did to me. About the gun. I'll end you," I rage through gritted teeth.

"You're out of your fucking mind," he seethes back. "When did you turn into a crazy bitch?"

"I'm out of my mind? Me?! You turned us in! You put my mom in jail! Why? Why the *fuck* would you do this? Was it revenge?"

His brows furrow as he shakes his head.

"What?" he says at the same time as Billie behind me.

"Don't act innocent now!" I shout with fury. "Why did you do it?! Is it because I slept with Nathan? Is it because of Cole? You broke up with me, Jake. *You* broke *my* heart. You shouldn't have cared how I fixed it."

When he doesn't say anything, I press my hands against his chest to give him a big push.

"Answer me! Why did you do it?! You told me you had deleted that document. Why would you lie to me? Was this all a game to you? Break my heart all you want, humiliate *me*, play with *me*, terrify *me*. But my mom? My mom, Jake..." My voice starts breaking as the tears rise to my eyes.

"Jamie, I didn't—"

"Don't lie to me! She's being interrogated as we speak. All we did was steal a few thousand from billionaires! Do you really think it is going to change their lives? Because it changed ours. It allowed me to pay for my uniform and the lacrosse tournaments. It allowed me to buy new clothes to look pretty for you. My phone, my bike repairs when your ex bullied me." I shake my head, still not being able to swallow the news properly.

He takes a step back as if finally realizing the extent of what he's done. His mouth opens and closes but nothing comes out.

I came here to shout, to hurt him, to threaten him with actions I well intend to take if my mom doesn't get out of this situation. But facing him like that, my defenses still go down, like wanting to prove to him that he just went too far.

"She's all I have, Jake," I finish with a trembling voice. I can't even pretend to be strong right now because I have nothing and no one.

"Jamie," he starts but Billie is now standing beside me. I can feel her presence, she's small physically but has the aura of a six-foot man.

"Did you send her mom to jail, Jake?" she asks, shock weighing heavy in her voice.

"No!" he finally shouts after multiple rounds of not being able to say a word. "Fuck, I would never."

"Don't lie," I shake my head as tears start freefalling. "You're a really good liar. All you Whites are."

"Jake, what the fuck!" Billie jumps in. "That's a fucking snitch move, we don't take none of that on the North Shore."

Is she...is she defending me?

"I *didn't* snitch," he growls at her. "Do you know the kind of things I'm involved with? Do you really think I would want to get anywhere near a police station?"

He takes a step toward me again, reaching out and trying to grab my hand but I step away.

"You were the only one with that document, Jake. The proof of what we stole, you created it."

"Created it?" Billie chokes. "What the fuck is wrong with you?"

"I...It's a long story," he says to her. "Jamie, I would never want to separate you from your mom. I would never share it...I-I know I threatened to but that's all it was: empty threats. I promise you that document is *gone*."

"You're a liar, Jake. You're full of hate, you hold a grudge on your brother, on *life,* so deep that no one can ever fix it. Fuck your way through life, threaten girls, do whatever the fuck you want but stay away from me. And make sure you hold onto that hate because, without it, you're nothing."

I don't wait for him to reply, I turn around and leave the room hoping no one follows me.

I hurry through the now half-empty hallway and desperately try to wipe the tears from my face, but new ones keep coming.

"Jamie!" I hear behind me.

But I don't turn around for Jake. Not anymore. I keep going, accelerating my pace.

"Jamie, please!"

He's on me as I go down the stairs to join Chris in his car. His grip on my arm halts me in my steps and I'm forced to turn around.

"I promise you on my *life*, on Ozy's life, that I didn't send that document to the police. Please, believe me. I will find out what happened, I will talk to Luke's dad."

"I don't *care* what you do! You ruined my fucking life! You're dead to me." I try to snatch my arm away, but he won't let go.

"Let go," I growl. "Let me go! That's all I ever wanted. I just wanted to be left alone, I just wanted to finish school and go to UPenn. I just wanted you to stop harassing me. I just wanted you to let me go. I never asked for this." I take a shaky breath as his eyes beg me not to leave. "Oh my God just let me go!" I scream from the top of my lungs.

That scream is everything.

It's everything I've ever wanted to say to him. It's every silent cry, every begging that I did when he was bullying me. It's all the questions he never answered when I tried to understand him, all the frustrations that built up as I tried to fix him. It's for all the times he pushed me past my limits, all the times I let him make me feel good, all the times I let him turn pain into pleasure.

It's a scream that lets out the dying love I have for him. Everything he threw away, a memory of all the times he made me laugh, he made me feel safe. It's a disappointment so loud it burns my lungs. A fear that if even Jake couldn't fix me, no one will. If even broken Jake White couldn't love me, no one will ever love me.

It's my heart screaming for help. Begging me to let go and leave this all behind. It's my brain remembering how much that broken heart loved Jake. Pure love. A drug more addictive than anything else.

And that scream is loud enough to attract everyone's attention. It only takes a few seconds for Xi to run toward us. It only takes a moment for Chris to jump out of the car and grab me just before I hit the ground from my knees going weak. I vaguely see Xi pulling Jake away by the shoulder. Telling him something about leaving me alone. But God, the tears are falling so hard, the sobs are wrecking my body in convulsions I can't control.

As long as your heart beats, mine will beat along with it.

That's what he had told me.

Tell me, Jake. Has your heart stopped beating yet? Because you completely annihilated mine.

My body is so numb on the way back, I don't really know where we are going or how long it takes us. Chris tries to ask me a few questions, but I don't say anything. When I finally notice we're stopping in front of the Murrays' gates I shake my head no.

"I'll walk to my house," I say as I open the door.

"Jamie, your house is too far to walk."

"I need the fresh air," I reply weakly as I let my feet take me away from the car.

I hear his door close and he calls after me. "Let me drive you!"

I shake my head again. "I need to be alone, Chris, please."

I don't really notice if he's agreeing or not. I just keep walking. I keep walking until I finally recognize where my feet have taken me. A half-smile breaks on my lips when I see the only place I could have gone to. The only place my heart has chosen.

The relief relaxes my body, and the numbness slowly fades away. I stop in front of him, but I know the respite is short-lived when a spike of pain comes back. I shouldn't be here.

"Hey," I breathe.

The expected silence is still heavy, and I completely give up as I fall to my knees.

"Hey, Dad," I sob as my knees hit the ground next to my dad's grave.

I don't visit often. There is still the flicker of a flame of anger toward my dad. The fact that he's dead doesn't take away the fact that he was willing to sacrifice us for this city. All Aaron and I wanted was to get out alive. All my dad wanted was to defend Stoneview. A city that paid him back by letting us all down.

But I miss him.

I miss him so much and I have nothing left.

All I have are the memories of him and me. I feel like he left us yesterday and yet our memories now feel like old tales. Like stories you tell your kids without truly remembering them.

'Oh yeah, I remember that time Dad took me to that steak place in Silver Falls.'

'Sure, I remember when he, Aaron, and I watched the All-Star game on the big TV.'

Yes, I remember how he was. He respected Filipino culture, taught us Tagalog, and cooked delicious meals for us. He taught us to get blessed by putting his knuckles to our forehead. He would never go to work without doing it. He talked about his parents being from Laguna in the Philippines and used to tell us about the Villa Escadero where there was a restaurant at the bottom of the waterfalls.

He hated shoes in the house, loved macaroni and cheese, and couldn't watch one football game without falling asleep. He liked fixing things, objects, people, cities. He respected the law, he had a sharp moral compass. He and Aaron didn't get along. Aaron was too rebellious, like my mom when she was younger. They both thought me and my dad were boring rule followers.

He wasn't very tall, and Aaron had already outgrown him by the time he was fourteen years old.

I do remember him. But every day it fades a little more. His voice isn't so clear anymore, I can't remember the exact effect it had on me. I don't remember how much darker his skin was from mine.

Was my head to his chest or his shoulder? Did he hug with his arms around my neck or around my waist? I can only remember my mom reading me stories, did he ever do it? Was he as beautiful as the pictures remember him? I don't remember the sound his steps made around our old house. I know I used to wake up to the sound of his boots walking past my room when he came back from a night shift. But why can't I remember the sound they made? Were they squeaky? Heavy? Dragging?

"I'm sorry, Dad," I sob. "I just don't remember anymore."

I curl both my arms on the hard headstone and rest my head on them. I can feel the cold emanating from the stone.

"You're cold," I cry.

It takes me a few minutes to admit why I came.

"We're in trouble, Dad." I grab a snail that is making its way up the stone and put it on the grass. "Mom..."

I don't want to admit it. Is he going to be disappointed? Is he going to hate us?

"Mom and I did something bad. We stole from the Bakers. And now she got caught. I don't know what to do. I'm so lost. I'm so lost without you and Aaron. Without Mom."

I take a deep shaky breath. "I don't even know if you noticed, but Mom didn't give Aaron a place to rest. She thinks he's still alive. Does it make me a horrible sister if I think he isn't? Because if he is, why didn't he come back for us?"

I readjust myself and completely sit on the damp ground.

"I sometimes read in books people saying that they can *feel* that someone is still alive. I don't feel anything, Dad. I just know he's not here and we still haven't found him."

Another set of tears breach the barrier of my eyelids when I admit the shameful truth.

"I've stopped looking for him. I thought I never could, but after everything that happened this year. I stopped. What is the point? I'm just...me. You used to say I was smart because of my grades. But I'm not that smart, I just work really hard. Nothing comes naturally. I can't fix people, I can't investigate everything. I just have a really toxic curiosity. You used to love it when I played detective, remember? Before the incident, I wanted to become a police officer like

Chapter 18

you. I wanted to become a detective. Now I want to be a surgeon, Dad, did you know that?"

You stopped being my hero when a surgeon had to save my life because you didn't want to choose us over your city.

I don't tell him that. I know he knows it already. I know he regrets his choice. I know he never wanted to leave us behind.

"I don't know what to do anymore. I fell in love, and I broke my own heart. Mom isn't here to patch it back together. I'm all alone."

A heavy silence falls on me.

My dad won't reply. He's dead.

I really am all alone.

"You're not alone," someone whispers behind me as a hand lands on my shoulder. "I got you, 'Me."

I look over my shoulder and let out another sob as my best friend sits down next to me to take me in her arms.

"You'll never be alone. I promise you." Emily whispers, her head nuzzled in my hair.

19

JAKE

911 – Ellise

I'm so fucking exhausted.

Bianco is a smart man. Very fucking smart. He threatens my twin and then plays me like a puppet. He's been working me out, using me to move drugs, to collect money, to bring him money from underground fights. I'm too tired to fucking think anymore and it's not even been a week of it yet.

The Cosa Nostra has a strict hierarchy. Boss, underboss, captains, soldiers. With the way Bianco is treating me he's added a new layer under soldier; Bianco's personal little bitch.

But at least Ozy is not moving to D.C. Not for now. Not as long as I behave, not as long as Nate is in the way. It forces me to wonder how long he has been putting himself between Bianco and us. I still hate him. I just wonder if he's been on our side all along. What sort of intimidation has Bianco threatened him with during our childhood?

The day after our drunken night at Chris', I texted Billie.

Chapter 19

I took her on a date, showed her a bit of my sweet side, fucked her the way she loves, and let her sleep in my bed. And that was us turning official.

Because that's what would hurt Jamie the most. And a hurt Jamie stays away from me. Stays safe. This is not the kind of battle I will win. There is no point telling her everything because she loves me too much and she will convince me to love each other despite the danger. I can't have that.

Billie became the second woman to ever spend the night in my bed. But when I woke up from a nightmare, she didn't move. She didn't soothe me, she didn't ask what was wrong, she didn't sense my distress. She was sleeping soundly like she should have. The issue with Billie and every single other girl on this planet is harshly simple: they're not Jamie.

So when Xi texted to say Jamie was showing up to our school and wanted to see me. I knew it was time to hit hard. It wasn't an accident she entered the room when Billie was on her knees for me. It's called perfect timing.

Except I could have never imagined in a million years the reason she came. Her mom's in jail. And she thinks I did it.

That's all I wanted, wasn't it? For her to stay away. But to think I did anything to put her mom in jail? Never.

So now, I'm running after her. Not because I want to get her back. I'm running after her because I can't stand her thinking I would do something so *wrong*. Yeah, after everything I put her through, I found my limit.

The tears and the screaming when I catch up with her drive a knife through my heart.

She's done with me, for good. For something I didn't even do.

I only notice Chris was here when I see his car leave. I shrug Xi off me and turn to him.

"Why the fuck would you let her in there? Aren't you supposed to be controlling entrances into the school?!"

I don't even listen to his answer. I've got places to be.

There are two guys from the Kings Crew when I get to my car. North Shore knows by now who the nice car belongs to, and yet these two fuckers have a death wish.

The violence in my steps is already putting fear in them as I approach. I don't even stop for them. I open the door and turn to them before I settle in.

"Look at this car too closely again, and I'll give you nice holes to go with those tattoos on your necks," I hiss, pointing at the crowns on their necks.

I take my gun out and put it on the passenger's seat for effect, and then I'm out of here.

It takes three tries for Ozy to pick up.

"Where the *fuck* are you?" I snap. Why is she always so slow at picking up?

"On my way to Chris'. I'm not exactly liking your North Shore gangster attitude. Why the anger?"

"I'll meet you there," I growl as I hung up.

I floor it to my best friend's house, but it still takes me too long to my liking.

The moment I walk into the basement den, Chris is on me, grabbing me by the t-shirt and pushing me against the wall.

"I hope you have really fucking good explanations," he growls in my ear.

"You know what," I rage. "I don't have to explain shit to you!" I push back and he easily lets go, taking a couple steps back, but the anger is palpable.

"I don't want to fight with you, man. I just want to get this sorted," I admit.

"She told me everything, Jake. Everything you did.

Chapter 19

Everything she forgave, and that's what you give back? You destroy her life?"

"I didn't fucking do it!" I shout. "That document has been gone for months!"

"The girl is sick of love for you! Do you understand that? She'd fucking die for you, for the toxic bastard you are. You broke her. You knew there was no hope for you two and you kept going, kept pushing like a greedy fucker."

A loud, hysterical laugh breaks out of my lungs. "I'm a toxic bastard? A greedy fucker? Then, *please*, my friend, tell me what you are?" I extend an arm as if presenting a show. I even slightly bow my head to push the sarcasm.

"What the fuck are you on about?" he fights back.

"Ah, come on Chris, we're between bastards who break girls for their own pleasures here. Don't be shy."

He shakes his head, but I know he's starting to see where I'm going with this.

"I don't know what you're talking about," he lies.

"I'm talking about Ella. Your *secret* girlfriend."

He takes a step back, wind knocked out of him, as his eyes widen.

"Looks like I hit the jackpot of all the deadly secrets," I smile. "So you want to tell me again how there's no hope for me and Jamie? Tell me, Chris, do you think there's a lot of hope for you and your best friend's sister?"

He shakes his head. "Don't fucking bring her into this."

"You're lying to Luke every day while you fuck her behind his back! Bro, you fucked her while we were all sleeping at your house. You're a shit friend."

"I–"

"You always talk to me like you're an almighty god that never does anything wrong. But I think just this once, it'd be good if you take a seat."

He runs a hand behind his neck, kneading at it, his big sign that he's stressed, before looking at me again.

"How did you find out?" he asks quietly.

"You know what, it was only a suspicion until last weekend. I just knew you guys went to the gym at the same time in the morning and I thought that was interesting. It was in the way she looked at you and the way you always avoided touching her. Then you punched her date at the Winter Ball, and I thought that was strange. And *then* you got drunk last weekend. And you got sloppy as fuck. Couldn't help yourself but touch her...and fuck if she blushes when you do. You fucking called her *Sweets*. How cute. The way you tried to save the situation..."

"Alright. Enough."

"I guess there's also the fact that I heard you guys fuck in the guest bedroom. Those moans...bro, did you grow a golden dick since our last sexcapade?"

"You're about a second away from losing your teeth."

"Fine," I smile. "I'll stop. But I must say, it's cute that she knows how you eat your eggs."

"Jake—"

"Luke will kill you. I know he's small, and I know you could take him. But you underestimate what it's like to want to protect your sister. Luke *will* kill you if he finds out."

"Are you done with avoiding the topic?" he asks in a guttural voice.

"I didn't do it," I answer in my most serious voice.

He turns toward the sofa, shaking his head at the same time. "Did he do it?"

Ozy is on the sofa, twisted so she can watch us, with her arms on the back of it and her head resting on her forearms. She doesn't even bother straightening up, she just shakes her head in negation.

"The fact that you have to ask me is beyond my understanding," she replies. "Of course he didn't."

I let out a much needed sigh of relief. Finally someone on my side. My twin never lets me down.

"The problem isn't if Jake did it or not," Ozy says as she gets up. "It's *who* fucking did it. Because while you two fuck girls you shouldn't, Jamie is now parentless. I have nothing in common with the girl and, really, I wasn't hoping this would be the first thing we bond over."

I nod to her. "Where is she? I need to talk to her."

"No, you need to leave her the fuck alone and sort it out."

"But—"

"Fix it, Jake," she seethes.

"I will!" I defend myself.

"Who did it?" she asks.

"I don't know—"

"Then fucking *think*."

"I was the only one with that document."

"Who did it, Jake."

"I'm thinking, Rose!" I rage at her. She's on me the next second, in my fucking face, pulling at my nerves.

"When did you delete it?"

Images flash in my head. Of the night of the Winter Ball. Jamie and I in my bedroom, the party at the pool house. So many fucking people.

"Are you thinking? Or are you daydreaming?"

"Shut up!"

"Tell me who fucking did it then!"

I hate when she pushes me like that. I want to slap her in the face and push her away. She keeps getting in my space, keeps snapping questions at me.

I took Jamie outside and she had forgotten her purse. I

put her in the limo and went back in for it.

"God, your brain is so fucking slow," Rose snaps at me again.

I ignore her this time, close to my goal. I went back to my room, but Camila was there. She tried to seduce me. She was threatening Jamie. And when I got rid of her, I decided to delete the document because I wanted to start fresh with Jamie. Because I realized how much I loved her and I wanted to make sure she was with me because she loved me back, not because of what I was holding above her head. But when I went to my computer that night, the screen was lit up despite not having used it in hours...

"Jake!" My sister rages. "You're so fucking useless sometimes. Can't even figure out who did it!"

...and only one person was in my room.

"Camila," I whisper in disbelief. "But you already knew that. Didn't you?"

"Had my suspicions," Ozy admits. "I had to get you to figure it out though. I couldn't point you in the wrong direction."

I knew she was jealous, but I never thought she would go that far. I should have, she was already putting notes in Jamie's locker and shit. Telling her to stay away from me. I shouldn't be surprised. But why wait until now?

"I'm so fucking done with the cunt," Rose growls.

"Yeah. Me too," I say as I grab my phone from my back pocket.

"Don't." She puts a hand on my phone. "You go to Luke and sort this shit out. Leave Camila to Chris and me."

My brows furrow and I turn to my friend, sure that he'll scold Ozy for insinuating she's going to hurt Camila but he just nods.

"Sort it out," he confirms calmly.

I don't need another word. I run back to my car and call Luke as I drive to his house. His dad needs to drop the charges and he needs to do it now.

We might not be able to be together, but I won't let her down when I have the means to help her.

Jamie

"Forgive me Father, for I have sinned. My last confession was three months ago."

I know exactly who sits on the other side of the screen in the confessional. Pastor Gilligan has been a pillar for me and Mom for years, but he has no idea what we've been doing. Admitting the theft to him is not only a need for relief, it's also a cry for help.

So I let it out. I don't say Mom's name, but I know he understands who I'm talking about. I know he understands everything I'm saying. We pray together and he gives me time to stop crying. He gives me more prayers to repeat at home and I just nod even if he can't see me.

What else is there to do? Mom and Dad would have prayed in my place. Aaron would have turned the town upside down, but I've never had his penchant for rebellion. No, I quietly do wrong. I keep an innocent face and break rules and people in silence.

It's praying that convinces me of the next step I should take. I wish I could say it's because I found the right path in there. But I never do. No, I always realize how...it doesn't change anything. I must be rotten so deeply to the core. Respecting the rules, respecting the law, where did that ever take me?

Nowhere.

The people who run this town, above and underground are covered in sins. They are corrupted, they are dangerous, lawless, and megalomaniacs.

I'm not going to save my mother with prayers. No, I will save her by being like them. Ruthless and anarchic.

And I know exactly who to call for that. It's like every time I'm in here, I'm brought back to him. Funny since he's probably destined for an eternity in hell. I'm surprised he never burned to ashes walking in here.

I grab my phone as I push the doors to exit the Church. My heart somersaults seeing I have a text from Jake, but I don't even open it. I can't let myself be weak to him anymore. Today was the harshest lesson of all. Instead, I call another number. He picks up on the first ring.

"I need your help," I say. And that's all it takes.

Half an hour later, I'm sitting down at the kitchen island of Nathan's house. His face is bruised, like he's been beaten up, but I don't bother asking what happened. He can keep his secrets to himself. He listened attentively when I told him what happened, but he still hasn't answered anything.

"So," I snap. "Are you going to say something? Are you going to help me?"

His saccharine smile already announces I shouldn't have made myself vulnerable.

"Didn't you break up with me because you couldn't be with the boss of the new gang in town?" he says, using my own words against me. "Didn't your mom tell you to stay away from gangbangers?"

I have to take a deep breath to keep my calm. Now is not the moment to play smart.

Chapter 19

"I broke up with you because of the lies. My mom was just trying to keep me safe. And now she's in big trouble, Nathan. I want to keep her safe as well."

He shifts slightly in his chair while he thinks, rubbing the back of his ear like he always does when he works out his next words.

"For what it's worth," he finally tells me. "I don't think Jake did it."

I let out a loud cackle. "Really?! After all the backstabbing and fights, now is the time you choose to act like a protective older brother? Jake was the only one in possession of this file. Don't try to defend him to me."

He shrugs. "I don't care what you think of him. I told you he would break your heart. I won't pick up the pieces."

Said heart skips a beat. It always does when it's reminded that it wants to beat for Jake and Jake only.

"I'll get your mother out of trouble. In fact, she'll be back home by lunch tomorrow. I just need to make a few phone calls and it'll all be gone."

"It will?" I light up at the idea.

"Sure," he smiles.

"What about Mr. Baker? He might not want to drop the charges."

Nathan laughs, undoes his bun and redoes it. "Gerald Baker does what I tell him to do. Trust me, he doesn't want his dirty secrets exposed."

"Dirty secrets? Like...what?"

He shakes his head and adjusts his glasses with his index finger. "I wouldn't worry about that if I were you. Instead, why don't you worry about what you're gonna give me in exchange for my big favor?"

"What?" I choke. He has to be kidding me.

"I don't do anything for free, 'Me. You should know that by now."

"I'm asking you a favor. As a friend."

He gets up slowly, walks around the island until he's standing right in front of me and bends down slightly to look me in the eyes. "I am *not* your friend, Jamie. You can see me as your ex if you wish. You can see me as your enemy. Or you could see me as the first guy who ever gave you an orgasm. But if you think I'm your friend, you got me all wrong, baby."

My gulp is a little too loud and his smile widens.

"So let me ask you again. What will you give me in exchange for getting your mom out of trouble?"

My heart picks up and my stomach coils with knots of apprehension.

Apprehension or anticipation?

My hands join on my lap, and I find some relief in twisting my fingers together. God, his eyes are so dark and so blue. Will the Whites forever be set on destroying any will I try to hold on to?

"What do you want?" I rasp.

He chuckles low and I want to push him to the floor for making fun of me.

"Why, I want you of course."

"You had me." I reply instantly. I knew exactly what he was going to say. I was ready for at least that. "You threw it away, remember? You know? When you used me to spy on your siblings."

He shakes his head and straightens up. I have to stretch my neck to look into his eyes.

"I don't want another relationship with you, 'Me. I want *you*. I want all of you, all night. I promise after sending you home tomorrow, I will get your mom out of jail."

Chapter 19

I shake my head in disbelief. "You can't be serious."

"Oh I am, believe me. Do it and when I let you go in the morning, you will never be the same again. There are things I've been dying to do to you, beautiful. I've held myself back and pretended to be the sweet guy when we were together. I was taken by surprise last time, when we had sex, and I held back *again*, by fear of scaring you away. But tonight...tonight you're all mine and I will show you just how far you can be pushed. How much you love being used as a little slut."

"Fuck you," I rage as I push him away and get off the stool. "God, you're the worst, Nathan. You...you...ugh." I stumble on my words from the fury.

Why am I letting him affect me still?

"How hard has it been to stay away from me since you and Jake broke up?" he asks out of topic.

"I'm not getting into that."

"You've been dying for me to fuck you. You're scared of losing Jake forever and so you don't. You want to keep a semblance of strength, but you *know* you want to do this. Deep down you know you're not getting Jake back and you're ready to go for the other person you can't resist."

"Stop it." My voice trembles under the forceful truth.

"I'm offering you an out, 'Me. An excuse. I'm holding something over you, you can pretend you don't have a choice."

He takes a quick step toward me, grabbing my hips and pushing me against the edge of the island.

"If you get caught, you can scream that I blackmailed you, that I'm just a horrible guy. Come on, 'Me. Let go. Completely."

My breathing is too fast, it's stopping my thoughts from functioning.

I shake my head one last time, but it's not very convincing. He puts both his hands on each side of my cheeks and stops my head movement.

"I *am* a horrible guy. I will keep you locked here, I will use you, I will abuse your body, and I will give you no chance of respite."

A soft whimper escapes my lips. This sounds too real.

"And you know what the worst thing will be?"

I try to shake my head no, but he's stopping me anyway.

"You're going to love it," he concludes.

He thinks he's got me. He really believes he's got me all figured out, like his brother. How many times do they think they can play me like that?

"No." I finally say. I'm not about to let another White play with my need for submission and my darkest fantasies. I'm not-

"Fine. I hope your mom likes prison food."

"What?!" I choke. "You can't do this you can't...you're evil!"

"When did you start thinking I was a good guy?" His grip on my head becomes tighter, pouting my lips. "Give yourself to me, Jamie. You're going to fucking love it, *and* your mom will be free. Win-win."

There was something I had never quite realized. That if I *didn't* give into my sick need to be dominated. Nathan would simply take it.

And what are you meant to do when all you want is save the person who means the most to you in this entire world?

His head drops, his lips are just below my ear. His breath on my skin burns, his soft soapy scent invades me.

"So, do we have a deal?"

And what a deal it is.

My nod is almost imperceptible, but I know he feels it

between his palms because I feel his lips stretching into a smile against my neck, and his next words are my demise.

"That's my good girl."

20

JAKE

Gods & Monsters – Lana Del Rey

"Bro, stop calling. I told you my dad won't be back until after dinner."

"I just want to check with you one last time. Are you sure you're okay talking to him?"

Luke is too good. Of course as soon as I told him what happened with Jamie's mom he said he would sort it out with his dad, but I know it's not safe. His father is an abusive piece of shit and I'm worried for my friend. I wanted to be there, and he insisted it would go more smoothly if it was kept between his family.

"Yeah, of course. My mom came home as well, it's all chill, man. Don't worry about me. I'll call you to let you know what he says."

I nod to myself before hanging up. I've got a missed call from Ozy, so I call her back.

Chapter 20

"I'm having the best day of my life," she says as soon as she picks up.

"Catch me up on Camila." I might be cold to her, but I don't really care about her fun right now.

"Oh you mean the girl whose daddy is going to find her naked and cuffed to her own bed with a note that says 'I'm a bad slut, I deserve this.'? Did you know she gets wet when she cries? And I'm not talking about her cheeks."

Yes. I know. But I don't reply to that.

"What else?"

The level of satisfaction I'm reaching right now is still not enough to drown out my hate for her.

"Someone's a greedy fucker."

"I want her dead, Ozy. So a little bit of humiliation is not gonna cut it for me."

"She's got all her stashes of coke spread out around her and the police on their way to her house."

"What. Else." I growl. Her dad is one of the most important people in this town. Being caught with a few grams of coke won't change shit for her.

"Hey Chris, I'm just gonna get something from the pool house." I'm assuming she has something to say she doesn't want him to know. I hear some doors, some walking and finally her voice again. *"We heard some noise at some point. Chris went outside to check if we were gonna get caught and left me alone with her."*

"And?"

"And I carved her. With the X."

"You what?!"

This is sadistic, dangerous...perfect. My twin took a knife and carved the tattoo we both have on our skins. Well, a simpler version. An X with the W under it. Only enemies of the Bianco family have that X as a scar.

"Too far?" she asks.

"Yes and no."

"It's on her hip bone, no one can see it if she's dressed."

"Yeah, but that means we stoop down to the gangster level."

"Next time she'll think twice before crossing us."

"She better."

I hang up.

I'm not going to feel bad for Camila. She put Jamie's mom in jail. She's crossed so many lines at this point, I'm not sure what else would bring her back to reality.

I'm driving aimlessly around Stoneview now. I don't want to go back to Chris' and there's no way I'm going home to Nate or Sam. I'm not even sure they're there but I won't take the risk.

The only person I want to see is Jamie. I want to explain myself, I want her to know that no matter how much of an asshole I am... I didn't do this to her and her mom.

When I get out of my own head, I recognize Silver Falls and enter the parking lot at the bottom of the trail that leads to the top of the falls. It's automatic for me to grab my phone and text Jamie.

> Jake: I fucked up a lot of things when it comes to you. But I didn't send that document to the police. I think we should talk. I'll wait for you where we had our first date, we can watch the sunset together.

My thumbs hover over the keyboard for a few seconds of hesitation before I send the text and make my way up the falls.

Chapter 20

But two hours later, when she hasn't shown up and the sun has gone down, panic overtakes me. What if...what if Bianco finally put his threats into actions? I try calling her a few times, but she doesn't pick up. So I call Emily instead.

"*How dare you try to talk to me,*" she snaps.

"Em, I didn't send that document!"

"*I don't care. You wrote it up in the first place!*"

I let out a long huff, really fucking tired of justifying myself.

"Look, I called to check if she's okay."

"*She's not with me. I picked her up from the cemetery. We spent a little time at her house so she could pick up her phone and then I dropped her at church. She wants to be left alone.*"

"The cemetery?"

"*It's the anniversary of her dad's death. Did you guys even date?! God, you're such a prick.*"

She hangs up on me and I can't really blame her. How did I not know that today was her dad's death anniversary? It also means it's the same date she got kidnapped. That her brother *disappeared*.

I walk back down to my car, settle behind the wheel and look at my phone. Still nothing from her. I'll try her again and if she doesn't pick up, I'm showing up at her house.

The ringing drives me crazy with anxiety. Come on, Angel. I hear her pick up, but she says nothing.

"Jamie? I've been trying to get through to you. Are you still at church?"

"*Ah, sorry brother. She's not at church anymore, but she's definitely on her knees.*"

I almost drop my cell, my blood turning freezing cold. Nate's voice is so smug I want to cut his tongue and feed it to him.

"You're lying," I whisper in disbelief.

"Stop calling her, Jake."

"Put her on the phone. Right fucking now." I grit my teeth.

"I'm afraid she can't talk. You know, mouth full and all that. It's rude to."

"I'm going to fucking kill you."

"I think I'm already in heaven," he chuckles. *"I can't believe I almost let you take her away from me."*

I throw my phone to my right. It hits the window and falls on the passenger seat beside me. Fucking asshole. I punch the steering wheel hard enough to make it scream in a loud honk. I do it enough times that some people around the parking lot start to look at me.

I'm going to find my brother.

And I'm going to kill him.

I burst into our house with a violence I didn't know I had. And I once broke someone's eye socket in the ring so that says a lot.

"Nate!" I shout to the empty foyer.

No answer.

"Nate, I swear to god you're a dead man! Where are you?!"

I run up the stairs and toward his room. I've never actually been in there. Up the stairs, there is a long hallway that goes to the left where mine and Ozy's bedrooms are, and to the right there is another even longer hallway that leads to a different wing of his mansion. I know it's down there, but I'm not even sure where.

I kick open every door I walk past like a crazy man. Jamie's managed to bring out the maddest parts of me.

"I'm going to find you," I growl as I kick open another

door. "And I'm going to make you watch while I fuck her!" I bark in fury when it turns out to be another empty room. "And then," I growl low. "I'm going to slit. Your." Kick open a door. Empty. "Fucking." Kick open another door. Empty. "Throat!"

I kick open the last door to find Nate's bedroom. It's gigantic. I feel like I've opened the door to the presidential suite at the Four Seasons.

His bed is not even in view. It's a sort of living room with a wooden, glossy coffee table. There is a sofa facing my way and at both ends of the table there is an armchair.

Nate is sitting in one of those armchairs. Jamie in the other. They're facing each other. He's fully dressed in his usual suit, his hair is tied in a small bun, like always, his glasses impeccable. The only thing that looks off is his beaten up face from last weekend, when Bianco unleashed some of his strongest men on him.

He's in complete control of himself, which makes me hate him even more when I compare it to the state of uncontrollable fury I'm in.

I'm panting with anger while he's casually sitting on the armchair, an arm resting on his thigh and the other dangling over the armrest. On the other side of the long coffee table, Jamie is sitting in the second armchair, only wearing the sexiest fucking black lace bra and a skirt.

I clench my teeth, desperately trying to control my dick that is hardening in my jeans. I notice her hands tight around the armrests straight away. Her nails are digging into them, like she's scared or frustrated.

"Jake," Nate smiles at me like a king on his throne. "I thought you'd join us. I wasn't sure about a threesome, but you know what? I'm feeling generous today."

"And I'm feeling murderous," I growl back. I turn back to

Jamie as soon as I'm done addressing myself to him. "Get the fuck out of this chair."

Her glassy eyes turn to me. Is she about to cry? What did he fucking do to her? And why is she not jumping on the occasion to escape him?

"Jamie!" I shout and she jumps in surprise, but she still doesn't move.

"She won't get up, Jake. She's mine for the night and she knows it. Don't you, beautiful?"

Her gaze goes back to him, and she only nods before proceeding to bite her bottom lip in the sexiest way I've ever seen.

"Jamie," I growl. "You better get your ass out of that chair before I make you."

I don't know if I'm saying this to protect her from him, to save her...or because my cock is now dying to be buried inside her pussy.

"Do you want to get up and join him, beautiful?" Nate asks.

She shakes her head no and that's when I see it. Her short pants, her blushed cheeks, her glossy eyes. The way her nails are digging into the armrests...

She's not in pain.

She's writhing in pleasure.

"She doesn't want to leave, Jake. She just wants to come."

Nate looks at her with a smile that is begging me to punch him. His right arm, that is dangling over the armrest, shifts and it makes her gasp. "So desperate to come, aren't you?"

She bites her lip but still, she can't control the moan that comes out as she loudly begs, "Please!"

"Motherfucker," I whisper when he brings his hand onto

Chapter 20 345

his lap. He's holding a small remote and I know exactly what it's connected to.

The shock is too great. The anger has turned into irresistible lust, and I can't utter a word. I should be flipping shit upside down right now. I should be on him, beating the shit out of him. I should be...fuck...what did I want when I walked in again? I wanted to fuck her in front of him. I wanted to make her scream with pleasure and pain while he watched. And then I wanted to kill him.

Well, what's stopping you from fucking her then?

Everything.

And nothing.

The beast in me is fully waking up for other reasons than my hatred for Nate. It's ready to shred Jamie into pieces. It's ready to use her over and over again until I'm imprinted on her like a fucking animal. The need for her, and to take over the situation is visceral.

She lets out a needy groan that makes Nate chuckle.

"Not yet, beautiful."

She opens her mouth to talk but he cuts her off. "I said no talking." His voice is harsh enough to make her clamp her mouth shut. "I let one go. I won't again."

She nods quickly and squirms on her chair. Fuck she is absolutely loving this.

"Jamie isn't allowed to come until I say so. And she knows once she does, she'll come over and over again until I deem she's had enough."

My jaw clenches hard, my hands fold into tight fists, and yet my cock begs for release.

"And you know what she said to me before we started? That she's already done overstimulation. That *you* had already done that to her...with Lik!" He explodes laughing like it's the funniest joke of the century, but my eyes don't leave the goddess being edged repeatedly.

"You're fine sharing her with Lik but not with me?" he insists.

"I didn't share her. Lik is gay, you asshole," I growl back. "Last time I checked you were fairly interested in my girl's pussy."

His tongue clicks as he tuts me. "Look at her, Jake. She's not yours. She's ours."

I want to retort something...but he's right.

"God, *look* at her. She's dying for both of us to ruin her."

My breath is coming out in short pants and I'm not even touching her. She moans a wordless complaint and I struggle to gulp down the desire building up in my throat.

Nate's voice is low with craving when he talks again. "Ruin her."

I don't know if he's talking to himself or me. I don't know if it's an order or a suggestion. I don't fucking care.

I get to Jamie in two long strides, grab her by the throat and lift her up. She screams in surprise but doesn't fight me.

"I see the little slut is out to play," I hiss in her ear.

I think I hate her as much as I love her. I sit down on the armchair, pull her down on my lap and spread her legs open with mine, completely aware that I'm exposing her to Nate.

"Is this what you want, Angel? You can't pick, so you want both?"

There's a beat before she nods. I don't know what that pause meant, but I don't care anymore. Keeping my legs against her inner thighs to make sure she doesn't close hers, I slip a hand under her skirt while the other one stays wrapped around her neck.

My stomach somersaults, my dick goes rock hard and

my spine tingles in appreciation when I feel how wet she is. Fucking dripping.

"Oh, Angel," I sigh against her neck. "You're such a bad girl."

My fingers wrap around the bit of silicone coming out of her pussy and that I know is attached to the vibrator Nate is controlling. I pull gently on it until I feel the largest bit stretch out the entrance of her pussy. She moans in delight, her muscles tensing against mine.

"Fuck," Nate whispers, his eyes trained on her pussy.

The view he must have...

I let go and the toy is sucked right back in. Her thighs are trembling around mine and my hard cock digs into her ass.

"You want to act like a brave girl, huh?" I taunt her. "You want to play us and beg for two dicks? My god, Jamie. We're going to destroy you."

Jamie

"My god, Jamie. We're going to destroy you."

I moan so loudly when Jake pulls at the sex toy again that his hand squeezes my throat until he cuts off the sound completely. My eyes dart to Nathan and I see him grab his hard length through his suit pants.

Oh my Gosh, Jamie. What are you doing?

This was never the plan. Yes, I'm undeniably attracted to both. And yes, I fucked both. But I never thought it would ever happen at the same time. I don't even know if I'm ready for this. Nathan is, but I know Jake isn't. I know because his grip is too tight, his heartbeat too fast, his possession too familiar.

Jake believes too firmly deep inside him that I belong to him and him only. He has never wanted to share me and neither did I...until now. The thought of the only two men to have ever made me come touching me all over, using my body for their pleasure, bringing me to the brink of sanity.

I've never been so wet in my life.

The vibrator in me accelerates and brings another scream out of me. I need to come. I need to come so bad I'm ready to do anything.

But Nathan oversees my fate tonight. He was very clear about that.

'I have many kinks, beautiful. I'm big on dominating my women. When I'm with Kay, I make her my captive. Fuck, she loves it so much. But you...you can just be my toy for the night.'

And out of all the things he said, I only replied one thing. *'Who's Kay?'*

He laughed and said, *'Toys don't talk. They just obey.'* He made sure to slip words of reassurance in my ear though. *'Your safe word is release.'*

Release.

So here we are.

I squeeze my eyes tightly shut, the pleasure is so overwhelming I want to cry, I want to beg to come. I want to go on my knees and prostrate myself at their altar if only they'd just let me fucking come!

"Did you suck his dick, Angel? While I was waiting for you at the falls, were you sucking his dick?"

What is he talking about? Jake's grip on my throat is lethal and I'm not sure how much longer I can take it.

"Answer me," he growls as he releases my throat. I cough but don't say anything. "Talk, Jamie. Show me you'd rather follow my rules than his." His fingers slip between my folds, and he pinches my clit.

"Yes," I hiss. "Yes, I did."

"Tsk, tsk, tsk," Nathan says as he shakes his head, and the vibrations stop suddenly.

"No," I whimper.

Jake chuckles behind me and lets go of my clit before stroking it gently, making me squirm on his lap.

"Bad girl," he says loud enough for Nate to hear. "Didn't he tell you not to talk?"

"But you–"

"I was just testing which one of us has a tighter control on you."

I feel his lips spread into a smile against my neck before his teeth clamp around my skin. I squeal before the pain subsides and his tongue draws more pleasure out of me.

"I like marking you, Angel," he murmurs against my skin, and I melt into his touch.

Nathan snaps his fingers, and my eyes go to him instantly.

"Over here. Now."

I feel Jake tense before he lets me go. I get onto my shaking legs, trembling with the need for release, and take one step but he tuts me again.

"Crawl."

I hesitate one second too long and the vibrating inside me starts again, making my legs weak and forcing me to my knees anyway.

"Atta girl. Get on the table."

I gasp with pleasure as the vibrator gets into a deliciously slow but sharp rhythm. I awkwardly get from the floor to the coffee table and crawl closer to him.

"You're gonna show him how you did it, beautiful."

I'm confused as to what he means until he gets up and undoes his pants, pulling out his gorgeous cock. Pleasure is spreading everywhere in my body, and I lick my lips at the sight in front of me.

On all fours on the coffee table, it puts my mouth precisely in front of his erection. I open wide for him and move closer to lick him, but he suddenly takes a step back.

"Stay," he orders low.

I don't move one bit as he comes back to me. His dick is a temptation I'm not sure I can resist, and I have to lick my lips again. From the corner of my eyes, I see his thumb pressing the remote and the vibrations get even sharper. I bite my lips to not let out any words. I look up at him as he strokes his length right in front of my face. I watch pre-cum bead at the tip, and it takes everything in me not to lick.

I look back up, whimper with need, my eyes heavy and yet still not leaving his. He smiles down at me from his mighty position and rubs the tip against my right cheek, spreading the sticky liquid and tempting me further. I squirm, I press my legs together, ready to come from his teasing only.

The vibrations stop suddenly, I open eyes I wasn't aware had closed and his full smile greets me.

"You may," he whispers, and I feel like it's Christmas morning.

My tongue unleashes on him, and I lick the whole of his length, completely forgetting about anything else. I drench him in my spit before taking him in and moaning around his cock.

Has he always tasted so good? Or is it only since he turned out to be a psychopathic piece of shit? My love compass is non-existent.

Bobbing my head up and down, I feel him slide a gentle hand in my hair and stroke my scalp. This feels too good. The toy is now completely still in me, and yet I can feel

Chapter 20

myself clenching hard around it. I'm ready to come, just from sucking his dick, just from clenching around a toy I know is so much smaller than he is.

"If you come, 'Me. I will force that vibrator on you all fucking night, you hear me? Your clit will be so raw you'll beg for me to end your life."

I whimper around him, desperately trying to control my rebellious body.

Please, please just let me come.

I'm so focused on giving Nathan pleasure that I don't hear the movement behind me. One hand comes on the small of my back and the simple gesture makes me moan. My tongue vibrates on Nathan's cock, and he groans in reply.

Jake's hand reaches between my legs, caresses my clit with the pad of his finger and then grabs the toy. He fucks me with it three or four times before slowly taking it out, making sure to stretch me as much as possible.

"You're dripping, Angel." Jake's voice makes me shiver hard enough that my thighs graze against each other. "Ssh, stay still," he soothes me as he runs his hand along my spine.

His hand goes away.

It reappears on my ass cheek, kneading and pinching before spreading them.

The only warning I get is the tip of his cock sliding against my lips before he slams into me so hard, I'm pushed forward and Nathan's dick goes to the back of my throat, choking me along with the shock of Jake's violent move.

Both their gasps of pleasure make me tighten around Jake. Nathan's grip on my hair intensifies, keeping me close against him and stopping my breathing.

Jake grabs my hips and pulls me back toward him,

easing the fullness of Nathan down my throat but making the grip on my hair painful.

I moan a complaint that makes them both chuckle and for a moment I'm not sure which chuckle is whose.

Jake picks up his pace, forcing my head to bob along Nathan's dick and he hisses in pleasure.

"Are you dying to come, beautiful?" Nathan pants. "Are you proud of being our slut tonight?"

I clench around Jake, and I feel him slow down.

No!

For the love of God don't slow down.

He relaxes a little behind me and I start moving my hips to pick up where he left off.

"Such a greedy slut," Jake rasps with desire. "Go on, fuck yourself on my dick, Angel."

I keep going, harder, quicker, moving my hips to a crazy rhythm while sucking Nathan's cock.

Nathan suddenly takes a step back, groaning as if he was a second away from coming down my throat.

"On your back."

Jake lets go of me and I execute so quickly, Nathan looks at me in surprise. Instead of keeping my face on Nathan's side, I switch, lay down on my back, and offer my mouth to Jake. He looks down at me with a half-smile on his face but somehow, it's a different one than usual. He's not satisfied, I can read it on his features.

Jake grabs me under my armpits and pulls me until my head is hanging from the table and all I can see are his ankles.

I feel hands on my thighs, Nathan must be getting on his knees because I hear a soft thump. The next second, I scream in pleasure as Nathan's tongue licks my pussy.

"How long can you hold until I let you come, beautiful?"

Chapter 20

"I can't hold!" I scream in frustration.

I only get a sharp slap on my clit in return. "What did I say about toys? They don't talk."

I'm on the verge of coming, tears springing in my eyes from the pleasure, when Nathan's tongue leaves me. Jake's ankles disappear from view, Nathan's cock slides along my pussy lips.

"Are you ready to come, baby?"

I only nod, not wanting another slap against my sensitive clit. I squeeze my eyes, ready to be full again but all I hear is a loud knock and Nathan's pained groan.

I jump into a sitting position, lightheaded from the sudden movement. Looking around I find Nathan on the floor, holding the side of his head. There's blood coating his fingers. Jake is standing next to him, his jeans back on, looking down at him with a smile on his face. That one I recognize. His winning smile.

He's holding his gun close to him.

"Did you...did you just hit him?"

Jake chuckles low and squats next to Nathan, bringing his gun to his brother's head.

"I can't believe you thought I was going to let you fuck my girl. And in front of me."

He breaks into a laugh, and I hop off the table, suddenly too aware that I'm only in a skirt and bra.

"Jake," I rasp as I walk to him. My throat is sore from sucking Nathan, my pussy still throbbing with the need for release. "What are you doing?"

He ignores me and just keeps talking to Nathan, who is now looking straight at the gun.

"Why do you have to be such a jealous fucker, Jake?" he asks, his voice carrying mockery. "Can't you see she was enjoying herself? Your need for control is a little pathetic. It just shows how desperate for it you are. It shows you can never truly grasp it."

Nathan can mock him all he wants but right now, he's the one on the floor with a gun pointed to his head and a bleeding temple.

"Turns out I'm just a tad too possessive to share her. But I did warn you, brother. What did I say again? Oh, that's right, I said I'd fuck her in front of you." He gestures in the air, pretending he's holding a pen and ticking. "Ticked. And then..." the poisonous smile that spreads on Jake's lips makes me gulp in fear. "...then I said I'd slit your throat."

He gets up, still pointing the gun down at Nathan. "Forgive me for the lack of knife. I hope shooting you will be just as satisfying."

The bang is so sudden, so smooth, so doubtless that I almost miss it.

Almost.

But I don't.

My ears ring, my heart jumps in my throat. My legs shake, my stomach sinks.

Just like that day.

The smell of gunpowder and copper makes me gag and I take steps back until my back crashes violently against shelves of books behind me.

I can see Nathan rolling to his side and the blood pouring out of him.

Everything is a mix of blur and unbearable screeching in my ears.

Jake turns to me. He's talking, he's moving toward me in strides so smooth I struggle to register them.

God, when did he become so dangerous? When did he get the upper hand on Nathan? Jake is a strong man, but when it came to his brother, he was always the weaker one.

Chapter 20

Stuck in his hate, stuck in a fear that was imposed on him since his childhood. Where was this lethal strength hiding all the time I was in love with him?

What are you talking about, Jamie?

It's been here all along, right in front of you, shining so bright it blinded you.

Jake White is the devil. He never tried to hide it. In fact, he's been desperate for you to know he was nothing else but!

"Did you hear me? I said come here," he tells me in the calmest voice I've ever heard from him. "I'm not done with you."

Why is he so calm?

I try to talk but I can't formulate any words. The ringing is too loud, the whole place is shaking and...no it's me, I'm shivering so hard my teeth are clattering and my vision blurred. I open my mouth to say something, but nothing comes out. My eyes dart to Nathan on the floor.

Is he conscious? Is he still alive? How long has it been since he got shot? A minute? Fifteen? An hour? I've lost all concept of time and space.

That's why I don't understand how close Jake is. And when his firm hand wraps around my upper arm I jump in fear.

"Don't worry about him. He won't get more than exactly what he deserves."

That doesn't help. Jake has wanted his brother dead for too long.

"And *you* need to be taught a lesson on who you belong to."

I shake my head, feeling tears spring to my eyes. My voice is a hoarse whisper when I finally manage to push words out.

"I don't belong to you. You betrayed me."

He pushes me hard into the shelves, his hips digging into my stomach. His anger spikes again.

"I didn't betray you," he growls. "All I've been trying to do since being back in Stoneview is protect you. And all you did in return was fuck my brother."

I push back at him without success. "I bet you were loving protecting me when you were balls deep into Billie's pussy," I wheeze from fury.

He laughs as his mouth comes to my ear. "Her cunt had nothing on yours, Angel."

One second his lips are against the shell of my ear, the next he's dragging me out of the room, across the countless hallways of the mansion. He pushes open the door I'm assuming leads to his room and pushes me face down onto his bed.

"There you go. Exactly where you belong."

He doesn't let me up, no matter how hard I fight, no matter how deep my insults go.

I feel him look for something in-between the sheets, but I can't see. He's got both my arms bent behind my back, pressing my wrists against my spine and keeping me tight against the mattress.

"You're fucking insane," I rage. "Let me go! Life is not about taking everything without asking."

"You let him take without asking," he retorts behind me.

My stomach twists as fear grips my guts. "Jake, you don't understand. My mom...he's going to get her out of jail. I owe him!"

He cackles loudly and I feel his weight shift slightly.

"That's the excuse you're giving yourself? That's the bullshit you're feeding *me*? Do you think I don't fucking know you? That I don't know how wet you get for him when he asserts power over you?"

Chapter 20

The shame that fills me chokes me. It stops me from answering, which confirms the truths he spat at me.

"You know how much you want him, Jamie. And I know how he loves taking advantage of people. What, you were going to spend the night with him, and he frees your mom in the morning? Do you even see how fucked up this is! Who says he was even going to do it?"

"Well he sure can't do it now that you left him for dead!" I rage. "You can't let him die, Jake. He's your brother!"

"Please, while you were sucking his cock on all fours like a bitch in heat. I texted Sam to tell him I was going to hurt Nate. Don't worry, he'll come in no time to help his boss. Let's hope Nate hasn't bled to death by the time he shows up. Either way, you won't need him to free your mom."

"What?"

"I already took care of it." His phone lands right next to my face and I rear my head back to look at the screen. My mouth falls open in shock.

> Luke: It's done, bro. He's dropping the charges. She'll be fine.

"W-what? But...but..."

I'm so shocked, so lost in my own head, I don't register the metal slipping around my wrists until I hear the gradual snap locking in place.

"But, but, but," he mocks me. "I told you I didn't send that fucking document to the police."

And the fact that he kept saying he didn't send it to the *police* should have told me it was the truth. Because the document wasn't sent to the police as he thinks, it was sent to Mr. Baker. Mom said so.

"But why do we care now," he continues. "You wanted to

give that tight pussy to the guy who got you out of trouble. Time to deliver."

His fingers enter me violently and I gasp in shock. My arms try to move, I tense against what I'm assuming are handcuffs. Not funny, furry handcuffs that anyone could break. No, these ones bite into my skin, hurt my bones.

I'm still so wet from our previous play and my need to orgasm comes back just as strong.

"Oh, God," I moan loudly.

"That would be me," he chuckles.

Two fingers turn into three and I scream at the pleasurable intrusion. From behind, his palm is cupping the underside of my ass cheeks, slapping against me from how harsh his fingers are moving inside me. He curls his fingers, rubs his rough knuckles against the magic spot and the scream that comes out of me is unrecognizable. My whole body is impossible to control anymore, and I push back against his hand.

But then panic overtakes me.

"Jake...I..." I pant. He puts more pressure on my g-spot and I shriek. "Wait I–"

He releases the pressure and I take a deep breath. "I think I need to-" This is the most embarrassing thing that has ever happened to me, and I can't get myself to say it. "I need a break..."

He chuckles behind me. He rubs his knuckles again, puts slight pressure on the spot and I melt against the mattress.

"Who decides when you come, Angel?" My lack of response makes him press slightly harder. It's too much and yet barely enough. "Who gives you the most pleasure? Who allows your orgasms," he insists in a growl.

"You!" I scream with need. "It's you! You, you, you, always you!"

He laughs at my admission. "I know."

"Jake, I think I need to go to the bathroom," I admit in shame as he stops.

"No, you don't," he bends over my back, whispering in my ear, "you can come now. Release."

I don't know what he means until he accelerates and forces my body to release in the most soul-shattering orgasm I've ever had. I can feel myself wetter than usual, I can feel myself shamelessly leaking onto his hand and...I don't even care. The pleasure is too strong for my mind to protest. I melt into his hand, the never-ending pleasure overpowering everything.

"That's my girl. God, Jamie you're so fucking hot squirting all over my hand."

I gulp a deep breath when he retrieves his hand. One second he's pulling at my hips, the next I'm on my knees, cheek against the mattress.

Time stops when he spreads my ass cheeks and feel his mouth against my burning core. I don't even understand if I'm still coming or if it's a new pleasure but when his tongue starts fucking my pussy, I rub against his face shamelessly. He then unleashes on my clit, makes out with my pussy, eats me out like he's got a degree in cunnilingus from Make Me Come University.

And when he breaks away, and I'm panting for more, still high on the pleasure he grants me, his dick enters me with the most loving, slow stroke we've ever experienced together. I moan, I writhe for more and he keeps going at a torturous pace. He takes a long break once he's completely in and even just being full of him and not moving keeps some of that orgasm alive.

When he starts moving, it's slow and sensual, making both of us moan desperately. He's torturing us and he knows it, he's keeping us on the fine edge between loving and possessing.

"I need more," I whisper, afraid to break the background noise of our panting.

"Ssh," he says as he folds over me and starts kissing my neck.

His dexterous fingers unclasp my bra, but it can't fall off completely because of my hands cuffed behind my back. It's still enough for him to slip a hand under and grab my right nipple, rolling it between his thumb and index finger.

A groan pushes its way past my constricted lungs. I need to come again, or still? I'm orgasmically confused since I squirted all over his hand, the pleasure doesn't start or end, it's a continuous thrill that just won't come down.

"Your right nipple is always so much more sensitive than the left," he whispers just before sucking at the skin where my neck and shoulder join.

I never even realized that. I always trust him with my pleasure without wondering which buttons he should push to work me up.

"And your skin doesn't mark easily. I always have to bite hard to leave my mark on you."

Why is he saying all this?

His next thrust is harder than the previous, making me moan louder.

"You always get wetter if I go harder, but not as much if I go quicker."

"Jake," I moan.

His hot breath on the skin he just bit sends shivers down my spine.

I feel him straighten up, leaving my abused nipple and

bringing his hand to my clit while the other goes up to my throat. He pulls until I straighten up and my back hits his chest. It would be impossible for me to stay upright without his hand wrapped around my neck.

My hands are secured tightly behind me, and I can feel his abs tensing against my fingers. His hand against my clit flattens and he delivers a soft slap. The pleasure spiking from it makes my stomach and pussy tighten. He does it again, and again...and again. He enters a comforting rhythm that I fall in complete sync with.

"Fuck, you get so tight around me when I slap that beautiful cunt."

I hear him, but I can't focus anymore. I know my body is present and feeling all the pleasure he's imposing on me, but my mind has drifted to a place of pure peace. His voice soothes me, his strokes take me higher every time they land. Is this what heaven feels like?

I feel a harsher slap and I know it should bring me back down, but instead it pushes me further into that space of relaxation. The slaps stop, I feel him retreat slightly and when he enters me again, I scream as I orgasm.

He says something but I don't really hear it. Next thing I know, I receive a little slap on my face. It doesn't hurt but it's sharp enough to bring me back down.

"Don't leave for too long. I need you with me when I use you."

He pulls out of me which gives me more room to balance myself on my own. Now completely naked, he lies down on the bed and strokes his dick.

"Suck me."

I don't hesitate one second, I bend down, working my core muscles to not crash on him, and wrap my lips around his length. He gathers my hair in a ponytail and wraps it tightly around his fist. When he pulls, I go up, and when he pushes on the back of my head, I go down. No questions asked, no fighting, no rebellion. I'm just dying to please him.

He fucks my mouth relentlessly, the exact opposite of how he fucked my pussy. He pushes me down and chokes me with his dick, he pulls me up violently, he makes me beg to let me suck him. I drip saliva on him, I gag hard enough to make my whole body tighten. And still, he doesn't come.

He pulls at my hair one last time until he's completely out of my mouth and lets go of me. I sit back on my heels, and he grabs my hips positioning my entrance right above his dick.

"You're going to fuck yourself on my dick, Angel. And you're not gonna stop until we're both coming."

I nod, twist slightly to find more comfort in my bent wrist and start lowering on his dick. He holds his shaft until I'm low enough that his fist meets my pussy. He lets go and I sink deeper.

"Oh God," I moan as I sit completely on him and have him buried deep down.

"Get to work," he growls. Both hands now on my hips, he squeezes until I start moving.

I start slow, until the pleasure builds up so tightly that I force my burning thighs to move harder. When it gets too much, I stay down and roll my hips. I feel him tighten and he suddenly stops me from moving all together, keeping me tight against him as his hips move up to meet me harshly.

He accelerates, until I watch his head fall back in a loud groan. I come as he releases in me, his hips frozen mid-air, and both our bodies trembling.

He finally relaxes and falls back on the bed. I fall forward, my head hitting right in the crook of his neck and his arms wrap around my back, holding my cuffed hands.

Chapter 20

"I really fucking hate you," he whispers.

It should hurt but it doesn't.

"Me too," I reply weakly. I am spent.

"Almost as much as I love you."

"Me too," I conclude. My voice is barely a sigh. I can feel my heavy eyes struggling to open again.

I feel him uncuff me and I feel myself slipping onto the mattress as he moves away.

Stay awake, Jamie. You can't let your guard down now. You should check on Nathan. Make sure he isn't dead. You should go home. Don't stay around Jake now. He's lethal when he's like this and you...should...

My sleep is deep. It always is when I'm sleeping next to Jake, and especially after the orgasms we gave each other. The memory goes on repeat in my profound dreams. Then, slowly, the memory comes back alive, and my sleep lightens. My wrists still hurt, and it keeps the need for him awake.

My insides are still twisted with desire, and I feel myself clench. I'm vaguely aware I'm having a wet dream about the very man sleeping next to me and yet I just let it happen. My thighs tighten and I sigh in pleasure. Jake is asleep, I know that. I can just slide my hand-

I can't.

Reality mixes with the realm of my lustful dream when the pain in my wrists becomes too genuine and I can't move my arms.

What the hell is happening?

A little more awake but with sleep still prominent in my brain, I try to move my hands again.

Nope, definitely impossible.

That's when I feel it. The presence between my legs.

I slowly understand that my arms are stuck above my head and my legs are spread. Something is pressing against my clit, and I moan at the sudden pleasure that overwhelms me.

"Wake up, Angel. You're about to get fucked."

Jake's voice wakes me up fully and I open my eyes.

"Jake," I moan in a groggy voice.

I look above me. My wrists are back in the cuffs and locked to the headboard. Jake presses the heel of his palm against my clit again and I let the ecstasy seep through my veins.

His raw, low voice is in my ear next, and I understand he must have just woken too. "You woke me up with your little moans. Were you dreaming about me?"

I only nod. That's all he needs to press his hard dick against me. His hands slide behind my thighs and just above the back of my knees. He pushes my legs up and further apart until my knees are practically by my ears. My ass lifts from the mattress and he enters me in one violent stroke.

"Ah!" I scream with pleasure.

Entirely, pleasure. That's what makes me realize how wet I am. This didn't hurt even a little bit. I feel swollen around him, and I know I must have been getting wetter and wetter in my dream.

"Waking up to you being all wet and bothered while you sleep? I could get used to this," he rasps as he pumps in and out of me with a force that makes the bed shake and tests my flexibility.

His upper teeth come to bite on his bottom lip and my eyes get heavier with pleasure. God, he is so beautiful. His ink black hair is tousled from his sleep, his eyes are closed while he enjoys and gives into his own pleasure. When they

Chapter 20

open, the dark blue sucks me in. I want to love him forever. That's all I want.

I want to wake up by his side every day, I want his love and his support. I want the way he always lifts me up when I'm down, I want him to let go of the demons.

Every time I think of all the curves life has thrown at me, I get exhausted. Do us humans never get to rest? Do we always have to suffer from the agonies of being alive? Life took my dad away, it took my brother. It traumatized me from the world. It threw lies and fake hopes at me. But Jake? I'm not saying it always feels good, simply that I know it's genuine. And if life must hurt, why can't I be in pain by his side?

That's all I want. To be by his side through it all.

But I know despite tonight, despite the orgasms and the words. By tomorrow morning, he will be back to the words he told me every time we got close since he's been back: We're not getting back together.

I know he felt me slip away because his next stroke is harder, it makes me scream in agonizing pleasure. He brings my legs back and locks them around his waist before sitting back on his heels. The position makes him hit straight into my g-spot and my eyes roll to the back of my head. He accelerates his pace and so does my breathing.

I have to wrap my fingers against the handcuffs chain to feel somewhat grounded because I can feel myself going back into pleasurable heaven. His strokes come harder, and I come undone. The orgasm lights up my veins, explodes into my heart, fills my lungs with unexplainable screams of pleasure, and keeps me in a drugged-up state. He finishes in a barely audible groan and freezes.

"My wrists hurt," I rasp when he finally moves off me.

"Tough," he says as he starts walking away.

"Jake?" I panic, pulling at the cuffs.

He turns back my way straight away. "I'm only joking."

His smile is lit up by the moonlight as he hurries back to me. He rests his palms on both my cheeks and gives me a long, loving kiss.

He retreats slightly and observes my face. I see his eyes darting from mine to my lips, my nose. He looks at my neck, my cheeks, and back to my eyes, completely lost in his own world.

"So...those cuffs?" I whisper.

He shakes his head, as if surprised that I am not a silent little doll and rather an actual human being. He nods and undoes them, before rubbing my wrists with his warm fingers. I go to clean myself in his ensuite and come back to bed.

He hugs me tightly in silence, his hands moving around my body. Not in a sexual way anymore. He explores me as if it was the first time he ever felt my body and its shape. I fall asleep with my head on his chest, my leg around his waist and his hand massaging my thigh.

21

JAMIE

Shadow Preachers – Zella Day

I wake up from the sunlight hitting the bed. Memories of my moments with Jake warm my heart, but they're too quickly overcome by the anxiety of knowing what happened to Nathan.

I slowly open my eyes to find Jake is not next to me. Gradually getting up and rubbing my eyes, I jump in surprise when I see him in front of the bed, sitting on his desk chair and watching me. I instantly know who I'm dealing with. Closed Jake, sociopathic Jake. The one with the secrets and the darkness. The one who doesn't care if I'm hurting.

"Hi," I say just before I swallow the rock stuck in my throat.

"We need to talk," he simply replies. His voice sends a shiver down my spine, and I instantly think of his words from last night.

I hate you almost as much as I love you.

Is that a good or a bad thing?

"Yeah," I say as I get off the bed.

I find his t-shirt from yesterday and slip it on. I'm not about to have a serious talk naked. Especially when he's wearing his signature gray sweatpants. With nothing else of course. Jake hates wearing a top in the morning, he's always too hot.

The fact that I know this about him makes me sad. We were so happy together. Why did he have to ruin everything?

"Is that the same tattoo as Chris?" I say as I point to his upper arm.

He looks at the bottle of whiskey as if he forgot it was there and then back at me. "Rose shouldn't be allowed near a tattoo gun when drunk," he shrugs.

I smile at that. "Must have been a wild night."

"I don't want pointless chit-chat, Jamie," he scolds me, and it makes me roll my eyes.

"What do you want to talk about then? I'm guessing this isn't a declaration of love." I say as I cross my arms and pop a hip.

Jake is so used to me bending to his whims. He needs to understand this is not going to be the kind of conversation he's used to.

I've changed this year. And I like the new me, especially if it means I can stand up to him.

"No it's not."

"And we're not getting back together."

"No. We're not."

He slowly gets up, making me too aware of his height. But I don't let it impress me.

"We can't keep doing this," he explains. "We ignore each other until we can't hold back anymore. We argue and have sex, or the other way around, and go back to staying away for a little while. That's not how breakups work."

"Now, how would I know that? It looks exactly like how you did it with your ex."

He doesn't appreciate the reminder of how badly he handled his breakup with Camila, but he doesn't deepen the topic. He defends himself instead.

"Yeah," he says bitterly. "Apparently that's what you did with yours too. You know, how you went and fucked Nate and all that."

"We weren't together anymore. You shouldn't have cared."

"Except I did," he growls. "And you know that. If not to hurt me, I don't know why you did it."

"Maybe it wasn't to hurt you, Jake. Maybe I don't do everything to please or hurt you. Maybe *I* wanted to have a break from the pain for a moment."

He chuckles and I have to turn away for a second. I'm already getting worked up and I don't want to be the first to lose my sanity. Even if we know it's inevitable for both of us.

"Fine," he snaps before running a hand through his messy hair. "You did it because I was so mean to you, boohoo. But-"

"You weren't *mean* to me," I cut him off. "Mean is Camila leaving pointless threatening notes in my locker or breaking my bike. But the way you left me? What you did to me? That wasn't mean, Jake. You completely *obliterated* me. You crushed my heart. You broke it in so many pieces there are some bits of myself I'm still looking for among the splinters and crumbs."

He stays silent for a few seconds, his eyes flooded with pain and his mouth twisted with regret. I know he's only realizing now how much he hurt me, but I'm done pretending to him that he didn't. If he wants to act like a big boy, then he should know the consequences of what he did. And some of those are breaking me.

I keep going. "So where are you going with this conversation? Is it an apology for how you treated me?"

"It's-"

But I can't even let him talk anymore. "But wait, if it is. Is it for the bullying *before* we were together? Is it for the way you wouldn't let me in while we were dating? For always keeping me at arm's length when it came to the real you? Is it for the fuckboy way you broke up with me? Or is it for the post-breakup humiliation you put me through?"

"Don't!" he barks. "You can hate me for how shitty I was to you at the beginning of the year. Yeah, it was really fucking questionable. And you can hate me for the shit breakup and for Billie. But fuck, Jamie, you can't hate me for keeping my past to myself."

"I don't hate you for keeping it to yourself," I correct him. My voice is getting angrier by the second. "I blame you for the dangerous way you let it control you. For the toxic traits you just won't let me help you with."

"Yes, because you are such a saint. You never lied to me. Always squeaky clean. Little Miss Goody Two Shoes."

"I never lied to you."

"Think again," he replies straight away. "The night my brother came to your house, huh? The night he came to tell you that he would never let you be with me. See, Jamie, that's how toxic my past is. That's why I don't want to include you."

My hands slide in my hair and grip the roots out of frustration.

"You are such an asshole," I growl. "You mean the same night you beat him up and never told me about it?!"

"Why do you care if I beat him up, huh?! Why do you care about him so much? For fuck's sake after everything he did. Why would you give him your heart when I'm right here begging for it!"

"You're not begging for it, you keep pushing me away!" I hiss.

"Because I *have* to!" His voice thunders into the room and I'm surprised the windows don't tremble. "And I know I can't have you, but I'm asking you to not run to him. You belong to me and if I can't have you, he shouldn't either. Choose anyone you want just," his pitch rises with pain, "just don't choose him."

"I never chose him over you," I reply calmly.

"You did!" he rages. "You slept with him and—"

"And you slept with Billie!"

Pushing all pride away, I assault him with the only truth I have left.

"My heart belongs to *you,* Jake. And you know how I know it? Because Nathan lied to me, he betrayed me... *once.* And I never forgave him."

I take a deep breath before admitting the rest to both him and myself.

"But you? My God, you put me through hell. You bullied me, you used me, you mocked me. I let you humiliate me in front of everyone. I let you play with me like a willing toy. And yet, I don't regret any of it. After everything you've done my heart still whispers your name as it beats. I still love you and it kills me. So yeah, that's how I know it's you and not him."

"Don't say this, please."

"That's what you just begged me to say!" I scream in frustration. My voice sounds hysterical. "What kind of game are you playing?!"

He turns around and pushes his chair away in frustration. "Fuck this shit," he grumbles quietly "I can't do this."

"The reason you can't take this is because I'm not letting you walk all over me anymore! You don't want a girl who talks back, a girl who refuses you. You want someone that will bow to you and always agree. That's not me anymore! Not for you, not for anyone."

"You're right." When he turns around, his voice levels back to normal. As if he's desperate to keep the peace. "But this is not what this conversation is about."

"Please enlighten me," I scoff. "What is this about?"

"It's about stopping this shit! All the arguing and the hurting and the...the..." he huffs and falls back in the chair. "Jamie..." his voice wavers slightly. "I have to tell you something."

He sits back down, his elbows land on his knees, and he takes his whole face in his hands. His next words are muffled. "And you're going to hate me for it."

I frown as I shake my head. Did he listen to anything I just said?

"But when you do, when you hate me with your whole being. Please, *please* I'm begging you don't go back to him. Because he hid just as much as I did."

My heart picks up as I understand there really is something awful coming.

"What are you talking about?" I whisper in fear.

"I'm not allowed to tell you this. And I shouldn't for both our sakes. But I can't keep this to myself anymore, it's eating me from the inside."

"Jake, you're scaring me."

He shakes his head. "Don't be scared."

"What is it?"

Chapter 21

"Angel, your brother..." he gulps so loudly my eyes widen. "He isn't dead."

Nothingness.

That is the only way I can describe what I'm feeling right now. There is nothing. I'm all empty.

"Jamie?" he asks, trying to bring me back to reality.

"Liar."

"What?" He jumps off his chair and comes toward me, but I take a step back. "I'm not lying."

"You're lying! You and Nathan convinced me I was wrong. You both told me he was dead, that he was buried with other corpses Volkov leaves behind."

"I know...I know I said that but-"

"I accepted he was dead. He's dead."

The back of my knees hit the bed and I let myself fall until I'm sitting. Jake's hands grab me at the nape of my neck, his fingers interlock in my hair and his thumbs rub my cheeks as he squats in front of me.

"He's alive, baby. I've known since your birthday, and... and I haven't said anything." He quickly tries to justify himself. "But I was trying to look for him, I promise you, I was just trying to find him. I still am."

"No," I shake my head as my throat tightens. "That's not true."

Then why can't I stop the tears from building up in my eyes.

"If it was true, you would not have hidden it from me. You wouldn't do this to me. You wouldn't, right you wouldn't?"

But the answer is clear in his eyes.

"Jake!" The sob that explodes out of my throat surprises both of us. "Wh-How could you?" I get up so suddenly he almost falls to the floor.

"Jamie," he falters as he gets up. "I-I wanted to tell you. Fuck, I was dying to. But Bianco...the things he said he would do. Please, you have to understand. I know you hate me right now, but I was trying to protect you. I still am!"

I shake my head, utter devastation raging in my heart.

"This is not as simple as it seems. Aaron isn't just alive," he explains. "He works for Volkov. He's a Wolf, Jamie."

There is a long pause before I howl hysterically. The laugh ringing out in the room must belong to someone else because I would never sound like this.

"My brother is a Wolf," I cry out. "Now I *know* you're lying."

But he's not. He's not lying.

God, he's not lying.

My whole world crumbles around me. This is impossible.

A ruffle coming from the door makes us both jump. Someone is trying to open the locked door. A loud knock resonates before Nathan's voice snaps at us.

"Open the fucking door, Jake."

Nathan. At least he's alive.

"Not the time," Jake snaps back.

"Bianco is downstairs, it really is fucking time."

My heart drops in my stomach and I run to the door, snapping it open. "He's here? Now? Downstairs?"

"My my, she's still here," Nathan smiles. His eyes dart to Jake before they come back to me.

Mine go to the sling around his shoulder. It keeps his arm folded against his stomach, bandages peek from underneath it. "Don't look at me like that, 'Me. It's really hard to kill me, and Jake can't aim for shit."

"I didn't try to kill you," Jake grumbles behind me.

This family is so fucked up I don't even try to under-

Chapter 21

stand their relationship anymore. Why has shooting your siblings become so normal to the Whites?

"You need to leave, Jamie," Nathan orders low.

"I need to see Bianco. He knows about my brother." Everything I say feels so neutral. My lips feel numb, and my mouth feels like I've been injected with an anesthetic.

Nathan's behavior takes a dramatic turn as he pushes me out of the way and threateningly strides to Jake. "You told her?" he snarls.

"She had to know," Jake replies.

"No she didn't. You told her because you can't stand her hating you. You told her because you wanted to be a fucking hero. This is no time to be a hero, Jake."

"I told her because her brother is alive. I wish someone had told me you were still around when you were meant to be six-feet under."

Once again, the White brothers become so obsessed with each other they forget I'm in the room. But it works to my advantage this time.

They're still arguing when I slip out of the room and sprint through the hallway. When I reach the stairs, I slow down and take a breath. I'm going to meet Mateo Bianco for the second time in my life. But this time I'm ready and he has something I need.

I take every step like my life depends on it, like Aaron is the one I'm going to meet downstairs. Now that I know he's alive, he could be anywhere. And if he's really a Wolf...he could be in Stoneview.

When I finally reach the last step, Bianco is facing the hallway I know is leading to the kitchen and he doesn't see me approach in his peripheral vision.

My whole body is trembling. Partly because he's a terrifying man, mainly because I know he holds information I'm desperate to know.

He must feel my presence because he turns to me as I try to discreetly approach him.

His saccharine smile spreads wide on his face. He is handsome in a wicked way. It must be so easy for him to charm everyone. It must be hard to grasps that he is a truly horrible man. But I know.

"Jamie Williams," he enunciates clearly, pointing out he knows exactly who I am.

He's not even surprised to see me here, or he hides it extremely well.

I suck in a breath when he takes a step toward me. He's not very tall or big. In fact, he is very average. His skin is tanned like the Whites and it's like he could really be their family.

I want to say something. I know what I came downstairs for, but God he is petrifying. I couldn't pinpoint exactly where it is physically, maybe it's just knowing the things he is capable of.

"Did you want to talk to me, Jamie?" he asks lowly.

I try to swallow the sand sticking to my throat, but my voice comes out breathless. "My brother...wh—" I have to swallow again before I continue. "Where is he?"

He only smiles at me. No answer. But it's a knowing smile. He's happy because he knows he has something on me.

"I need to know," I insist in what sounds barely above a whisper.

"Jamie, what are you doing here?" I recognize the husky voice before I even take my eyes away from Bianco.

Rose is now standing next to him, having come back

Chapter 21

from the kitchen. She's handing out a small espresso cup to him.

"I—"

"You can't stay," she chastises me. "Leave and—" Bianco puts a hand up and she stops talking right away.

The frustration that rises out of me when he turns her into the opposite of who she truly is makes my blood boil.

"I-I want to know where my brother is," I say a little louder.

My fingers are digging into my palms, leaving crescents on my skin and giving me courage.

"Your brother?" Rose asks. She clearly has no idea what this is about. She isn't in on the secret Bianco shared with her brothers.

"Who told you about him?" he asks.

I stay quiet, not willing to give more information than necessary.

"Which one was it? Nate?" his chin points to something above my left shoulder. "Or was it Jake?" This time to my right.

I turn around to find the White brothers standing behind me, expressions shut, chins raised. The perfect masks on.

"I just want to find my family," I explain quietly, feeling the storm coming. "I don't care about..." how do I put this? "...what you do. Your business is your business. My brother is mine."

He slowly drinks his coffee and I feel a hand on the small of my back. "Time to go," Jake's voice is low in my ear and it's vibrating with fear. For himself? Or for me?

"I just want to know," I insist.

"Jamie, please," he implores as he pushes me slightly, trying to get me to take a step.

It's not Jake that gets me to move. It's Rose's pleading eyes. She is so breakable next to Bianco. The quicker I leave, the quicker he'll leave.

My body guides me to the door slowly, but I don't turn back. Not until Jake opens the door for me and Bianco's voice calls for me.

"I don't know where exactly your brother is, Jamie. I just know my men have seen him in Stoneview. He doesn't work for me, after all, he works for my enemy. I don't know where he is at all times."

I gulp as my stomach twists. Aaron is in Stoneview. Or at least he's been recently.

I nod in response, but he doesn't stop there.

"What I do know, however, is that you're a very curious girl. I'm sure you've heard of the saying 'curiosity killed the cat'." His tone is still light and my brows furrow. Is this a game to him?

"I have," I snap. I'm ready to leave now. I'm not here to play his stupid games.

"I think someone should warn you," his voice turns low and ominous, "that sometimes it's a long and painful death."

My nostrils flare as my heart picks up and the need for air becomes more prominent. Is that a threat?

Of course it is, you stupid girl.

I don't have time to reply, Jake drags me out of the house.

"Do you understand now?" he whispers to me. "Why I can't be with you?" He slams the door in my face.

I'm not halfway down the driveway that I can hear the shouting resonating within the walls of Nate's mansion. My whole body is begging me to go back and get the twins out of that house.

But I have my own problems to deal with, my own family to save.

22

JAMIE

If You Want Love – NF

How hard can finding someone be? It took me hours last night to process the news. Mom came home and I couldn't bring myself to say it to her. Because what if it isn't true? What if Bianco is playing all of us? I've spent so long hoping he was alive that I can't quite believe it's real.

But lying on my bed for hours, hoping Aaron would magically appear, hoping I would suddenly forgive Jake for keeping this from me. It's not taking me anywhere.

So as I get dressed to go to town today, I only have one thing on my mind: Aaron.

I have to go to the shops around town to drop off my resume. It's one thing that Mom is out of jail and Gerald Baker has dropped the charges but we both got fired.

Biking along the cars on my way to the town center, I check into every single one that overtakes me. Going from shop to shop, I keep hoping there's a chance for me to bump into Aaron. For him to magically appear. But is he even in Stoneview? Our small town has never felt so big.

Jake was right all along, he was either dead or he didn't want to be found. And he isn't dead. Aaron being alive doesn't mean I'm going to see him anytime soon.

I come out of His&Hers with a heaviness in my heart. Why would I walk into the fanciest shop in town and hope they even look at me when I hand out my resume.

'You don't have the look,' they said.

Yeah, I thought so in a shop kept by a handful of model-like-fake-influencer white girls.

You don't have the look.

Probably a bit too young. A bit too poor looking. A bit too non-Caucasian.

"Whatever," I mumble as I head out.

Mom has been crying on the phone to Pastor Gilligan all morning. She thinks I don't know, that I don't hear her if she locks herself in her room. The pressure of finding a job weighs heavy right now.

My phone ringing drags me out of my dark thoughts.

"Nathan?" I check when I pick up. As if his name on my screen wasn't proof enough that it was him.

"We should talk," he tells me. *"You know where Silver's is, right? Meet me there in an hour."*

He doesn't even give me time to answer. He knows I'll go anyway.

Nathan is just as guilty of keeping that secret from me and I know that. But I wasn't expecting anything from him. I know he only cares about what benefits him and him only.

Jake was meant to be the one. He was meant to protect me and keep me safe. He was meant to be honest and truthful.

And he lied.

Not about anything, he lied about Aaron being alive for fuck's sake. How am I meant to forget that?

Chapter 22

But Nathan...I almost expected that from him. So what could he possibly want to talk about now?

I walk across Silver's parking lot on trembling legs. I don't know if I can face Nathan after everything that happened yesterday. I can see through the window that he's sitting at a booth on his own. He looks so tired and pale. His sling-wrapped shoulder still makes my stomach twist with guilt. I didn't shoot him, but I might as well have. Bringing Jake's wrath on him wasn't intentional but going back to Nathan when it didn't work out with Jake wasn't a wise decision, especially knowing that Jake will always be my one and only choice.

I discovered the difference between love and simple lust, and Nathan paid for it. Now I face the consequences.

Nate

Jamie is twenty minutes late when she hops out of the taxi that drove her to Silver's. I can see her from the booth I chose by the window. She's just as gorgeous as usual.

And fuck if she is gorgeous.

When she comes in, her gaze looks around before it lands on me. She's got that worried look on her, the one that just makes me want to take her in my arms and kill whoever put that look on her face.

Problem is...it's me.

I've never found it hard to make decisions purely based on what *I* want. It's easy, I'm always given two choices: The one that will please anyone but me. The one that would please me. Simple math, really.

Then Jamie came into the picture.

Well she didn't exactly come in, I found her. And I really wasn't meant to fall for her.

But fuck she's got that way about her. She's strong willed and powerful and yet her heart is begging you to save her. She doesn't even realize she's doing it, but she's subconsciously screaming *'help me I never recovered from my trauma'*. And I guess if there is one thing I know about, that would be trauma.

She pulled at my weaknesses. The ones I wasn't even aware I had. She dug her way into my heart, found her residence, settled herself, and redid the decoration. Now she lives there rent free.

"Sorry, I'm late," she huffs as she sits on the bench opposite me. "I had to drop my bike home and wait for a taxi. They're rare in Stoneview."

She's wearing a light pink blouse with a short, black skater skirt and my brain is already running a million scenarios of how I could take her on this table. I bet she's wearing those lace booty shorts she loves so much. I hope it's the red ones.

"You wanted to talk," she says, cutting off an imaginary image of her bent over the table.

"Yeah," I sigh back. I've got a headache and my arm is killing me. I need more painkillers.

All that because Jake decided to suddenly grow a pair of balls and use his new braveness to shoot me out of jealousy rather than to fight back against Bianco. Stupid fucking kid.

Jamie is looking at me with a million questions in her eyes and I know it's time to admit what I've been up to. I just know she's going to be confused after that. Not that she won't get it, she's incredibly smart, but her heart will be torn, and I can't have that. I need her focused.

"My Stoneview stay is coming to an end," I admit.

Chapter 22

Her brows furrow in that way that would make anyone want to rub their thumb between them to smooth them out.

"What do you mean?" she asks, completely lost.

"I think it's about time I explain myself, isn't it? If anyone deserves the truth, it sure is you. Would you like to eat or drink something?" I point at the nachos in front of me. "You were right, these are amazing."

"Just get to the point, please."

I'm always smitten with how polite Jamie stays. Even when she's impatient, or angry or sad. Her elocution and her civility rarely take a fall.

She settles back in her seat and crosses her arms, waiting for me to start.

"As much as this is going to hurt you, I did come to Stoneview to find the twins. And I did use you to spy on them."

Her jaw clenches but she doesn't say anything.

"That day Sam found them, he saw you being...well you. Eavesdropping and being a little detective. He saw Jake trying to scare you away, and he told me."

"Did you come to find me at Church?" she instantly asks.

"I did, yeah."

She shakes her head, the disappointment so clear in her eyes it actually pinches my heart.

"There's no need to go over how much I fucked up," I say. "I wanted to use you to be closer to the twins and I fell in love with you like a fucking rookie. Period."

Her brows lift in surprise. I guess I had stopped telling her how much I love her. I wish I had just stopped loving her.

"The facts are what they are. I used you, I played myself, and now you hate me."

"I don't hate you for what you did to me. Well, I can't

forgive you for that. But I hate you for what you did to the twins."

A smile pulls at the corner of my lips. "And what did I do to the twins, please tell me."

I can see the anger rising in her. Angry Jamie is so damn hot. But why does she only get angry for others? It's for Jake, or for Rose. What about herself?

"You forced them to stay at Bianco's for your own benefit. You abused them, and when they managed to leave, you dragged them back into a life you know they don't want. You *still* abuse them. You hit Rose, you beat up Jake. You-"

"I do a lot of things for my own benefit, beautiful. But the way I treated or currently treat my siblings is not part of them."

"Right," she scoffs as she rolls her eyes.

"Don't." My voice becomes so threatening she straightens herself in her seat. "You don't get to judge me on how I treat them or the sacrifices I made for them."

She's speechless. I use the occasion to let my eyes roam over her whole body and her beautiful face. She is magnificent.

Those beautiful green almond eyes are full of curiosity for life. Desperate for answers about everything that piques her interest. They sparkle with a need to live that she's not even aware she has.

Her long lashes bring me back memories of every single time she's sucked my cock and looked up at me.

She knows how to use her cuteness and make the best puppy face to get what she wants, those long black lashes help with that.

And those plump lips...damn I'm just desperate to bite and lick them. To pull them between my teeth until she moans into my mouth.

Chapter 22

Jamie is so fuckable. So breakable. She doesn't understand where Jake's and my attraction for her comes from.

It comes from the need to control someone so deeply they would do anything for you. It comes from the need to open up to someone and have them stay despite them knowing your darkest secrets. And I don't want to kill the light inside Jamie, but fuck I want to possess her and never let her go.

But I won't, because I'm leaving.

"No matter how good of a detective you are, 'Me, you could never guess the things my siblings and I have been through. And I'm not here to tell you about Jake's secrets. Because the things he did, that's between him and his conscience. I just need to tell you my side of the story, so you stop losing sleep over trying to save and fix everyone. Spoiler alert, it's impossible. Especially not for broken souls like us Whites."

She readjusts herself and puts her forearms on the table. "Okay," she nods and looks around. "I'll have a vanilla milkshake please. Then you talk."

I smile at her and call over the old waitress. They exchange a few words about her mom and when she's back with the milkshake I finally lay back against my seat.

"Tell me, Nathan. Why are you so sure you're the hero of this story?"

I shake my head in a chuckle. "I'm no hero, beautiful. Just some kid who let a grown man threaten and groom him into becoming the one and only person that will be his downfall."

Fuck, she is so confused it almost makes me want to laugh. If only this all wasn't so sad.

"Are you saying you will be Bianco's downfall?"

"Inevitably. The student always surpasses the master."

"What are you talking about, Nathan?"

"How do you think you destroy a monster, Jamie?"

Her lips part slightly as she sucks in a breath, but she doesn't reply. So I do it for her. "Why, by becoming one of course."

I huff. It's a bit shit to go down memory lane, but I guess I'll make an exception for Jamie.

"You know, before we went to Bianco's, Ozy, Jake and I were inseparable. We loved each other so strongly, care workers would never put us in a foster house if they knew we would be separated." I take a sip of my coffee and settle back against my seat.

"But people rarely want to adopt three kids. We grew older, going from one foster home to another. When Bianco showed up, I was twelve and they were eight. Our chances of all three of us being adopted – especially with me being a teenager and them losing that baby cuteness – were next to none. But Bianco said he would take us in and talked big talks about adopting us when the time was right. So off we went." I take a moment to let the memories overtake me.

"When did you realize something was wrong?" she encourages me.

"A few months in, when I saw he was collecting kids. A lot of young ones, about the same age as the twins. Jake can tell you more about what happened to them. I was mostly worried about him and Ozy."

"Is that how you met Sam?"

"Yes, but he wasn't one of Bianco's kids. He was always around though. His dad worked for him."

Sam is my best friend. He's my brother and I would die before I let anything happen to him. His story is all kinds of fucked up, just not mine to tell.

"Life wasn't bad at first, but it only lasted a few months. I realized too quickly that Bianco was growing a toxic obsession toward Rose. Back then he was also fascinated with Jake for other reasons."

And this is where it gets real fucking hard. I straighten the cutlery around my plate, turn the cup of coffee so the handle is to the right and look back up at Jamie.

"When he started getting violent, the twins had the only response they were taught to have if something goes wrong with your foster parent. Let an adult know. *I* was their adult. But I was in the same shit as them, 'Me."

I hate the way my voice breaks when I recall what happened the first time I got in-between Bianco and the twins.

"The first time he got Ozy alone with him. She came to me crying the next morning. I tried to make her feel better, but it was too late. He had already broken her. Too much pain and violence for a little girl to handle."

By the nod of her head and the tears building in her eyes, I know Jamie is aware of the pain that fucker has inflicted on my sister.

"We had already been with him for almost a year then."

I chuckle coldly. Fuck I hadn't talked about this in years. Only Sam knows.

"He was, and still is, so dangerously obsessed with her. He is never going to let anyone get in the way of him and her. Least of all me. In his eyes, I should have been thankful to him. He was teaching me the ropes, he was showing me the way. And fuck, yeah at first, I felt special. I felt like someone was finally taking the time to take care of me and I thought I was the most fucking badass thirteen-year-old on the planet. But even I could see he had gone too far. Even I couldn't stay silent after what he did to her."

I bring up the sleeves of my shirt to my elbows and Jamie looks at me like she knows it's something I do. Is it?

"Anyway," I say to try and sound unaffected. "I had to confront him about it. What kind of brother would I be if I didn't?"

This is much harder than I thought it would be. I stay silent for too long, images of my nightmare flashing at the back of my mind and cementing terror in my stomach.

"Nathan?" Jamie whispers as she puts a hand on the table. She slides it until she's grabbing mine and I think my eyes are shining with tears when I look at her. I think she can sense what's coming. She feels it in the air.

"Do you know what he said when he raped me that morning?"

Her eyes squeeze hard at my words, but it still doesn't stop her tears from falling.

"He told me that's exactly what he would do to my siblings if I ever helped them escape. He said he would sell Jake to the highest bidder. That if he ever caught us trying to escape, I'd watch him rape my little sister and then he'd keep Rose to himself forever."

I wipe the single tear that has dared to make its way along my cheek.

"He said we should all be thankful to be with him and that thanks to him I would become a big mobster one day. That I would control everyone and everything, but until then, I had everything to learn from him. That everything he was doing were just the hardships of being taught to be tough."

"Nathan," she sobs as her hand tightens around mine. It squeezes hard enough that I can feel her nails dig in.

What she doesn't understand is, that's not what helps.

That isn't what gives me strength and power. My voice is so grave when I talk again, she almost winces.

"And that's when I started planning my revenge. It's been so long it won't be cold, it'll be freezing. And oh my god, Jamie, it's going to taste delicious when I serve it to him."

"What are you going to do?" she wonders quietly.

It's like she's been waiting for the happy ending we all deserve, and she can't wait for me to finally give it to all of us.

"You know, the only way I've managed to keep the twins safe was by following what Bianco wanted out of me. And I took my share of pleasure doing so. Then Rose shot me. It wasn't meant to happen, but it was actually genius. Bianco never blamed it on me that they managed to get away from him. But then he found them, and he sent me after them again."

I am aware I slightly avoided her question, but I need her to know everything.

"I am Bianco's most trusted member of his organization. He believes that I would lay my life to save his. And I've managed that by turning the twins against me. It's a terrifying balance of keeping them close enough that he believes I'm on his side, but not too close that he would put his most dangerous threats into action."

"It's making sacrifices, it's making him believe I was doing it because he ordered me to. I wasn't. I was keeping them close, but always far enough. Like when I convinced Bianco to leave Ozy alone until she was eighteen. Like when I told him to send Jake to L.A. so he wouldn't use him for more dangerous things here."

She shakes her head, completely confused.

"I was biding my time, I was protecting them, I was building my case against him. And fuck I have everything I need, Jamie. Everything the FBI and the OCGS have been asking to take him down."

"What?" she chokes on her breath.

"They've been using me as their informant since I came back from the dead. Some sort of deal so I can escape prison while he will go away for the rest of his life. And trust me, the kind of place he'll be in...he'll get a taste of his own medicine."

"Nathan, that's insane...that's...how?"

Ignoring her shock, I get to where I finally wanted to.

"I must apologize, though. In my quest for revenge, by wanting to protect my siblings, I've put you in danger."

"You didn-"

"I did. I sent the Wolves after you because they knew you were important to me. But mainly, I put you on Bianco's radar."

"How?"

"There are a few people Bianco trusts. People that will never turn their back on him. When Bianco falls, I will take his place, and those people will never ally with me. I've been slowly getting rid of them."

"Getting rid of them?"

I roll my eyes because she has been through so much and yet her youth still makes her so gullible sometimes.

"I've been killing them, Jamie. Or Sam has. I need them out of the way for my plans to work. Plans you don't need to be made aware of."

"Nathan-"

"Bianco started clocking that his most trusted people were disappearing. It's been driving him sick with paranoia. Now, this is a sick twist of fate, but it happens to have been at the same time that your brother has been back in Stoneview. Don't ask me why he's here, or how, I really don't fucking know. I didn't know he was alive until Bianco told Jake and I."

"But he is. And he is a Wolf, our enemies. Bianco has been putting those deaths on him. And he associates you with him. It's my fault and I'm sorry but I promise you I will never let anything happen to you. You have to trust me on that. I am ready to take Bianco down and he will be gone before he can put his hands on you, I promise you, on my life."

I can tell this is a lot to take by the way her eyes keep darting from one of my eyes to the other, playing ping-pong, trying to figure out if I just made up the craziest story of her fucking life or if it's true.

The problem with life is, the wildest stories, the most unbelievable ones are usually the real ones. People tend to either make up half-assed lies for more attention, or tone down their crazy stories so people believe them.

"I can't believe this... I... I thought I was hating you for good reasons. I thought it would be morally wrong to keep seeing you," she sighs. "But you're not the bad guy."

I laugh loud enough that some heads turn our way.

"Come on, 'Me, you know me by now. I am a horrible man. I'm selfish and borderline psychopathic. I'm a megalomaniac and I don't care in the slightest about people's feelings. But if by not being bad you mean I don't want my siblings to have a horrible life, then yeah, I guess I'm not *that* bad."

My phone rings on the table and the name *Kay* shows up on the screen. Huh, talking about being bad, here's one girl who gets my worst side. A side I would never show Jamie. I turn my phone face down on the table, but Jamie already saw.

Her brows furrow, her eyes dart to the side and she pinches her lips.

She's jealous.

"Everything all right?" I ask.

"Who's Kay?" she huffs in reply. She already asked before, and I already ignored it.

"Oh, 'Me,' I chuckle. "Will you ever be able to make your choice?"

"I'm not in love with you, Nathan," she answers.

"Just possessive," I smile back.

"I'm not possessive," she growls. "It's not easy to erase someone who made you feel such strong feelings for the first time in your life. It doesn't mean I'm not completely and hopelessly in love with Jake."

"I just keep getting in the way," I chuckle. I stare at her in silence before carrying on. "That's because you're right. It *is* hard to forget someone who makes you feel so strongly…for the first time."

Her eyes widen slightly at my admission. It's hard to be in love with Jamie Williams. She has that kind of flawed perfection that leaves a mark on your soul. It's a beauty that radiates from the inside and blinds you until you completely forget who you are, who you're meant to be, and just become a soul living through her.

"Kay is my girlfriend," I lie. "I do have to get over you at some point, don't I?"

It's hard to keep a straight face saying that. Kay is one of the best fucks of my life, but she could never be my girlfriend. She's rude and cunning. She's a tough, dangerous girl. She's untamable and the fact that I take immense pleasures trying doesn't mean I could ever achieve it.

"Your girlfriend?" Jamie repeats slowly as if tasting the words on her lips.

Chapter 22

"'Me, I know I wasn't a great guy to you, but I'll never forget what I experienced with you, and I know you won't either. I love you..." She opens her mouth to say something, but I don't let her. "...*but* I love my brother more. And Jake? He loves you more than life itself."

"He doesn't want to be with me," she whispers in shame. "I know what it looks like from the outside, we break up and we can't keep away from each other. But every time he touches me, he makes sure to remind me we're not getting back together."

"Believe me, everything he has done was to protect you. There are reasons we are all so scared of Bianco. He wasn't just an abusive foster parent. He is a psychopathic sadist with unlimited resources. Jake was a good kid. Bianco killed that kid and replaced him with the Jake you know. He's terrified of him like a child of the monster under their bed. As clumsy as his ways were, Jake was trying to protect you from that monster. More than I was, that's for sure."

It's not as hard as I thought to step down. I think deep down I've always known that Jake loves Jamie with the kind of love you only find once in your life. He'd sacrifice everything for her and the way it's heading right now, he'll probably sacrifice both him and her.

If I don't try to help them, I would have failed my brother *and* Jamie. All the sacrifices, all the years trying to keep their heads above water, they would have been for nothing.

"Here's what you're going to do tonight. Jake is fighting on the North Shore of the Falls. You're going to go there and talk him out of it, you're both going to go to your house and wait until I tell you that Bianco has been dealt with."

She nods strongly, ready to follow the plan. "What about Rose?"

I wish I had met someone as selfless as Jamie earlier in my life. It's a breath of fresh air, maybe I wouldn't have ended up with no moral compass. Who knows?

"Rose is safe," I smile. "She's spending the weekend at the Murrays."

"I thought you'd have asked Sam to keep an eye on her," she smiles knowingly, telling me that she knows the strong feelings they have for each other.

"Sam is in love with my sister. He loses his head around her and becomes useless. Besides, I need him with me. What's the point of having a giant friend made of only muscles if you can't use him to your advantage occasionally?"

She breaks a small smile, but her face stays worried.

"I don't know how to talk Jake out of a fight. He does anything Bianco says. He's scared of him."

"As he should be. Jamie, listen to me. Bianco is out of his damn mind. Nothing he does is rational anymore. He was fuming after seeing you at our house. The kind of fight he's forcing Jake into, everyone sends their best fighters. Their beasts. Sam is the only one Bianco ever sent to this place..." Fuck, I'm actually scared to say the worlds out loud. "...I don't know if Jake can handle it."

Aka, I don't know if Jake will come out of it alive.

"Jake is a really strong fighter," I add to reassure the both of us. "But he's not invincible. The kind of fights Bianco puts together on the North Shore are to impose his reign on any gangs that dare go against him. And other gangs use it to try and take over him. It's not the kind of fights Jake should get into."

Her loud gulp stirs something in my guts. I guess that would be guilt for putting her in this situation. I don't tell

Chapter 22

her the one detail that will make her mission particularly difficult. She doesn't have to know.

"I will drop you off and go handle Bianco. You get Jake out of there and stay at your house. Got it?"

She only nods in return.

"Nathan? You said you finally had everything you needed against Bianco. Why not before? What changed?"

I smile at her awareness. Jamie is such a smart girl, I always wonder how she loses her brain so easily when it comes to love.

"Last weekend, he found Rose and Chris Murray alone at home. That evening, while the twins had escaped to the Murrays', Mateo invited some guys over. There was a lot of alcohol, a lot of anger. I got a real good beating from him and his friends. But Mateo wasn't satisfied, he still had that rage in him. So... he killed one of his guys with his bare hands."

Her eyes are so wide I wonder how they haven't popped out yet.

"That had never happened before. Bianco always uses people to do his bidding. Not that night. The free life is over for him."

Yeah. That fucker got what was coming for him. And it might have taken me nine fucking years, but shit it feels so good to know that he's going to end up in the worst penitentiary being raped by his cellmates.

And mostly, my siblings will live the carefree life they deserve.

Jamie

. . .

I jump out of Nathan's car like my life depends on it. I think it does. Because my life is directly linked to Jake's, and if anything happens to him tonight, I will not be able to carry on without him.

The industrial park on the North Shore is made of two hangars and an abandoned factory. I think it was an old paint factory, but it shut down after the crash of 2008, and that's when most people on the North Shore of the Falls lost their jobs.

Nathan said Jake was in the factory, that the hangars were for petty fights and training.

I can't believe this is actually happening. All this time Jake wanted to keep me out, to protect me, and here I am about to be the one who saves him. Or at least I hope so.

It is clear what Nathan meant, Jake could die going into that fight and I won't let that happen.

There is no way I'm letting that happen.

My heart is beating hard in my chest, to the drums of impending action. The fear of inevitable doom.

My stomach is twisted in knots no sailor could understand. The kind of anxiety coursing through me is worse than what I was feeling when I was waiting for Volkov's men to trap my dad. It's different this time, because underneath the fear there is braveness. It's buzzing under my skin, it's tickling my throat making me want to scream a war roar.

If I can take out anything from being involved with the Whites, it's the courage it has brought me. I'm not the little girl I was when I met Jake. I'm not the meek and quiet goody-two-shoes who fears that *something* will happen to her, who waits for fate to decide her future.

No, I'm stronger, I'm braver. This year I've let go of parts of myself I had always believed were qualities when they actually were lies. They helped me hide who I truly was in order to survive following the trauma and fear of death.

Jake brought out parts of me I wish I had never hidden. I'm not a shy girl, and I'm not weak. I like having my voice heard. I'm a leader – or I wouldn't enjoy leading my lacrosse team so much. I'm a decision maker, a problem solver. I have strength running through my veins, accepting that this year has made me more calculating and less accepting of people trying to step over my feet. And the best thing was not only discovering that but learning that I can let all of them go when I want and for who I want.

Like Jake.

I learned that it feels delicious to be strong and then submit to him. That the best thing isn't letting him take over my life and control everything I am. No, the best is being exactly who I'm supposed to be, and then giving him the gift of controlling my body. That's the fine line we are slowly learning together. He is finally starting to understand I won't be a doll he can control all the time and use for his every whims, and I'm finally understanding when I will fight him back and when I will happily give in.

It took me long minutes to cross the industrial park and reach the old factory. All the windows that would have been in use before are covered with metal plates that make it impossible to see inside. A huge sign hangs on the only accessible door that remains:

DANGER KEEP OUT – DANGEROUS SITE

Yup, dangerous alright if people are fighting to death in there.

The door is large and made of metal with only a rectangular window at the top of it.

Nathan laughed when I asked if there was a password or something. He said to knock and walk in like I know what I'm doing. They rarely ask questions, and they usually check the tattoos of people who come in – to see who they belong with – but just leave it if it's hidden under clothes.

It'll be fine, it'll be fine, it'll be fine, I chant in my head.

It will, right? Because after everything we've been through, Jake and I deserve our happy ending.

Please, Lord, we really deserve it.

I check my watch, I only have ten minutes before Jake starts his fight. That's ten minutes to get in and talk him out of it. To convince him that Nathan has got his back. In short, ten minutes to achieve the impossible. Jake hates his brother with a passion, it's what drives him.

I have to convince him.

I knock three times hard on the door and check myself. I was looking for a job on the main street this morning. My outfit screamed Stoneview when I met up with Nathan.

He opened all the buttons of my blouse and instead tied it in a knot at the front, my red silk-like bra showing. We borrowed scissors from Silver's and he shortened the length of my skater skirt so much that my red lace booty shorts show every time I take a step. I look like Britney Spears in the Baby One More Time music video. A petite version with less shape, I guess.

The head of a man appears behind the high rectangular window, and I frown. How does his head reach this high? Please tell me he's standing on a step or something.

He opens the heavy metal door, and it takes everything in me not to widen my eyes. Nope, no step. Just a giant, bald man that is about three times my size.

Chapter 22

I keep my face blank, and ignore him, walking in as if I should be here. I walk with a sure step into a long, thin, dark hallway. The walls used to be painted white and there are only peelings of paint left on them.

Keeping my head high, I can see a black curtain at the end and my heart somersaults knowing I'm practically in. I'm walking past the curtain, looking at another steel door, when I hear bald-man's voice.

"Hey!"

Pretend you didn't hear him, just open the door.

I push the door open and I can already hear a rowdy crowd at the back. The sound was imperceptible in the hallway but that's all I can hear now. That and...

"Hey! Come back here, little bitch!"

What the actual fuck.

I turn around in a split second.

"What the *fuck* did you just say?" I rage.

"You look lost, little girl, you clearly don't belong here." His voice isn't that threatening but as he walks toward me, his size makes me want to shrink into myself.

Stay strong, stay strong.

"Are you from the North Shore? And if so, which crew are you with?"

I open my mouth to answer when a voice rises behind me.

"She's with me, Shawn. And I'll make sure to give you a free nose job if you call her a little bitch again."

A hand wraps around my arm and pulls me through the steel door. The heat hits me in the chest, the lights are strobes that blind my eyes, a mix of black and white on repeat, and the sound of the loud crowd renders me deaf for a few seconds.

I'm pulled through another door and the sound dies.

The strobes are replaced by a blinding, industrial, white light and I have to put my other hand in front of my eyes. My steps resonate in the empty hallway until the person pulls me through another door, stops and lets go of my arm. I blink a few times before the familiar face clears in front of me.

"Jamie fucking Williams, the last person I expected to see here," Billie says with a smirk on her face as she crosses her arms over her chest.

Shit.

I was ready to fight a giant that looked like he was about six-foot-eleven. But tiny Billie Scott with her big doe eyes and unthreatening face, that might be a little harder than I would like. Because I've received a punch from Billie before, and I don't know where this girl hides her strength, but I know I don't want to be on the receiving end of her fist another time in my life.

"I don't want trouble, Billie. I'm here to talk to Jake."

"Jake is busy," she replies coldly.

"I know, but he's about to make a huge mistake."

She laughs at me, mocking my naivety. "Trust me, no one here is making a huge mistake. They're just being forced into it."

"Where is he?" I implore. "Please, we can put our differences aside for one night if it means saving someone's life."

"God you really are just a privileged naïve bitch."

"I'm just trying to help!" I rebut. "You don't even have a reason to hate me except that your 'boyfriend'," I make sure to quote-unquote with my fingers, "was mine before he was yours."

God, I sound so damn childish right now.

I do, but what is she even doing? She helped me go past

Shawn, defended me for what? Just so she can hate on me herself?

She shakes her head as she laughs. "You're fucking delusional."

"Are you seriously not going to tell me where he is?"

"What are you gonna do? Do you want to try to fight me, Williams?"

The groan of frustration that comes out of me sounds like anything but myself, but every second counts and she is making this longer than it should be.

"Why are you making this so difficult? Nathan said-"

"*Nathan* doesn't make the final decisions. Bianco does, and he put this fight together. Do you think I want to watch Jake risk his life tonight? I do what I'm told, that's how you survive outside of that rose-colored glasses world of yours."

"Stop," I snap at her. "Stop talking to me like I'm this privileged girl when you know that's not the way I grew up. You know my life is shit in Stoneview, my mom just got out of jail for fuck's sake."

"And that wasn't even Jake's fault! You accused him when it was one of your bitchy friends from your bitchy preppy school. Fuck you," she snorts. "You think you can dress like a slut and that means you fit with the North Shore girls here? You think that's what we're all reduced to? You're not like us, you don't know what it's like to fight every fucking day for the right to exist because someone else might take it from you. And you don't know what it's like to watch your back all the time, to be forced into the life of petty gangs and stupid crimes just because you know there is no other way."

She shakes her head. "Jake and I know that. We share a strength that you guys never will."

She turns around and searches through her bag on one of the benches behind her. "I really don't fucking get him," she keeps talking as she searches. "I never asked anything from him but a good fuck. But he was so adamant to hurt you. And yeah, fuck, I fell for it because when he shows you his sweet side it's impossible not to."

I gulp, my stomach twisting when I think of the sweet things Jake might have said to Billie. Maybe some he never said to me, maybe the same. Both make me feel sick.

"But his heart was never in it," she says as she turns around. She's got something in her closed fist, but I can't see what it is. "He's just too fucking in love with you for that."

She opens her fist and presents her palm to me. The gold necklace Jake had given me for Christmas is shining from the industrial light. That night, he told me he was in love with me for the first time. And it felt like the realest thing I ever felt.

"How-what-where?" I stutter as I grab it tightly in my hand.

"He keeps it on his nightstand. I took it earlier."

My heart breaks all over knowing she was at his place. She must see the pain in my eyes because she keeps going.

"I was only there for support. He was in pieces after your argument, he was dead inside when Bianco told him he had to fight here. He loves you, Jamie. *You*. No one else." She shakes her head again. "And only God knows why, you're nothing special."

My throat constricts knowing Jake has kept the necklace. That means he went to look for it in the yard that night after he tore it off of me. He's been holding on to me as much as I've been to him.

"I think that's the thing with love, Billie," I rasp. "It doesn't take someone special, just the right person."

"I don't like you," she confirms. "It's shit that bitchy girl

Chapter 22

sent your mom to jail. It's fucking annoying cause now I can't even hate you knowing you two had to steal to survive."

It makes me chuckle. "Yeah, how unfortunate."

There's a short silence before she points at a door opposite from the one we came in from.

"He's about to get on, you better hurry."

I don't think, I just sprint to the other door.

He's sitting topless on a bench, his back to me. I don't need the X tattoo between his shoulder blades to know it's him. I know those muscles by heart. The way they tense when he makes love to me and tries to hold himself back. The way they bulge under my weight when he picks me up and throws me over his shoulder.

He's got his elbows on his thighs, his hands hanging between his legs and his head bowed.

He's already defeated. I can sense it from here.

The man in front of him was talking to him when I walked in, but he stopped as soon as I stepped inside and is now looking at me.

"Wrong door," he snaps at me in a broken voice, like his vocal cords are damaged. He's much older than Jake, old enough that he could be a dad.

"Jake." My whisper is just as broken as Jake looks. Emotions are begging to be let out, fears taking over, anxiety poisoning my veins.

It's like his ears perk up at the sound of my voice. His back straightens like a rod, his muscles tensing. He gets up and turns to me, fury painting his beautiful features.

"What the hell are you doing here," he hisses.

"I need to talk to you," I rush the words out of my mouth, knowing my time is limited. "You don't have to go into that ring I-"

"Get her out of here, Dickie," he spits at the man next to him.

Dickie takes a step toward me, and I shoot to the other side of the room.

"Please I just need a minute-"

A loud sound makes another metal door tremble, and I jump in surprise.

"You're on, White!" A voice shouts from the other side.

"Jamie, *leave*," he snaps at me in rage.

"No! No, you have to listen to me. I spoke to Nathan, he wants you out of that fight. He sent me here, Jake. I know the bad blood there is between you two, but you have to trust him just this once. He's getting you out of this, I promise you. He's getting both you and Rose out of Bianco's clutches, please believe me."

There is a slight surprise in Jake's eyes before he reels it in. He shakes his head in a sarcastic chuckle.

"Angel," he murmurs as he slowly walks toward me.

He takes my face in-between his hands, making me notice the wraps he's wearing from his wrists to his knuckles. "After everything that happened, how can you still be so naïve?"

He drops a kiss on my forehead and smiles. God that smile, it's broken, it's from someone who's completely given up. It's crushed and accepted loss.

"I love you," he whispers before letting me go.

"No," my voice wavers with sobs that are slowly taking over as tears start pouring. "No, Jake, you could die out there."

And it's insane, because two days ago, I wished he was dead. Two days ago I thought he had put my mom in jail. But he didn't, he saved her instead, and him? He didn't ask for anything in exchange.

He turns around with a hand on the door handle, and shrugs. "I don't think our story was ever meant to have a happy ending, Angel. If it was, we would have known it by now."

"That's not true! Please," I cry. "Don't go, do it for me. For me!" But he's not listening anymore.

I grab his arm and pull back with all my strength. "It's insane, isn't it?"

He raises an eyebrow and I keep going while I know I have his attention.

"The things one would do for love. It's terrifying. We think we're safe from the craziness that hides within ourselves." I take a shaky breath, so scared to let this sort of truth pass between us. "That madness that comes out when we fall in love. Had I known that the first time I fell in love I would become this crazy, obsessed, addicted woman, the complete opposite of myself, I would have avoided it at all cost. Spending my life as a nun would have been a better idea than falling deeply in love like I did with you."

"I let our love consume me, it left me with nothing of my true self. Or maybe...I don't know, maybe it showed my true self. Had I known I would be left with a consummating burn, a fire of hell ready to destroy everything in its way. Then I guess I would have stayed away. From you, from Nathan. From the Whites."

I shake my head, chuckling sadly. "I wouldn't have. Thinking about it, if I could, I'd do it all over again. All for love. For *you*. Stay with me, Jake. Don't go."

He takes a deep breath, and I watch his strong chest rising and falling. I watch his defined shoulders tensing and releasing. He runs a hand through his ink-black hair, and his sharp jaw tenses.

Come on, Jake. Give in to me like I did to you.

"Don't let her watch," he orders Dickie before freeing himself of my hold and disappearing down another hallway.

I run after him in a last desperate attempt. Dickie grabs me but I knee him in the crotch right away. He folds in two in a groan, and it gives me time to run after Jake.

"Please, Jake!" I scream in a frenzy. "Please!"

The hallway leads to a huge industrial room. It looks like it used to be the main room, but all the machines have been taken away. All there is left is a large hangar that fits what looks like more than a hundred people. They've all parted to leave a path in the middle for Jake to walk. I look to the end of the path.

It's not just a boxing ring.

It's a cage.

The kind they use for UFC fights. Except it looks old and neglected. There are four steps to get him in that cage and if I don't make him turn back before then that's it. He'll either be dead, or a murderer.

The crowd is rowdy and loud. They're screaming encouragements or insults at Jake. Some guy tries to make it past the barrier of people to grab Jake, but he's stopped straight away by someone else, starting their own fight.

"Jake!" I scream but my voice gets lost in the intensity of the crowd.

Someone unlocks the door of the cage, and he climbs the steps. I break into a sprint, I'm about to grab him. He's going to come back home with me whether he wants it or not.

"Ow!" I wince as someone slams into me hard enough to make me fall to the ground just before the steps.

Two arms wrap around my waist before lifting me up. Just like that, my feet aren't touching the floor anymore and

Chapter 22

I'm watching helplessly as the guy locks the cage shut behind Jake. I writhe and kick my legs but I'm just too weak. I don't compare.

The screams and roars from the crowd are piercing holes in my heart.

I can't believe it.

I didn't do it, I didn't save him.

I didn't save us.

"I'm sorry," Dickie's broken voice rings behind me. I've gone limp against him in defeat, but his arms are still keeping me well above the ground. "This is bigger than the two of you kids. There was nothing you could have done."

But the last thing I expected happens. Jake suddenly turns around in the cage, his wide eyes meeting mine. He's panicking, something's wrong.

I understand what when I look past him, at his opponent. My breath hitches.

My heart doesn't stop.

It doesn't break.

It completely shatters.

This can't be real.

23

JAKE

I Found – Amber Run

This can't be real.

I look behind me at Jamie, and after locking her eyes with mine, she looks behind me. The pain on her face breaks my heart. I need to be with her. I need to hold her in my arms right this second.

But I don't get that option. The man in the middle of the cage calls me over. I'm stuck, I'm fucking stuck in here and I have to fight.

The death cage.

That's what they call this place. Gangs organize fights between their soldiers to prove their power. Bets are made, big business decisions are completed, and unimportant people like me die. Pawns in bigger games.

All my life I thought Bianco was too obsessed with me and my siblings to kill us. That was until I got in the way too much. Tonight, he's throwing me into shark infested waters to prove a point; don't ever rise against him, you won't live to tell the tale.

Tonight, I'm just a fucking lesson for Ozy and Nate. For all his other soldiers.

I never fucking asked for this. I never asked to be born to parents that didn't want me.

I never asked to be put in foster care.

I never asked to be taken in by Mateo Bianco.

I never asked to become his experimental toy.

I just wanted to leave, I just wanted to be free.

Really, I just wanted to be happy.

Happiness is Jamie. It's in the way she wraps her leg around my waist when she sleeps. It's the sound of her moans and her giggles. It's how she opens up to me when she's about to fall asleep, a simple truth here and there.

Happiness is the small things she likes. Chocolate ice-cream, the scent of rain on the hot asphalt, listening to my heart beating, tracing letters on my back for me to guess.

Happiness is laughing at her for the way she writes her W's. It's inhaling her lavender and citrus body spray. It's watching reality TV despite hating it. It's observing her when she buries herself in homework because she won't let anyone take her place at UPenn. It's the way she subtly rolls her eyes and winks at me when I wait for her to finish work at the café and there's an annoying customer.

It's a dream-like state to be with Jamie. An unattainable fantasy. Fiction written for the books and films and series on Netflix.

Not for me.

I'm by the 'ref' without realizing, facing my opponent like I'm ready for this. I don't remember walking to the middle of the cage. He checks my wraps and then my opponent's to make sure we're not hiding anything.

I'm back in my fight state. Chopped, blackout moments

wishing I was somewhere else and somehow trying to survive at the same time.

"No weapons allowed. Except for that, no rules. Winner is the last one standing."

I look at the floor while the crowd chants 'fight to death' on repeat. Before I jumped into the cage, I still had hope I would win. I'm a great fighter, even better since L.A. I thought, it'll change me forever but at least I'll still be alive.

Not a fucking chance now. I'm going to die tonight. Some sort of self-sacrifice I know I'll never regret.

I look up into the green eyes staring daggers at me. Jamie is so fucking tiny, I never expected Aaron Williams to be so big. After months of looking for him to try and reunite him with the love of my life, I'm still in shock to see him face to face.

They look so alike. His hair is the same chocolate color, his skin tanned like hers. That mix of southeast Asian and white. And the eyes…fuck they're exactly the same. A green that glints with golden thoughts. And his are lethal. He clearly knows who I am.

But the big difference is that, while shorter than me, he is still tall and big. He's not the skinny teenager that is smiling in the pictures in Jamie's living room. No, this guy has a square jaw held so tight it's like he's imagining crushing me between his teeth. The tattoo of the six phases of the moon is exactly where it's supposed to be on his neck, just like the picture Bianco has shown us.

It's him, it's really him.

The bell rings, announcing the beginning of the fight. It's not going to be a fight with rounds and water breaks. Underground fighting is one bell to announce the start, and one to announce the end. Tonight, the second will announce death.

Chapter 23

Before we both start taking our distances, he smiles carnally at me.

"I tried to keep her away from you," he growls. "But since neither of you will take the fucking hint, I guess killing you will do."

He throws the first punch and I take it like a fucking rookie, too shocked by his words to do anything.

Shit, that hurts.

Adrenaline kicks in and I don't feel the second one. I take a few steps back, shake my head and take back my defensive stance, dancing on my feet so I can bide my time.

"What do you mean you tried to keep her away?"

He's surprised I'm talking back. I guess he thought I'd just accept my fate. He shouldn't have piqued my interest then.

"How?" I repeat.

"The fucking notes I left her on repeat. Didn't they clearly state to stay the fuck away from you? You think I want my little sister involved with the Bianco family?"

He goes for my head again, but I block his attack. I throw a punch to his ribs to keep him back slightly.

"That was you?" I reply in shock. "The bullshit threatening notes left in her stuff were from you?"

He goes for me again and I take a step to the side. My fury is rising and my beast roaring. He's got to be fucking kidding me.

"*That's* how you protected her," I rage. "With fucking notes?!"

My punch lands on his nose and he takes a few steps back as I go for him again. He knees me in the stomach and my breath stops as I fall backwards.

I catch myself against the cage and we both take a few steps away from the other to catch our breaths.

But I can't control the beast that's woken up. The piece of shit is the first one who put her in danger and then dares try to keep me away from her.

"I don't give a shit what you think, White. I need her safe, and that's away from you."

I can't avoid his next punch. It's right in my jaw and I get dizzy for a few seconds. I was willing to sacrifice myself for Jamie. But fuck I never imagined her brother was such an asshole.

I should have, he's a selfish cunt who put her life in danger.

So I fight back.

"You're a fucking hypocrite," I fume as I sway his way. He blocks my jab, but not my right hook. "You fucking disappeared on her." My uppercut gets him right in the chin and his head rears back. "You put her life in danger because you were a stupid teen who got involved with the wrong guys."

While he's recovering from my punch, I grab the back of his head and punch him in the nose. Blood spurts all over me and my beast roars, feeding on it.

"You brought the Wolves on your family," I rage. "You got your dad killed and then you dared leave Jamie behind!" My cross lands on his temple and he falls to the floor.

The crowd is shouting but my beast is screaming louder.

"Do you know what that did to her?" My voice is slightly broken from shouting at him so he can hear me over the crowd. "It broke her. She's scared of the world and still kills herself trying to understand it."

He's folded over on the floor, trying to recover from my attack, but I don't stop. I kick him in the ribs.

"You're her fucking brother. Where were you?" Maybe there's something else, maybe the anger at my own brother is coming out too. Because where was Nate when I needed him the most? I jump on the other side of him and kick him in the kidneys. "I was there when she woke up from her nightmares. I was there when she had panic attacks, reliving the night she got shot because of *you*."

Jamie is so sure the Wolves were after her dad because he was trying to end them. But if Aaron is part of them now, he must have been back then too. He simply didn't have the tattoo to show it.

I'm not the one who lifts my foot to crush his face under it, it's the monster in me. The one who is so addicted to Jamie it won't let anyone get in the way. Not even her own flesh and blood.

But before it can bring my foot down on him, the beast's ears perk up to the only sound it would recognize among those hundreds of screams in the crowd.

"Jake, please don't!"

Her cries kill the beast and bring me back. I look around, searching for her face in the wave of unfamiliar people. Before I can find her, my leg is grabbed from under me, and I fall to the floor.

The beast roars, it's mad at me for letting myself lower our defenses.

MMA is a complex art. Everyone has their strengths and weaknesses. Mine rests in boxing, not in floor and close body fighting.

Aaron Williams is clearly the opposite. He's on me in a split second, his blood dripping on my face and torso. My legs are stuck before I can move, and I receive two punches to the face.

I barely manage to escape before the third but I'm not out of trouble. My heart is kicking with fear, sensing I'm not getting away from danger. He grabs me from the back and an arm wraps around my neck.

This is the most dangerous position to be in in MMA. In a normal fight, he'd make me tap out.

This isn't a normal fight.

His panting voice is in my ear too soon, I'm not fucking ready to die. I still need to defend Jamie, I still need to fight for her.

"What do you want, White? A thank you for taking care of her while I was fighting other battles? Thanks for reminding me I got my dad killed, it helped me remember why you're a sociopathic piece of shit that needs to be put down."

His hold tightens and I throw punches behind me, but I can't reach him properly.

Shit. I can't breathe. I can't fucking breathe.

"I've been watching you, Jake. And if you think the way you treated my sister was the right one, you're gonna have a big surprise when you wake up in hell."

My airways constrict and my ears start ringing. My heart beats wildly, running around and wondering where is that fucking oxygen I need.

"And tell me, who do you think you are to judge?" he insists as his arm tightens even more. "I know the things you've done. You're a murderer, White. You'll always be a murderer."

His words make it past the ringing in my ears and I'm assaulted with images of what he means.

'He's right,' Bianco's voice echoes in my head. *You're a murderer, Jake. You killed him. You killed that kid.*

My visions blurs, it darkens with spots everywhere.

The gun.

The blood.

The screaming.

It's all mixing together. The taste of blood in my mouth,

Chapter 23

the crowd shouting. I don't even know if it's tears or blood dripping down my cheeks. And whose blood is it? His? Mine? That kid? My eyes close and I know they won't open again.

"Time to die, Jake," he growls in my ear.

"I love her," I rasp as I feel myself slipping away, high on the lack of oxygen.

Will he tell her? Will he let her know I died for her love when he sees her after the fight? That all I've ever wanted was to love her.

I didn't even get to see her face out there one last time.

"I love her so fucking mu..." I don't hear my own last words.

But I hear Jamie's laugh. It's beautiful. It sounds like crystal in my ears. And I feel her kisses on my lips, like those of an angel.

It's so peaceful to die.

24

JAMIE

Paralyzed - NF

"Die, die, die!!!" Aaron screams as he brings down a giant stick on a sunflower.

"Stop!" I scream in a giggle. "That's a sunflower! They're nice, you silly poohead."

He drops the stick he was using as a sword and turns to me, holding his head high like a knight who just saved a princess in distress.

"You said it hurt you M'Lady, I was bound to defend your honor."

"I could have defended myself," I pout as I cross my arms and stomp my feet.

"You're too young," he argues back. "You're six, you're just a baby."

"Am not!" I stick my tongue out and pick up the stick he just dropped. "Watch me." I bring it up, but he grabs it.

"No, 'Me! You're gonna hurt yourself. Leave the defending to me, I'm strong."

Chapter 24

"But you killed Mr. Sunflower, and he was nice. He hurt me but it wasn't on purpose."

"On purpose or not, he should have never hurt you. Plus, he disrespected you behind your back. I saw it."

My eyes widen, my pout growing stronger. "Did he?"

"Yah, but I took care of it now. See?"

He points at the destroyed sunflower now lying on the ground with his stick. Its yellow petals and seeds are spread everywhere. It's a massacre.

"Mr. Sunflower will never disrespect you again."

"Wow," I gasp. "You're my hero! My favorite poohead hero."

I break into a laugh as his face falls.

"Call me a poohead once more," he growls. "I'll tell Dad you made me destroy Mr. Diaz' sunflowers."

"But I didn't ask you to," I argue back.

"I had to, 'Me. A big brother always defends his sister. I'll always defend you, okay?"

I nod quickly, proud to have my personal knight. "Okay," I smile.

"Now I'll race you to the house. Loser is a stinky poohead."

"Hey!!!" I scream as I break into a sprint after him.

They push and they push, and they push at me. All the people around me are moving, either because they're escaping the room or celebrating. Some people chose the wrong side, and they need to leave in a hurry. Some people are laughing and shouting as we all watch Jake's body being carried out of the cage.

My heart does not know how to feel anymore.

What are you meant to feel when you just watched your long-lost brother kill the love of your life?

When you watched the life slip away from him, when

you screamed helplessly knowing he couldn't hear you anymore?

My family was always meant to be everything to me. But as time passed, family lost its meaning. It was a mix of my own experience and learning about Jake's one.

I love Jake with all my being. With a soul-shattering bond that can never be broken. Not as long as we're both here for the other.

But Jake is gone. He's gone.

There are no tears on my cheeks, no sobs breaking from my chest. I'm a standing pillar as everyone moves around me. This is too confusing, too much to take in.

I was not meant to see this fight. Dickie kicked me out of the building, and I found my way back in.

I was not meant to see Aaron's blood spill as Jake beat him up.

I was not meant to watch Jake fall to the floor.

It rang so loudly in my ears when he did. The fall of a God shaking the earth and pushing my whole body to bow in pain.

What is the point of my brother being back if my reason to live is gone?

I'm in shock. That's the only explanation as to why I am incapable of moving or feeling. It doesn't make sense. Jake can't die. He's mine.

He can't die because we're meant to be. Our hearts beat in unison, when he breathes, I breathe. Our souls are linked, when he shines, I shine.

So what happens when his heart stops beating? What happens when his soul leaves us?

"Jamie, *Jamie!*" A voice hisses at me. "Wake the fuck up, we need to leave. This place is about to turn into Wolf central and if we stay one more minute, we're dead meat."

Chapter 24

My eyes focus on Billie, but my mouth can't function, and my body can't move.

"Come on, don't make me regret trying to save your ass," she growls as she grabs my hand. She forces me into motion, pushing people away and making her way through the crowd.

The industrial light in the hallway doesn't even blind me anymore. I'm so numb, I'm scared at how numb I am.

I'm a problem solver, I'm a down to earth solving machine who is constantly in search of explanations. My brain simply cannot process what just happened. It doesn't work, the scenario is broken, the problem unsolvable.

I'm bugging out. My brain is overheating, desperate to find a solution that means Jake is not dead.

As soon as we're outside, voices call after us.

"Fuck," Billie curses. "Fuck. Fuck. Jamie...*RUN.*"

Her hand is still holding mine as she breaks into a run. My feet are forced to follow and we both sprint.

My lungs are burning, and my legs feel like jelly when we stop. We're in a dark alley that can't even fit two people standing next to each other. I'm not even scared. So what if we're being chased by Wolves? Kill me for all I care.

The alley is made of brick walls on either side of us and Billie is leaning against one of them, holding her ribs as she tries to catch her breath.

She faces me. "We almost fucking died!"

I shake my head, incapable of formulating anything.

"You need to catch up, Jamie. I know...I know this is hard." Her own voice breaks. "But it happened."

The silence stretches for far too long.

"No," I finally whisper.

"Yes," she insists. Tears run down her face as she puts

both her hands on my shoulders. "He's gone, Jamie. I'm sorry."

A thousand thoughts run through my rational mind.

"But..." I attempt to talk. A sob suddenly rises.

No, no, no. Don't cry. If you cry, it's real. And it's not real.

"Who's going to tell Rose," I finally say.

And that's when it hits me.

Jake is dead.

"Oh my God," I explode crying. My legs give up under me and I fall to the floor. "Who's going to tell her?" I sob. "He was almost out...Nathan was going to...and Chris... Chris will lose it. Luke...but Rose can't take it...she will, she will..."

"Ssh," she crouches in front of me and rubs my shoulders, but her face is streaked with tears. "I'm sorry," she whispers.

"I can't...I can't, it hurts." I grab at my chest, at my belly, everything hurts. I can't breathe. I'm choking. I think I'm choking. "It hurts, it hurts, it hurts...Jake..." I wail.

It comes from deep in my soul. I need him right now. I need him.

"Jamie, I'm so sorry," she cries with me. "You're strong, it's going to be okay."

I can't reply, I just scream. I scream from the physical pain currently burying itself in my soul. I scream because this is too much, I couldn't take anymore. Life threw its last twist at me, and I couldn't take it.

"Ssh, ssh," Billie says as she grabs me closer to her. "I know this hurts, baby. I know. But please, you need to keep quiet. The Wolves have sent the Kings after us right now. The Bianco Family lost an important fight, and the night is turning into a fucking hunt for North Shore Crew and anyone else affiliated with Bianco. We need to keep low

Chapter 24

right now. If they find us..." I hear her gulp and it slightly calms my cries.

I want to die right now, but I'm not allowed to take someone down with me.

"Leave me here," I rasp. "Just leave me, please."

"I can't," she whispers back. "Jake would have never let me. I can't do this to him."

"Jake is gone," I sob loudly. In my pain, I forgot she asked me to be quiet.

Hurried footsteps can be heard at one end of the alley.

"Right here!" someone shouts.

"It's Scott," someone else adds.

"Shit, shit, shit," Billie panics. "Jamie, get up. *Please* get up."

She helps me up, but I've completely lost my will to live. Billie looks at the three shadows walking toward us and back at me.

"Come out, come out, Billie," one of them sing-songs in a threatening melody. "We're hunting NSC bitches tonight."

"That's Caden King, we need to leave. We need to leave *now*."

We hurry toward the other end of the never-ending alley but stop dead in our tracks. Someone is coming from the other side, a shadow covering their face. They seem miles away, but they're there.

She lets go of me and runs a hand over her face. "Shit," she whispers in defeat.

She turns back to the three guys and crosses her arms over her chest. That's her way of making herself look threatening, I guess. I'm just a mess next to her.

"Billie Scott," one of the guys says as they stop right in front of us. "Who's that?" he asks, pointing at me with his chin.

"I know who that is," another says. "That's Jake White's girl. Well...*was*."

I feel sick to my stomach. Everyone knows.

Everyone knows because it's real.

"Looks like we got the best catch of the night," the first one mocks.

One of them grabs my arm and I jerk away in a whimper.

"Leave her alone," Billie growls.

The first guy takes a threatening step toward Billie and smiles. "Now, why would I do that?"

"The girl just lost her boyfriend. Don't be a dick, Caden," she insists.

So that one would be Caden King.

"Talking about dicks, how about I ram mine down her throat. She's single now."

Another stab at my heart. This one deep enough I feel it in my stomach. I feel so sick I have to put a hand on the brick wall next to me.

"He's gone," I whisper to myself.

I bend to the side, against the wall and it all comes out.

I throw up until I can't breathe and I'm heaving. Until my stomach shrinks on itself.

The guys in front of us make fun of me, and Billie puts a hand on my back.

"How about you play your fucking games with someone who can take them," she rages at him.

"Yeah? You think you can take me, Billie? With the state we found Kay in after she visited you guys, you're not gonna like what's to come."

Billie gulps, but she doesn't move, her courage unbreakable.

I feel a presence behind me before I hear a voice. Busy

Chapter 24

with these guys, we had forgotten another person was coming.

"Take your catch and go away, King."

I barely recognize Aaron's voice. I hadn't heard it in so long. It sends a shiver down my spine and my heart goes into its confused state again.

You missed him. He left you behind.

You've been looking for him for so long. He didn't want to be found.

He's your brother, you cried his loss. He killed Jake.

My God, he killed Jake.

Caden grabs Billie by the upper arm and brings her close to him with a force that makes her cry out.

"Hey!" I snap, but my brother's hand is on my shoulder. The other grabs my arm, keeping me in place.

His touch is so unfamiliar. He's a stranger, a murderer.

I can only watch helplessly as the group of three boys take Billie away. As soon as they've left the alley, he lets me go.

I wasn't sure what my reaction would be, but it's instinctual.

I turn around and slap him hard across the face.

"You fucking bastard," I cry out. I push him, I claw at him. His face is already beaten up from the fight and I add to it.

He lets me for a few seconds, until he grabs my wrists and keeps me at a safe distance. When did he become so strong? When did he get tattoos? When did he grow tall and big?

This isn't my brother, it can't be.

"Calm down. Fucking calm down, 'Me."

The mention of my nickname brings me down. I can't do

this, I'm just not strong enough. My legs give up for a second, but he keeps me up with his hold.

"Calm down, please," he whispers.

He grabs a small bottle of water in his back pocket and gives it to me.

"Here, you've been sick, you should hydrate yourself."

What a fucking joke. How can he pretend to care? I still take the bottle and clean my mouth. But as soon as this silence is over, my rage is aimed at him again.

"How could you? *Who are you?*"

Visions of the past years without him hit me. All the tears my mom and I have spilled. All the times looking for him. All the trouble I got myself in.

"How could you?!" I shout. "Do you have any idea? Do you...how could you..." I let my cries take over my words while I struggle to take a much-needed breath. "I hate you! I hate you, I hate you, I hate you," I sob on repeat.

He lets me. He doesn't say anything.

"You have no idea what I've been through..." I'm getting whiplash from my brain switching from hating him for disappearing to hating him for what he did to Jake. "You killed him," I cry out. "You murdering piece of shit. Oh my God Aaron you just broke my heart, you just took everything from me!"

His name seems foreign on my lips, but the hate is real.

"I didn't kill him."

His voice is so calm, so quiet, that I almost don't hear his words.

The silence that falls between us is my brain completely shutting down. I just don't understand anything anymore.

"What?"

"I didn't kill him," he repeats a little louder.

"I-I saw it," I stutter.

"I put him to sleep. Someone had to look like they were dying or that fight would not have stopped."

"Where is he?" I sob. "You're lying, aren't you?" I push him again. "Where is he?!"

"Me, you and I need to catch up before you go and lose yourself again."

How can he keep so calm? Doesn't he understand my life means nothing anymore?

"I'm not losing myself! I don't need to catch up with you, I need to see Jake!"

"Jake is going to be fine."

"I want to see him," I insist. I can't hold onto false hope. I need to see it with my own eyes.

"I'm not lying, Jamie."

"I don't know you! I don't know who you are, I don't trust you," I rage.

I can see my words hurt him. And I try not to care, but I do.

Aaron is right in front of me, and all I want is to see Jake. I need it like my next breath. I don't care if we're meant to be together or not, I just want him to be okay.

"It's me," he rasps. "It's still me. I promise."

The truth hits me so hard I struggle to breathe.

"Where were you?" I demand. "All this time...all this time I looked for you, you really were with Volkov?"

He nods his answer. I don't think I could take the words anyway.

"Why?"

"Let's get you home. You're in shock, you're tired."

"I can't go home, Mom is there. I don't want her to see you."

He takes a step back at my words, but he nods again, and

I know exactly what he's not saying. I haven't seen him in years, but I can still read him like an open book.

"You're not staying, are you?"

"I can't."

"Then why did you come back?!" I shout.

"Because you were in danger. Because Volkov wants to weaken Bianco and ordered me to kill Jake. Because the Wolves and the Bianco Family are at war, and no one is safe from them. Especially if you're involved with Nate or Jake White."

"I'm not *involved* with Jake," I attest. "I'm in love with him."

"Fuck, I get it okay?! You two are in love with each other, trust me I felt it in that ring. That's the only reason I didn't kill him."

"Volkov asked you to kill him..." I swallow the news. "Is that what you do? You fight for Volkov? You kill people for him? You...after what happened to us? After what they did to Dad, to me?" I point at the tattoo on his neck. "That's who you are, isn't it?"

"Let me take you somewhere you can sit down and rest. Somewhere we can talk."

"If Emily knew you were here..."

"Don't." He goes rigid. "Don't mention her."

"She loves you, Aaron."

"I didn't come back for her, 'Me. I came back because I was forced to."

"Please, don't sound so happy to be reunited," I spit sarcastically.

"This isn't a reunion!" He rages in frustration. "This is me, telling you my situation so you understand why I can't fucking stay."

"If you're not here to stay, I don't want to see you," I reply coldly. "Leave. Disappear again, we were doing fine without you."

"Clearly," he deadpans.

I shake my head with disappointment. This is not my brother.

His shoulders sag and he looks at the ground then back up at me. "'Me," he whispers. "I missed you. I miss you every day."

I shake my head again. "Don't," I reply as my throat constricts again.

"I live every day with the guilt of having destroyed our family."

"Stop talking," I cry.

"I need to tell you."

"I know!" I seethe. "Do you think I haven't figured it out by now? You were a shitty rebellious asshole who got involved with the Wolves and somehow it didn't end up well. They had a grudge on you, and you turned to dad for help. You got him killed, you got me shot. You got yourself too deep and then you couldn't come back because of the guilt. I know, Aaron. I know, I know. What do you think? That I'll forgive you because you feel like shit? Because you come back three years later with half-assed apologies? Because your boss asked you to kill Jake and you realized I was in love with him so you spared his life? It's too little, too late. You're not even planning on staying."

He clenches his jaw and I almost feel him bite his tongue. "You're right. It's too late."

My phone rings, making me jump. Seeing Jake's name on the screen makes the panic come back tenfold. It's mixed with some relief, and I don't know if it's going to be him on the other side, or someone announcing his death.

"Jake?" I pant into the phone. My heart is beating out of my chest.

"Where are you, baby?" His voice is small, but I recognize it. It's raw and hoarse. Like... someone who's been strangled would sound like.

"Jake," I cry. "Are you okay? Where are you?"

"I'm still at the factory, but I'm okay."

"I'll come to you. I'm not far," I answer in a hurry.

"No," he cuts me off. "Go home. I don't want you on the North Shore tonight, it's too dangerous. I'll meet you at your house." I could confuse his words with care, but his tone is so cold. I can hear he's still trying to protect me.

"Promise me. Promise me you'll come. Promise me you're okay."

"I promise." But it still sounds so detached, he's still keeping an emotional distance between us. "How will you make it home?" I hear him cough and I know he called me as soon as he could.

I look at my brother, hesitation on the tip of my tongue. "I'm with Aaron," I admit.

"Angel," his voice softens. There's a pause before he talks again. "Don't be too hard on him."

I want to agree, but I can't.

I want to tell him I love him, but I know I won't hear it back. So I just hang up and turn to my brother.

"I want to go home. You're not allowed to come. If Mom sees you, she'll lose it. She can only take so much."

"Okay," he whispers in shame. "I'll take you home."

The drive is completely silent. The opposite of what I had imagined reuniting with my brother would be. In my head, we would hug and cry together. We would catch up on all the wasted time. I would bring him home to my mother so she could find happiness again.

Chapter 24

No.

He knows the way to mine and Mom's house because he's been spying on us. Because he was around and never let himself known.

Tonight I watched him be everything I didn't want him to be. He betrayed this family. He has no excuses.

He parks down the street so his car isn't in front of the house.

I think I hate my brother.

Then why can't you get out of the car?

"'Me-"

"Do you miss her?" I cut him off. "Mom."

"Of course I miss her. I miss both of you."

"She drove herself, and me, crazy over you. She couldn't put a grave next to Dad in your name. Kept telling everyone she knew you were alive, that she could feel it. People call her crazy behind her back. 'Poor Caroline, she can't get over her son's death'."

I take a deep breath. "You're not even dead," I spit with venom. I almost sound disappointed that he isn't. "She was right all along."

"I'm sorry," he says.

The silence falls on us again. What does sorry even mean? Sorry's never fix anything.

And yet, I still can't get out of the car. Because when I do, it'll be over. I know he'll leave again. For the past three years, the last image I had of my brother was him sacrificing himself for me.

If I leave now, for the rest of my life I will have an image of him choking Jake. Of his dark voice, his tattoos and his cold calmness. The image of a man who made the wrong choices and sacrificed everything, including me.

"I asked them for money," he cuts the silence.

I don't say anything.

"One night I heard Mom and Dad argue about money. *Again.* But that one was serious, they were talking about having to move back to the North Shore. The move to Stoneview was always a struggle. They thought they could afford it with Dad's new job, but they couldn't. Stoneview was just too expensive for people like us. And Mom didn't have a job. I wanted to help them out. I just asked the Wolves for a few thousand. I didn't even have to give it back. All they asked in return was that I do a few jobs for them."

My heart squeezes. I know what it's like to do something illegal to help our struggling family.

"Mom and Dad had no idea. I would move packages for them. Pick up big ones from their hangars and bring small ones to their distributors. I was just a driver really."

He runs a hand through his short hair. It's the same color as mine.

"One time, I got robbed. They took everything from me. All the drugs, all the money. I had nothing left. I was in deep fucking trouble. Volkov's guy threatened me, they threatened our family. I was seventeen, I was lost, I didn't know what to do."

He shakes his head at his mistake. "So I told Dad." His voice tightens. "He just wanted to protect me, *us*. He decided it was time to take down the Wolves. But you can't take down Volkov. It's impossible."

"Aaron," I whisper in compassion as I watch tears stroll down his face.

"They took us down instead. Dad died because of me. I know that. You got shot. I'm your older brother, I was meant to protect you and you got shot because of me."

I put a hand on his arm. "I'm alive," I reassure him. "Mom and I survived."

Chapter 24

"You were meant to live a happy life, not survive your way through it. I fucked everything up."

"You were just trying to help," I defend. "Mom and I did the same. We stole from the Bakers because we were struggling. Life is unfair like that."

"I was too stupid. Once you're with the Wolves, you can't get out. I don't know why I thought it would be different for me. They took me that day. I woke up with them and they didn't let me leave. Not until I had done enough jobs to pay everything I lost, plus everything they had lost due to Dad running a task force against them."

"Did you? Pay it all back?"

"Of course I did. But at what price? Once you've done the worst, how can you go back to your family? It's not just that I couldn't face Mom after having Dad killed. It's what I did while I was with them, it's the fear of bringing bigger enemies back home. I couldn't come back. I can't, I never will."

I shake my head in defeat. There's no point arguing, I know he means it.

"We miss you so much," I admit. "Me, mom…Em."

"I miss you too."

We hold hands for long minutes. I know the separation is coming, but it's too hard.

"Will I ever see you again?" I ask with a tight throat.

"Who knows? Maybe one day someone will take Volkov down. Until then, there's no way out for me. With the Wolves it's blood in and blood out."

"I can't believe it," I murmur.

"I'll always keep an eye on you. From afar."

"Is that what you've been doing?" One thing comes to my mind. "That text I got from an unknown number. That text telling me Nathan was dangerous. The one that said to look for his tattoo. Was that you?"

He nods. "And the notes in your stuff, telling you to stay away from Jake."

"No that was Camila D-" I stop short when I see the knowing look on his face. "It was you," I whisper.

"Yup. Can't say it worked."

"I should have listened. I should have stayed away from him. From both of them."

"We can't really choose who we fall in love with. But I wish you had just picked a good guy that wouldn't have dragged you into this."

"Don't worry." I explain, "he's not *a* good guy, but he was good to me. He might have broken my heart doing so, but I can't say he didn't try to protect me from all this."

"He '*was*' good to you?"

"Jake and I..." I take a deep breath. "He won't let me close until he knows it's safe. And like you said, who knows when that'll happen."

"That's real love, 'Me. Letting someone go because it's best for them. It's selfless."

I nod slowly. "There are all these stories and these books where the guy wants to protect the girl, but in the end, he says fuck it and they find each other again. I...I don't think this is us. I think he loves me too much to stop protecting me."

He gives me a sorry smile.

"I guess no '*fuck it*' for me and Jake. Just 'have a good life and stay safe'."

"For fuck's sake, when did you start swearing so much?" he scolds me.

"Oh my Gosh, you sound like dad!"

Chapter 24

We both explode laughing and it lifts some of the pain off my chest. It hurts, just not as much.

When our laughs die, another stretched silence fills the car.

"I can't tell Mom I saw you," I say.

"No, you can't."

"I love you, Aaron."

"I love you too, 'Me."

Our hug lasts forever, and yet it's not enough. I need an infinity of hours with him, just to feel his arms around me and his heart beating in his chest.

"'Me," he calls out just before I close the car door. "Will you..." he scratches his throat. "Will you tell Em I love her? Or at least that I haven't forgotten our promise."

I don't know what that promise is, but I shake my head. "No, Aaron. I'm sorry, but if you're not coming back, she's allowed to move on."

He nods. "Yeah," he chuckles sadly "You're right."

"You should too," I advise before closing the door.

He follows me with his car as I make my way to our house. When I reach the steps that lead to our small cottage, Jake is waiting for me, sitting on them.

"Hey," he tells me in his newly broken voice as he gets up. It's as broken as my heart.

I look behind me, Aaron's car is already gone. I look back at Jake, trying to keep strong, but losing my brother a second time is not something I'm sure I can handle.

"He's not coming back, is he?" Jake understands straight away.

I shake my head 'no' and fall into his arms. I hear his slight wince, but he holds me tight.

"I got you," he whispers in my hair.

"Is it over now?" I sniffle.

He doesn't reply. And that's how I know that it doesn't matter that he just almost died. It doesn't matter that I know deep down in my heart I will never love someone else. This is too dangerous for both of us. And as long as Mateo Bianco is out there, as long as the Wolves could come after us, we aren't meant to be together.

"Let's get you inside," he rasps in a tight voice.

"Will you stay with me?" I ask as soon as we're inside. "Just tonight."

"I can't stay over, Jamie. I haven't done it since we broke up and I won't now. If anything, now is the time to protect you more than ever."

"Do you love me?" I croak, tears still streaming down my face. "Can you at least tell me the truth?"

He shakes his head. "Does it matter?"

"It does to me."

"I won't put your life in danger," he avoids the answer. "Tonight has proved that this is bigger than me, it's bigger than us. I'm fighting against threats I didn't even know existed. Volkov and Bianco are at war, and as much as I hate it, I will always be associated with Bianco."

A loud knock on my front door makes us both jump in surprise.

It bangs again, more harshly.

"Stay here," he orders low.

He walks to the door slowly, but when he opens it, Rose pushes inside with a strength I didn't know she had.

"Your gun?" she pants. Did she just run?

"What?" Jake replies completely lost.

"Your fucking gun, where is it?!"

"In my car, what's going on?" he asks in a panic.

She doesn't stop, she goes out to Jake's car in a hurried

Chapter 24

step. We both follow. "Volkov." She takes a short breath. "He's got Nate."

"Whoa, what are you doing?" he says as she opens the door and looks for the gun. "You're not going to confront Volkov," he raises his voice at her.

"I'm not having an argument with you now, Jake. Either you drive, or you fucking leave, but don't delay me."

"How do you know?" he insists.

"Because they called Sam and I was with him. He left me to go get him. This is a giant fucking trap to kill the biggest guys that work with Bianco." She pauses, looks at her twin in the eyes, and continues. "I can't, Jake...I can't let him die."

Jake takes a moment, hesitation and hatred too strong in his eyes.

Then he nods. "Let's go. Jamie, go back inside." He turns to where he thinks I am, right behind him. He didn't realize I was already at the back of the car. "Jamie," he snaps.

"Stop wasting time! Just get in the car," I scold.

"Where are they?" Jake asks as he takes the wheel.

Rose is taking his gun from in-between the driver's seat and the gearbox, and checking the magazine.

"Ozy, you can't put yourself in danger, we-"

"They're at the old painting factory. In one of the hangars," she cuts him off. "Press the fucking gas pedal," she hisses.

We get there in record time and the wheels scream as Jake skids to a halt in front of one of the hangars. It's surrounded by three black cars.

"This is a suicide mission," Jake whispers.

"Then I'll fucking die," Rose rages.

"Ozy, I know you love him, but we'll all die going in there. We need to think clearly for a fucking second. We need a plan."

Too late.

"Jake!!!" I shout as one of the black cars suddenly accelerates towards us. It crashes into our left side, the one where Jake is sitting.

Jake turns around straight away. "I'm okay..." I say in a shaken voice.

The impact was hard, but we weren't moving anymore. Except another car comes from the other side and crashes into us again. This time it hits Rose and me.

I scream in pain as the bit I'm sitting against pushes in and the window shatters, covering me in glass. Something is wrong with my arm, I feel it straight away, the pain is too intense to think.

Two people come out of the cars, one on each side of us and they aim guns at us.

"Great plan, Ozy," Jake groans. "Pleasure to die in such a stupid fucking way."

There is no escape from this. We're dead.

Two bangs ring outside and I squeeze my eyes.

But nothing comes.

Instead, Sam appears with a handgun and opens Rose's door.

"Get the fuck out of here," he hisses in fury as he grabs Jake's gun from her.

Jake is on my door in a split second and helps me out. "Are you okay?" he asks me.

We all sit behind the car, hidden from the front of the hangar where some of Volkov's men are coming out.

"I think so," I reply, my whole body trembling.

His eyes land on my arm and widen. "No, no you're not."

I look down at my bleeding arm. Right, maybe I'm not okay.

"I can't feel it," I reassure him. And I really can't anymore.

"That's the adrenaline! You're fucking bleeding gallons right now!"

"I'm okay," I insist.

I look up behind the car and my eyes widen. Sam is committing a massacre with the few of Volkov's men that came outside. His aim is perfect, his focus lethal.

He grabs another magazine out of his pocket and turns to Rose. "If I wasn't short on bullets, you'd be receiving one too."

She rolls her eyes and turns to me. "We'll get you help, Jamie."

"I'm fine," I repeat. But I feel a little more lightheaded.

"They're all coming this way," Sam rages. "We need a distraction."

"Give me that," Jake grabs the empty gun.

"It's empty, mate."

"I fucking know that, asshole. Give me more."

He slides him another magazine and Jake escapes with it, slipping behind one of the black cars that crashed into us.

There are three men left in front of the hangar. I don't know how many inside.

Jake shows his head from the side and one of the men sees him.

"One here!" he says as he changes his trajectory.

Understanding his plan, Rose grabs Sam's gun and gives it to me. I nod straight away and crawl to the other car that crashed into us. I show my face and another guy catches me. "And here," he says before coming my way.

The last one is still heading toward Sam and Rose. Sam slips to one side of our car and Rose to the other, still staying out of view.

Rose suddenly gets up. She whistles at the man coming their way and smiles at him. "Here, dickhead."

The guy aims the gun at her but he's too late, Sam is already on him from the back and the snap of his neck rings loud on the empty parking lot.

The two guys that were watching Jake and I suddenly run to Sam. Jake and I use the distraction to make a run for it. We sprint toward the warehouse with all our strength. By the time they react, we're too far for them to aim at us.

I slip into a side door and hope Jake is doing the same on the other side.

I hear some gunshots outside and shudder. Please, let it be Sam killing more of Volkov's men and not the other way around.

I stop dead in my tracks as I slide in. I can see Jake coming in from the other side. The problem is, in the middle of the hangar, three people are surrounding Nate. He's in a fetal position on the floor, blood pouring out of his already injured shoulder. His bruised, swollen face is barely recognizable.

One of the men is older, his hair all white, his face wrinkled. He's wearing an all-black suit and stands a little further away with a smug smile on his face. It has to be Volkov.

"The downfall of the Bianco family is the sweetest thing to watch," he says in a strong Russian accent. His foot lands on Nathan's face hard enough to make him gargle a whimper.

I have to put a hand in front of my mouth to stop the whimper from escaping. Jake looks straight into my eyes and puts a finger against his lips. I nod at him and stay silent in my corner as Jake keeps creeping in closer with his gun tucked against him. I slip the gun at the back of my shorts and plaster myself against the wall.

That would have worked, if only Sam and Rose hadn't suddenly burst through the main door. Sam's shirt is bloody, but he looks like he's still got the situation under control.

"Your men are a little too easy to kill, Dimitri," he smiles. "I thought you'd offer us a real challenge." His British accent makes him sound even more smug than he intends. But he isn't holding a gun anymore.

"Why do you need a challenge? You've already lost. Look at your boss," Volkov chuckles as he kicks Nathan in the ribs. "He flew too close to the sun."

The groan of pain that escapes Nathan brings tears to my eyes.

"That's not my boss," Sam calmly replies. "That's my brother. And you made a big mistake going after him." He nods and Jake gets the message straight away.

While the three men's attention was on Sam and Rose, Jake got closer and in one swift move, he shoots both of Volkov's bodyguards.

In a panic, Volkov pulls out his gun and grabs Nathan. He forces him up, brings his back to his chest, and wraps an arm around his neck before putting the gun against his temple.

"No!" Rose cries out. Her arm extends, her fingers desperately trying to grab the brother she can't reach.

"Alright, this is over for you." He backs away until he's facing all of us and we all gather closer. "Drop your gun," he shouts at Jake.

He doesn't hesitate one second, he drops it to the floor and slides it toward Volkov with his foot.

Jake puts me behind him, and we all watch helplessly as Volkov takes steps closer to the door.

"This is what is going to happen," he snarls. "You're all going to get on your knees with your hands behind your neck."

Is this how we die? After everything that happened? Everything we've been through? Shot because Volkov is taking over Bianco?

I can hardly believe it.

"Don't do it," Nathan growls. "Let him fucking kill me."

He's barely conscious, but he's still aware we're all about to get sacrificed like lambs.

Despite Nathan's request, we all get on our knees. I lock my hands behind my neck and suck in a breath. This looks too familiar. The feeling I had that night with my dad on his knees, with Aaron and I shrinking into the corner of the room.

"It's going to be okay, Angel," Jake whispers as he puts his own hands behind his neck.

I heave for a breath that doesn't come.

"Jamie," Rose says as sweetly as her hoarse voice allows her. She puts a hand behind my shoulder blades and rubs up and down.

"I said hands behind your neck," Volkov shouts as he presses the gun harder against Nate's temple.

"She's having a panic attack," Rose snaps back. "Give me a fucking minute."

Volkov replies something about not caring about panic attacks when I'll be dead in a minute, but I can't really hear him. My senses are all focused on Rose and her hand that suddenly stops rubbing. She's just grabbed the gun that I forgot was tucked in the back of my shorts.

My ears are ringing from fear. She can't do this, it's too dangerous.

But it's our last resort.

Chapter 24

I see her sharing a look with Nate and he smiles. His teeth are covered in blood, it's dripping from his mouth.

"Ozy," he coughs. I can still hear the warning behind it, the understanding of what she's about to do. I really think he's going to tell her not to move. But all he says is, "Don't miss."

It happens so fast, Volkov can't even realize she's moving. She's like lightning, one second her hand is on the small of my back, the next the bang is echoing in the room.

Blood spurts from where Volkov and Nathan are standing, and Sam jumps to his feet. Jake is on me as I try to get up. I feel myself lose my footing, but I need to know. They're both down, there's blood everywhere. We were far, she was on her knees.

She killed both of them.

She must have.

That's what my brain repeats until I hear some more coughing. Nathan's to be precise. He rolls to his side, out of Volkov's hold. But Volkov doesn't move.

As we all approach, we can see the distinct hole in his throat and the blood spilling out of it.

And Nathan is absolutely fine.

Sam helps him up and we all turn to Rose.

"Thank fuck," she whispers in a broken voice.

Her legs give up and she sits on the floor before wiping her eyebrow with her wrist.

But we don't get a break. Nathan limps toward her and pulls her back up.

"Give me that," he says as he takes the gun.

He grabs the handle multiple times, putting his fingerprints all over it, and rubs it against his bloody button down, spreading his own blood on it.

"What are you doing?" Rose chokes.

"Not letting you take the fall for saving my life," he retorts. "Now get yourself home and leave this to Sam and I."

He looks to me and Jake before his eyes zero in on my arm. "'Me, you're hurt."

"I..." my eyes drop to my bloodied arm and when they come back up, white dots cloud my vision. "Yeah, I think so."

Blackout.

25

JAMIE

Arcade – Duncan Laurence

That beeping is my worst enemy. It goes on repeat, letting me know I'm alive through my sleepy haze. It makes me believe that everything is going to be okay. That when I open my eyes, my brother and my dad will be alive too. I know it's a lie. Did Aaron make it? I know Dad didn't. They're going to tell me soon. And for the rest of my life, I'm going to have a scar on my shoulder that reminds me of that dreadful night.

Beep. Beep. Beep.

I feel a hand on my cheek, and I recognize the slim fingers, the rugged fingertips from burning yourself on coffee cups too many times. Time to face reality.

I slowly open my eyes and turn my head to where I think my mom is.

"'Me," she smiles with tears in her eyes. "Hi, sweetie."

"Hi, Mom," I rasp.

I try to smile at her, but the haze is too much. My whole body feels heavy and my muscles unmovable.

"You're okay," she whispers to me as she pushes some strands of hair away from my face. "You're all okay."

I think she's insisting for herself more than me.

"I am," I reassure her.

"I'm going to get the nurse, sweetie. Is your arm hurting?"

"My arm?" Her eyebrows furrow and I insist. "It's my shoulder."

She pauses and can't hold back a sob. "Aw, baby. My baby," she cries as she takes me in her arms. "It's not, sweetie, your shoulder is fine. That nightmare was over a long time ago."

Memories hit me, the fog spreading quicker now. Another night with the Wolves. Another nightmare to add to the previous one.

Mom leaves to get the nurse and I look around for my phone. Where are Jake and Rose? Where is Nathan? Is he alive?

The pain in my forearm springs to life and I cry out.

Shit...shit that hurts. I sit up and look down. I've got a cast.

The nurse walks in and he smiles at me reassuringly.

"Miss Williams, you're awake."

I nod but he can sense the panic in me. "I'm Johnathan, I'm your nurse. Dr. Fernandez will be with us in just a second. Are you hurting anywhere? I'll get you some water for now."

"Just my arm," I rasp, now realizing how thirsty I am.

He gives me a plastic cup filled with water. "Drink slowly."

I execute, taking small sips in silence until a short woman in a white blouse walks in.

"Miss Williams, how's the arm?"

"Painful," I reply.

Her dark skin matches mine and I recognize her features right away.

"Are you Filipina?" I ask, not caring about how rude I sound.

She smiles and nods. "From El Nido." She looks at my mom and back at me. "Is Dad from the Philippines?" she asks lightly.

I nod. "He was, yes."

She nods in acknowledgement that my dad isn't with us anymore and playfully carries on. "Kamusta Tagalog mo?" she says, cheekiness in her voice, wondering how good my Tagalog is.

"It's not very good," I mumble, my cheeks burning. Dad had taught me, but I haven't practiced in a while.

She winks at me. "Good, because I don't know how good my medical talk is in my own mother tongue," she chuckles. "Let's do this in English, shall we? You were in a car accident, do you remember? That was Sunday night. You had a good sleep, it's Monday now. Do you remember all that?"

I remember Volkov's men driving into Jake's car and attempting to kill us, yes.

"Y-yes," I murmur.

"Good, and you remember what month, right? Can you tell me that?"

"April."

"Very good. How are you feeling? Apart from the arm." she asks. I only shrug and she pushes. "A little shaken maybe?"

"Where are my friends?"

"They're waiting outside," she waves her hand toward the door. "We checked your head and for internal injuries.

You're all fine, no concussion, no bleeding. You fractured your ulna. It's the-"

"The bone in my forearm, apart from the radius," I cut her off like the know-it-all that I am.

She nods enthusiastically. "You bet it is." She turns to Mom. "You've got yourself a very bright girl Ms. Williams."

Mom smiles proudly. "She's going to UPenn on a full scholarship."

"I want to go to medical school," I add.

"How wonderful. Well, before that, I'm afraid you'll be wearing this cast for four weeks. We'll see how it looks after that and might keep it for six. You also had many cuts from the glass shattering. There was a lot of bleeding, so you had a very small transfusion. We had to put some stitches, if you feel superficial pain around here," she points at the cast just below my elbow, "it's normal. But if you see some blood leaking through, then you need to contact us. The stitches will dissolve on their own in a week or so."

She looks at me and I nod. Her face turns a little more serious. "It can be very traumatizing to be in a car accident, Jamie. You're physically healthy enough to be released but we'll leave you with some information about groups and doctors you can call if you feel mentally unwell. It's important to talk about it, yes?"

"Yeah," I nod again. "I've been through that bit before."

"Yes," she smiles. "I saw your records. You're a very brave girl, I hope you know that."

"I don't know," I shrug. "Maybe I should have joined those groups."

"It's never too late," she reassures me.

She taps my leg with her hand and gives me and mom an encouraging smile.

"Let me know if you need anything. I'll sign the release

documents, but you can take your time. I'll let your friends in, they've been worried sick."

Dr. Fernandez leaves and the nurse takes the drip out of my arm. When he leaves, Mom turns to me. "I need to talk to them about insurance. I'll be back, Sweetie."

Insurance...or lack thereof.

Mom leaves in a hurry and I fall back against the pillow. How are we ever going to pay for this? I rub my eyes before the tears fall.

I sit up and slide my legs across the hospital bed, letting them hang. I need to leave asap. We can't afford to stay here.

The door opens and I look up. Emily hurries in.

"'Me!" she gasps. "Are you okay? Let me see your arm."

She stops in front of me and reaches out to grab my arm but stops herself. "I guess I shouldn't touch," she chuckles. "How are you feeling?"

"Just a bit drowsy from the drugs," I admit. "I'll be fine."

I start standing up and she takes me in her arms. "You scared the shit out of me. *Again*."

"Sorry," I mumble into her shoulder.

"You're okay. That's all that counts," she says as she pulls away. "Are you sure you're okay to walk? The nurse said you can stay as long as you need. You don't need to run away from the hospital."

"I'm fine," I reply, my stomach twisting as I think of the amount of money we probably already owe to the hospital. I find some fresh clothes Mom brought and slip into my leggings. I take the gown off and put on the large t-shirt she put in the plastic bag.

Emily starts gathering the clothes I was wearing yesterday and puts them in the bag. She grabs my phone and the charger Mom also brought.

Em looks at me with a smile and I know there's something to say.

"What?" I nudge.

"Jake is here."

My heart drops. Of course, there was a possibility. But he's been so adamant in trying to keep me away from him. Even practically dying didn't change his mind. If anything, it reassured him in his position that we shouldn't be together.

"...your mom won't let him see you. She keeps trying to send him away, but he won't leave." She's excited, I can feel it. She thinks we're about to get back together.

But we won't.

I nod but don't say anything.

"You'll be able to see him later today, I'm sure."

"Yeah...maybe later."

"Are you okay? You do want to see him, right?" she chuckles quietly.

It doesn't matter if I do, even if he does. He knows we can't be together. And I know too.

"I...I don't think this is going to end how we want it," I admit.

"'Me after everything that happened...you guys can't give up now."

"I guess. I mean, yeah. I need to think about it. I just...I don't know. Maybe it's the meds, I'm feeling weird."

I can't really get more into it, Mom comes back into the room in a pure state of shock.

"Mom, are you okay?" I say as I put a hand on her shoulder.

"I'm perfectly fine. Just..."

"Is it the bill?" I whisper.

"It's the fact that it's been settled," she replies.

"What?"

"Oh yeah," Em admits. "Chris, Luke, and I took care of it. Split it by three," she smiles.

My eyes almost pop out of my head. "Em..."

"We can't accept that," Mom cuts me off.

"Caroline, I hate to be that kind of Stoneview kid." Em's mouth twists before she even speaks her next words. "But it's spare change for us, truly."

I shake my head as I put it between my hands. "Em, you can't say that," I mumble.

But Mom just laughs. "Spoiled brat," she chuckles. "Thank you," she nods more seriously. "We'll pay back every cent."

"No need. Oh, and Mom wants to talk to you about an opening at her friend's shop," Emily insists.

"Okay, one thing at a time," Mom says. "Let's get Jamie home. Why don't you bring the truck around." She gives the keys to Em and shoos her.

As soon as Em has passed the door, my mom turns to me.

"Sweetie, I know this might not be the time to talk about this, but I need to be very clear on my next point."

"Yeah..." I already know what she's about to tell me.

"Jake White is waiting outside."

"I know," I say.

"I don't want you to see him, Jamie. I don't want you to be involved with him. And I mean I don't want you guys to talk or be friends."

I open my mouth to talk but she cuts me off. "And yes, I know you're eighteen. But you're still a child, 'Me. You're my child, you'll always be. And as long as I can, I will steer you toward what I believe is the right choice for you. I have to put my foot down here. As long as you're here, as long as I'm around, you will not see this boy."

"Mom, I know what you think-"

"No actually, you don't. Because you never lost a child, you never almost lost another one *twice*. This boy is nothing but trouble. You've got your whole life ahead of you, Jamie. And I know you, you're not the kind of girl who throws everything away for a guy."

"Am I not?" I say, my bottom lip trembling. I can see the disappointment in her eyes. "Didn't I?"

"You made a mistake, you chose the wrong person. It's not too late to turn this all around. You're going to UPenn in just a few months. He won't be there, he'll be stirring trouble somewhere else and you'll be moving on. He's a weight you don't want to carry, 'Me."

"I love him," I whisper in shame.

"I know," she nods. "And I know how much the first heartbreak hurts. We've all been there." She smiles with the truest smile I've ever seen on her. It's burning with agonizing sadness.

"Was it dad?"

"My first heartbreak? Why, yes of course. That man truly took everything he could out of me. And I survived. So will you."

She can sense I'm still not on her side, she can sense how strong I feel about Jake. She takes a few seconds before talking again.

"Do you know what it's like, Jamie? For someone to ring at your door one day just to tell you the love of your life is gone."

My heart stops. I don't want to imagine it.

"It's different," I try to convince her...or me. "Dad was a cop and..."

"The good or the bad guys...they fight the same war, just on different sides."

"Mom, with what happened tonight, trust me...I'm ready to fight for him. He's spent the last months doing everything to protect me and...I want to be there for him, I want *him*. I'm ready to-"

"One day he won't come back, Sweetie. One day, all this gang activity will be the end of him. And you'll be alone. All alone, having loved the wrong person and hurting for it. You lost your dad and your brother. I don't want you to lose him too. You think you're hurting now? Imagine the kind of pain you will be in if you give this a chance just so he ends up dead one day. And then all your fighting, all this strength you've put in it. It'll all be for nothing. It's not worth it, Sweetie. It will only end in heartbreak, I know it."

Have you ever been in this situation? I think it happens to people who have a very close relationship with their parents. When you know something isn't good for you, but you truly realize it when they point it out. Because you know they have your best interest at heart.

And suddenly it all becomes clear, how much you've been hurting yourself and the ones who love you the most.

For what?

I love Jake with all my heart, but how many times will we survive danger getting in the way? Doom follows us wrapped in a dark cloak, waiting to strike when it'll hurt the most. We're just not meant to be. He accepted it all this time, it's my turn.

There will always be something. And it gets bigger every time. Camila, his past, Bianco, Volkov. He got strangled in a fight against Aaron. We almost all lost our lives yesterday.

I simply can't do this anymore.

"High school sweethearts rarely make it past graduation, Sweetie. It's nothing wrong with you. And that boy, he put your life at risk too many times. As your mother, I am asking you to take a step back. To leave it for now, go live your life, go to college, get out of this town and make new friends. You need to broaden your horizons."

I start nodding as tears run down my face.

"I think you're right."

She takes me tightly in her arms and speaks softly in my ears. "I will always be there for you."

She steps back and wipes the tears from my eyes. "I will be waiting for you outside."

I have to sit down on the bed when she leaves. I need to collect myself before I see Jake. Before I end it all for good. I don't get to, the door is already opening and I can already feel his presence. It's powerful, it's destructive.

Jake

In the space of twenty-four hours, I almost died. Twice.

The first time in the ring. The second when Jamie dropped in front of me, blood pouring out of her arm.

I spent the last few months trying to push her away from me, trying to protect her, trying to put an end to this madness. I spent weeks hating her for sleeping with Nate, jealousy turning my blood black and poisonous. I tried to treat her like a girl I have meaningless sex with. I tried to hurt her, I tried to break her. And I did.

But it is pointless to try to break someone that is already shattered.

I should have tried harder at breaking the bond between us rather than the person. Only, there's one thing I didn't take into account in my equation.

Our bond is unbreakable.

Chapter 25

Sometimes, it takes the scariest moment of your life to realize something. Jamie and I are going to be together. There is nothing anyone can do about that. Because no matter how hard I tried to stay away to protect her, she almost died.

She almost fucking died.

Is that how she felt when she thought *I* died? Shit, when I woke up after the fight, my choice to keep her at arm's length was only fortified. But how did *she* feel? Because the way I'm feeling right now, there is just no way I'm ever taking my eyes off her again. *Never.*

The Wolves are done. Volkov is dead and he'll never be a threat again.

So, fuck Bianco and his rules. Fuck Nate trying to get in-between us.

Jamie and I are a forever kind of thing. I would fight and kill for her. And I'm not talking death do us apart sort of shit. No, I'll follow my Angel to heaven, bring her back down, and drag her to hell with me. Exactly where I belong. Mine today, mine tomorrow, and mine forever.

God, it's like something in me is pulling and pulling, desperate to get out and get to her. It's controlling my body into a desperate need to submit to her love.

And she almost died. She almost died thinking I didn't want her, that I didn't love her enough to fight against all of this.

I shake my head, look around, and let my eyes fall on my twin's identical ones.

"We shouldn't be here," she tells me.

And she's right. I don't reply, I just look down.

"You tried," she adds.

"Tried what?" I ask as I focus on a spot on the hospital linoleum floor.

"To stay away." It's like she can read my mind. She can sense I'm changing direction, she knows I'm about to go in there and declare my undying love to a girl I've pushed away since I've come back to Stoneview.

I shrug and direct my gaze to my shoes.

"Some people are like magnets," she says. "You can fight all you want, the second you lose focus, the second you put your guard down, it'll find its way back to the other."

I nod, showing I see what she's saying. Understanding that even if she knows I make my own decisions, she's giving me her blessing to go ahead with my crazy thoughts. To take Jamie for myself despite the dangers. To make the most selfish decision of my life. And she might not think it matters, but her blessing means everything to me.

"That pull, Jakey, you'll feel it forever. Time, distance, *danger*. Nothing will dull it. I get it, truly. I have it too."

I look up and scowl at her. "You better be talking about Rachel and not Sam."

She cackles a raspy laugh as her head falls back. When she looks at me again, she's got that cheeky smile on. "Who said I'm only talking about one person?"

It's my turn to laugh. "Oh, Ozy. You're just going to keep breaking hearts, aren't you?"

She stretches, fatigue spreading into her body. "Yeah, I guess. At least until I find someone who's willing to put a heavy crown on and reign on my little heart."

"They'd have to find it first."

"The crown?"

"The heart," I mock her.

The door to Jamie's room opens and her mom comes out. She walks past us and throws a glare my way.

Yep. Fair.

I wait until she's in the elevator to jump out of my seat.

Chapter 25

"Wish me luck," I smile at Ozy. "I'm getting my girl back and bringing her into our fucked-up world for good."

I walk into the room and feel like I can finally take a breath. It's like I've been holding it all my life. Jamie is sitting on her hospital bed, already dressed and ready to go.

I've been trying to see her for hours, long before she woke up. Caroline Williams just wouldn't let me in. I've been torn between respecting her mom's choices, and fucking everything up and forcing my way in.

"Angel," I say in the most reassuring voice possible.

I still sound raspy from the fight with Aaron and I'm starting to wonder if it will ever go away. My throat is swollen, the bruises are at their deepest purple, and I guess only time will tell.

She looks up and when I see the tears on her face, I want to die right here and then. Seeing Jamie sad is the deepest pain that can pierce my heart. I practically teleport myself next to her and grab her face in mine, but she shrugs me away.

"Angel, what's wrong? Are you hurting?"

I would cut my arm off if it meant Jamie wouldn't be in pain. She looks so distressed, and I need to know what's going on.

"Jake," she says in a tight voice.

"Yes, baby?"

She shakes her head and more tears come.

That's when I get it. That's when I realize the tears aren't because of physical pain.

She's heartbroken.

"Jamie..."

"Don't, please. Don't speak. Don't be sweet."

"Jamie, you're about to make a big mistake," I say in a rush, ignoring her request. "Don't do this to us."

"We can't do this," she insists.

"I love you," I cut her off. I need her to know. "I...that means something. I don't just love you, you're my everything."

My heart is beating so fast, I think I'm about to have a panic attack. I've never felt this way before. Not out of *love*. The fear is so real, my hands are trembling. I try to keep my face blank, but I can feel my features starting to twist from the pain.

"We tried, Jake. We tried and we couldn't make it work."

"That's okay, that's okay," I panic.

I take her hands in mine and take a step to be as close to her as possible. Her head is right below my chest, exactly where it's supposed to be. I look down at her as she looks up. "We'll start all over again-"

"Jake," she tries.

I don't let her.

"We'll go back to the very beginning, Jamie. I don't care, we'll be friends first if that's what you want. All this? It was my fault, I was meant to leave you alone and I couldn't. I tried to end us and I failed, I dragged you along..."

"Jake-"

Don't let her talk! She'll break your heart!

Jamie broke down all my walls, I have no defenses left. I only have my purest form of emotions. I only have her to give my love to.

"Let's be friends. We can do that because it means there's still hope. Right? Tell me there's still hope, Angel."

"If we could be friends, we would have been," she replies.

She pushes me off with one hand and gets up. She walks past me, but I grab her wrist. I only realize after that it could have been the one in the cast. I could have hurt her.

Chapter 25

"We can be friends. I need to be in your life, Jamie, you can't just give up on us like that."

Like that. As if we haven't been through hell and back. My heart is getting harder, denying her will to break it. I can feel the asshole taking over, refusing to not get what he wants.

"We love each other too much to be friends, Jake." Her voice is so soft, like she's already accepted it and she wants to let me down easy. "All we can do is destroy each other."

She shakes her head in a sad chuckle. "Think about it. That's all we've ever done. Honestly, I can't take it anymore. We can't be together, we can't be friends, we can't be anything. Because I love too hard. I just do. And you? You feed on people's weaknesses. And you're my biggest weakness, Jake. You'll always be."

"You have got to be fucking kidding me," I snap. "Yesterday you declared your undying love for me. You poured your heart out to me before the fight and now that I finally say yes you've changed your mind?!"

Control. Control. Control.

I smile at her, and I know what kind of smile it must be because I can see the excited fear in her eyes. It's the carnal kind, the kind she loves without admitting.

"I won't let you get away, Angel. I won't."

"You can't-" My grip on her wrist tightens, scaring her quiet.

"Is that what you want? I'll fucking bully you into being mine, Jamie. I've done it once, I'll do it again."

"You can't do this..." she squeaks in fear.

"But I fucking will if you don't let us love each other. I decide. When I say we're off, we're off. And when I say we're back together-"

"I'm not stopping us from loving each other! It's just

impossible. I think you were right, we aren't meant to have a happy ending."

"That's fucking bullshit," I raise my voice and she tenses under it. But I can't control it, my beast is roaring from the heart ache. "Happy ending is a stupid expression," I add. "That's for stories that *end*. Our story doesn't fucking end. Not until I say so." I pull her close and she hits my chest hard. "And guess what, baby. That's never," I seethe.

"It is the end, Jake." She looks up, a single tear rolling down her cheek and I understand she really means it.

She won't let me push her. She won't let me control this situation like I desperately need to.

She pulls on her wrist, and I'm forced to let go. The smile on her face is too fucking sad. I turn my head, incapable of looking at it.

"It doesn't mean it has to be a bad thing," she murmurs. "When a story ends, you get to close the book and start another one. Isn't that the beauty of stories?"

"No..." I try desperately, looking back at her. "You... there's no logic."

"It's the first rational decision I've made since meeting you, Jake. I'm sorry. After the summer, I'll be starting my new life at UPenn and you don't get to be part of it."

It's insane, the way I'm feeling. I can live without ever knowing my parents, because I was never aware of what it felt like to have them in my life. But Jamie? No. I can't live another day without her in my life. It's impossible.

Except I'll have to. Because she doesn't add another word, she just leaves.

She just...leaves.

Jamie Williams brought me to my knees, and then she left me there. Aching for her, aching for her love.

26

JAMIE

Give Me a Reason – Jillian Rossi

Mom opens the door to the house, and I walk in feeling completely empty. We stopped by Silver's on the way back from Silver Falls and got nachos and a milkshake to takeaway.

But I'm not hungry. I'm too numb, too far gone. I don't think anything will make me smile ever again.

Only Jake's beautiful beam can. Those dimples that would never fully come out at school when he would wear his mask and then would show themselves when we spent time together.

I never realized the privilege I had to have him open to me. Even the small bits he did. He never told me what really happened during his childhood, he never brought back the stuff he really didn't want to. I could only make them up from his sleep-talking. But he still let me in like he never did anyone before.

And I'm aware I broke his heart. I'm aware I pushed him to give it to me and then crushed it in the palm of my hand.

But he did the same, he only did it extremely slowly. At a pace where I wouldn't realize until it was too late. At least I ripped the band-aid hard and fast.

It will only sting for a short time.

It doesn't seem like it now, but we'll both survive. And who knows, maybe one day we'll find each other again. And maybe we can be friends.

But not now.

"I'm gonna have a shower," I tell my mom as I head straight for the hallway leading to the bathroom.

"Watch your cast," I hear her shout back from the kitchen.

I sigh and lock myself in the bathroom.

I cry in the shower, but I know these will be the last tears I ever shed for Jake and in some way, it's kind of reassuring. To know that I will be capable of moving forward. To know that it's officially over.

It's stupid that it took this much for me to realize how incompatible we were. Jake turned me into the meekest girl on the planet before I found myself as a strong woman. In some ways I can thank him for that.

He helped me grow, he showed me what love is.

I'll never forget that. I'll never forget him.

Fuck, who am I kidding. I'll never forget him.

I hear the door shutting as I attempt to dry my hair with one hand.

"Mom?" I shout.

No response. Weird.

Gripping the towel around me I walk to the kitchen and find a note on the counter.

Went to get your aloe vera drink from the store. Love you xoxo

I shake my head. She really didn't have to. I guess I'll be happy to have my favorite drink when she's back.

I walk back to my room, leaving drops of water in my trail. I turn the light on, walk to my mirror and observe myself. My casted arm is all bruised and I hope these will fade away soon. I just want to forget about that night. At least the drugs they gave me are strong enough that I'm not feeling anything right now.

The light suddenly turns off, but it doesn't surprise me. It's either an old bulb or we haven't paid for electricity. That happens more often than we care to admit.

"That's annoying," I mumble to myself.

I jump in fear when a hooded shadow appears behind me. I can see it in my mirror.

A hand gripping my wet hair ruthlessly makes me shriek in pain and my head is pulled back.

"Not as annoying as you thinking I'd let you get away from me," Jake whispers behind me.

"Jake," I whimper. "You can't be here." My working hand is holding my towel and I have to put my other one in my hair to attempt and ease the pull. "I was clear, we're done."

But shit, his presence behind me. His hot body against my almost naked one. His scent of pine and spice. That scent drives me absolutely insane.

And his voice is so dark. His vocal cords sound damaged, exactly like he should always have sounded. Unapologetically broken...sinful.

"You know what's funny, Angel," he growls in my ear. "That after everything, you still think you have a say in this relationship."

My insides tighten at his words, and I can already feel the wetness between my pussy lips.

"I do, I—"

"Here's what's going to happen. I'm going to use you one last time. I'm going to bring my little slut out. I'm going to abuse your body until you completely forget why you even wanted this to end in the first place. You're going to give me control... One." He pulls me harshly, my back hitting his chest.

"Last." His hand goes up my thigh slowly.

"Time." He grips my pussy harshly and I whimper with need. I'm already wet enough that I know he can feel it.

"And then you can tell me if you want to break up or not. Got it?"

I try to nod but his grip is too tight.

"Words."

"Y-yes," I whimper with need.

"Good girl," he purrs in my ear. "Now drop the towel."

I drop it.

So quickly that he chuckles.

"You're so desperate for my dick, baby. How were you even planning to live without it?"

His fingers enter my pussy harshly and I moan my need for him to keep going.

"My little slut is so wet for me, isn't she? I love bringing her out of you, Angel. I love that she only comes out for me."

He works me slowly, forcing me to roll my hips to try and accelerate the rhythm.

"More," I beg.

"Ssh," he says from behind. "Should we play one of our games? If you make a sound, that's another minute I'll be edging you. If you come before I allow you, I'm fucking your ass raw. How does that sound?"

Chapter 26

My heart kicks happily at the idea of playing one of our games. I love it so much. My pussy tightens around his fingers, my lower belly drops.

But I've played these with him enough times that I know not to reply. So I only nod.

"Sounds good?"

I nod again and he pulls at my hair. "I *said,* sounds good?" He stops moving his fingers and I cry out.

"Yes, yes sounds good! Please keep going."

"Tsk tsk," he tuts me. "Why is it so easy to win against you, baby? That's an extra minute." He flicks my clit with his thumb, and I tremble all over.

The torture is so delicious, the need to beg unbearable.

I bite my lips, letting him play with my pussy how he sees fit. He curls his fingers inside me, and I can't help the moan.

"Aw, baby. You were so close to your minute being over. I guess that's another one."

"Y-You're cheating," I pant with need.

"Another," he says coldly. "You need to take this seriously, or I'll stop being gentle."

He takes his fingers out and it takes all of me not to scream for more.

He pulls on my hair, steering me toward the bed, but before pushing me down, he brings his fingers to my lips.

"Don't make me tell you what to do, slut."

I part my lips and lick his fingers. He pushes them in, flattens my tongue with them and stretches my mouth before letting me suck on them.

"Such a good girl." His erection is pushing hard on my lower back, and I grind my ass against him.

"These should count as making a sound. You're begging to be fucked way too hard."

I shake my head silently but don't say anything. Unexpectedly, he turns me around, brings his fingers out of my mouth and slams his lips against mine. His tongue pushes through and mixes with mine. I dance the dance of the devil with him. That lustful tango that brings heat to my cheeks and wetness to my pussy. He bites down on my lower lip and makes me shriek in pain. He slaps my ass as a warning to keep quiet and I bite his lip back.

He grunts and pulls away. "Fuck," he says as he puts his hand to his bleeding lip.

"Not that easy to stay quiet, is it?" I pant.

"Oh, baby. You have no idea how bad you're going to pay for this," he smirks. "And that's another two minutes by the way."

I stomp my foot on the floor for lack of being able to do anything else to show my rebellion.

He grabs my throat tightly and pushes me. My back hits the bed and he's on his knees the next second. He puts one of my legs on his shoulders and disappears between my thighs.

When his tongue goes flat against my pussy and goes from my entrance to my clit, devouring me in one go, I have to bite my lower lip to keep quiet. I squirm with need, but he grabs my hips tightly, no doubt bruising me.

He bites the inside of my thigh and licks away the wound. Then he does it again, sucking at my skin with a visceral need.

He's back on my pussy after leaving his mark. He grazes my clit with his teeth, nibbles on it and licks it, his spit mixing with my already soaking wet pussy.

I grind against his tongue as he plays with my clit.

Fuck. Fuck. Fuck, I'm so close.

"Not now, Angel," he murmurs, and the vibration alone could have sent me over the edge.

But when he inserts his fingers at the same time as his tongue hardens against my clit, I cry out.

"I can't, I can't..." I pant. "I can't hold it."

He doesn't reply, he simply curls his fingers and I explode against his tongue. I scream my release until my voice is raw. I ride his face shamelessly, abusing every last drop of my orgasm.

His face reappears from in-between my legs, proof of my arousal glistening on his lips. He licks his lips and wipes what he can't get with the back of his hand.

"Oh no," he fakes pout. "Now I'm gonna have to fuck your ass."

"Jake..." I breathe out. "You...that was unfair."

"Turn around," he orders in a low voice.

My body follows his order. He pulls at my hips and my feet hit the floor. I end up being bent over the bed.

"Mm," he groans. "That's a tight little hole, Angel. I'm the only one who ever took your ass, aren't I?"

"Yes..." I whisper back. I squirm, embarrassment heating my cheeks from having him observing me so closely.

"Watching you squirm is my favorite show. I want ten seasons of it."

He slaps my right ass cheek and I jump in surprise. My pussy tightens at how much I love it when he does that.

He inserts two fingers in my pussy and spreads them, rubbing against my walls.

"Make them nice and wet, baby. We don't want it to hurt. Well... at least you don't..." I moan when shoves them deeper in a harsh movement. "Or do you?"

His thumb is next, and I know what's about to happen.

He spreads my cheeks and starts massaging my back hole with his thumb, spreading my own wetness against it.

"Mm, Angel. I have bad news for you."

He pauses with his thumb and lets the suspense ring silently in the room.

"I'm never letting you go," he says just before he pushes his thumb in.

I groan at the strange pleasure I had forgotten. Jake can make any pain turn into bliss. That's a power of his.

I feel him loosen me up and I start grinding against his thumb. My clit is screaming to be touched and I rub against the mattress. I moan from the pleasure it brings me and it makes him chuckle. He retrieves his thumb and inserts a finger, then another, spreading exactly how he wants me.

I feel him shift, hear the zipper and squeeze my eyes, anticipating the intrusion. But instead, he slams into my pussy with force, making me scream.

"Jake!!" I gasp.

The orgasm comes less than a minute later, with him pounding my pussy relentlessly, his fingers in my ass, and my clit rubbing against the mattress.

I scream loudly, I scream his name and the curses that go with having a God making you orgasm so hard.

He leaves my pussy, takes out his fingers, and slowly enters my ass.

"My cum is going to drip from this tight hole, Angel. And you're going to thank me for it. Now say thank you."

He pushes harder and my muscles tighten before relaxing. He starts slow, making sure to not tear me. But when I don't say anything he pushes harder.

"Have you gone deaf?" he growls.

"No!" I scream. "Thank you! Thank you, thank you!"

He pulls hard on my hips and digs himself deeper. The

pleasure comes back tenfold, my clit is swollen and throbbing, my pussy leaking.

"Jake...." I moan. "I need to come, I need to..."

One of his hands comes around and slaps my clit hard, bringing me to the very edge.

"More..." I push myself hard against him, making his dick go in me more forcefully. "More...please hurt me more," I beg.

"There it is," he gloats triumphantly. "You did it, baby."

I don't understand what he means so I groan with need and push myself against him again. It's primal, inevitable, I *need* him to be harsher.

"It's the first time you asked to be hurt. It's the beginning of greater things, my Angel."

He slaps my pussy again, harder, stronger. Again, and again. It hurts. It hurts so bad but fuck it feels so good. He moves onto my thighs, my ass cheeks, all the while he rams, his dick so deep in my ass he might leave permanent damage.

It's horribly delicious, sensually depraved. I crave the pain he's giving me like my next breath, I know it's the only thing that will ever bring me the orgasm I desperately need.

He stops suddenly, pinches my clit harshly, and I come hard. Tightening all around him. He grunts with pleasure, pumps into me again, making me scream my release as he empties himself in my ass.

When he comes out, I feel the cum dripping, exactly like he promised.

"What do you say?" he growls as he pinches my ass cheek.

"Thank you," I sigh blissfully.

"Good girl."

. . .

We shower together and come back to my bed.

"I guess...we should talk," I suggest.

He smiles wickedly at me and gets up from the bed taking a few steps back.

"Angel," he sing-songs. "You know what happens when you want to have deep talks at the wrong moments."

My heart drops in my stomach, and the lust is back instantly.

I am more than ready for this.

He snaps his fingers toward the floor and smiles. "On your knees, my little slut."

I execute quicker than lightning. This is what I need, pleasure without thinking.

I lick Jake's erection all over before sliding him inside me. He tastes like fresh soap, and it mixes with his natural scent, making him taste heavenly.

He grabs my hair and brings himself deep in my throat. I gag and spit against him, but I don't want to move. I just want him to use my mouth so I can forget about everything else.

I just want to feel safe and owned.

And Jake never disappoints when it comes to owning me.

He doesn't come down my throat though. He pulls out and ejaculates all over my face. I swallow every single drop that lands on my tongue with an instinctive need.

I wash myself, but there's no point.

Jake dirties me again. All night, he uses and abuses my body. Holding up to his promise.

I can't think straight, I can't remember what I was so scared of. I don't think of the big world that always hurts me and makes me afraid. I beg for him to hurt me over and over again, to bruise me and mark me. And he does, he forces orgasm after orgasm as my skin reddens and bruises. When we hear my mom come home and we have to keep quiet, he gags me with some of my pantyhose and I come even harder after that.

Funnily enough, he makes sure not to touch my casted arm. He makes sure it's always in a comfortable position and not hurting.

But for the rest, he lets his beast out, and so do I. I become the woman I've always wanted, I grow stronger as I give myself over to him knowing it's because I chose to. Knowing it's because it's him, and I. No one else. Nothing else.

The sun is rising when Jake and I come out of the shower. We gave up showering the second time he came all over me. He kept taking pictures of me covered in his cum and I still wonder why I loved it?

I settle in my bed, but he doesn't follow. My heart stops when I see him put his clothes on.

"Are-are you leaving?" I stutter in fear.

He smiles at me as he puts his hoodie on. "Leaving you? Absolutely fucking never. I'm just getting something from my car."

"Oh," I chuckle with embarrassment. "Right."

He drops a kiss on my forehead. "You don't have to worry about me leaving, Angel. Never again. What I did was to protect you from an evil I'm not scared of anymore."

"You're not?"

He shakes his head. "I almost died, and so did you. They tried their worst and still didn't get us. We're invincible."

And when he says it, it makes so much more sense than the talk I had with my mom yesterday.

"We're starting over, Angel. And this time I'm not letting you go. This is our time. Finally." He comes on top of me and hugs me.

"Are we really doing this?" Bliss is bubbling in my chest. It's insane, but I feel it, it's replaced the fear I let overtake me after what my mom said to me.

"Yeah," he nods in the crook of my neck.

He stays there, hiding, and I sense the shift in him as soon as it happens.

"Remember when I opened up in that supply closet?"

"Yes, of course I do."

"I want to do it again."

My heart almost stops, but I keep a calm breath. "We can use my closet. No one will hear you there. Just me and you."

He pauses before lifting up his head and looking down at me. "Okay." I recognize this tone of voice. It's the kid that's dying to find an ally in his misery.

I look at him as if it was the first time I ever did. He is gorgeous. A God among us humans. His dark blue eyes are searching for something in mine. His long lashes blink at me in a need for reassurance.

Jake never got to have a childhood. He's a broken child inside, one that never got to grow up and instead had to build walls around him to protect himself.

I nudge him so we can both get up and I grab his hand, guiding him to my closet. We barely fit in there with his big shoulders and height, but we manage. We even manage to slide to the bottom so we can see each other under my hanging dresses.

"It's okay," I whisper. "You can do it."

"I need to confess," he says as his voice breaks. "I did something horrible, Angel. Something that might make you hate me."

Chapter 26

"I know," I reassure him. "I know, Jake."

"No, you don't."

My heart accelerates even though I am sure I'm right.

"You talk in your sleep," I explain. "Your nightmares are as clear as if you were talking to me."

"But I want them gone," he admits. With his raspy voice and his constricted chest, it makes him sound so breakable.

"Then say it," I tell him. "Because I have already accepted it."

"I..." he hesitates, looks away and back at me.

"You can do it, baby."

"I killed someone," he murmurs.

"I know," I whisper back. "And I still love you." I'm holding his hand so tightly, his knuckles are bound to break.

Sitting cross-legged in front of each other, he drops his head on my shoulder.

"He was just a kid," he sobs against me, his voice muffled against my skin. "And I took the gun Bianco handed me and I shot him. I shot him because Bianco said so. Because he said it was him or me. I was only twelve, but I did it. And I missed the first time. There was blood everywhere because I got his ear. His screams still haunt me. His sister was next to him, and she was begging me not to. But I did it. I emptied the gun on him. It was slow, and bloody, and painful. But he died. He died because I killed him."

"It wasn't your fault," I tell him as I rub my hand up and down his back. "You were abused, and you were forced. You didn't kill him, Bianco did."

"His name was Tim."

"I know," I comfort him. I heard that name so many times in his sleep. Tim is the ghost of his past that still haunts him. "I love you, Jake."

We spend the next hour in the closet together. He

explains how obsessed Bianco was with him. Because Jake was strong and survived so much Bianco put him through. He tells me how he used to make him compete with other kids he would take in. How they would drop like flies after he'd put them through awful physical activities. How Tim and his sister were the last ones left and Bianco made Jake get rid of him. Then he called the police on him and made him spend a night in jail. He let him have his first charges and put his name on police records before paying them to forget about it all and taking him back in.

Bianco spent the rest of his life threatening Jake to put him in jail for killing Tim. That's how he kept him in check all along. That and pure fear.

But in this closet, together, he doesn't feel that fear. He frees himself word by word, letter by letter, with his head sometimes on my shoulder and sometimes in his own palms to hide his tears.

It's our own made-up therapy. And with time, he might want to see a professional, or he might want to keep hiding in a closet with me. It doesn't matter. Either way, I'll love him.

After a while, he sighs and looks directly in my eyes. "It feels good to open up, Angel. I feel...shit I feel so good."

"You can open up to me anytime, Jake. I'll always be here."

"Always," he repeats. "That sounds perfect."

We hug in silence until he's ready for us to get out and face the world. He stretches and helps me out.

"Anyway, I was supposed to get something from my car," he chuckles. It makes me scoff a laugh too. He sniffs and runs a hand over his face. His eyes are red from crying, but they're not as haunted as they used to be. "I'll be back."

. . .

Chapter 26

He comes back with a large cardboard box that he awkwardly holds.

"What the hell is this?" I giggle.

"Your birthday present," he answers as he puts the box on the floor. "I never got to give it to you, and eighteen is quite a big one."

We both look at the box and he huffs. "I just wish I could have given it to you all those months ago. Chris had to keep it and I'm not sure how this is going to go down."

Just as he finishes his sentence, the box barks.

Wait.

The box...

Woof! Woof!

"Jake," I say with excitement as I get off my bed. "Why is the box barking?"

Except I know why the box is barking.

"I think you know why," he smiles. He gives me a peck on the forehead.

"I do, I do, I do!" I shriek jumping on the spot.

"Open it, then! Before that thing dies in there."

I run to the box and open it with both arms, making myself wince in the process.

"Be careful," he scolds me. "Don't hurt yourself."

"I won't!" I argue back as the small head of a German Shepherd puppy appears. It has a grey eye and a brown one.

"Oh my Goooosh," I melt as it jumps in my arms.

It's a puppy, but I can see it's a few months old. It must have been a baby on my birthday.

"Jake...I can't believe this! Why?!"

"Back in January you were living on your own. I was worried for you, and German Shepherds are great guard dogs."

"This is amazing, I can't believe it!" I repeat. "Is it a boy or a girl?"

"A girl, of course. Do you think I'd let another male live so close to you." I pause for a second thinking he's serious, until I see the pinch at the corner of his lips, indicating the joke.

"You're insane," I explode laughing. "Mom is going to be so happy!"

"That one reminded me of us," he says as he comes closer. "Look at her eyes, the exact balance of light and dark. If that's not us, I don't know what is."

I nod in agreement, but I'm barely listening anymore. The puppy jumps from my arms and goes to Jake.

"Ugh," he groans. "I need to admit something. I fucking hate dogs."

"What?" I choke. "You're a sociopath!"

He raises an eyebrow and I bite my lip to avoid laughing. "That still a surprise to you?"

I shake my head and smile at him. "You're going to love her. Just like you love me."

"I really do love you," he huffs. "Way too fucking much."

There's a moment of silence, intense love traveling like electricity between us.

"So," he finally says. "What's her name?"

"I need to think about it."

I get up, still crazy with excitement. The puppy is barking and jumping everywhere, grabbing some clothes that were left on the floor and rolling around in it.

"She's so beautiful," I whisper to myself.

"Just like you." Jake grabs my hips and carries me until we both fall on the bed. He stays above me, caging me in.

"Maganda," I say.

"What?" He pulls away and looks at me like I grew another head.

"Maganda," I giggle. "That's what I'm calling her. It means beautiful in Tagalog."

"Maganda," he tastes the word on his lips. "I like it. A lot actually."

Woof!

"I think she likes it too," I smile back. I grab her from the floor where she keeps trying to jump on the bed.

"You, me, and Maganda. I'm truly happy." I admit. And I feel like this is something I hadn't felt in forever.

"You, me, and that little puppy. Always," he says, his ocean eyes sucking at my green ones. His darkness embracing mine. His lightness shining through despite everything.

After all, Jake and I, we just fit perfectly.

One broken piece at a time.

One shard after another.

They all fit.

"I can't believe all I had to do was walk into your house and bully you into being my girlfriend *again*," he chuckles.

"Wow," I deadpan. "I was actually starting to have nice thoughts about you…"

We laugh. It's deep, loud, *magical.*

THE END

EPILOGUE
JAKE

Cruel Summer – Taylor Swift

Graduation day...

"And you just walked out?" Ozy's raspy voice chokes on the other end of the phone.

"Yeah," I say as I straighten my tie, the phone stuck between my ear and shoulder.

My voice matches hers now. It never went back to normal after being strangled by Aaron Williams. Permanent vocal cord damage. I have the same hoarseness as her. Well, the boy version. It's kind of funny, Rose and I are more alike than ever now.

"Why didn't you call me? Why do you hate me?"

"I love you with all my heart," I answer. "We're free, Ozy. We don't need revenge, we just need to move on. And the day I leave you alone in a room with him again hasn't arrived."

She huffs loudly. *"Yeah, whatever we'll rise above it and all that shit. But it was my right to kick Bianco in the balls before he's off to his prison vacation. You've gone soft, Jakey. It's Jamie and that ugly dog of yours, they've changed you."*

I laugh so loudly my phone falls. I pick it up and run a hand through my hair. Meh, it's probably gonna go back to being messy anyway. It's too hard to keep it back.

"Yeah, I'm not angry anymore, Ozy. That's what Jamie did. And Maggie is gorgeous," I argue back. Jamie's stupid nickname for Maganda is starting to stick. "But seriously, why do we hate dogs so much?"

I have a soft spot for Maganda, but why do Ozy and I not like dogs? Are we that mean?

"I'm a cat person."

"Yeah, all lesbians are," I sigh, trying to work her up. "Maybe it's 'cause Nate loves dogs so much."

"This conversation is boring. Bye."

"See you at school."

But she's already hung up and I chuckle, shaking my head. Just Rose being Rose.

Chris walks into my room in his suit, all ready to go.

"Are you trying to make me fall in love with you?" I say looking at him. "Chris, bro, you look way too handsome."

He runs a hand behind his neck and smiles at me. "Maybe that handsomeness will help me find some girls at Harvard."

My mouth twists. "Still hurting?"

"Does it ever stop?" he chuckles sarcastically.

"You made the right decision, man." I reassure him.

"I'd say it was the coward decision. Breaking up with Ella instead of telling Luke what was happening behind his back." He winces at the reminder. "Not my best."

I shake my head. "You did what you had to. It'll be our

little secret." I wink at him, and it brings a genuine smile out of him.

His eyes land on my right hand and he frowns. "What happened to your hand?"

I quickly grab a towel and wipe my bloody knuckles.

"Jake," my friend says in a low warning. "You said you just left."

Yesterday, Mateo Bianco got sentenced to a lifetime in Leavenworth Federal Penitentiary, one of the most violent prisons in our country. And that's all thanks to Nate. I never thought I would ever say that, but he did it, he redeemed himself to me by freeing us from the man that scarred us.

It happened the day after Jamie and I accepted our fate was to be together, and fuck I'm so glad it didn't happen a minute before. Because it shows we were ready to face everything and anything together. Even Bianco.

I couldn't believe the news, Jamie kept showing the titles to me. I still remember them by heart.

Head of crime family, Mateo Bianco, arrested at his D.C. home this morning.

Mateo Bianco, dangerous head of the Bianco Family, arrested in Washington D.C. on multiple accounts.

At 4am this morning, the clocks stopped at Mateo Bianco's house in Washington D.C.

FBI arrests violent criminal, Mateo Bianco, in another hit against organized crime.

Epilogue

Because of his high profile, known criminal activities, and the war against organized crime – plus because of mine and my siblings' statements – his trial was swift and unforgivable.

Tomorrow, he'll be in prison. Forever.

An hour ago, my brother called me. He said he had a graduation gift for me. Turns out, through his dodgy relations, he managed to get me in a room alone with Bianco. No camera, no witnesses. Just me and him.

I told Ozy, Chris, and Luke that I walked in, looked him up and down and walked out. I've moved on.

"Okay, maybe one punch," I admit to my friend. "He was just there proud and all smug, saying how he'll never be in there his whole life. Fuck, Chris I was just dying to kill him."

I punched him so hard, a tooth flew out of his mouth. But after one punch, I realized it didn't feel that good.

I realized some other things in life just feel so much better than revenge on Bianco. Focusing on my girl makes me so much happier than fucking up my ex foster parent.

"You...*didn't* kill him, right?" he asks, worried.

I chuckle and smile. "Nah, man. I had to get ready to watch my girlfriend give her Valedictorian speech."

He nods and smiles back. "And we'll *never* tell her how she got that spot."

"Nope," I confirm.

Ozy missed one question on her last exam so she wouldn't be Valedictorian instead of Jamie. We all know how she deserves the spot way more than my sister. It was tight, but Jamie worked her ass off. Ozy just showed up and was her arrogant self.

"Are we ready?" Luke shouts as he walks past my room.

We moved back with the Murrays. Inside the house this time. Nate is still our guardian, but he's been leaving us to do whatever we want now that Bianco is gone. He just checks on us every now and then. We have lunch with him sometimes, but he doesn't live in Stoneview anymore. He's got his own agenda now that he put Bianco away and got his deal with the FBI. But I don't believe the FBI would like his agenda if they knew...

"Is Rose meeting us there?" Luke asks, looking around the room. "She wasn't in her room."

"Yeah, she's at Rachel's."

"Cool, cool. Let's hope she doesn't disappear on us."

"BAH!"

Luke jumps in fright, and we all explode laughing as Ozy comes from behind him in the hallway.

"What the fuck is wrong with you?" he rages her.

"You guys didn't think I was gonna let you show up to my school without me, did you?"

"Your school," I scoff. "You mean my kingdom."

"Rach must be sad," Chris cuts in.

"Meh, I was a bit done pretending to be her bestie to her parents. At least if we meet at school, I can make out with her behind the bleachers."

"So cliché," Luke chuckles.

"Wasn't it yours and Em's favorite spot this year?" she mocks back.

"Leave the past in the past, please," Luke pouts.

"Come on, we're going to be late," Chris says.

"That dress is ugly as fuck," I tell my twin as I walk past her. Floral isn't her thing.

She gasps. "It's Jamie's, you fucking idiot."

"Yeah? I guess it's you that's ugly then. Cause it fits Jamie perfectly."

"Yeah, yeah," she mumbles. "You, your girl and your fucking dog can f-"

"Okay let's go!" Luke shouts as he clasps his hands.

Jamie

"No, not that close," Mom scolds as Jake and I stand side by side so she can take our picture.

We've been acting extra good in front of her. She's not best friends with him, but let's say she hates him a little less every day and that's progress. It became easier when we started explaining everything to her. She doesn't like it, but she was understanding, as always. Especially when we told her the danger was gone. Keeping her little girl safe, that's all she cares about.

We stand like two straight rods next to each other as she takes the first picture. But as she takes more, Jake suddenly grabs my waist, tilts me until my back is bent, puts a hand between my shoulders so I don't fall, and kisses me.

I put my arms around his shoulders to not end up ass first on the floor and squeal before his lips meet mine. But as soon as they do, I melt into his embrace.

"No! No! That's enough," Mom shouts.

We separate and giggle like two teenagers caught in the act.

Well, I guess that's exactly what it was.

"I'm sorry Ms. Williams, she's irresistible. And I know who she gets it from." He winks at her, and my mom can't help the blush creeping onto her cheeks.

"Stop it, Jake," she tries to reprimand him as seriously as possible.

I slap his shoulder and giggle into his arm. "You're the worst."

"Choose better next time, 'cause you're stuck with me now."

"Oh no," I fake pout. "Well, can't do anything about it now!"

"Where's Maggie?" he asks, looking around as if looking for his kid.

"Running around the lacrosse field. Driving Coach T. insane."

"He loves her."

"Your silly dog ate my *tsinelas* yesterday again," Mom complains.

"Slippers," I translate for Jake. Some words we're just too used to saying in Tagalog, even with Dad gone.

"I'll get you some new ones, Ms. Williams."

"Don't bother, she'll eat them again. Untamable this dog. Untamable."

Jake shrugs. "But she protects you ladies."

Mom rolls her eyes. "Sure."

She pretends she hates her, and so does Jake. But really, they both have a soft spot for her. She's too amazing not to.

"The Diaz just gave Camila a new car for her graduation and I'm starting to wonder what she does with all those cars," Rose says as she approaches us. "Hi Ms. Williams, Jamie's speech was wonderful. Wasn't it?"

I blush slightly from the compliment.

"It was, wasn't it? My baby's the best. Thanks for noticing, Rose."

I can see Jake's mouth twisting. He's complimented my speech a thousand times in front of Mom, but she just nods.

She loves Rose so much more than she does him, it's driving him insane. He's just never had people disliking him before. He doesn't know what to do and it's giving me great entertainment.

Epilogue

"'Me!" Em shouts as she runs to us.

She's with her parents and they come wearing their best smiles, but I know deep down they're unhappy.

Em is going to Julliard in September, and while we're all so proud of her, it doesn't go with her parent's plan to keep her in Stoneview.

"Let's open the champagne," she beams as she shows us a bottle.

"I've got flutes," Luke says as he joins us with Chris.

Him and Em smile kindly at each other. The king and queen of clean break ups. I guess they're the high school sweethearts Mom had mentioned, the ones that don't make it past graduation.

Thomas and Hannah Murray are with us, but not Luke's parents. They didn't come back to Stoneview for the big day. At least Luke has his sister, Ella. She's around here somewhere.

We pop the champagne, drink some, and talk about our futures. We're all excited, bubbling with an energy that seems like it'll never run out.

We've got our lives ahead of ourselves, and I feel giddy thinking about mine with Jake.

"Hey, Angel. I need to show you something," he tells me.

We slip away from the group, but not too far. We're still on the grass, among parents and students celebrating.

He takes a letter out of his jacket and hands it to me.

"Remember when you were like," his voice gets higher to imitate me in a mocking way, "I'm gonna have a new life in UPenn, you're not invited 'cause you don't have parents and all that."

"Jake," I gasp. "I did *not* say that." Him and Rose are way too comfortable making jokes about being orphans and I really am not.

He laughs and I fall in love with him all over again. "Yeah, whatever, you didn't want me."

"Thanks for reminding us of this beautiful day," I deadpan. "I'm guessing you're coming to UPenn seeing you're holding a letter from them and took me to the side."

"Well now that ruins the surprise, Angel."

"That was a shit surprise. You've been avoiding college talks for a few weeks now, it was pretty obvious you were following me." I fake a sigh. "I guess I'll text all those other guys I was planning on seeing there and tell them our plans are cancelled."

He smiles at me but the possessiveness in his eyes is clear. "I *will* chain you to our bed and only feed you my cum. See how you enjoy UPenn from our bedroom."

"*Our* bedroom?"

He shrugs. "Why not? You, me, and Maggie."

My heart swells way too much at the idea. "I don't want to leave her in Stoneview," I admit.

"Okay, how about the idea of moving in with me?"

"Yeah, I guess that's alright too."

He laughs at my stupid joke, and we rejoin our group. From afar, Jake and I both notice Nathan and Sam standing at the edge of the crowd, their eyes on us. Well, Nathan's eyes are on us. Sam's are glued to Rose, as usual.

My phone beeps and I look down. It's a text from Nathan.

> Nathan: Your boyfriend is very average. Ever thought of going for a better version?

I pinch my lips not to laugh. I know Nathan has moved on, but the way he still tries to work Jake up is hilarious. Jake falls for it every time and this time doesn't miss.

He snatches my phone from my hands and starts typing a reply.

Jamie: Don't fucking text her you fucking...

He pauses, looks up at his brother, and shakes his head smiling. He deletes everything and types another message.

> Jamie: Love you too, brother.

I look up at Jake and smile.

"Get that smile off your face. If you text him so much as a smiley face," he lowers his voice and slips the next words in my ear so no one hears. "I'll have to bring my little slut out so I can punish her. You don't want that now, do you?"

My stomach tightens at his words, my pussy already ready to beg for pleasure.

I grab my phone, open the conversation with Nathan and type a smiling emoji.

"You're playing with fire, Angel."

I look at him straight in the eyes when I send it, and I could swear I see his beast wake up. The one that is going to ravage me so deliciously.

"To your future, kids," Hannah Murray shouts as she raises another flute of champagne.

Jake and I raise ours, but our eyes stay on each other.

"To together forever," I say.

We clink our glasses and drink a sip before he kisses me deeply. He puts a hand on my hip and squeezes tighter than he should. He bends lower, his lips to my ear.

"Now wait until I get you alone," he growls lowly.

He misses the wicked grin that spreads on my lips, his face is too close to my ear, but he doesn't need to see it to know I'm more than ready.

Ready to be alone with my favorite monster.

KING OF MY HEART: ROSE'S DUET BOOK ONE

PROLOGUE

Hate you for a lifetime – Connor Kauffman

Graduation Day...

"You've packed your bags, right?" I ask as I put a strand of hair behind her ear. Blonde, below her shoulders, with a habit of tickling my nose when I hug her.

She nods, biting her lip and looking up at me. The hope shining in her eyes makes my chest buzz with warmth.

"I just need to grab some last-minute things. Charger, laptop, some cash I've got hidden. I didn't want my parents to understand something's going on." She accompanies her words with her arms wrapping around my narrow waist.

Sliding my hand behind her neck, I bring her closer until her cheek is against my own neck and I can drop a kiss at the top of her head. She smells of chamomile and honey because of the shampoo she uses. No one smells more like comfort than Rachel Harris does.

"You go," I tell her. "My brother will drop me off at your house. Are we still good to take your car?"

She smiles and nods again. I can see the images of freedom and adventure reflecting in her eyes. She is speechless, light, hopeful.

My gaze catches on the groups of parents and Stoneview Prep students around us. Everyone is celebrating our graduation. Everyone is jovial and ready for their new life.

So are Rachel and me. This town is already in the past for us. Our future is somewhere else together. Far from her restricting, homophobic parents. Far from the rich kids and their poisonous families. Far from the power-hungry wealthy criminals who control the underbelly of a town that is spotless on the surface.

My friends will be going to college, and my twin will be following the love of his life. While I will be going to Duke, taking Rachel with me even though she hasn't applied to any colleges. She'll be with me, and we'll figure it out.

Three years of ups and downs. Of secrets and toxicity that we need to leave behind. It's the only chance we have to flourish peacefully.

"Ready to say goodbye to Stoneview?"

She looks around, too, taking in our beautiful campus. Then, she locks her eyes with mine in that way she does to tell me she's going to say something she means. I see her losing herself in my midnight blue eyes for a few seconds, incapable of resisting and melting for me. She finds her focus again and her stare hardens.

"I'll be waiting, Rose. My parents said we have dinner with the McGills tonight. I know what they want. They'll try to start the process of my engagement to Conor."

I nod. "I'll be there. Trust me." I put everything I have into those words, but I know the number of times I've asked her to trust me just for her to be disappointed.

Not this time.

"Don't disappear on me," she whispers, her throat clogged with pains from the past. From all the times I hurt her. "Not again."

"I'll be there," I repeat. "Nate is driving me. I'll be right behind you."

Words are not enough for Rachel anymore, even from someone as charming and convincing as me. She knows my promises don't often mean much, that I use human language as a weapon and turn people's emotions against them. I can see in her eyes that it's not enough right now. But it will be very soon.

I observe her going back to her parents with a watchful eye. We didn't hide from anyone but them in the last three years. Her mom looks back at where Rachel just walked from and then stares at me.

She knows.

She's always known I wasn't just the best friend coming for sleepovers. Rachel is helpless when it comes to me. She has this impossibility of hiding her infinite love for me no matter how much she tries. And her mom is a hawk. She sees and hears everything. She plans, schemes, manipulates, and poisons minds like a creature of nightmares.

I smile in response to her glare. Her plan to lock her daughter in a loveless marriage so she can gain more power in our corrupted city is going to crumble under her. A house of cards she spent years building that I will destroy with a whispered breath.

I go my own way and join my older brother waiting for me in his car.

"Look at that. Look at that fucking offer," I laugh as I slide inside.

I show my Duke acceptance letter to Nate. I'm going on a

lacrosse scholarship. I'm never going to go pro, but I've now got access to my dream college. And then it'll be law school.

Now that I'm out of the harpy's orbit, I feel myself relax again. Mine and Rachel's future awaits us.

The excitement makes my ears whistle with the melody of freedom.

"Congrats. I can't wait for you to become my bribed attorney," he smiles back at me.

"Ha. Very funny," I say as I put my seatbelt on.

The silence is a little too long.

"Are you for fucking real," I snap. "In your dreams."

He chuckles and starts the car. "You sure you don't want to go to the Murrays'? They're gonna be celebrating all of your guys' achievements."

"Nah." I let my head fall against the headrest and glance outside. The weather is beautiful, it's warm and sunny. Students from Stoneview Prep are walking around with diplomas and hats in their hands. Everyone is blissful.

And the best thing in all of that?

Bianco is gone.

I let a long breath of relief escape my lungs.

"I can't believe it," I smile. "He's gone."

I never imagined a life without Mateo Bianco. I never imagined what freedom would feel like.

Light.

I've got butterflies in my stomach, and I can't stop smiling. I'm going straight to Rachel's house. I can hardly believe her mom didn't think I'd get in the way of her plan. She wanted her to do some dumbass online course and get engaged to Conor McGill. I chuckle to myself. As if.

It doesn't matter, though. She's escaping Stoneview with me. We'll figure something out. We always do. I'm going to marry this girl one day.

"Are you not dropping me off at Rachel's?" I ask as we pass the sign that says, 'Thank you for Visiting Stoneview – See you soon!'

Nate simply shakes his head and keeps driving. My heart drops in my stomach from fear and my brain starts to overwork itself with that fucking listing coping mechanism.

2019, 36,120 – 2018, 36,560 – 2017 37,473 – 2016...

"Fuck," I groan as I shake my head.

"Relax, Ozy." His voice is soft, and I'm not used to it sounding that way. "I can hear you listing shit in your head. Will you stop?" I don't reply, and so he keeps going. "What is it?"

I huff and run a hand through my hair. It's so fucking annoying. "Motor vehicle deaths in the U.S. by year."

"God, your head is a dark place," he cackles. "I'm not going to get us killed."

"It's not that. You said you were taking me somewhere, and you're not. You don't exactly have a record of planning lovely surprises."

"Don't worry, I'm not kidnapping you."

I nod and look out through the window again. "I don't know how to live life without worrying about what's going to happen next," I admit in a quiet voice.

"I know." He sounds like a man full of regrets. Yet, how could he when he's just saved all of us? "You'll get used to it. You've got your whole life in front of you, and no one will take that away. Or I will fucking end them, trust me. We didn't go through all this shit for something to happen now."

It makes me laugh as I look at him. His bun is perfect, keeping his dark blond hair away from his face. He's wearing a night blue suit that matches his eyes and a slight smile stays on my lips. Women probably fall head over heels for him.

"I bet you fuck a lot," I drop.

His eyes snap to me, shooting daggers. "Don't say that to your older brother. I'm not talking about sex with you."

I laugh so hard my head hits the window. "Jake and I talk about everything. I mean, not in detail, but it's good to check from time to time. Make sure we don't fuck the same girl."

"Yeah, well, you and your twin have always been weirdos. I'm normal. One out of three, thank fuck."

"So fucking normal," I mock in sarcasm.

It's nice to talk to him like everything is fine. Nate and I have been through a lot, but it doesn't matter anymore. Because it was all one man's fault, Mateo Bianco, our ex-foster dad, whose been put away for good now.

Half an hour later, Nate slows down as he enters Silver Falls. I recognize the street he takes, and I turn to him.

"Why are we going to Sam's?"

"Why do you know where Sam lives?"

I roll my eyes but don't grant him a response. I want mine before he gets his.

When he parks in front of the building instead of going into the underground garage, I raise an eyebrow.

He takes a deep breath and shifts so he's facing me. "I'm sorry."

"Wh—"

"For every time I've hurt you, physically or mentally. For not telling you what my plan was even though I knew you were smart enough to understand it. I'm sorry for all the times I wasn't here when Mateo hurt you. I knew what he was doing all along and I sacrificed you for the bigger picture."

It takes all of me not to flashback to the past. My hands

land on my thighs and I'm grabbing them so tightly I feel my heart beating in them.

"Nate, I don't hate you..."

"You should. You have all the reasons to. Jake does. He knows. He understands but won't forget. And I get that. I'm not asking for forgiveness. I just want to let you know that everything I did was so we could get to this point. And I will hate myself forever for some of the stuff I've done, but if it means that it leads to this," he points at me then him. "Then I'd do it all again."

I nod, feeling some tears springing in my eyes. None of them fall. I won't be crying today, for it's a beautiful day.

"I love you," I tell him. I feel like I never did. Not in this lifetime. "Thank you for saving us."

"I didn't save you. I fixed mistakes."

"You didn't put us at Bianco's in the first place. The system failed us. And when I say you saved us, I don't mean just Jake and me. I mean all of us. You included."

He nods, pushes his glasses up his nose, and pulls his sleeves up to his elbows.

"I'm not staying, Ozy. Stoneview and all that, it's done for me."

I could say so many things. I could beg him to leave his life of crime behind. Cry and tell him I'm scared for him. That I want him to be happy.

We're not the kind of family that cries and begs. We're ruthless sociopaths. Myself included.

"You're going to build up illegal shit somewhere else, and I'm telling you now that it's not a good idea. The deal you got with the FBI for giving them Bianco is not valid on future crimes."

"No, it's not," he agrees. "But I'm not planning on ever getting caught."

"You'd end up in prison, Nate. A cell right next to Bianco's."

My attempts to scare him only make him smirk. He's the worst of us. So fucked in the head that he would love to end up in prison just to prove he can get out.

"Cool. I can keep on torturing him there."

I shake my head. What's the point? A gangster, that's what he is. That's all he knows.

"Sam and I are leaving tonight. I thought you'd want to say bye." He runs a hand in his hair, undoing and redoing his bun. I can tell he doesn't like this situation and is trying to keep a hold of his patience.

When I don't answer, he explains further.

"I won't come in. You guys can just...whatever I don't want to know. I don't approve of any of this shit. I just think if you say bye then you won't look for him."

"Right," I chuckle coldly.

"You've got so much waiting for you, Ozy. That girl you're seeing, she's a fucking angel. You need to take care of her, and you need to cherish what you guys have."

"I know that." I don't need him to tell me how to live my life. I know what's best for me, even when I make the wrong decisions.

"Do you want to say bye to him? He can drive you back to Stoneview, or I can come to pick you up later. I can even wait here if you want."

I take a deep breath and nod. "Don't wait. I'll call you."

I enter the code and take the elevator all the way to Sam's apartment. This whole situation is fucked up. I can't help the pain in my chest knowing it's going to be the second time I put myself through saying goodbye to him.

I gulp when he answers the door. Why does he have to look so irresistible? Why does he have to be exactly what I want out of him. Dark, dangerous, *lethal*.

There will never be a single word that can describe Sam to me. Childhood best friend, hero, savior, first love. He's all and none of these things. Really, he just happened to have been linked to Bianco at the same time I was. Fate and criminal organizations. That's all that connects us. He's Nate's best friend, not mine.

He looks at me, then throws his head back, looking at the ceiling while he thinks over what he's going to tell me. Sam thinks a lot, his words are never wasted. When he looks back down, he gives me a pinched smile.

"He told you we're leaving, didn't he?"

"Let me in."

He nods and shifts out of the way. I walk in and take in the familiar penthouse that looks nothing like him. The modern white furniture, the Scandinavian rugs, and comfortable nooks everywhere. This is Sam's deep need for comfort, the kind he doesn't show to anyone.

Except me. I know this place by heart. I'm special to him and I know it. We often spend precious time together, where we laugh. I make Sam fucking Thomas *laugh*. And no one knows how exquisite it sounds.

We walk together to the living room and sit on the L-shaped sofa, a safe distance from each other. The silence is a little too loud and I hate when he makes me feel like this. Like I have to say something.

I cave about thirty seconds later. "So, bye, I guess."

It makes him laugh and I smile while butterflies flare up in my stomach. It's beautiful. He gets up and stretches his arm above his head, cracking his neck. His top rises and gives me a beautiful view of his lower abs and his marked V.

They're covered in tattoos, his whole body is, and it makes me shiver with need. Why can't I just feel normal around him? Why do I always feel like this young girl discovering love and pleasure for the first time? The effect he has on me is unavoidable, no matter how hard I try.

"Would you like a beer or something?"

I shake my head. "I had champagne at graduation, and I'd like to stay sober." It's needed around him.

"Champagne. Such a Stoneview girl now," he throws as he walks to his open-plan kitchen and opens the fridge.

He grabs a beer, pours me a glass of water, and comes back. This time, he sits a little closer. Close enough that I feel his warmth. It's strange because he's so cold, so dark, that I'm always surprised when I feel his body heat.

"Congratulations," he finally says. "For graduating."

I nod and take a sip of water. "Thanks."

Fuck, this is too awkward.

"Look, let's just get it over with," I snap. "Have a good life. See you, probably never, and don't call me if you ever need an attorney."

He doesn't reply. He puts his beer down, locks his black eyes with mine...and kisses me.

I gasp in shock at the last thing I expected from him. My glass slips from my hand, dropping to the floor, the clink barely audible when the beating of my own heart deafens my ears. One hand tangles with the hair at the back of my head. One grabs my jaw to angle me and adapt to his height. And he deepens the kiss.

He kisses me like I've always dreamed of him kissing me. Like he loves me. Like he reciprocates the feelings he knows I've always had toward him.

At first, it's the kiss I always wanted from him as a little girl. It's loving and tender as he plays with my lips and shows me the romance he never showed anyone.

And then, it's the kiss I've begged for as a woman since he's been back. His tongue breaches the barrier of my lips and intertwines with mine in a passionate embrace. I moan into his mouth from sheer satisfaction. I pull myself closer to him as my hands land on his chest and tighten around his t-shirt.

He groans when I bite his bottom lip and he pushes back harder, dominating the kiss with a strength he rarely uses toward me. His hand in my hair becomes painful, our teeth clash and my lungs beg for air, but he doesn't stop. He ravages my mouth, my lips, and causes havoc in my heart.

He ravages *me*. And that's all I've ever wanted.

In this moment, nothing else matters. Just him. The British prick who stole my heart when I barely knew how to use it. Who stormed back into my life and never let me get away from him.

Finally. Fucking finally.

For a minute, all my dreams come true. My life becomes clearer, my brain takes a rest, and my fears fly away.

Until he breaks the kiss so suddenly my body shivers.

"Shit," he hisses as he gets up and steps away.

I can't help my eyes from widening in shock. Is that regret in his features?

We're both panting and looking at each other, but I have nothing to tell him for once, and he looks like he has everything to say.

"I shouldn't have done that. I...fuck." He huffs as he runs a hand through his black hair. Always short on the side and long on the top. Always gelled back.

I slowly get up and walk to him. "Don't!" he snaps. "Stop it, Rose."

"What? I don't get it."

I'm trembling, because I was so close to my wildest dreams coming true, and I can currently see them fading away.

"I can't do this. Don't you get it? Stop it. Stop pleading with your eyes every time you see me. I see the imploration in them. I see how much you're in love with me. I can't give that love back, do you understand? I cannot love you, Rose."

"But...why?" I rasp.

I'm not even going to deny I'm in love with him. I've always been; this isn't news to anyone. I've tried lying to myself too many times to pretend anymore.

"I'm leaving," he tells me. "You just got a lacrosse scholarship to Duke. I'm leaving, and you're going to go to college and have a life free of all the shit I'm involved with. I *kill* people for a living, Rose. Do you think I want you involved with that? Do you think Nate wants that for you after everything he's put himself through to free you from Bianco?" His British accent is so strong when he starts talking fast. His T's are sharp, his consonants a true hit to the heart.

It's a real struggle to swallow the rock stuck in my throat.

"All these things are to protect me, and I get it." I try to keep calm, try to hold on to the hope I felt a minute ago. "But what do *you* want? You're in love with me too. You're not a liar, and you can't deny it."

He shakes his head but stays silent.

"Come on, admit it," I rage.

"You fell in love with me at such a young age." He sounds so sorry. Why does he sound so sorry? "You needed someone to protect you, needed to escape the reality Bianco put you in. I can understand that. I was happy to fill that role for you."

"No," I try to cut him off. I don't like where this is going.

"We got separated suddenly. It was a rough fracture, and you couldn't get rid of those feelings because of that. Because you kept imagining where it would have led if we had still been in each other's lives."

"That's not t—"

"Nowhere. You loved enough for the both of us, but I never reciprocated those feelings." His voice is so cold.

I'm still panting, but this time it's from all the rage and sadness flooding me. "You're a liar," I push past my tight throat. "I know you feel the same as I do."

"I've got a boyfriend, Rose. I'm in love with him, and I can tell you that what I feel for you is nothing like what I feel for him."

My whole world comes crashing down. Because, while Sam always kept me at arm's length, I had convinced myself it was to protect me, except it was actually because Nate was keeping him away. I was wrong all along. I'm so used to people falling for me. I'm so used to getting my way when it comes to love, that I have no idea how to accept rejection anymore. I fucked my way through all the people around me out of pure greed. Since I knew I could. And the one person I truly want? I was delusional; I made it all up. I thought he loved me because I loved him so greatly.

"Why would you kiss me if you have a boyfriend," I rasp.

I want to know who he is. I want to know why he's so special.

"Why would you do this?!" I shout in fury.

"I shouldn't have. I'm sorry. I wanted to make sure there was nothing. I apologize for that."

"You...you apologize?!" I imitate his pathetic accent as the rage takes over. "You're fucking breaking my heart, but, hey...you apologize!"

I take out my phone and text my brother to come pick me up.

"I hope you have the life you deserve, Rose," he says quietly. It makes me cackle a sarcastic laugh.

"I hope you fucking die on a job. One day, someone is going to ask you to kill the wrong person. And they will end you."

He nods slowly. "I know."

I shake my head and hurry to the door then stop dead in my tracks. "Who is it? What does he have that I don't? Apart from a fucking dick."

"Nothing. You're perfect, you know you are. He's just the person I fell in love with."

I take a shaky breath to stop the tears from falling. I haven't cried in so long. Sam will *not* be the one who gets them out of me.

"It should have been me," I conclude. I walk out with my head high and close the door inaudibly.

This is unfair. Sam was mine. He was always mine. And some guy just took him from right under me.

The warm air that crashes into my lungs when I leave his building does nothing to help. I feel a little dizzy and hot from the argument, and the temperature is making it worse.

The street is quiet, the view of the river slightly calming. I lean against the barrier while I smoke a cigarette. That river leads straight to Stoneview lake on one side and the Silver Falls on the other. I could just jump in and let it take me somewhere nicer.

I sigh and look at my phone. This was meant to be a good day. I've got a missed call from Rachel and a text, making my heart drop from the shame and guilt.

> Rach <3: Are you still coming? My parents want to celebrate with Conor's family tonight. We're leaving for dinner at 6:30.

I put my phone in my back pocket and huff the smoke out of my lungs. How can I face Rachel now? When I was ready to throw it all away for Sam.

Rachel is the love of my new life. Sam of the old one.

The first car I've heard in a while drives behind me and I look around. A black SUV with blacked-out windows. How not creepy.

I peer back at the river, finishing my cigarette and stubbing it against the sole of my sneaker, and then put it back in the pack. Let's not pollute. I need to bring a nicer karma on me.

I turn around and freeze on the spot. That black SUV is back, driving slowly past me. I look around me. No one. No other car.

I shake my head and relax. It's the middle of the afternoon, no one is going to fucking kidnap me now.

But I know.

I know something is wrong because that's just how we women are. We grow up having to be careful. We learn to trust our instincts when we're outside.

The SUV comes back to stop right in front of me, and I take a step back, but it all happens too fast.

The two men dressed in all black come out of the back door.

One grabs my arm as I try to run away.

The other one makes it behind me and slams a hand over my mouth when I try to scream.

I fight with all I have. I kick, and I drop my weight to the ground. Lists and lists of the things I should be doing in case of attempted kidnapping run through my brain, but one is highlighted in red: *do not let them take you to another location.*

I manage to kick the guy in front of me in the balls, but the other one is already dragging me toward the car. He's got one hand pulling my hair, ripping strands out. When I manage to bite the palm pressing against my lips, he curses and drags it to my neck.

I don't hesitate one second. I scream.

"Help!! Help!!" Sam's building stands tall at the corner of my eye, and I push my vocal cords past their capacities. "Sam!!! Sam!! Help me!"

I don't give up when I'm thrown to the back of the car through the open door they both came out of. I feel dizzy, the world lopsided as I'm forced to lay down on the back seats.

No, no, no. The driver is ready to go. One hand on the steering wheel, one holding a phone to his ear.

One of the two guys sits in the front passenger seat while the other pushes my legs so he can sit with me and close the door. I don't fucking let him. I kick at him, extend my hands above me and pull at the handle. The door opens, and I put all my strength into going out the other way, but he grabs my legs. And while he does so, the guy who sat at the front comes out, rounds the car, and grabs my hair again. He holds my head in place and a rag in his other hand.

"No!!" I shriek in complete panic. "Help!!"

"No one's coming for you, baby." The guy with the rag chuckles. The next second, it's on my face. "Night-night now."

It's suffocating, disgusting. It burns my lungs and makes me cough as tears fill up my eyes from the asphyxiating fumes.

I try to hold my breath as long as possible. Long enough to hear the driver talk to someone on the phone.

"Yes, it's her. She's got the Bianco family tattoo."

I fight in the men's hold despite my limbs going numb by the second. The driver turns around, and my eyes grow wide when he talks again. I know him. I know this face it's...it's...

"We've got the girl who killed your father, Mr. Volkov."

It's Aaron Williams, my brain whispers as blackness engulfs me.

After that...It's a complete blackout.

Want more? King of My Heart: Rose's Duet Book One is available on Kindle Unlimited!

ALSO BY LOLA KING

All books unfold in the same world at different times.

This is the recommended reading order.

STONVEVIEW STORIES

Stoneview Trilogy (MF Bully):

Giving In

Giving Away

Giving Up

Rose's Duet (FFMM why-choose):

Queen Of Broken Hearts (Prequel novella)

King of My Heart

Ace of All Hearts

AFTERWORD

This is it. Jake and Jamie's story is officially written and no more cliffhangers.

If you followed Jake and Jamie from the beginning. Thank you so much. Giving In was my first ever published book, and here we are almost seven months later with a complete trilogy. Thank you for your support, for giving my writing and characters a chance, and for sticking until the conclusion of their story. Jake and Jamie will forever hold a special place in my heart for allowing me to publish my first book.

There is so much more to come from the Stoneview Stories. Rose's book will be the next one, and if you truly know her...you will know she struggles to stick to one person...that is all I will say for now. If you've read Rose's epilogue, I hope you enjoy cliffhangers because that book is far from ready. She deserves her story to be told the right way, and it takes time!

Other characters will get their story, especially our favourite villain, Nate. It's all in my head, don't worry. And if you paid attention, you already know who will be his next victim.

I cannot express what it means to me if you have stuck with this trilogy. I hope you enjoyed yourself, and I hope it was everything you deserved.

Please, keep in touch!

IG: @lolaking_author
      FB: Lola's Kings

Lots of Love,

Lola ♡

AKNOWLEDGEMENT

Papa & Maman, thank you for your endless support and for the strength you put in me every day. Thank you for raising me the way you did, with all my qualities and flaws. And no, you will never read those books. I love you.

My King, you bring me up when I'm down, and lift me higher when I'm up. You share my passion, inspire me, support me. Mostly, you love me for who I am, and that is irreplaceable.

Lauren, my alpha and dear friend, thank you for your hard work. Thank you for making sense of my weird words and polishing my book. One of my favourite thing in life is discussing sex scenes and wondering what would work and not work? Should we put the gun safety on? If a position is possible? Which way would her arms go if the rope is pulling? That shit is important.

Thank you so much to LJ Findlay, Gabby, Zoe, for beta reading and helping me put that big thing into shape!

Kat, your advice and passionate words have honestly changed this book for the better. This would have not been possible without you. Thank you. I hope you still read

Nathan's book despite your hatred toward him. I promise it'll be worth it.

Thank you to my amazing street team. Guys, your support means absolutely everything.

Julia, my lovely Julia, thank you so much for your help with the release and EVERYTHING else.

Thank you to my siblings for always checking up on the books.

And obviously....thank you to every. single. person who read this book. You have no idea the sort of feeling I get knowing someone reads my words. When you read those words is when I'm at my most vulnerable. I want every single one of those words to make it past the page and into your world. You're making that possible. You're bringing Stoneview to life and its characters' stories become real thanks to you.

So, truly, *thank you.*

ABOUT THE AUTHOR

Lola King is a dark, steamy romance author who loves giving 'happy ever after's to antiheroes. She writes flawed, and deeply broken characters, and focuses some of her stories around queer love. Her books are sometimes cute, sometimes angsty, but always sexy! Lola lives in London and if she isn't writing, she is most likely keeping her mind busy putting together a play or making music.

Let's keep in touch on IG @lolaking_author or on FB readers' group *Lola's Kings* !

Made in the USA
Monee, IL
04 May 2025